MELA[NIE] ... when sh[e] ... the bed ... horrible [message] scrawled in lipstick on the mirror:

MOMMY AND DADDY
KILL BAD CHILDREN

Alicen's terrifying reflection appeared in the mirror. "They're all going to die," she sneered.

"No!" Melanie shrieked. "What have you done with my children? Where are they? Where are my children?"

Alicen laughed hideously. "Mommy's going to kill them," she said. "They're bad. . . ."

GHOST HOUSE
REVENGE

GHOST HOUSE REVENGE

by
Clare McNally

AN ONYX BOOK

ONYX
Published by the Penguin Group
Penguin Books USA Inc., 375 Hudson Street,
New York, New York 10014, U.S.A.
Penguin Books Ltd, 27 Wrights Lane,
London W8 5TZ, England
Penguin Books Australia Ltd, Ringwood,
Victoria, Australia
Penguin Books Canada Ltd, 10 Alcorn Avenue,
Toronto, Ontario, Canada M4V 3B2
Penguin Books (N.Z.) Ltd, 182–190 Wairau Road,
Auckland 10, New Zealand

Penguin Books Ltd, Registered Offices:
Harmondsworth, Middlesex, England

Published by Onyx,
an imprint of New American Library,
a division of Penguin Books USA Inc.

First Onyx Printing, May, 1992
10 9 8 7 6 5 4 3 2 1

REGISTERED TRADEMARK—MARCA REGISTRADA

Printed in the United States of America

PUBLISHER'S NOTE
This is a work of fiction. Names, characters, places, and incidents either are
the product of the author's imagination or are used fictitiously, and any
resemblance to actual persons, living or dead, events, or locales is entirely
coincidental.

PROLOGUE
Summer, 1975

The little girl clung to her father's hand, feeling a warmth that made her happy and secure. It was a beautiful afternoon to be seven years old, and Alicen Miller was very happy. Her father smiled down at her, seeing the anticipation in her brown eyes. She was such a cheerful little girl!

They were standing on a corner, a block away from their apartment building, watching the cars that sped down the highway. Alicen and Derek were looking for one car in particular, a blue sedan that belonged to Alicen's mother, Elaine. She had spent the last week in Maryland, attending the funeral of her only relative, Alicen's great-aunt. Both Derek and Alicen missed her terribly.

"Now, listen," Derek said. "Mommy might still be very sad, losing her aunt like that. After all, your great-aunt practically raised her. Now all she has are you and me."

"I'll be extra-special nice to her," the little girl said in a sing-song tone.

Just then, they spotted Elaine's car. Alicen jumped up and

down, waving excitedly. Derek raised his arm to wave, too, but he never completed the gesture.

There was another car behind Elaine's, about thirty yards away. It was weaving erratically across the highway and coming up on Elaine's car—fast, too fast.

Desperately, Derek tried to signal her off the road. Reading his gestures, Elaine looked up into her rear-view mirror and saw the car behind her. Quickly she tried to turn out of its path, but it was too late. There was a loud crash, a screech of tires, and a scream.

Elaine's car flew over a road divider, tumbling down a deep embankment. Derek felt his legs pull him forward. His arms stretched out as if he could grab his wife and save her.

"Elaine!"

This couldn't really be happening. . . .

Derek's legs gave way from under him as Elaine's car went up in flames, and he fell to the sidewalk. His mouth dropped open, and his palms pressed hard against the warm sidewalk as he gazed at the inferno. He vaguely heard sirens, barely registered the sight of fire trucks and water-gushing hoses. He was too busy watching the fire and praying.

Please let it be a mistake. Please don't let it be Elaine.

He pulled himself up onto his feet, his legs as heavy as tree trunks. Derek hardly felt the sidewalk underneath him as he walked toward the car. He heard humming in his ears—was it the whispers of the curious bystanders or the shouts of the paramedics? Or maybe it was the hacksaw they were using to get Elaine's door open.

That's not my wife, he thought.

Two hoses at last managed to still the flames enough for firemen to get inside the car and pull out Elaine. Or what was left of her. What had once been a beautiful woman was now a blackened mass. Not a woman. Not his Elaine.

Then he noticed the blackened hand. On one finger was a diamond ring—the ring Derek had given Elaine the day he had asked her to marry him.

He threw back his head and screamed. And then he felt a small, cool hand in his. He looked down and to his horror saw his little daughter standing at his side, staring at the flame-engulfed car.

"Oh, my God," he whispered.

He grabbed Alicen into his arms and turned her away from the sight, hugging her tightly as if to protect her. If only someone would protect him . . .

2

He heard laughter. Sweet, childish laughter that rose above the sirens and screams. It was Alicen's laughter.

"Oh, daddy," she said, "I made a mistake. Mommy isn't coming home today at all. She's coming home later on."

She's in shock, Derek thought. Thank God she's being spared from all this. Thank God we both don't have to suffer.

"Mommy will come home when she's ready," Alicen said. "When she wants to see me again, mommy will come for me."

1

When the noon sun struck the mansion at the top of Starbine Court Road, its whiteness seemed to glow like a holy vestment, and anyone seeing it might have thought: "There is a good, beautiful old house." And on this April Saturday, it seemed everything *was* good about the 185-year-old structure. Nothing set it apart from dozens of other Long Island mansions. Its large front porch faced the town of Belle Bay. Magenta azalea bushes ran from either side of the wooden steps to the rounded towers at its sides. These towers, added over a hundred years after the original Colonial mansion was built, made the house all the more breathtaking.

But those who had the powers to see beyond pretty flowers and inviting front porches would have known the house harbored a terrifying evil and that those who lived within its walls faced unspeakable dangers.

For now, though, all was well. Behind the house, two children were working on a corner of the back yard, which stretched for an acre to the thick woodlands that surrounded the house on three sides. Kyle and Gina VanBuren tugged hard at weeds and dug up rocks in preparation for a spring garden. Kyle found a fat grub and dangled it in front of his sister's nose.

"Daddy, make him stop!" Gina cried, her mouth turning down in a grimace.

Their father looked up from the legal papers he was reading. Kyle was giggling, but he had put the worm down again. Gary smiled at him.

"You're a rip, Kyle," he said. "Be nice to your sister."

Gina decided the incident had been funny after all and started to laugh. Both children rolled around merrily on the newly cut grass. Gary grinned at them, forgetting his work long enough to watch them play. He felt a surge of love for his two oldest children and decided that in the long run it had been a good idea to move from the city into this house. They would have to put last year out of their minds. It was over, and now it was time to enjoy their new home.

Gary looked up at the house. Although the front was somewhat gingerbready, the back was more true to the original Colonial style. His eyes roamed proudly across the back of the house. Suddenly they stopped at one particular window, which stood out because of its modern construction. The odd window brought back memories that made Gary shudder, and he forced them out of his mind. He quickly raised his eyes higher.

The weather vane at the peak of the roof needed straightening, he thought. Someone would have to come and fix the whole roof. The shingles were all curling up at the edges. Gary sighed to think that less than a year ago, he could have been the one to climb up there and do the job. But that was impossible now. He couldn't even climb stairs.

Gary looked down at his legs, muscular after so many painful hours of exercise, and yet useless. His fingers wrapped around the arms of his wheelchair. He'd been confined to it for four torturous months, ever since an—*intruder*—had pushed him out of that hated upstairs window. That November night, when he had become a cripple, had been so horrible that he and his family never talked of it.

He shivered, then pushed the accident from his mind and went back to his paper work. Gary refused to let the wheelchair hinder him. Maybe he couldn't go to his office in the city, but he wasn't about to give up on the law practice he had had for fifteen years. He had arranged with his partner to have all paper work sent to the house. Clients were handled over the phone and were invited to the house to discuss divorce settlements in his upstairs office. But he still longed to get back to his Manhattan office.

Well, Gary thought, sighing, that was impossible right now. As part of his rehabilitation program, he had to go to physical therapy sessions four days a week at a distant medical center. Gary worked himself hard and amazed the doctors by his progress. His bones were mended by now, and they said he would soon be able to walk on crutches. Nothing would make him happier.

"Daddy," Gina said, interrupting his thoughts, "would you hold the bag open for us?"

"Sure," Gary said.

He closed his briefcase. Lad, the Weimaraner puppy at his feet, jumped up from his nap, and Gary patted the puppy's smooth, silver-brown head, then unlatched the brake of his chair. He wheeled himself toward the children. "When's Mom coming home, anyway?" Kyle asked, obviously hungry for lunch.

"In a while," Gary said, looking at his watch. "It's just noon now."

Gina had something else on her mind as she filled the plastic bag with debris. "Daddy, the school glee club is singing next Wednesday afternoon," she said. "Can you come?"

"Oh, honey, I'm sorry," Gary said. "I have therapy that day. I can't miss it."

"It's okay," Gina mumbled, though it was clear she was disappointed. A moment later she looked up and asked, "Do you mind going to the hospital so much?"

"I'd much rather jog on the beach," Gary said, playfully flicking the long dark braid that hung down his thirteen-year-old's back. "But therapy helps me, and the sooner I get out of this wheelchair the better."

Having finished cleaning up the debris, Kyle put a twist tie on the bag and carried it to the barn. Gary couldn't help smiling to see the grim expression on his son's face. Though he was barely nine, Kyle was already a go-getter who considered no job too big. God bless my kids, Gary thought. They make it so much easier.

As Kyle turned back to the house, he saw someone move past the bay window of the dining room. She stopped, and through the lace curtains Kyle made out her blond hair. He waved. She did not wave back.

"Mom's home!" he cried, racing toward the house. Lad ran after him, barking and wagging his tail.

Gary, wondering why he hadn't heard his wife's car, wheeled himself around the side of the house. The driveway was empty. For a few moments he stared in confusion at the strip of gravel.

5

"Hi, honey!" someone cried.

Gary jumped a little when an arm wrapped around him from behind and a kiss landed on top of his head. He turned so abruptly that his wife, Melanie, backed away from him.

"I'm sorry," she said. "I didn't mean to startle you."

"It's okay," Gary said. "I was lost in thought. Where's the car?"

"You wouldn't believe the trouble it's been giving me. It stalled three times this morning, and then it died completely down on Houston Street. Nancy and I had to walk up the hill."

"I'm glad you were close to home," Gary said.

"Well," Melanie said, shrugging it off, "the station wagon's an old car. It was bound to start giving us trouble some time."

"We'll have the garage check her over," Gary said. "Tell them to do a complete overhaul. I don't want my wife driving a dangerous car."

With that, he reached out and slid his hand around Melanie's small waist, pulling her onto his lap. Before she could protest, his fingers weaved through her hair and squeezed the back of her neck. He brought her face to his and kissed her warmly.

"Love you," he said.

"I love you, Gary," Melanie replied. "Now, let me up. I'm much to heavy for you."

Gary snarled playfully but let her go. He wouldn't admit that under the weight of her body pain had shot through his legs. No less a man because of his wheelchair, Gary winked up at his wife.

"Never mind, Romeo," Melanie said, turning him around. She pushed the chair toward the ramp. "I know that look in your eyes, but I've got three hungry kids in the house and a car full of groceries down the road."

In the kitchen Melanie poured Gary a glass of beer, then steered Kyle and Gina out to help fetch the abandoned groceries. Gary grinned at his five year old, Nancy, who sat on the floor playing imaginary games with a stuffed yellow rabbit. "You've got a mustache, daddy," she said, pointing a chubby finger.

Gary erased the offending stripe of foam with the back of his hand. Then he opened his arms, and Nancy ran to him.

"I want a ride!" she squealed, wriggling onto his lap.

Gary laughed, kissing her golden curls. He wheeled the

chair toward the kitchen door, into the dining room and down the hallway. Nancy laughed with delight, trying to touch each brass doorknob as they raced past. Neither Gary nor his daughter knew they were being watched by a pair of malevolent eyes. A beautiful young woman stared at them, her heart almost set aflame with desire to destroy their happiness and their lives.

On Monday Melanie dropped Nancy off at kindergarten, then headed toward the medical center with Gary. She hummed softly as she drove, enjoying the scenery.

"Long Island is so beautiful in the spring," she commented. "I'm so glad we moved here from the city."

Gary mumbled a reply, staring out the window. He was thinking how much he hated these long drives. In truth, he hated them less than the fact that he himself was not doing the driving. Melanie recognized his frustration and tried to cheer him up.

"Dr. Norton says you're doing remarkably well," she said. "Pretty soon, you'll be able to stop coming here."

"Nothing would make me happier," Gary said.

At the clinic Gary was greeted by his doctor, a middle-aged woman with a perpetually sunny disposition.

"My colleagues and I had a meeting about you this morning," she said. "We're all very impressed by the progress you've made. Looks like you'll be out of this wheelchair in a few weeks, Gary. And there isn't anything you're doing here that couldn't be done at home, under the care of a private therapist."

Gary smiled broadly and said excitedly, "When do I start?"

Dr. Norton laughed. "Next week, possibly. I know a fine therapist who is available. His name is Derek Miller, and I recommend him highly."

"Then he's the one," Gary said. "Uh, what sort of setup will it be? Does he live near Belle Bay?"

"He's from New Jersey," Dr. Norton said. "I'm sure he could find an apartment near your house."

"When we've got lots of extra bedrooms? He'd be welcome to stay with us."

"I haven't finished telling you about him," she cautioned.

"Why would I have any objections?"

"Because Derek hasn't done private work in three years,"

7

Dr. Norton said. "You see, he's a widower with a teen-age daughter. If you were to board Derek, you'd have to take in Alicen, too."

"That's okay," Gary said. "There's nothing wrong with the kid, is there?"

"No, nothing really. She's rather shy. She wouldn't be any trouble."

"I'm sure," Gary said. "Listen, I want to discuss this with Melanie before I give my final answer. But I can't see any problems."

The entire family was sitting around the dinner table that night when Gary announced his news. The children were delighted. Now their father would be able to spend more time at home. They asked dozens of questions about the therapist and his daughter. Melanie, however, remained silent. Gary looked at her, not understanding the worry in her eyes. But he decided it was best to discuss her objections in private.

Later that night, as they lay in bed, their arms entwined, Melanie told Gary of her fears. "I just don't think it's safe to bring people into this house," she confessed.

"Why not?" Gary asked. "We certainly have enough room. And if the extra housework is too much for you, we'll hire a maid."

"I can get along fine without a maid," Melaine said. "Gary, you know what I'm talking about. You know what happened last year! What if it happened again? What if . . ."

"That is over, darling," Gary said. "We promised not to talk about it, remember?"

"Perhaps we *should* talk about it," Melanie said. "Let's get the statement out in the open, Gary. Our house was haunted. And not by nice harmless ghosts flitting around in white sheets. What's our guarantee that the ghost won't come back again?"

"I just don't think it will," Gary said firmly. "You know, lightning doesn't strike the same place twice."

"Yes, it does," Melanie protested.

"What do you expect me to tell the man?" he demanded. " 'You're taking this job at your own risk, Miller. We once had a ghost in our house who may come back again'?"

"Stop making fun of me," Melanie said. "I think my fears are justified."

Gary's expression softened as he bent to kiss his wife. "I'm sorry," he said. "But don't you see how much this means to me? I *hate* going to that medical center. It would be easier for me—and for you. Just look at all the time you take out of your painting just to drive me."

"That never bothered me," Melanie said.

"Look, Melanie," Gary said. "Nothing is going to happen. I want this so badly that I'll go ahead and do it in spite of your objections. But please say it's all right with you!"

His eyes were so like a little boy's that Melanie felt herself melting. She nodded slowly.

"All right," she said. "All right, do what you want. I'm just being ridiculous."

"No, you're not," Gary said. "But don't worry. Everything's going to be fine."

2

"Are they here yet?" Gary asked as he wheeled himself into the living room.

"Not yet," Melanie said. She was standing near the bay window, her slender hands resting on the back of an antique chair. Gary came up beside her.

"Are you still worried?" he asked.

"No, I've gotten used to the idea of house guests," Melanie said.

"They'll turn out fine," Gary insisted. "You'll see."

"From the looks of that rain," Melanie said, "they may not make it here today."

But just then, through the heavy downpour, they heard the sound of an engine. A few minutes later, a green Volvo came over the top of the hill and stopped in the driveway. Melanie and Gary watched as Derek Miller got out. He was wearing a raincoat with an upturned collar, which hid his face. He opened his daughter's door, and the two shared an umbrella up to the porch.

Derek was shaking the rain from his umbrella when Melanie opened the door. He looked up and smiled.

"I'm Derek Miller," he said.

"I know," Melanie answered. "Come in out of that rain, will you?"

Derek immediately introduced his daughter, then bent down to shake Gary's hand. Doctor Norton had told him about his patient, and Derek was impressed by the firmness of Gary's grip. Gary, in turn, was scrutinizing his therapist. After Derek removed his coat, Gary saw he was a well-built man of about thirty-five. The muscle lines under his cardigan told Gary he was a man who cared as much for his own body as those of his patients.

"Can I get you some coffee?" Melanie asked. "Or hot chocolate?"

"Not for me," Derek said. "Thanks."

Alicen declined with a shake of her head. Melanie folded their coats over her arm, thinking how handsome Derek was with his boyish features and dark, wavy hair. Unfortunately, none of his good looks had been passed on to his daughter. Alicen was the sorriest-looking child Melanie had ever seen, with a chubby body and stringy black hair. Melanie noticed she was staring at the mirror backplate of an elaborate wall lamp that hung in the hallway.

"That's called a girandole," she said. "It's an eighteenth century antique. Isn't it lovely?"

Alicen nodded but said nothing. Gary led the group into the living room and indicated seats for everyone. Derek sat on the overstuffed burgundy-colored couch. Alicen kept her distance, choosing a huge slat-back rocking chair near the fireplace.

"You collect antiques, Mrs. VanBuren?" Derek asked.

"Oh, no," Melanie said. "Gary does. He decorated this entire house."

"Some of the furniture came with it," Gary said. "That table there, for instance. It was built around 1795, the same year as this house."

Abruptly Gary changed the subject. "How was your trip?"

"Not bad," Derek said. "It's only two hours from Engle-wood."

He stood up and went to the fireplace, looking at the portraits that hung over it. There was one of a blond boy and another depicting two little girls looking out a window.

"Dr. Norton said you had three children?" he asked.

"Kyle, Gina, and Nancy," Gary said, pointing to each in turn. "They're in school right now."

"Gina's your age," Melanie said to Alicen.

10

The little girl mumbled, "I know."

"I guess that's one reason you let me bring Alicen," Derek said. He picked up a pewter vase and fingered its smooth rim. "Most people think she'd be in the way, even before they meet her."

"But you seem like a well-behaved girl, Alicen," Melanie said, smiling at her. Alicen had left her rocking chair and was now sitting on the window seat, watching the rain pummel the azaleas. She said nothing.

"She's a teen-ager, though," Derek said, "and that bothers people. They think she'd bring drugs into their houses or something. It's idiotic. I prefer private work, but it's impossible to get it with a kid in tow. I've been stuck in a clinic for three years."

"We like children," Melanie said, thinking it was very rude of Derek to speak that way in front of his daughter.

"Well, your call was a godsend, Mr. VanBuren," Derek said, ignoring the glare in Melanie's eyes.

"It's Gary," was the reply, "Mr. VanBuren is for clients and children. I'm hoping we'll be friends."

"After a few days of therapy with me," Derek said, laughing, "you may not want to be friends."

Alicen suddenly spoke up, in a clear voice that surprised Melanie.

"Who lives in that house down the road?" she asked, still staring out the window.

"It's empty," Melanie said. "The owner—the owner died last year."

As if to indicate she didn't wish to discuss it, Melanie stood up abruptly. "Well! How about letting me show you your rooms?"

"Sounds good," Derek said.

Gary had rigged a lift along the stairs so that he could get up and down them easily, and was quite adept at sliding himself into it. Melanie started to push the wheelchair up, as she usually did, but Derek took the handles from her.

"You're too pretty for work like this," he said, putting his suitcases on the seat.

"I've been doing it for months," Melanie said. "I'm not a weakling."

Derek agreed, but still held fast to the chair. They ascended the stairs slowly, so that Gary could keep up with them. As they walked down the hall, Derek stopped to look at the paintings that lined the walls. He saw Melanie's name on a few of them and complimented her. When he saw

11

that the others depicted naval scenes, he asked if they had an interest in that field.

Melanie and Gary exchanged glances, and after a moment's hesitation, Gary said, "The original owner of this house was a captain in the eighteenth-century British navy. Someday I'll tell you about him."

When they came to the last door in the hall, Melanie opened it and led Derek inside. The room was sparsely furnished with only a bed and dresser.

"We can bring other pieces down from the attic," Melanie said. "I thought it would be best to ask what you needed, first."

"This is just fine," Derek answered.

"Now, Alicen," Melanie said, "come across the hall and see your room."

Thinking the original furnishings had been too plain for a young girl, Melanie had added pretty yellow curtains and a white desk. There was a big bouquet of flowers on the window seat. Alicen looked around, then sat down on the bed, which was covered with a yellow and white quilt.

"Well, how do you like it, Alicen?" Melanie asked.

"It's nice," Alicen said in a soft tone.

Derek shook his head in a gesture of eternal patience, then left the room. Out in the hall he turned to Melanie and said, "You'll have to forgive my daughter's lack of enthusiasm. She's been withdrawn like that since my wife died. It's been six years, but . . ."

"Don't make excuses," Melanie said. "I promise, Alicen will get along just fine here. My children are very friendly."

Indeed, Gina lost no time in making Alicen feel at home. After dinner, she showed the girl her collection of records and stuffed animals. They sat on Gina's bed in their robes, Gina's frilly quilted one a sharp contrast to Alicen's flannel robe.

"Do you like Billy Joel?" Gina asked.

"I—I don't know any boys yet," Alicen faltered.

"I mean Billy Joel the singer!" Gina cried. Seeing the confused look on Alicen's face, she said, "Never mind. I'll play some of his records for you later. Don't you listen to the radio?"

"I like to read," Alicen replied. Thinking Gina might ridicule her for being a bookworm, she climbed from the bed and busied herself with a stuffed kangaroo.

"We have lots of books," Gina said, coming up next to her. "Come on downstairs and I'll show you our library."

"You have a library?" Alicen asked incredulously as she followed Gina from the room.

"Uh-huh," Gina answered. "It's got hundreds of books, but we kids have our own special shelf."

Alicen's brown eyes became very round when she and Gina entered the room. Arched bookshelves decorated with carved cherubs' heads lined three of the walls, while a fourth held built-in stands for maps and atlases.

"It's beautiful," Alicen whispered.

"This is our shelf," Gina said. She stood on her tiptoes and pulled a book down. It was so huge that she had to use both hands to carry it to the brown Chesterfield sofa. She laid it down on the long table before her, and Alicen saw the title: *Collected Works of Charles Dickens.*

"Grandpa said the pictures were painted by hand," Gina said. "See the date? 1850!"

"It's just beautiful," Alicen said again.

"My favorite story is *A Christmas Carol,*" Gina said. "See this picture of Scrooge? There's this guy named Mr. Percy at school who looks just like him. And he's just as mean."

"Will I get him?" Alicen asked, worried.

"I hope not," Gina said. "You'll probably be in my class. We live together, don't we?"

"Are the kids in your class nice?"

"Real nice," Gina said. "How come you look so worried?"

"I hate school," Alicen said. "All the teachers I've ever had have been mean to me."

"My teacher is nice," Gina said. "So stop worrying."

A knock on the door interrupted their conversation. Melanie poked her head in and said, "Do you know it's almost eleven? Come on up to bed."

"Let me put this book away first," Gina said.

"Well, Alicen," Melanie said, "how do you like our fancy library?"

"Oh, I love it," Alicen said, with more enthusiasm than Melanie had witnessed all day.

"You're welcome to use it any time you like," Melanie said. "If you don't find what you want, I can drive you to the library in town."

"Thanks," Alicen said.

Melanie leaned against the door as the two girls filed out of the room. She hadn't been near the public library since—well, since Gary's accident. Libraries depressed her. They reminded her of a librarian friend she'd had. But that friend

13

had died last year, violently. And though it wasn't her fault that Janice was dead, she still felt guilt twisting at her stomach whenever she thought of her. Why? Why so much guilt?

Stop that, Melaine told herself. *It's the past. It's over!*

With memories of Janice still heavy on her mind, she went to Alicen's room. The girl was surprised to see her and jumped under the covers as if ashamed of the pretty gown that hung over her fat body.

"How do you like it here so far?" Melanie asked.

"It's nice," Alicen said softly.

"I'm glad you like it," Melanie said, wanting to put her arms around the girl. But something in her manner held her back, and she simply said good night.

Alicen settled back against her pillow, all the while thinking how nice everything seemed to be. She hoped Gina would become her friend. Then, exhausted after a long day, she fell asleep immediately. Her dreams, of her mother, were sweet. Alicen was completely unaware of the woman standing over her, considering her as a pawn in a diabolical scheme.

3

Alicen's fears about her first day at Saint Anne's were completely justified. It began when she learned that she had been assigned to the dreaded Mr. Percy, who really did look like the Scrooge in Gina's book. He had white hair and a pointy nose, and he seemed to always be scowling.

He had put her in the seat directly in front of his desk, wanting to keep an eye on his new student. Alicen sensed he was watching her, waiting for her to do something wrong. She looked around the room, lost and afraid among unfamiliar faces. Alicen began to chew her lower lip as she studied the pretty blond girl next to her.

"Eyes front, Miss Miller," Percy snapped. "Let me tell you, I don't tolerate daydreamers in my classroom. Don't let me catch you again, unless you want to spend your first day in the principal's office."

"Yes, sir," Alicen said, feeling tears of humiliation burning in her eyes. She blinked them away.

She tried her best to concentrate that morning, although her mind wandered whenever Percy had his back to her for too long. She knew already that she hated him. Why did she have to be in his class? The principal had said Gina's class was too full, but couldn't they have made room for one more student? And worse than that, Gina's lunch hour was later than hers. So, this first day, she was forced to eat alone.

As she sipped at a container of milk, she noticed a nice-looking boy with red hair approaching her. Not wanting to talk to him, she ducked her eyes and pretended to be busy with her sandwich. When she next looked up, he was sitting across the room.

The afternoon passed more quickly than the morning, since Percy was concentrating on literature. Alicen became caught up in a story, but she was still glad when the bell rang. Like a drill sergeant, Percy barked at them to get on two separate lines. Alicen was surprised to find the red-haired boy from the cafeteria standing next to her.

"Hey!" he hissed. Alicen ignored him, but the boy persisted. "Don't let Percy get you down. No one else listens to him, either."

Alicen managed a smile but didn't say anything. A few minutes later, they were outside, and the two lines broke as children scattered across the schoolyard. The redhead was still with her.

"My name's Jamie Hutchinson," he said. Alicen noticed the braces on his teeth and felt a little less flawed herself.

"I'm Alicen Miller," she said.

"Where do you live?" Jamie asked. "Did you just move to Belle Bay?"

"I came here yesterday," Alicen told him. Then, surprised that she was suddenly talking so much, she added, "I live with Gina VanBuren. Do you know her?"

"Not really," Jamie admitted. "I've heard of her, though."

Alicen looked around uncomfortably. "There's Gina now!" she cried. She left Jamie without saying goodbye.

"Nice meeting you," Jamie called as he watched her run toward the bus.

Gina grabbed Alicen's arm and took a quick glance at Jamie. "Who was that?" she asked. "He's so cute!"

"His name is Jamie Hutchinson," Alicen reported.

"Gee, you've got a boyfriend already!" Gina squealed.

"He's not my boyfriend," Alicen said, annoyed.

15

When they arrived home, they found Gary and Derek in one of the upstairs hallways, supervising a group of carpenters at work on Gary's therapy room. The banging of hammers and buzzing of saws was deafening.

In the studio Melanie, in a blue smock, was busy at work on a new painting. A photograph of Belle Bay's town square was pinned to a bulletin board beside her easel.

"Hi, mom!" Gina cried. "What're you painting?"

"A picture of the town square," Melanie said. "I hope to sell it to the mayor or some other local politician. Oh, guess what? I'm going to have another one-woman show. I'll have to paint a lot of pictures of Long Island since it's my home now."

She promised the girls they could go with her to visit Montauk Point and Jones Beach and other local sights. Gina started enthusiastically to plan her summer vacation, talking of nothing else for the rest of the day. But all Alicen could think about was school and how much she dreaded going back.

When she went to bed that night, she whispered out loud, as if her mother were there to hear her, "You'd make it okay, wouldn't you? I wish you'd come back to me, mommy! I need you!"

Tears filled her eyes, and she turned and stared out the window. The moon was bright and full. Alicen gazed at it and tried to remember her mother. The memory of her mother's beautiful, smiling face was still with her; Alicen had made it a point never to forget that face. She had heard adults at the funeral whispering that her mother had been horribly disfigured in the car accident, but she refused to believe they were talking about her. She stamped a picture of her mother in her mind that showed her always smiling, always willing to play with her little daughter. Not like her father.

Alicen's thoughts were suddenly interrupted by a strange, high-pitched laughter. Terrified, she pulled her quilt over her head and held her breath. Was someone in the room, listening to the thumping of her heart? The laughter came again, and she realized it wasn't in her room at all. It had come from the kitchen below, filtering through the grating in the floor.

Alicen was about to get up and tell her father, but she was afraid. This was his first private job in three years, and he'd warned her she had better not do anything to jeopardize it. *Anything.*

"And that means acting like a baby, the way you did at the Laines' house," her father had said.

Alicen had awakened in the middle of the night, crying out for her mother. Her screams had so frightened the Laine children that their parents decided she couldn't stay with them any longer. Derek couldn't afford to send her to a boarding school, so the two packed their bags together. Alicen knew it was her fault that her father had lost his job. So tonight, she pretended she didn't hear the laughter. This time, she swore, she wouldn't have nightmares.

Trembling, she put her fingers in her ears and blocked out the sound. She didn't hear the click of Derek's door across the hall. He had also heard the strange cries and was on his way downstairs to investigate. The long hallway that led to the stairs was pitch black, lit only by dim moonlight filtering through an amber stained-glass window at its end. Obviously the VanBurens were fast asleep, too far at the front of the house to have heard the noise. Derek, deciding he could handle the situation himself, groped his way down the dark staircase.

He stopped short when he heard the laughter again. Then he took a deep breath and burst into the dining room, switching on the overhead light. He scanned the room, taking in the table, chairs, and bay windows. The windows were locked tight. Everything seemed to be in order. Even the fireplace, black and yawning, gave no hint of hiding an intruder. Everything was so silent that Derek could hear a ringing in his ears.

"I must have been dreaming," he said softly, running his fingers through his tousled hair. But then he noticed the kitchen door. Could the prowler be hiding in the kitchen? It suddenly occurred to him that if there was an intruder, he might be armed. Derek wasn't afraid, but he wasn't about to take chances. He needed a weapon.

Looking around, he spotted a pearl-handled pistol on the mantel. It looked like an antique, and Derek prayed the intruder wouldn't know the difference. Refusing to let himself be frightened, he shoved through the kitchen door and switched on the light. The white refrigerator and oven gleamed innocently. He could see his reflection in the back-door window as he moved carefully around the kitchen. No one was hiding here. He went to the back door and twisted the lock. It was one of those doors where one needed a key to get out as well as in. There had been no time for a prowler to escape—if indeed it was a prowler he had heard.

He sank into a wooden chair. "I'm sure I heard something."

It might have been his imagination. After all, this was an old house, with creaking boards and drafts. He had heard some explainable noises, and nothing more. Laughing at himself, he stood up and headed out of the kitchen.

The door to the basement started to rattle.

Derek turned abruptly, aiming the gun. Why hadn't he thought to check the cellar? Was that just the wind? He heard a scratching noise. The wind didn't scratch. . . .

Derek refused to be afraid. He reached and jerked the door open. His gun was pointed at the black, shiny nose of a puppy.

"I don't believe this," Derek groaned, putting the gun on the counter. He knelt down and stroked the little Weimaraner's ears.

"How'd you get stuck down there?" he asked, wondering if a puppy's high-pitched yapping could sound like laughter. "There's a good boy. Poor doggy, locked in a cellar."

He peered down the stairs into the inklike blackness. "Locked in a dark and cold cellar, too," he said. He stood up and beckoned the dog. Lad followed him from the room. Derek returned the gun to its stand on the mantel, then headed upstairs, Lad at his side. Feeling somewhat embarrassed by the incident, he decided to keep it to himself. Afraid of a little puppy!

He had no idea that Lad hadn't barked once that night.

The therapy room was completed just a few days later.

"It'll be best to get your muscles toned," Derek said as he fastened a cushioned leather cuff to Gary's left ankle. "Once you're used to this equipment, you can move on to bigger and better things."

"Like walking, I hope," Gary said. His leg moved up and down with little difficulty, the cable squeaking from newness.

"Let me add a little more weight to that," Derek said. "It looks too easy." He added a ten-pound weight. This time Gary groaned when he moved his leg.

"Pretty soon," Derek said, "you won't feel it. For a guy who broke both legs, you're in pretty good shape, Gary. Say, nobody ever told me the details of your accident. If you don't mind, I'd be interested."

"They didn't tell you what kind of injury you'd be dealing with?" Gary asked impatiently.

"Of course," Derek said. "But part of therapy is knowing how the accident occurred. I want to know on a professional basis, but if you feel uncomfortable about it, then—"

"No, it's not that," Gary said. "It's just that we don't like to talk about it. Let's just say I came into one of the rooms up here one night and found a prowler. We had a fight, and he pushed me out the window. That's all you need to know, isn't it?"

"Probably," Derek said, wondering why Gary was so reluctant to talk about the accident. He decided it was some family matter and did not pursue it.

Gary asked when he would be able to start using crutches.

"I want to warn you," Derek said, "practicing with crutches is a frustrating and sometimes painful process. You'll probably fall down a lot, and you'll need your muscle strength to get back up again. But don't worry. One of these days, you'll be playing racquet ball with me."

"I don't know how to play," Gary said.

"If you promise to cooperate with me," Derek said, "I promise to teach you the game."

The two men shook on it and continued with the routine. They could hear Melanie down the hall, singing as she worked in her studio.

"Melanie's a beautiful woman," Derek said. "You're lucky to have her."

"I know," Gary said. He studied the sadness in his therapist's eyes for a moment, then asked, "What was your wife's name?"

"Elaine," Derek said. "She was beautiful, too. Her hair was clear down to her hips, and the lightest blond color. She was only thirty-two when she died. Her car was—uh, was struck by a drunk driver doing ninety. The engine exploded."

"I'm sorry," Gary said, feeling uncomfortable. Grasping at straws, he said, "Do you play a lot of racquet ball?"

"Three nights a week and every Saturday, when I lived in Jersey," Derek said, smiling again. "There was a little gymnasium there that didn't charge too much for court time. I miss it."

"I sometimes see ads for a local health club in our town paper," Gary said. "It has a court. Why don't you join?"

On Saturday Derek did drive into town to look up the club. Halfway there, he spotted a young woman hitchhiking. Derek, who never picked up strangers, ignored her. Silver

19

lampposts and patches of sand and sparse, scrubby foliage shot passed him. Something about this barren section of Belle Bay made Derek uneasy. Why was that? He was never unsure of anything!

It was the woman, of course. She had looked like a pitiful refugee, her eyes huge and staring. Derek looked in his rear-view mirror, his breath catching in his throat when he saw her eyes. They seemed to be pulling him, making him turn the car around and drive back to her. Without understanding why, he stopped and opened the door for her.

"Where do you want to go?"

The woman said nothing. She stared straight ahead through vacant blue eyes. There was a strange smell about her, a faint mixture of sea wind and rotted meat. Rotted meat? Derek was disgusted at the thought. Close-up, the young woman's appearance disgusted him even more. She was so pale it was painful to look at her, especially since he could see the veins beneath her skin. Her eyes had a filmy quality, and the blond hair that hung around her shoulders looked as if it hadn't been combed in weeks. Even stranger were the clothes she wore—corduroy pants, a flannel shirt, and fur boots. On a warm spring day.

God, have I ever picked up a loser, Derek thought, starting the car again.

"Just tell me where you want to get off," he said as he drove down the road. He was annoyed at himself for giving in to a ridiculous impulse and letting this stranger into his car.

All of a sudden, the woman pressed her hand on top of his. It was as cold as ice. Derek looked down at it, keeping a firm grip on the steering wheel, although he wanted to pull away from the freezing touch of her fingers. Her hand was chapped red. It was as if she had just stepped out of a snowstorm.

"Hey, let go!" Derek cried. "What's wrong with you? Do you need a doctor?"

She made no reply, but took her hand away. Derek turned his eyes from the road for a split second. The woman was making gestures as if she were crying. Derek couldn't see any tears, though her small mouth hung open and her shoulders heaved. She stared down the road.

"Mel . . . Mel . . . Mel . . ." she moaned.

Derek, his eyes on the road once more, patted her arm and told her he would get help. She stiffened. Her sobbing stopped with a huge gasp, and she doubled over as if she were

20

going to be sick. Derek quickly pulled the car off the road, got out, and ran to open the door. But when he tried to help her out, she collapsed to the ground. Her eyes stared glassily, and she made no sound.

"Jesus in Heaven," Derek whispered.

He hesitated, afraid to touch her. All sorts of visions came to his head. Everyone would start asking questions, and they might even accuse him of killing this woman. She had been in his car—how could they think otherwise? Why should he jeopardize his life and career for one crazy addict? He didn't need that kind of trouble.

Derek looked up and down the road, surprised at how calm he was. There was no one around, no one to see him lift her—why was she so stiff, he wondered?—and carry her to a nearby clump of bushes. He put her down there, glad to be rid of her.

"Sorry, lady," he said as he hurried back to his car, "but I don't know you from Adam. I don't need your problems."

He thought at first about forgetting the entire incident, but his sense of decency got the better of him. He parked his car in the center of town and walked to a phone booth.

"Belle Bay police department," a voice said. "Bryan Davis."

"I—I want to report a body," Derek said carefully, keeping his voice low so that passers-by wouldn't hear him.

"A what?"

"A body," Derek repeated. "I saw it behind some bushes on Houston Street, near Walher."

"Hey, wait!" Bryan cried. "Who are you?"

But Derek had already hung up. By the time he reached the health spa and signed the membership papers, he had pushed the incident with the girl from his mind. He was choosing a racket even as Bryan Davis reached the designated intersection.

"Over there," Bryan said to the cop with him. "I think I see something, Jack."

"It's just an old towel," Jack said, kicking it aside to show that the ground beneath was empty. "You suppose this is what our caller saw?"

"I don't know," Bryan said. "He sounded pretty upset. Let's look a little further."

As he poked through the clumps of bushes scattered here and there on the roadside, Bryan took note of the fact that no cars had passed them. Chances were, no one else had seen the body—if indeed there was one. After a few more minutes of searching, Bryan straightened himself and sighed.

21

"Jack, we're wasting our time," he said. "It was just a wild-goose chase."

"That doesn't surprise me," Jack said. He was looking at some point behind his captain. "Nothing surprises me anymore."

Bryan turned around and followed Jack's gaze. He could see the huge VanBuren mansion at the top of the nearby hill. Bryan wondered how the family was doing, especially Gary.

"I sometimes see his wife driving him through town," Jack said, as if reading Bryan's thoughts. "He's still in a wheelchair, you know."

"It was a hell of a fall he had," Bryan said grimly. He clapped Jack on the shoulder. "Let's get back to the station. We'll just assume the caller was seeing things, okay?"

"If it's all the same to you," Jack said, "I'd like to believe we aren't going to have any more trouble here."

"I couldn't agree with you more," Bryan said as he got into his car.

4

As soon as breakfast was over, Derek turned to Gary and said, "Why don't we get started now?"

"Right away," Gary said. "I'm having some clients here this afternoon, so I want to get this done early."

Melanie looked over her shoulder. "Honey, I'm going to be taking my new painting into town today. Do you mind if I'm not here?"

"I'm sure I'll be okay," Gary said. Melanie often helped him by answering phones or bringing coffee when he was with his clients.

"I hope you sell that painting," Derek said.

"Thanks," Melanie said. "If I do, I'll probably sell a few more. The mayor's wife is filthy rich."

"Then don't take less than five hundred dollars," Gary said laughing.

Later that morning, Melanie carefully laid the painting in

the back of the station wagon. As she walked around to her door, she looked up at the ominous gray clouds in the sky. A faint rumble of thunder told her it would rain within the next hour.

Melanie switched on the radio as she drove down Starbine Court and thought how pretty everything looked that afternoon. The approaching storm gave the air a clean, cool scent. She could see the stretch of beach through the sparse woods; it was empty except for a young couple and their dog. The usually still waters of the bay were churning now, and sea gulls anticipated the storm with high-pitched cries.

Melanie shuddered suddenly. Though it was April, she had felt a wind so cold that goose bumps crept over her skin. Keeping one hand on the wheel as she turned a corner, she tightened the belt on her raincoat. She heard something thump behind her and looked quickly over her shoulder. The painting had shifted a little, but no harm had been done.

"I sure hope I sell that," she said out loud as she drove through the center of town. She pulled into the parking lot next to the town hall, surprised to see how full it was on this gloomy day. She found a spot at last, then switched off the engine. Crossing her fingers for luck, she went around to the back of the car to retrieve the painting. But when she pulled it out, she nearly dropped it. There was an ugly red smudge mark right in the middle of it.

"Oh, no!" Melanie whimpered, propping it against the door. "I don't understand. I worked so hard on it. And I *know* that paint was dry!"

Something told her, though, that this wasn't paint. Carefully she touched the spot. It was thick, but not as thick as oil paint. Melanie brought her finger to her nose. It wasn't paint at all. It was blood.

Quickly she examined her own hands and arms for signs of a cut. That was fresh blood—it wasn't as if one of the kids had touched it earlier on and had been too scared to tell anyone about it. Yet Melanie's skin was unbroken. It was almost as if someone had done this on purpose. But that was impossible.

Suddenly she heard a voice right behind her. "What happened to your lovely painting?"

An attractive, well-dressed middle-aged woman was at her side. The woman was shaking her head.

"Who'd do such a thing?" she demanded. "It looks as if someone rubbed red paint on it."

23

"It's—" Melanie stopped. Why should she tell this stranger the red mark was blood? How could she, when she hardly believed it herself?

"Did you paint it?" the woman asked. "It's beautiful, in spite of . . ."

Melanie nodded. "I was going to sell it to the mayor. I don't think I could even give it to him, now."

"It's really not a big smudge," the woman said. "Do you think you could paint over it?"

"I don't know," Melanie said sadly. "I don't know if it would do any good."

"Yes, it would," the woman said, taking Melanie's arm. "Come inside with me, and we'll talk about it. I'm Sarah Kaufman; I'm the mayor's wife."

Melanie and Sarah shared coffee in an empty office, discussing her work as a painter.

At last, to Melanie' delight, Sarah wrote a check for one thousand dollars, explaining that she wanted Melanie to do two paintings for her, one of the duck pond and one of the local church. She asked if Melanie could put pink roses in that one. They were her favorite flowers, she explained. They also agreed that four hundred and fifty dollars would be a fair price for the damaged painting if Melanie could repair it successfully. Sarah Kaufman was a sympathetic woman, and Melanie found herself lingering on after they had completed the transaction, talking about her home and Gary's unfortunate accident.

When Melanie left the town hall, it was starting to rain, so she pulled up the hood of her raincoat and ran down the steps to her car. She was surprised to see a young woman sitting on the back fender. Melanie, feeling elated with the check in her purse, smiled at her. The woman did not return the smile, but watched Melanie as she walked to her door and got in the car.

When Melanie started the car, the woman was still sitting on the fender. Melanie hit the horn, to no avail. Sighing in exasperation, she got out of her car. She tapped the woman's shoulder.

"If you don't mind," she said, "I'd like to move my car."

The young woman said nothing, but stared up at Melanie. There was something in her glassy blue eyes, something cold and vicious, that made Melanie shudder. The woman seemed strangely familiar. Melanie studied her for a moment, then decided she didn't know her after all. "What is it you want?" Melanie asked. "Money? A ride?"

The young woman shook her head and smiled for the first time. It was a thin evil smile.

"I want you to die," she said.

Melanie gasped and turned quickly to run into the hall. She found a security guard and brought him outside. But when they reached the car, the woman was gone. Droplets of rain covered up any indication that she had been sitting there.

"She was right there," Melanie said, pointing.

"She probably ran away when she saw me coming," the guard said. "I wouldn't worry about it. You know kids these days. Probably some smart-ass teen-ager."

"You're right," Melanie said. "I'm sorry I bothered you."

"It's my job, lady," the guard said.

When she arrived home, Melanie gathered the family together and held up the check for everyone to see. She told about her meeting with Sarah Kaufman and how the mayor's wife had commissioned her to paint two pictures.

"That's a lot of money," Kyle said.

"But what about the other picture?" Gary asked.

"I couldn't sell it," Melanie said sighing. "Somehow, part of it wasn't dry yet, and it got smudged." There was no point upsetting everyone with the truth.

"But you finished that several days ago," Gary pointed out.

"I know," Melanie said. "I guess—well, I guess this damp weather we've been having kept it from drying. It's all right, though. Mrs. Kaufman says she'll pay four hundred and fifty dollars for it when I fix it."

Despite her feelings of misgiving, Melanie related the story about the strange young woman. She described the glassy blue eyes and scary smile and related how the girl had disappeared before the security guard could chase her away.

"Probably high on something," Derek said. He thought for a moment about the hitchhiker who had been in his car the other day. Belle Bay was such a nice town. Not the sort of place you'd expect to find a lot of drugged hippies.

"Well, let's forget it," Gary suggested. "This is too happy a day to dwell on something like that. Why don't we all go out to dinner, to celebrate?"

"It sounds great," Melanie said. "Derek and Alicen will come, too, I hope?"

Derek smiled. "Let me get my umbrella."

A short while later everyone headed out to the cars, laughing and talking about the good evening they would have.

25

The silence of the big house lulled Lad to sleep. His wiry body was stretched out near the front door, ready to waken and jump all over the children when they returned. A twitch of muscle would ripple his smooth gray-brown skin every once in a while, but the dog slept on.

And then something reached his ears, some strange sound that didn't belong in the house. As if he had never been asleep, the dog raised his head and shoulders with a jerk. He looked around, his ears alert for the noise.

Loud wailing was coming from Melanie's studio. With a loud series of barks, Lad jumped to his feet and ran upstairs. A sudden terror overtook him, and he cowered in the studio door and whined, smelling something, but seeing nothing.

Across the room, one of the paintings lifted off its stand as if by itself. It seemed to shake in midair.

She sells paintings, and that's all she cares about. She doesn't care that I was her friend once. She doesn't care about what happened to me.

The painting came crashing down against the easel.

She laughs with her family while I cry for life. But I will have vengeance.

Lad snarled as he saw the painting rise in the air again . . .

Vengeance!

. . . and come crashing down on the easel. But what he heard next was a human voice, disembodied and powerful. He scurried to hide underneath the couch.

"Vengeance! I'll kill them all. I'll make them suffer like I do."

There was a final crash, and then the house was silent once more.

"That was one terrific evening," Melanie said as she and the others walked up the porch steps. She was carrying Nancy, who was asleep, while Derek pushed Gary's wheelchair. "Thanks for everything, guys."

"I wonder why Lad isn't down here to greet us?" Kyle asked.

"Yeah, that's weird," Gina said. "He's always here when we go out."

"Well, he probably got tired of waiting," Melanie said, handing Nancy to Derek as she took off her coat. "We were out very late—so, up to bed!"

Derek offered to carry Nancy to her room. As Melanie

followed him down the hall, she noticed she had left her painting there that afternoon and picked it up. Upstairs, she put her sleeping daughter into a pair of pajamas, then tucked her in.

"Sleep good, love," she said, kissing the child's forehead.

She picked up her painting again and carried it down the hall to her studio. Slightly giddy from the wine she had been drinking all night, she was whistling a tune as she opened the door. Her whistling stopped short when she turned on the light.

The room was in complete disarray. Her paintings were scattered everywhere, easels were overturned, and a tube of bright yellow paint had oozed out all over the couch.

"What happened?" Melanie demanded out loud. She could feel her heart start to pound, but she breathed deeply and walked further into the room. She spotted one of her paintings lying on the floor. The frame had been bent completely out of shape, and there were long, ugly gashes running the length of the canvas.

Melanie dropped it as if it were boiling hot and ran out into the hallway. Somehow, common sense got the better of her, and she managed not to scream out in anger. How would she explain this to the children?

Gary was at the bottom of the steps with Derek.

"Gary, could you come to my studio with me?" Melanie forced her voice to remain calm.

"Sure," Gary said. "What's wrong?"

"Oh, nothing," Melanie insisted. "I just want to show you something." She looked at Derek. "Good night."

As she pushed him down the hallway, Gary asked what all the mystery was about. But Melanie refused to speak. Gary's answer came when she opened her studio door.

"My God, this place looks like a cyclone struck it," he said. "What the hell happened?"

"I don't know," Melanie said softly. She walked across the room and lifted the torn painting. "Look at this. This is a painting I did a few years ago of the three children." She brushed back one of the torn edges to reveal a little baby. "That's Nancy, remember?"

"It was one of my favorite pictures," Gary said sadly.

"Mine, too," Melanie answered. "Why, out of all my paintings, was it singled out for destruction?"

"Singled out?" Gary asked. "You say that as if someone did this on purpose. But no one's been home."

Melanie remained silent as she tried to straighten out the

mess. She propped her paintings and canvases back on their stands and righted the easels. Tears flowed down her cheeks, and she sniffled.

"Melanie, I'm sure there's some logical explanation," Gary said in a soothing tone.

"There always is," Melanie answered.

A long stretch of silence passed before she spoke again. She had her back to her husband, busily trying to scrape the yellow paint from the couch cover.

"It could be a ghost, Gary," she said.

"Oh, of course not! Some local kids probably broke in and got their kicks by vandalizing your studio," Gary said.

"It isn't impossible that the ghosts are back?" Melanie asked uncertainly.

"No, it isn't," Gary answered. "But it's improbable. Honey, there is no reason to believe all that happened here last year will happen again. You're just tired and upset. Why don't you wait until morning to think this out?"

Melanie burst into tears then and ran to put her head on Gary's shoulder.

"This wasn't supposed to happen to me!" she cried. "I was so happy!"

"It's okay," Gary said, rubbing her back. "Everything's gonna be okay."

He stared across the room. If only he had some proof that all this was the result of mortal hands. And then, as if in answer to his pleas, he saw a small brown paw poke out from under the couch. Then another, and then Lad slowly slithered out. Gary tapped Melanie's shoulder, and she looked up.

"There's your culprit," he said.

Lad slunked toward them, whining in terror.

"He must have been chasing a mouse," Gary said. "And he knocked everything over. The torn painting just caught on an edge of the easel—that's all."

Melanie looked into the dog's big brown eyes and saw fear there. Though she nodded her head in agreement for Gary's sake, she wasn't quite sure the dog was guilty.

An icy touch brought Melanie out of a dream sometime in the very early morning. Without opening her eyes, she tried to brush it away, groaning. But it stayed with her, insistent, pressed against her bare arm. Groggily she rolled over onto her back and squinted up through the darkness.

A woman was leaning over her.

Just a dream, Melanie thought, closing her eyes again. She sighed and opened them a second time to check the clock. The woman was still standing there, moonlight casting a glow over her face and dark hair. She let her hand slide down Melanie's arm and took her hand.

"Come," she said, simply.

Melanie opened her mouth to waken Gary, but no sound came from it. Still half-asleep, she didn't question, but got out of bed and followed the woman into the hallway. In the soft moonlight, colored amber through the stained-glass window at the end of the hall, she could see the woman was a head shorter than she. Could it be Alicen? What did she want? Melanie couldn't open her mouth to ask. She felt as if she were in a dream world, where everything is fuzzy and feet don't make contact with floors.

They went downstairs to the dining room. Now Melanie was beginning to become more fully conscious, and she was aware of the soft rug under her bare feet. But this was a dream, wasn't it?

She knew it wasn't a nightmare, because, somehow, she wasn't afraid.

They entered the kitchen. Someone had left the light on, and in its brilliance Melanie saw the woman's face. It was pretty and childish, framed by long, dark hair. The old-fashioned gown the woman wore was torn to shreds, and she had no shoes.

Encouraged by the gentleness of the woman's face, Melanie spoke at last. Her voice sounded hollow, far away, yet she had the feeling this was all really happening. She wished Gary were down here.

"Who are you?" Melanie asked.

"I have come to warn you," the woman said. "Leave this place!"

"Why?"

"There will be more sorrow," the woman said. "I take great risks coming here—for if she knew of me, she would conjure up the wrath of hell."

"Who would?" Melanie demanded. "Who's she? And who are you?"

Suddenly the woman gave a small cry. "I must go! She walks too near!"

"Wait!" Melanie cried.

The woman turned a panic-stricken face to Melanie and shook her head. Her hair waved slowly from side to side, as if it were floating in water. Then suddenly it started to fall out. The pretty white-and-pink skin began to shrivel and draw away from the skin. Brown eyes disintegrated, and the swan-like neck became a tree branch. Melanie watched in horror as the woman sank to the floor, drawing her arms and legs up in a fetal position. She was nothing but a black, shriveled blob. Then a skeleton. Then, nothing.

"Nnnnooo!"

Melanie screamed and screamed, falling back into a chair. She felt two hands on her arms and tried to pull away, but they held her tightly. And from the other side of her terror, she heard a comfortingly familiar voice.

"Melanie, wake up!"

She dared to open her eyes. Gary was leaning over her in his wheelchair.

"Gary?" she asked weakly. "Where did the woman go? Did you see the woman?"

"What woman?" Gary asked. "Here, calm down. There's no woman here."

Melanie looked around at the empty kitchen.

"Yes," she said, her voice weak but insistent. "Yes, I saw her! She led me down here."

"No one led you down here," Gary said. "I saw you get out of bed and leave the room—by yourself."

"You must have seen the woman, too," Melanie said. "Why didn't you follow us?"

Gary sighed. "Melanie, you were alone. You must have been sleepwalking, although I didn't realize it until I heard you screaming. Luckily, I was awake."

"What about the children? Did they hear me?" Melanie asked, her fears giving way for the moment to motherly concern.

"No one's awake," Gary said. "Now, come back to bed."

Melanie stood up.

"Gary, I saw a woman," she insisted. "She brought me down here. She even spoke to me, warned me to leave this place!" Melanie shuddered. "And then she turned into a skeleton."

"There was no woman," Gary said. "You were sleepwalking, that's all. And it's no wonder, after you found your studio torn apart like that. That was a frightening experience."

"It isn't happening again, is it, Gary?" Melanie asked, her voice almost childish in its pleading.

"Of course not," Gary said. "Come up to bed now, darling."

She did. But she laid awake for hours thinking of the woman. Who was she? What did she want?

No answers came. Melanie considered the possibility that she had been sleepwalking, as Gary said. She only wished she could be sure.

5

"Well, today's the day, Gary," Derek announced as the two entered Gary's therapy room the next morning. "I'm going to have you start on crutches."

"It's about time," Gary said eagerly.

"Here, wheel yourself to this mat," Derek said. "That's the way."

"What's it for?" Gary asked, looking down at the heavy vinyl mat.

"Hopefully for nothing," Derek said. "How do you feel this morning?"

"Fine," Gary said. He shrugged his shoulders. "Well, a little tired. Melanie and I were up late last night. She went into her studio and found it ransacked. It upset her pretty badly."

"Did someone break into the house?"

"Oh, no!" Gary said. "I found Lad cowering underneath the sofa. I think he knocked over a few things and got scared. Anyway, it's okay now—so let's get on with this."

Derek positioned a pair of crutches under each of his patient's arms, then lowered the footrest of the wheelchair. After warning Gary to go slowly this first time, he stepped back and said, "It's all yours."

Gary grinned at him, his face a mask of confidence. He had waited so long for this day that he was certain he would just get up and speed right across the room.

Suddenly, as he was leaning forward, the chair shot out from behind him. With a frantic cry, Gary dropped the crutches and grabbed for it, landing sideways in the seat. His hands clutched the back, and he looked up at his therapist with wide eyes.

"What happened?"

"Nothing," Derek said firmly. "Try again."

"I'm not so sure ..."

"Try again," Derek said, his voice firm.

"Yes, sir!" Gary answered, eyeing him suspiciously. Was he going to let him fall again?

He repositioned the crutches, then took a deep breath. Slowly he started to get up again. And then he sank back down into the chair, frozen.

Memories of his accident came flooding back to him. He saw himself flying through the window, shards of glass flying, sparkling all around him. Down and down and down ...

His eyes snapped open when his dream-self hit the trash cans below the window. He stared down at his hands, ashamed of his fears. But he still couldn't move.

"I can't do it," he said. "I just don't understand, but I can't do it!"

He was so frustrated that tears began to well in his eyes. Ashamed, he ran his fingers through his hair. This was supposed to be so easy!

Derek was kneeling beside him. "Of course you can do it," he said, with a strange gentleness that Gary had never heard before. "You see, Gary, you associate falling here with the fall that injured you."

Gary blinked and looked at him. "How did you know that?"

"Simple," Derek said, smiling as he stood again. "It's a very common thing with people who were hurt in falls. Why do you think I put that gym mat down?"

"But if you knew that," Gary asked, "why did you let me fall?"

"You didn't really fall," Derek said. "You just got up the wrong way. And I did tell you to be careful. These things take time, Gary."

Gary smiled. "Look at me, will you? An overgrown crybaby. I guess I'd better tackle those damned crutches right now, eh? Before I'm too scared to try them again?"

"That's the boy," Derek said, punching Gary's shoulder.

This time Derek showed Gary how to firmly plant the crutches and to lean forward in such a way that the chair remained stationary. After thirty or more frustrating attempts, Gary was finally able to stand up.

"Now, that's not so hard, is it?" Derek asked.

"What do I do now?" Gary could feel dull pain running up his legs through muscles that hadn't been in this position for months.

"Nothing. You've got a few more days to practice getting up before you try to walk. How do you feel?"

"Achy," Gary said. "But it's a good feeling. You know, like after you've played a hard game of ball?"

Suddenly a delighted yelp and a "Wonderful!" sounded from downstairs. Both Gary and Derek looked at the door, then at each other. Seconds later, Melanie burst into the room. There was a wide grin on her face, but she didn't say anything. She had stopped short to stare at Gary.

"You're standing up!" she cried. "Isn't it wonderful?"

"Isn't what wonderful?" Gary asked as Derek helped him back into the chair. "I'm not walking yet. And what's all the noise about?"

"Oh, Gary," Melanie said, hurrying to put her arms around her husband. "I just got the most wonderful news. My agent booked me into a very prestigious art gallery for the whole month of June—a one-woman show."

"Melanie, I'm so proud of you," Gary said. Melanie leaned down and kissed him. "What do you think of my talented wife, Derek?"

Derek wasn't in the room. He had stepped out, knowing Gary and Melanie might want to be alone at such an important moment. "What do you say we celebrate?" Melanie asked in a soft voice.,

Gary smiled. "What've you got in mind?"

"Come into the bedroom and I'll show you," Melanie said.

Though the rough workout that morning made his legs ache from toe to hip, Gary wouldn't let that hinder him. The joyous happenings of that morning made him want Melanie so much that he could ignore the pain. Melanie was the dominant one in their lovemaking now, but today, Gary used his strong arms to embrace her and fondle her more passionately than he had in months. His movements were forced into slowness by his crippled legs, yet Melanie seemed to revel in it.

A while later, when they were leaning against the headboard in a warm embrace, Melanie said, "This is the best of all. Everything is so wonderful."

"What is?"

"Being with you," Melanie said. "More than my art show,

33

more than the fact you're learning to walk again. I have everything I want, right here and now. I've never been happier in my life."

Gary kissed her. "That doesn't sound like the woman who insisted a ghost led her into the kitchen last night."

"I don't know," Melanie said. "I suppose everything that happened today pushed it out of my mind. I don't feel as apprehensive as I did."

"Have you decided it was all a dream?" Gary asked hopefully.

Melanie shrugged. "I suppose so. But even if it was a dream, I wonder who that woman was?"

"Don't even think about it," Gary said. "Everything is just perfect for us now, Melanie. We'll never be afraid again."

His embrace tightened. "I promise you that."

As Derek drove along Houston Street on the way to the racquetball club, he thought of Gary and Melanie and the love they shared. It had been six years since Elaine's death, and in that time he had never let another woman into his heart. Now he felt an emptiness deep within himself. He really needed to love again. A nice, smart, beautiful woman like Elaine.

"No one's like Elaine," Derek whispered.

But he did meet someone that very day. It happened when he was practicing his Z-shot. He was so mesmerized that he didn't pay attention to anyone else around him, and as he dove for the ball, he slammed into a woman, knocking her to the floor.

"I'm sorry!" he cried, turning quickly to look down at her. "I wasn't—"

He stopped talking for just a moment to look at her. She was a vision, a beautiful woman with high cheekbones and almond eyes. She was dressed in a pale green jogging suit, her long legs sprawled out in front of her. Looking at Derek through strands of dark brown hair that had fallen over her face, she held up her hand. Immediately, he broke from his spell and helped her to her feet.

"You have eyes just like Ava Gardner," he heard himself say.

"What?" the woman shrieked with an embarrassed grin.

Derek shook his head. "I'm sorry," he said. "I shouldn't have said that. Are you okay? Did I hurt you?"

"I'm a lot stronger than I look," the woman said, "although I've probably got a nice bruise on my backside."

"I was working on my Z-shot," Derek explained. "I wasn't paying attention. Is my court time over?"

"Well, no. I was watching you, and I guess I became so caught up that I didn't realize I was walking in here. It was my fault."

"I hope you liked what you saw," Derek said, "for the price you paid."

The woman smiled, showing brilliant white teeth. "I've been trying to get that damned Z-shot for weeks, but I can't seem to do it. You make it look so easy."

"Well, I could show you," Derek offered. "Here, stand like this. . . . By the way, what's your name?"

"Liza Crewe."

"I'm Derek Miller. Now, you hold the racket this way, and . . ."

He showed her a perfect shot. Liza tried to copy him, in vain. Laughing, she tried again and again. While she practiced, she and Derek talked. Liza seemed very interested in Derek's work as a therapist. In turn, she told Derek she was a dance student.

Liza missed the shot for the tenth time, and sighing in frustration, she took a step backward.

"See what I mean?" she cried, waving the racket a little. "I just can't get it."

"You're aiming too low," Derek said. "Here, like this."

"Well," Liza said as she tried again, "I may not be the world's best racquet ball player, but I know I can dance. You're looking at the next Fonteyn."

"You'll be better than Fonteyn," Derek said, though he wasn't quite sure who Fonteyn was.

Liza practiced the Z-shot a while longer, until she did it right a dozen times in a row. She squealed with delight and turned to flash a grin at Derek. She was positively the most gorgeous woman he had ever seen. For a moment he forgot about Elaine.

"Do you live here in town?"

"I have an apartment over a house," Liza said. "I'd like to live in the city, but there're just too many worries there. Belle Bay is so peaceful. It's a nice place to come home to after a long day."

"You don't seem like a worrier," Derek said as they walked off the court.

"Oh, I worry a lot," Liza admitted. "I worry that twenty-eight is too old to take ballet lessons. And stage fright is my pet phobia, believe it or don't."

"I don't," Derek said. "And I think it's great you're studying something you enjoy. Just one question—why did you wait so long?"

Liza sighed. "My father has been sick for many years, and I felt guilty about leaving him down in Florida. That, and the fact I couldn't afford it. But dad's better now, and he even paid half my tuition."

"I'm glad he did," Derek said.

They went off to their respective locker rooms. Thirty minutes later Liza reappeared wearing a lavender dress that showed off her figure beautifully.

"Will I see you here again, I hope?" Derek asked.

"Sure, when will you be here?"

"Saturday morning?"

Frowning, Liza shook her head. "Sorry, I have rehearsal. How about next Thursday?"

"I'll be here," Derek promised.

He grinned ear to ear all the way home, too caught up in his thoughts of Liza to notice the blond-haired woman watching him from the roadside.

6

Derek wasn't the only one falling in love that day. In the cafeteria of Saint Anne's school, Alicen was sitting with red-haired Jamie Hutchinson, much to her chagrin. Too shy to let the boy be her friend, she had tried to ignore him. But Jamie, who was naturally friendly, had followed her to the lunchroom every day to sit across from her. He tried to win her over with bags of cookies and potato chips, but Alicen always refused. She would stare down at her food, barely glancing up at him every once in a while.

"You're too weird, Alicen," Jamie said one day. He took something out of his lunch bag—a huge chocolate bar—and pushed it across the linoleum table. "That's for you. And don't tell me you don't like chocolate."

"I love chocolate," Alicen said, gingerly touching the

candy. She had never received a present from a boy before and didn't know how to react. Her "thank you" was barely audible.

"Don't mention it," said Jamie. "And listen, don't leave it in your desk. It'll melt."

Alicen nodded. Then suddenly she found her tongue. "Why are you doing this?"

"Doing what?"

"Being so nice to me," Alicen said.

Jamie clicked his tongue. "Because I like you, silly. Can't you take a hint?"

"Why?"

"Why shouldn't I?"

"Because I'm fat and—"

"You're not *that* fat," Jamie said.

Alicen started to protest, but he stopped her.

"You really want to know why I like you?" he asked. " 'Cause I knew from the minute you walked into our classroom that you weren't a phony. You weren't wearing designer jewelry, like all the other girls. I think those things are dumb."

"So do I," Alicen said. She was surprised to find herself smiling.

"Gee, you look pretty when you smile," Jamie said.

He was so charming that Alicen felt herself begin to relax. She learned in their conversation that his father owned a butcher shop in town, and when Jamie asked why she had come to Belle Bay, she told him that her father was a therapist. He became very excited when he learned she was living in the big white house on Starbine Court Road.

"But I already told you that," Alicen said.

"No, you didn't," Jamie said. "You just told me you were living with some girl named Gina."

"Her father's my father's patient," Alicen explained.

"Wow!" Jamie cried. "You live in that spooky old mansion? Did you know it was haunted?"

"That's silly," Alicen said, taking a bite of her sandwich.

"I heard stories," Jamie said. "See, it was built a zillion years ago, and everytime anyone moved into it they either left in a hurry, or"—his eyes became very round, and he spoke slowly, teasing Alicen—"they died."

"You're crazy!" Alicen cried.

"Quiet down there!" the cafeteria monitor yelled.

Jamie was snickering. Alicen frowned at him.

"It is not haunted," she said in a softer voice.

37

"A bunch of people died there last year," Jamie said. "And if you don't believe me, it was in the papers."

"Liar!" Alicen hissed. "I'm not going to make a jerk out of myself by looking up a story that never happened."

She was glad when the lunch bell rang. She moved quickly away from him, but he caught up with her.

"Hey, I'm really sorry I scared you," Jamie said. "But it is true."

"Well, I'll ask Mrs. VanBuren tonight," Alicen said. "And I still think you're lying."

But somehow, she was unable to ask Melanie. Dinner came, and still she hesitated. She was terrified that they'd make fun of her or that her father would become angry that she'd fall for such a story. Murders? In this beautiful old house?

Still, she wasn't quite so sure. . . .

"Alicen, pass me the bread?" Kyle asked.

Alicen started, jumping out of her thoughts.

"What's up?" Melanie asked. "Daydreaming?"

"No," Alicen said. She handed Kyle the bread basket.

"I'll bet she's thinking about that Jamie Hutchinson," Kyle teased.

Alicen looked at him.

"Kyle—" Gary said in a warning tone.

"Who's Jamie Hutchinson?" Derek asked.

"Just a boy in my class," Alicen said, embarrassed.

"Well, I hope he's just a friend," Derek said. "You're much too young for boys."

"How do you know about him, Kyle?" Melanie asked. "Do you eat lunch at the same time as Alicen?"

"No," Kyle said. "Jamie's brother Mikey is in my class. He told me Jamie talks about Alicen all the time."

Alicen sank lower into her chair.

"That's so neat," Gina said. "I wish a boy would talk about me."

"Somebody will, honey," Gary said. "When that day comes."

Nancy, who had been concentrating on her dinner, held out her empty plate. "Mommy, I want more spaghetti!"

Melanie took the plate from her daughter and went to the kitchen to refill it. She was surprised when she turned and saw Alicen behind her. Alicen shook her head when asked if she wanted more, too.

"Uh, Mrs. VanBuren?"

"What is it, Alicen?"

"I just wanted to know if, uhm—"

She shifted back and forth, staring down at her feet. "Oh, never mind!" she cried, hurrying back into the dining room.

"Now, what was that all about?" Melanie wondered out loud as she watched the door swing shut.

Alicen probably wanted to ask her something about boys but was too embarrassed. Considering she didn't have a mother, she probably didn't know what boys were all about. Derek didn't seem the type to sit down with his daughter and talk about the facts of life.

"The poor kid," Melanie said, picking up Nancy's dish. "It must be tough growing up without a mother."

Later, when Gina and Alicen were helping her with the dishes, she leaned over and whispered, "If you ever want to talk, I'm here. I can keep a secret."

"Okay," Alicen said. She appreciated that, but still couldn't bring herself to ask Melanie if the house was haunted. The more she thought, the more Alicen decided it was just a silly story.

Until that night, when she heard the laughter again. . . .

As before, she was in bed when the laughter started. She turned on her stomach and buried her head under her pillow. The laughter rose to a high pitch, filling her room. Finally, she couldn't stand it any more—she had to convince herself that it was only a draft blowing through the grating in the floor. She climbed out of her bed.

When she switched on her light, the glare blinded her, and she had to grope toward the grating. She was going to put her hands over it, to feel that there was air coming up through it. Then she would know there was nothing to fear.

She dropped to her knees on the carpet and put her hands out. No draft, though she could still hear the laughter. What *was* that? Something made her crawl nearer, and she looked down into the grating.

"EEEYYYAAA!"

She jumped back, screaming. A hideous face had smiled up at her! Even as she stumbled to her bed and sat there crying, she could see it in her mind's eye. The eyes had been blue and filmy, the smile revealing sharp teeth. There was blood caked on the blue-veined forehead.

The door opened just then. Alicen looked up through tears to see her father entering the room, his eyes shadowed with concern.

"What's wrong?" he asked, coming nearer to her bed. "Were you dreaming?"

"I—I saw a face," Alicen choked.

She pointed to the grating in the floor. "I heard funny noises, and when I went over to look, there was this ugly face under there!"

"Alicen, that's just ridiculous," Derek said. "You were dreaming."

Now Melanie was standing in the doorway. "I heard Alicen. What's wrong?"

"Nothing," Derek said. "My daughter was just having a bad dream. I hope it didn't wake the other children."

"They're sleeping soundly," Melanie said. She came up to Alicen's bed. "Honey, what on earth were you dreaming about?"

"It wasn't a dream," Alicen insisted, wishing they would just go away and leave her alone. "I saw a face staring at me under the floor grating."

"It was probably just a trick of the lights," Derek said, standing. He had Alicen firmly by the arm. "Come over here and I'll show you there's nothing there."

"NNNNOOOO!"

"Shut up!" Derek snapped. "You want to wake the other kids, like at the Laines' house?"

"I don't want to go over there!"

Melanie moved forward to intervene, but not quickly enough to stop Derek from dragging his screaming child to the floor grating. She stood stiffly, with her face turned away, an icy chill crawling over her.

"Look at it, Alicen," Derek ordered. "There is nothing there!"

"No!"

Derek, exasperated, twisted her arm a little. Alicen obeyed him at last and saw the grating was empty.

"Dad, I know I—"

"You were dreaming," Derek insisted.

Melanie felt something in her stomach go sour, something that told her Alicen hadn't been dreaming at all.

"What made you have such an awful dream?" she asked.

"Jamie Hutchinson," Alicen said. "He told me people were murdered in this house. Is that true?"

Melanie gasped a little, then quickly said, "No no, of course it isn't true. Now, you just lie down and go back to sleep. Would you like some tea or hot chocolate to help you relax?"

Alicen was looking into Derek's yes. The warning in them made her shake her head.

"No, I'll be okay," she said.

40

Seeing the girl shivering, Melanie went to the bureau and pulled out an extra blanket. To her surprise, Derek took it from her and laid it over his daughter. Then he bent and kissed her forehead.

"You'll be all right," he said.

He walked with Melanie out to the hall, closing Alicen's door very tightly before speaking. "I'm sorry," he said. "I don't know why she behaves so hysterically."

"It's all right," Melanie said, resisting the urge to tell Derek off for being so rough with the child. "I'm sure Alicen will forget all this by morning."

Derek waved his hand. "No. She's had nightmares before this—about Elaine's death. I was certain she was over them. Now she's probably wakened your children."

"I told you they were sleeping," Melanie said. She laughed, trying to ease the tension. "My kids sleep through wars."

"I just don't understand her," Derek said softly.

"It's no wonder she had nightmares," Melanie said. "After those stories Jamie Hutchinson told her about murders. What would possess a boy to do that?"

"Showing off, I guess," Derek said. But something in Melanie's face told him there was more to it than this. Her eyes were just a little too wide, and her smile was just a little too forced.

"Uh, there isn't any truth to that, is there?" he asked. "I know it's a stupid question, but—"

"Derek, nothing bad ever happened in this house," Melanie insisted. "Look, I'm really tired. I'll see you in the morning."

With that, she hurried down the dark hallway. She got into bed, closed her eyes, and pressed herself close to Gary, as if his body could act as a barrier against the darkness. She pulled the covers clear up to her chin, not wanting an inch of her body exposed to the night. Then she buried her face in Gary's chest and breathed deeply. Soon, out of sheer exhaustion, she fell asleep.

Someone touched her arm. Melanie opened her eyes slowly and looking at the clock radio vaguely noted that several hours had passed. She closed her eyes again and snuggled closer to Gary. But when she heard her name, she opened them again and turned around.

The dark-haired woman was standing next to her bed. "Come," she said, taking Melanie's hand.

Without protest, Melanie rose from the bed and followed the woman from the room. She felt sleepy and yet keenly aware of the noises in the house. The wind blew outside, rattling the windows. Nancy was mumbling in her sleep, and Lad gave one yelp from the kitchen.

But Lad was sound asleep when they entered that room. Once again, the light was shining brightly. Able to see her surroundings, Melanie felt stronger; her voice was somewhat harsh when she demanded, "What does all this mean?"

The woman shrank from her words.

"Please," Melanie said, more gently, "I know you're trying to tell me something. What is it?"

"It is not over yet," the woman said sadly.

"What isn't?" Melanie asked, though she felt something gnawing at her stomach. "Please tell me! I can't fight what I don't know!"

"You must leave this place!" the woman cried. She looked over her shoulder, her brown eyes wide with terror. Then she turned back to Melanie.

"I must go!" she cried, wringing her tattered gown. "She comes now. She is evil!"

"Who is she?" Melanie demanded.

But the woman disappeared. Melanie took a step forward, and as she did so, the room light went out. She swung around terrified, expecting to see something hovering behind her in the darkness. But no one was there.

"What do you want?" Melanie whispered. "Who are you?"

No answer. The clock above the sink began to tick loudly. Melanie stared up at it, unmoving. Her eyes began to droop, though she desperately wanted to stay awake. She sank down to the floor.

She forced her eyes open again. But she wasn't looking up at the clock. She was looking at the clock radio next to her bed. It was 7:30 A.M., and the sun was shining.

It was just another dream, she told herself insistently. I just had the horrible incidents of last year on my mind.

In broad daylight it was easier to convince herself not to be afraid.

Much to Alicen's relief, nothing was said about the incident at breakfast. Alicen sat with her head low to her cereal bowl, trying to make herself believe it had been a dream. But it had seemed so real!

Across the table, Derek was also thinking about it. He recalled the series of nightmares Alicen had had after her mother died. Was that happening again? Or was his daughter overly impressed by tall tales of a young boy? Funny, Melanie had seemed a little unnerved about it all, more than she should have been if it was only a dream. He looked over the rim of his coffee cup at her. She was reading an art magazine, nibbling on a piece of toast. Derek recalled the strange way she had behaved the night before. He wondered if she had been hiding a secret—something to do with the murders Alicen had spoken of. But that was just ridiculous, Derek thought. Melanie had flatly denied it, and the VanBurens were hardly the types to be involved in murders. No, it was just a dream. That was all there was to it.

"Mom, you have to sign a permission slip for me," Gina said then, interrupting his thoughts. She pulled a piece of blue paper from between the pages of a book.

"What's it for?" Melanie asked.

"The eighth grade is going on a trip to Vanderbilt Planetarium," Gina explained.

"Are you going?" Derek asked Alicen.

Alicen nodded and produced her own slip of paper. Derek and Melanie read and signed them. Gina smiled at Melanie. Alicen did not smile at her father.

"We'll have to do something special for your graduation," Gary said. "Maybe we could have a family reunion."

"What a good idea!" Melanie said. "Our family hasn't really seen this house yet."

"You never had a housewarming?" Derek asked.

"Well, we were kind of—*busy* the first months," Melanie faltered.

Alicen stirred her cereal. Without raising her head, she looked up at Melanie. What were they busy with? Murders?

"What's the matter?" Gina asked her.

"Nothing," Alicen said, shoving a spoonful of cereal into her mouth.

Later Gary and Derek left for a session of therapy and Gina and Kyle went out to the bus stop but Alicen dawdled, fingering the counter and finding excuses to delay. She bent down to tie a shoe that was already tied. Then she leaned heavily on the counter, finding a place for her elbow amid all the dishes and propping her chin on her hand. She looked up at Melanie.

"Do you think I could have another bedroom?"

"Why?" Melanie asked. "Because of last night?"

43

Alicen nodded. "I saw a face—I know I did! It had blond hair, and it was *ugly*. I don't want to stay in that room."

Melanie put her hand against Alicen's cheek.

"Honey, it's just a dream," she insisted. "This house is as safe as can be."

"Jamie Hutchinson said—"

"Jamie Hutchinson is a big fibber," Melanie said. "And if I get hold of him I'll—well, never mind. Just realize that boys often make up stories to impress the girls they like."

"They do?"

"They do," Melanie said. "Hey, here comes the bus! You'd better hurry and catch up with the others."

Alicen started to run out the door, but before she did she turned and kissed Melanie on the cheek. Melanie watched her race down the hill, thinking her weight made her look much younger than thirteen. She wasn't happy to hear about that boy teasing her. Wasn't it obvious that Alicen had enough problems? A mother who was dead, a father who had no patience with her?

Melanie went to the sink and tried to concentrate on the breakfast dishes. Somehow, alone in the kitchen with Alicen's "dream" on her mind, she was taken back to the night when Gary had been hurt. She saw a tall, dark-haired intruder fighting with her husband. She heard Gary's scream, then glass shattering.

Somehow, she could believe that Alicen had really seen a face. What had she said? That it was blond-haired and ugly? Now Melanie closed her eyes and saw a face herself. It was of a young, pretty blond woman. She was smiling, but then the smile faded and turned into an evil grimace. Melanie's eyes snapped open.

She felt her lungs constrict, and a weakness in her legs that came when she was feeling guilty about something. But why? She had nothing to do with the woman's death. Why did she always feel such pain to think about her? Last night, when Gary had mentioned the librarian's death, she had wanted to scream. If it wasn't her fault, why did she always feel such guilt about it?

"It isn't guilt," Melanie said. "It's sorrow."

She scrubbed hard at a frying pan. "Oh, Janice," she whispered. "Why did you have to die like that?"

Suddenly the frying pan slipped from her hand. It fell to the floor with a loud clatter and rocked there before settling at Melanie's feet. Sighing, she bent down to retrieve it.

"I've gotten myself so nervous I'm dropping things," Melanie said out loud. "I've got to stop thinking this way!"

She wiped at the pot with furious motions. "Everything is all right," she said.

She was unaware that an unseen hand had knocked the skillet from her, a gesture of anger at her words. Everything was not all right.

You killed me! the being shouted, as if Melanie could hear her. *It's your fault I walk in darkness, and you'll pay for it!*

But not yet, Melanie VanBuren. I won't let you discover me until it's too late.

7

Melanie decided the best way to conquer her fears was to work hard on her painting. She finished the two paintings for Sarah Kaufman sooner than she had expected. One day, she dropped Nancy off at kindergarten and headed toward the mayor's house. It was a mansion on the other side of town, as big as theirs, but much newer.

"Let me see the masterpieces," Sarah said, inviting Melanie to sit down in the living room. "I can't believe you finished them already!"

She tore the brown paper from the two canvases and propped them against the table. Sarah gasped and lifted one of them to study it. Then she carried it to the fireplace, setting it on the mantel in front of a portrait of some distant relative. She stepped back and admired Melanie's painting.

"Look at the detail!" she cried happily. "I love the way the sun's rays hit the church spire. And I can almost count every bud on the rosebushes."

She turned and smiled at Melanie. "They're pink."

"Well, of course," Melanie said. "That's what you asked for."

"Marc is going to be so pleased," Sarah said. "I haven't told him about these, yet. They're a surprise for his birthday."

As Sarah poured coffee into dainty gold demitasse cups, Melanie looked around the elegant living room. "Are these antiques family heirlooms?" she asked.

"Oh, no. I found them in antique shops over the years." Sarah said.

"My husband collects antiques, too," Melanie said. "That's one of the reasons he bought our house. It's the one at the top of Starbine Court."

"Oh, yes," Sarah said. "Marc and I nearly bought it a few years ago."

Melanie's eyebrows went up. She put her coffee cup back in its saucer. "Why didn't you?" she asked, curious.

"Well, I don't really know," Sarah said. She seemed embarrassed and turned to look out the French windows. "I just didn't like the place. There was something about it that made me feel uneasy."

Melanie stiffened. "What was that?"

"Oh, it was silly," Sarah said, waving her hand. The huge diamond she wore on her finger sparkled brightly in the sunlight. "I'd been ill at the time—perhaps I just wasn't receptive to it. Not to say it isn't a beautiful home. But this one is more to my tastes. Your house has a rather masculine air about it, don't you think?"

"I suppose that reflects the man who built it," Melanie said.

"Do you know about him?" Sarah asked, leaning forward eagerly.

"His name was Jacob Armand," Melanie said, not really wanting to talk about it, but there was no way out. "He was a captain in the British navy during the 1790s."

"How interesting," Sarah said.

"Yes, it is," Melanie said, taking a sip of coffee. "But that's all I know about him. Say, these roses are lovely. Do you have a garden?"

"I sure do," Sarah said eagerly. "Would you like to see it?"

They wandered in the garden, then sat outside talking, until Melanie realized her children would be home from school. But before she left Melanie invited Sarah and the mayor for dinner the following week. She liked Sarah, and it wouldn't hurt her career to have the mayor and his wife known as her patrons.

Melanie left the house in a happy mood, whistling as she drove home. All of a sudden, she spotted Alicen Miller trudging down the street. Wondering why she wasn't on the

46

school bus, Melanie honked the horn. Alicen turned and squinted at her. Melanie pulled the car over to the curb and let her in.

"What happened?"

"I missed the bus," Alicen said, wriggling in the seat to get comfortable.

"Wasn't Gina with you?"

"No, she must be home by now," said Alicen. She clicked her tongue and sighed. "Oh! I had to stay after school because I got into trouble today. That's the real reason I missed the bus."

"You?" Melanie asked. "How on earth did you get in trouble?"

"That dumb old Mr. Percy—that's my teacher—sent me to the principal's office. He said I never pay attention to him. I tried really hard, but I kept thinking about that dream I had."

Melanie took the girl's hand and squeezed it.

"Is that still bothering you?" she asked. "I know it was horrible, but it was just a dream. Keep telling yourself that, and you'll feel better."

"That's what I was doing this afternoon," Alicen said. "And I got into trouble 'cause of it."

"Did you explain the situation to the principal?"

"She didn't want to hear it," Alicen said. She stared down at the books on her lap. "No one wants to listen to me."

"And they call themselves teachers," Melanie grumbled. Louder, she said, "They should at least have driven you home. Your father must be frantic!"

"My father never worries about me," Alicen said. "He probably doesn't know I'm not home yet."

That evening when Derek left for the health club, he packed his jacket and a good shirt in his duffel bag. As he drove to the club, his thoughts were on Liza. He hoped she would accept an invitation to go out for a midnight snack. He was trying to decide where they should go when something made him look in his rear-view mirror. A few hundred yards behind, he saw the blond hitchhiker again. Sighing, he pushed his foot down on the gas pedal. At least he knew she was alive, he thought. But she'd never get in his car again.

He sped down the road a few more miles, putting a distance between himself and the girl before easing the pressure of his foot.

I don't know why I let that girl upset me, he thought as he entered the "safety" of the club.

One look at Liza made him forget the hitchhiker completely. She was sitting in the waiting room, dressed in white terry, racket in hand. She smiled at Derek and stood up.

"Am I late?" he asked.

"Not at all," Liza said. "Go put your things in a locker, and I'll meet you on the court."

Much to Derek's surprise, Liza turned out to be a terrific racquet ball player. She explained that the Z-shot he'd helped her with a week ago was her only problem and that she'd been playing the game for years. She beat him two out of three.

"I probably shouldn't admit this," Derek said as they walked off the court, "but my ego's been shattered."

"It'd be wrong to say I'm sorry," Liza teased. "I played fair and square."

"You play like a man," Derek said. "Just watch out next time, lady."

Liza put her hands on her hips and tossed back her dark hair.

"What do you mean I 'play like a man'?" she asked "I play to win, and that's all. You're sexist."

"Sorry," Derek said. "It's just that I've never been defeated by a woman."

Shut up, Derek, he told himself. *Before you blow it.*

"It isn't that painful, is it?" Liza asked.

Derek thought for a moment. "No, I guess not. Especially not when you're my partner. Say, would you like to relax in the whirlpool awhile?"

"I was thinking the same thing," Liza said. "Meet you there in ten minutes."

Derek was relieved to find the whirlpool unoccupied. He leaned back, letting the water massage his aching muscles. A day of therapy with Gary, and three games had made him sore all over. He opened his eyes and smiled lazily when Liza sat down beside him.

"That bathing suit is beautiful," Derek said. "Almost as beautiful as the woman in it."

"Okay," Liza said, laughing, "you've earned your Brownie points. I don't think you're sexist any more."

"I mean it," Derek said. "You look as if you're in top physical condition. I—uh—I'm speaking from a therapist's point of view, of course."

"Of course," Liza said, smiling. "Remember I'm a dancer, and I keep myself in shape."

"That's obvious," Derek said.

That's the understatement of the year, he thought. She was downright stunning. Her one-piece suit clung tightly to her, its shiny material showing off her curves. There was just enough fat on her body to make her soft looking, but not an ounce too much. She had rolled her hair up, and now her cheekbones stood out. Derek couldn't help staring at her.

"I've thought about you all week," he said.

"Really?" Liza asked, sounding pleased. "I was afraid you'd forget me."

"Are you kidding?" Derek asked. "I was hoping you'd want to see me again."

Liza moved a little closer to him. A second later, he felt her hand on his thigh. He gaped at her, then grinned. She smiled slightly, teasingly.

"I've only known you for a while," she said, "yet I know you're my kind of man."

"Thanks," Derek said. God, it had been so long since a woman had touched him this way. Unseen beneath the foamy waters, he slid his arm around Liza's waist.

"I think I'm falling in love," he said.

"Me, too," was the answer.

They stared at each other. Without another word, Derek leaned forward and kissed Liza. She moaned a little, pushing herself closer to him. They kissed passionately, so passionately that they suddenly slipped and went under the water. They quickly pulled each other up and sat there laughing hysterically.

"Do all great love affairs start this way?" Liza asked, rubbing her eyes.

"I don't know," Derek said. "But they ought to. I've never been kissed like that before."

He thought for a split second of Elaine, feeling a little guilty. Then he smiled again and took Liza's hand.

"Want to get dressed?" he asked.

"Sure," she said, a little breathlessly. "I've got to get home to practice."

"Practice?" Derek asked. "But I was hoping we could go out somewhere."

"Some other time," Liza said, giving him an apologetic smile. "I have a recital coming up tomorrow."

"You should have told me about it," Derek said. "I would have gone."

"It's private. Only for the dance instructor and class. I'll be advanced according to how I do on this."

"You'll do great," Derek said. "I just wish you could come with me tonight."

"Don't be disappointed, honey," Liza said, kissing him.

"I'll see you soon," Derek said.

"You bet."

They hugged for a few minutes, their wet bodies pressed so close that they could feel each other's heat rising. At last, Derek pulled away.

He didn't wait to see Liza again, but went straight to his Volvo. He unlocked the door, got behind the wheel, and drove out of the parking lot. The car had taken him halfway home when someone suddenly tapped his shoulder and said, "Hello."

Startled out of his thoughts of Liza, Derek turned around and saw the hitchhiker sitting in the back seat. She was grinning.

"What in the hell are you doing here?" Derek demanded angrily.

"I waited for you," the woman said. "I wanted to talk."

"What for?" Derek asked. "Why do you keep following me? We don't even know each other."

"Well, my name is Janice," she said. "And I know you very well."

Suddenly she jumped over the back of the seat. Her hand fell between Derek's legs, grabbing him. He jumped, feeling a pain in his groin as intense as if she had kicked him. The car jumped a curb, and Derek moved quickly to straighten it again.

"Are you crazy?" Derek shouted, pulling over and stopping. "Get the hell out of my car!"

"I want you," the woman said, unbuttoning his slacks.

Derek pushed her hand away. It was like moving cotton. He turned and looked at her, assessing her strength. She'd be easy enough to throw out of the car, but he didn't want to give her a chance to have him arrested for assault.

"Just get out," he said. "I don't want to hurt you. Just leave me alone."

"The way you left me alone?" she demanded as she opened the door. "You'll pay for that, Derek Miller."

She was out of the car before he realized he had never told

her his name. He jumped out of the car, calling out: "How'd you know my name?"

But the street was now completely deserted. Filled with curiosity, Derek walked up and down, looking for the strange woman. But she was nowhere to be found. Wondering how she could have slipped into the shadows so quickly, he returned to his car. He had never been a man to fear threats, and so he climbed into the car and tried to put the incident out of his mind.

"What could that crazy little bitch do to me?" he asked himself.

He drove home at a faster speed than usual, unwilling to admit that the thought of the woman knowing his name made his flesh crawl.

8

Derek stared up at the beam of dark wood that ran across his ceiling. He had been awake for an hour, trying to make sense of the evening's strange events. His hands were folded behind his head, and his teeth dug into his lower lip, pressing harder as his thoughts grew more intense. He had already decided how the woman had gotten into his car. It was old, and the lock didn't work very well. But how did she know where to find him? And more than that, how did she knew his name?

Derek shook his head roughly, driving away sleep that wanted to claim him. He wanted this mystery solved, *now*.

Thinking the comfortable bed was making his mind wander, he got out of it and pulled on his robe. Walking barefoot out to the hall, he closed the door softly. He stopped when he heard a whimpering noise—Alicen talking in her sleep. Derek ran his fingers through his hair, then reached for the knob of her door. His fingers held it but hesitated.

"Mommy!"

The kid sounded so frantic.

"Mommy, come home."

Derek pulled his hand away from the door. Another dream? When were those going to stop? When was Alicen going to face the fact that her mother wasn't ever going to come home?

But he knew Alicen would never accept the truth. Even though she had seen Elaine's car explode and had stood there watching as the twisted body was pulled from the wreck, she refused to believe it was her mother. That first year had been especially painful. Alicen would look outside every time a car stopped in front of the apartment house, hoping it was her mother.

Derek was struck with the painful memory of Alicen's eighth birthday. Elaine had only been dead a month.

"Mommy told me she'd buy me a new dress," Alicen had said.

Derek could almost feel her small arms around his waist. He closed his eyes.

"I know, darling," he had replied. "But mommy's gone now. And you know how expensive the funeral was. I'm afraid you'll have to wait for your dress."

"Oh, that's all right," the little girl said cheerfully. "I'll have a new dress when mommy comes home."

Derek recalled that he had given her a stuffed animal. Alicen had almost crushed him with her hug. She had once been such an affectionate child. But over the years she had drawn into a shell, until Derek could barely remember their last loving embrace.

He felt a pain for the child that used to be and drove it away.

He shuffled down the hall, then the stairs, and finally entered the kitchen. He always felt as if he were walking into another time zone. Despite the antiques in the rest of the house, the VanBurens had equipped their kitchen with every up-to-date convenience, from the white side-by-side freezer-refrigerator to the gleaming green and yellow tiled floor. The only antique in here was a wooden table with X-shaped legs. He sat down and propped his feet up on one of the X's. At that moment Lad jumped up and barked at him.

"Shh," Derek whispered. He slapped his thigh. "Come here, boy."

Lad rested his chin on Derek's knee. The soulful brown eyes looked up into Derek's, asking for affection. Derek stroked the dog's smooth head and spoke to him as if he were human.

"Can you figure this out?" he asked. "What do you suppose that woman wants from me?" Lad whined. "I don't know, either," Derek said, yawning.

He leaned back in the chair and turned to gaze through the back-door window at the moon. Sighing deeply, he just sat, waiting for an answer to come to him.

"Wait a minute," he said, turning to the dog again. "I know! Suppose, for some crazy reason she's been spying on me? She must know I go to the health club a few nights a week. She just followed me there and hid out in my car."

It made sense, but it didn't answer the most important question: *why?* What could she want from him? He had no money to speak of, and little of value—*nothing* of value, he corrected himself.

Suddenly Lad let out a growl and leaped for the back door. Startled, Derek pushed his chair back and went to investigate. The hitchhiker was staring through the back-door window! She was smiling at him, her pointy teeth glistening wetly. Her eyes, shining with malevolent delight, had a filmy look to them. She didn't move or make a sound. She just stood there grinning.

"You bitch!" Darek hissed.

He turned quickly to the cupboard behind him and removed the back-door key. As he twisted the lock, he glowered at the woman's hideous face. He wouldn't be afraid. He'd let her in and make her tell him....

But just as Derek got the door open, she ducked away. He stepped outside quickly and peered around through the darkness. He could see the silhouettes of the trees beyond the huge back yard; nothing seemed to be moving. The moon above cast a silver-gray glow over everything at such an angle that there were no shadows.

"She must have run into the woods," Derek reasoned, "and there is no way I'm going to chase her around out there."

Let her go, his mind ordered.

He locked the door behind him. It was all a sick joke, of course. He shuddered and rubbed his arms to ward off a sudden chill. Lad nudged him and after receiving a few strokes of reassurance, went under the table to sleep.

Oh, damn, Derek thought as he headed out of the kitchen.

Never a man to be easily frightened, he decided to forget the whole thing. How could he let it upset him? It was just some smart-ass kid in old clothes and Halloween makeup. He'd ignore her. He wouldn't give her the satisfaction of showing fear. Maybe she'd get bored and leave him alone.

He did not know that it wouldn't be that easy.

* * *

"God, you look like you've been through the mill," Gary said when he entered the kitchen the next morning to find Derek already up.

"I didn't sleep much last night," Derek answered, yawning into a cup of coffee. He poured another and set it in front of Gary.

"Thanks," Gary said, adjusting himself in his wheelchair. "I thought I heard Lad barking."

"I was here in the kitchen," Derek explained. He took a sip of coffee. "Hey, Gary, are there any other families around here?"

"Not for a mile or so. And we told you the house down the road's been empty for several months. Why?"

"Well, some crazy kid's been bothering me lately. I made the stupid mistake of giving her a lift in my car one day—right down on Houston—and she's been following me around ever since."

"Maybe she's got a crush on you?" Gary asked.

"Oh, no," Derek said, shaking his head. "This isn't infatuation, it's harassment. She is probably out of her mind. You should see her. She has stringy blond hair, blue eyes, and sickly pale skin. I mean, you can almost see her veins through it." He thought a little more, then said, "Oh, yeah, and her hands are always red. Like she has frostbite."

"It's a little late in the spring for frostbite, don't you think?"

"Of course," Derek said. "She's using some kind of makeup on her hands. And on her face, too. She's just too pale—like something out of a horror movie."

Melanie entered the kitchen just then. She greeted them cheerily as Kyle scooted around her to the refrigerator.

"What intense expressions!" she cried. "What's going on?"

"Some girl's been harassing Derek lately," Gary said. He cast a look at Kyle, who seemed to be busy filling his cereal bowl. "Do you know any young women with blond hair and pale skin?"

"Yea," Melanie said, laughing. "Me."

"Paler," Derek said. "Like death warmed over. And her hair was a lighter blond. It's down to her waist and looks like she hasn't combed it in a week or two."

Melanie shook her head. "No, I don't know anyone like that." She went to the refrigerator and took out a container of milk.

"Wait," Derek said. "She told me her name. Do you know anyone named Janice?"

The milk container fell to the floor, the white liquid spilling all over the floor. "Oh, God," Melanie said in a soft voice. She waved her hands. "No, damn it. I don't know anyone named Janice."

She went to the pantry for a mop. Her heart was beating rapidly, and she felt a chill crawling over her. She rubbed hard at the milk, keeping her back to the others. Derek eyed her, wondering why she had reacted so strangely to the mention of Janice's name. Perhaps she did know her?

Later Derek asked Gary about Melanie's reaction. Gary tried to explain it.

"See, Melanie had a good friend once named Janice," he said. "But she died the same night I was hurt. Uhm—I was unconscious at the time, but they told me later that the same—uhm—the same guy who pushed me from the window killed her."

"No wonder Melanie was upset. I probably brought back painful memories," Derek said apologetically.

"Melanie's sensitive about it," Gary said. "She somehow feels responsible for what happened to Janice, but of course that's ridiculous."

"What did happen to her?"

Gary stopped and stared into his eyes. "I don't really know," he said.

"Well, okay," Derek replied. "But I know of course that that Janice isn't the one who was in my car. Not if she's dead. There're no such things as ghosts."

Across the room, an unseen woman laughed silently.

Oh, but there are ghosts, my handsome Derek! she cried, unheard by him. *You'll soon learn how real I am! They'll all learn, and they'll pay for what they did to me.*

Derek decided he would simply ignore the woman the next time she showed up. But a week had gone by with no sign of her. Well, that was fine. Maybe she had seen him with Liza and decided he wasn't single and worth pursuing any more.

Tonight he was dressing in his best clothes for the dinner with Sarah and Marc Kaufman. He had bought Alicen a new dress (much to her surprise). His child shouldn't look like a street urchin around all this wealth.

Down the hallway, Melanie was in Nancy's room, busy tying and retying the blue sash to her daughter's best dress. Kyle bounced on the bed, whining about his seersucker suit.

Gina stood at the vanity table with Alicen, combing her friend's hair.

"Kyle, sit still," Melanie said, at last finishing the bow. "You'll mess up your clothes."

"How come I hafta wear these dumb pants?" Kyle asked, settling on the mattress. "They're scratchy!"

"Oh, Kyle," Gina said in a motherly tone, "stop complaining. You look very nice."

Kyle clicked his tongue and jumped from the bed, heading for the door. Just as he reached it, Gary entered the room, on crutches. Kyle stopped short to avoid a collision, his arms spread out at his sides.

"Where are you going so fast?" Gary asked, laughing.

"Downstairs to the kitchen," Kyle said, ducking past him.

"Stay out of the food!" Melanie called. She smiled at Gary. "Say, you look great. It's been a long time since you wore a suit."

"And a long time since I was walking," Gary said. "I hope I do okay tonight."

"You'll do fine," Melanie reassured him. This was the first time Gary would be using his crutches in front of strangers. Melanie went to him and slid her arms around his waist. They kissed warmly.

"We make a beautiful couple," she said.

"You're beautiful," Gary said, running his hands over her peach-colored jersey dress. "And you've really done a great job tonight. I've never seen the kids so immaculate."

He looked over his shoulder at his daughters. Gina was dressed in an eyelet-trimmed denim jumper, while Nancy wore a red-and-white flowered dress. Even Alicen was attired neatly. Her father had bought her a stylish shirtdress with tiny vertical stripes that made her chubby body look a little thinner.

"You'd think it was Easter Sunday," he said.

"It isn't going to kill you," Melanie responded, picking up a comb from Nancy's dresser to brush her hair for the fifth time.

Now Nancy opened her little jewelry box, revealing a tiny dancing ballerina. She lifted out a silver and turquoise bracelet. Gina offered to help her put it on, but Nancy refused, insisting that her father do it. Gary obliged, smiling at his little daughter.

"Why don't you kids go downstairs?" Melanie said after he had finished. "You can make sure everything looks right."

56

"Yea," Gary said. "Your mother's expecting the queen of England."

"It's just the mayor," Nancy said.

"The way your mother's got you kids dressed up," Gary said, "she might as well be the queen of England."

"Gary!" Melanie cried.

Gary left the room laughing. Melanie had to admit he was right, though.

Sarah arrived wearing a pale pink suit. Four gold chains hung from her neck, and gold earrings dangled from her ears.

"Boy, she looks rich," Kyle whispered.

Melanie aimed a swat behind her to hush her son, then smiled and greeted Sarah and Marc Kaufman. Marc, who had brown hair just turning gray and a thin mustache, offered a stark contrast to his wife in his plain, though expensive, gray suit.

"Sarah and Marc," she said, "I'd like you to meet my husband, Gary."

"Glad to know you," Sarah said.

Marc hesitated to extend his hand, seeing Gary's crutches. But Gary reached out and took his firmly. Marc grinned.

"This is Derek Miller," Gary said, "my therapist."

Derek and Marc shook hands, then Melanie introduced the children. Sarah leaned down to Nancy and chucked her under the chin.

"My, aren't you a pretty little thing?"

Melanie saw Alicen shuffling in the background and quickly said, "This is Alicen Miller, Derek's daughter. She and her father live with us."

"Hello, dear," Sarah said.

"Hello," Alicen replied, shyly averting her eyes from this stranger.

Sarah and Marc followed everyone down the long hallway. Sarah commented that something smelled luscious, and Melanie told her they were having rib roast for dinner. In the dining room, Sarah complimented Melanie on the centerpiece of azaleas and baby's breath as she settled herself into a massive oak chair. Melanie suddenly remembered Gary's comment about the queen of England and bit her lip to suppress a giggle. She turned into the kitchen to get the food, aided by Kyle and Gina.

57

Gary's chair had been placed near the sideboard so that he could serve the wine. He turned around and lifted a heavy crystal carafe, filling five matching goblets.

"Excellent wine," Marc said. "What is it?"

Gary laughed. "You're asking me? I hardly know the difference between red and rosé!"

"Well, let's see," Melanie said, leaning toward the sideboard.

She picked up the empty bottle that sat behind the carafe and brought it closer to read it.

There was a sudden crash, and giving a cry, Melanie jumped away from the table. The bottle had exploded in her hand. Shocked, she held out her palm to Gary, showing a trickle of blood that ran from a gash in her skin.

"Kyle, get the first-aid kit," Gary said quickly.

He reached for his crutches, but Derek was already on his feet and leading Melanie into the kitchen. He held a white napkin to her hand to stop the flow of blood. Melanie grimaced in pain.,

"I don't know how that happened," she cried as Derek put her hand under a running faucet to wash it.

"You'll be okay," Derek said, examining it. "It's a long cut, but not a very deep one."

Melanie shuddered. "It hurts."

Kyle entered the kitchen with the first-aid kit and put it on the counter. While Derek opened it to take out a bandage, the little boy stood on tiptoe to see his mother's hand. Gary, who was standing in the doorway, called to him.

"Kyle, leave your mother alone," he said.

"Is she gonna be okay?" Kyle asked. "Mom, does it hurt a lot?"

"It just stings," Melanie said, smiling for his benefit.

Derek wrapped the cut with gauze, then closed the first-aid kit. Holding her hand upright, Melanie reentered the dining room while Gary held the door open for her. She looked around at her guests. Sarah and Marc looked worried, Gina and Nancy were whispering, and Alicen kept her eyes on her lap.

"Wait until you see what I do for an encore," Melanie joked, hoping to ease the tension.

Everyone laughed. Melanie was glad, for this night was very important to her. She wouldn't spoil it by letting them know how much her hand hurt.

"What do you suppose happened?" Marc asked.

"Maybe a tremendous pressure built up inside the bottle while it was sitting there for so many months. Melanie just happened to pick it up at the wrong time," Gary theorized.

"That makes sense," Derek agreed.

"Yes, I'm sure that's what it was," Melanie said, a slight inflection in her voice betraying her uneasiness. She just wanted to forget the whole thing. "Come on, eat the food before it gets cold. Gary, will you carve the roast for us?"

"Yeah," Kyle said. "I'm hungry."

Beef, mashed potatoes, and peas made the rounds, and at last everyone settled down to eat. Sarah noticed Melanie was having problems and asked, "Would you like me to cut that meat for you? You really should rest your hand."

"I'd appreciate it" Melanie said. "It is kind of awkward."

"I know how frustrating it is to be helpless," Sarah said. "When I had a heart attack a few years ago, I was unable to do anything for myself for weeks."

"I never knew you had a heart condition," Melanie said. "You seem so healthy."

"I'm better now," Sarah said. "I haven't had a second attack."

"Thank God," Marc said, squeezing his wife's hand.

Sarah turned to smile at her husband, and as she did so she noticed that Alicen was staring intently at the diamond ring she wore. Sarah smiled a little at her, thinking how different she looked from the VanBuren children. While they were listening alertly to the conversation around them, Alicen seemed lost in another world. And while they were beautiful to look at, Alicen was plain and overweight. A feeling of pity ran through Sarah. Poor child, she thought, deciding to talk to her to make her feel comfortable.

"Do you like my ring?"

Alicen nodded, staring as if entranced by the reflection of the chandelier on the facets. Sarah took it off and handed it to her.

"It's beautiful," Alicen said softly. "My mother had one just like it."

Now Derek recalled the engagement ring he had given his wife. It hadn't been as big as this one, but it was as beautiful. He felt his stomach twist as he remembered the last time he had seen the ring on the charred, twisted remains of Elaine's hand.

"You were wearing that the other day, weren't you?" Melanie asked, cutting off Derek's gloomy thoughts.

59

"I always do," Sarah said. "It's a family heirloom, passed down to me from my great-grandmother. It's a very dear possession."

Alicen, responding to a prod from Gina, turned to show the brilliant gem to her friend. The two girls sighed over it.

"All right," Derek said then, "you'd better give that back." He didn't want the ring to make Alicen start talking about her mother.

"I'm sure Alicen wouldn't hurt it," Sarah said, accepting the ring and placing it on her finger.

After dinner, at Sarah's request, Melanie took her guests on a tour of the house. They ended up in Melanie's studio. Sarah noticed the yellow paint stain on the couch.

"Accident?" she asked, sympathetically, looking at Melanie.

"The dog ran through here one night and knocked over a few things," Melanie said. A glance at Gary produced a smile from him, as if he were telling her he was glad she had accepted that reasoning. It was one less thing for Melanie to worry about, he thought. He had expected her to be upset after hearing Derek mention Janice's name, but she hadn't said a word about it all week. In fact, she looked very sure of herself tonight. Gary wanted to kiss her but restrained himself.

"May I have a glass of water?" Sarah asked, coughing a little.

"Let me get it for you," Derek said.

"I'll manage," Sarah said. "I need to exercise to work off that delicious dinner."

She patted her stomach and went downstairs to the kitchen. Passing through the dining room, she paused to smell the flowers on the table. She was admiring the arrangement when she heard the voice from the kitchen.

"Murderers!"

Sarah tilted her head. The voice had certainly come from the kitchen, and yet it sounded so far away. Was it one of the children, playing tricks on her? Trying to frighten her?

"Murderers!"

"The little monkeys," Sarah said laughing, pushing through the kitchen door.

Her smile vanished in an instant. It wasn't a child at all, but a woman, one whom Sarah recognized. Horrified, she took in the stringy blond hair and pale skin. It couldn't be—this woman had been dead for six months!

"Oh, dear," Sarah moaned, touching her forehead. She felt the cold of her diamond against her skin. Trying to tell

60

herself it was only her imagination, she moved to leave the room. But an arm wrapped around her neck, drawing her back. Sarah grabbed it. Her fingers squished through flesh and blood and bone as if the arm were made of clay. But it wasn't clay. It was much too real, squeezing Sarah's neck tighter and tighter. She couldn't scream.

"You saw me," her assailant hissed.

"No," Sarah managed to whimper.

"You saw me, and you have to die now!"

Sarah's heart began to pound. Pain rushed from the center of her chest to her underarms. Sarah knew the pain—a heart attack. And she somehow knew also that she wouldn't survive this one.

Hail Mary full of grace . . .

Die!"

. . . the Lord is . . .

Something muddled her thoughts. Sarah saw lights flashing over her head, blinding lights. She couldn't close her eyes.

This can't be happening.

"DIE!"

Oh, please, God, I'm so afraid. I'm so fri—

Sarah Kaufman prayed no more. Her murderer stood back, letting the body sink to the floor, and looked at her handiwork. There were no marks on Sarah's neck.

The ghostly being grinned. She had taken life, and she wanted more. . . .

Marc Kaufman turned around from a painting of Fire Island and said to Melanie, "You don't suppose my wife got lost somewhere in this big house?"

Melanie laughed. "She probably stopped to talk with the children. I'll go rescue her."

She left the room. For some reason a sudden chill rushed over her as she descended the stairs, a cold feeling in her stomach. She had felt like that after hearing Derek mention the name Janice, but she had forced her fears away. After all, it was a very common name. It was only a coincidence that Derek had mentioned it. But why did she feel that same way right now, when nothing had happened?

Sarah wasn't in the playroom. Melanie went to the kitchen and pushed at the door. It wouldn't budge.

"Sarah?" Melanie called, pushing heavily against it with her shoulder. "Sarah, are you all right?"

No answer came, and Melanie stepped back to ram her

body against the door with all her strength. Breathing heavily from the effort, she stumbled into the kitchen—half-tripping over Sarah's prone form.

"Oh, my God," Melanie whispered.

Sarah was staring up at the ceiling, her mouth open in a silent scream. Her wide and glassy eyes were fixed on the overhead light.

Melanie sank to the floor, reaching to touch Sarah's face. Still warm. She looked so terrified—what had she just seen, Melanie wondered? She looked around nervously. But the kitchen was empty.

It was Kyle who broke her spell. Melanie jumped to her feet when she heard the door open, blocking her son's way. He looked up at her in confusion and said, "I just wanted a glass of milk. What's the matter?"

"Kyle, honey," Melanie said, pushing him gently from the door so that he wouldn't see Sarah, "run upstairs and get Mr. Kaufman. Tell him his wife had an—an accident."

"What happened to her?" Kyle asked, trying to look around his mother.

"Kyle, please—"

"I'm going," the little boy shouted, running away from her.

Melanie turned back to Sarah. Why couldn't she stop looking at her? What in the hell did she expect to find in that frightened expression?

Marc and Derek entered the kitchen a few moments later.

"Gary's calling a doctor," Marc said. "Kyle said my wife hurt herself?"

"I—I think she had a heart attack," Melanie said.

Marc's reaction upon seeing his wife was barely audible. "Oh, dear Lord, Sarah—"

Without wasting a moment, Derek pushed Marc aside and dropped down next to Sarah's body. At his instruction Melanie left the room to find a blanket. Derek pressed his mouth to Sarah's, vainly trying to get her breathing again. She did not respond.

"I'll try CPR," he said, looking up at Marc.

"Just help her, please!"

Now Derek pressed the palm of one hand against the back of the other, interwining his fingers. He positioned himself over Sarah and pushed down on her chest. The muscles in his arms trembled with the effort, yet none of that strength would seep through to Sarah's heart.

"I'm sorry," Derek said, standing. "There's nothing more I can do."

"Sarah . . ."

Sirens sounded in the distance just as Melanie returned with a blanket. Derek took it and laid it carefully over the woman. Marc watched all this, stunned and not believing. He hardly noticed the ambulance attendants when they lifted Sarah's body and carried it out of the house.

Marc rode in the back of the ambulance, biting his knuckles. He was so shocked that he did not notice the heirloom diamond missing from his wife's finger.

Melanie had another dream that night. She woke up with a start to feel a cold touch on her arm. But then she saw the woman with dark hair and somehow lost her fear. Without protest, she followed her downstairs. The woman turned to her. "It is beginning again."

"What is?"

But there was no answer. Melanie felt her eyes closing, unable to stay awake. When she opened them again, she was back in bed with Gary snoring beside her.

9

Sarah Kaufman was laid to rest in an ancient family plot two days later. On her death certificate, heart attack had been written under cause of death. Marc Kaufman, though deeply grieved, accepted that. It did not occur to him to ask if his wife's death had truly been from natural causes.

Melanie, feeling as great a loss as if Sarah had been a dear friend, walked slowly to her car from the graveside. She was sweating in the hot May sun, her dark brown suit making her uncomfortable. Underneath its bandage, her palm began to itch. Melanie tried to endure the pain, to make it dominate the memory of Sarah's face. But that look of horror hovered in her mind like a dark cloud, menacing her.

"Wait a minute," Melanie said to herself as she took off her jacket and got into the car. "Sarah had a heart attack. That's *all*. It has nothing to do with anything that ever happened in my house."

She turned on the radio to drown out her thoughts. But still her memory was overpowering. Vivid pictures came to her of the night of Gary's accident. She could hear the screams of her children, echoing her own screams. She could see Gary flying out the window, glass sparkling in the moonlight.

And she saw a blond-haired woman sitting in her kitchen, looking up at her with wide blue eyes. . . .

"GO AWAY!" Melanie shouted at her memories.

She gritted her teeth and concentrated on the road ahead, but still there were tears on her cheeks.

"You've been crying," Gary said when she got home. "Funeral upset you?"

"No," Melanie said. "I was thinking about the—well, remembering the look on Sarah's face."

"Why?" Gary asked. "It was sad that she died, and a shock, too. But she did say she had a heart condition."

"She looked *terrified*, Gary," Melanie said. "As if she had seen something."

Gary sighed very deeply and said with patience, "Melanie, she didn't see anything. What would she see in an empty kitchen? She had a heart attack—maybe she'd rushed down the stairs too quickly when she left us."

"I don't know, Gary," Melanie said. "I wish I could believe it was that simple. But I had another one of those 'dreams' last night."

"What dreams?" Gary asked with concern.

"Do you remember the night you found me in the kitchen? When you said I was sleepwalking?"

"Yes?"

"I had two more of those dreams," Melanie said. "Once that night Alicen saw a face under her floor grating, and again when Sarah died."

"Both highly emotional incidents," Gary pointed out.

"Maybe," Melanie said. "And maybe they *were* only dreams. But I heard once that recurring nightmares mean there's something heavy on your mind. What could a girl in old-fashioned, ragged clothes mean? Or the kitchen? It's always in the kitchen."

"Symbolism," Gary said. "Is the girl so hard to figure out? She represents the olden days—Jacob Armand's days. You're thinking too much of him, Melanie. No wonder you have nightmares."

"I don't know." Melanie sighed. "It seems the woman was trying to give us a warning. She even said: 'It's happening again.' "

"You're the one who always insists it's happening again," Gary said. "You just put those words in another woman's mouth. Your dreams simply state what's on your mind."

"Okay," Melanie said. "Then what does the kitchen symbolize?"

Gary waved his hands. "I don't know. Oh, God, Melanie! Don't start talking about evil doings in this house. Your dreams are simply the result of too much emotional stress. They aren't a warning of anything—except, maybe, that you need to get your mind off of all this."

"There's nothing wrong with my mind," Melanie said darkly.

"Melanie, look," Gary said, losing patience, "Sarah Kaufman died of a heart attack, that's all! People die in houses all the time."

"They seem to die more often in this house, don't they?" With that, Melanie turned abruptly and went to her studio.

What was wrong with him? Melanie pondered as she daubed paint on her canvas. Why couldn't he, just for once, give her the benefit of the doubt? Sarah *must* have seen something! It had started this way the last time, so subtly, the old lady next door dying on the hill between their houses.

But this time, Melanie vowed, *I'll be ready for it.*

As she worked on her painting and occasionally stopped to look out of the studio windows, the beautiful sunny day gradually overcame her fears and worries. When she saw the school bus pull up, she was no longer in a dour mood. She watched the children climb the hill, racing each other. Kyle was first to reach the steps, Alicen last. Just a few minutes later, Kyle burst into her room.

"Hi, mom!"

"Hi," Melanie said, laughing. "How'd you get up here so fast?"

"I ran all the way," Kyle panted. His fair skin was flushed red. "I told Gina I could beat her upstairs."

Gina entered the room a moment later, panting, too. Alicen, who had obviously given up, came in after her, breathing normally.

"You win, Kyle," Gina said. She fished in her pocket and produced a quarter for her victorious brother.

"My kid's a gambler?" Melanie asked.

"I didn't think he could do it," Gina admitted.

Now Kyle climbed onto one of the stools in the room, his book bag on his lap. From it he produced a box made from ice cream sticks, painted bright yellow. He held it out to his mother.

"Look what I made," he said proudly. "My teacher said it was the best one in the class."

"Well, good for you, Kyle," Melanie said. "It's very nice."

"I'm going to give it to dad," Kyle said. "To put in his office."

"You should give it to mom," Gina said. "Mother's Day is coming up soon."

She turned to Alicen and without thinking said, "What are you going to give your mother for—"

She cut herself off, her eyes opening wide. Looking at her mother for help, she began to blush. Then she turned back to Alicen and said, "Gosh, I'm sorry! I wasn't thinking, and—"

"It's okay," Alicen said, though she felt a pain deep inside. "It's okay."

Melanie, seeing how uncomfortable both girls were, quickly changed the subject. "Say, when is that class trip of yours?"

"It's tomorrow," Gina said.

"Already? Well, you'll have a great time."

"I can't wait to go," Gina said. "I've never been to a planetarium."

"You know," Melanie said, "I think there might be some books on the planets in our library. Why don't you go see?"

Gina pulled Alicen out of the room. "Let's go look, okay?"

Melanie laughed. With kids like that, how could she ever have sad thoughts?

Alicen had tried to pay attention when Gina read off the statistics of Jupiter and Saturn. She had tried to listen to the conversation at dinner and to laugh at a joke Kyle told. But she was still smarting from the way Gina had carelessly mentioned Mother's Day. She hated that holiday, when people sent cards and flowers to their mothers and stores were filled with sentimental posters. Why did they all have to remind her she didn't have a mother?

She put her forehead down on her desk and cried softly. It just wasn't fair! Some people had mothers and treated them horribly. But she wouldn't, if her mother was alive. She'd be good to her, better than her father had ever been.

"Oh, mommy," she whispered. "Why did Gina have to make me think of you dead?"

She sat up, shuddering. Drying her eyes, she looked over at her clock and noticed it was well past midnight. She'd have to fall asleep now, or she'd never be able to get up for the class trip. Trying to wear herself out, she got up and paced the floor. The rug felt soft and warm beneath her feet. She did not go near the grating.

"Mommy," she whispered. "Mommy, mommy . . ."

Something creaked behind her.

"Aaallliiicceeeennnn!"

The voice sounded hollow and far away. Her heart beating loudly, Alicen hurried to the door to lock it. Who was out there? Was it just Kyle, teasing her? Or was it someone else?

"The door is locked," she whispered aloud. "I'm safe in here. I'm safe."

But suddenly she didn't care who was in the hallway. Her muscles became like jelly, too weak to support her body. Her eyes drooped shut as she sank to the floor. Without warning, she had fallen asleep. But this wasn't a real sleep that took her over.

In a minute she was on her feet again. She unlocked the door and pulled it open. Though the hallway was pitch black, she didn't have to grope her way to the stairs. It was as if some unseen force had her by the hand and was leading the way downstairs.

Alicen heard laughter in the kitchen and pushed through its door. Obeying a silent command, she sank to the floor and waited. She didn't feel the cold of the linoleum.

There was a woman standing above her. Alicen couldn't see the features of her face. But she saw the blond hair and smiled, unafraid. Her mother had had blond hair.

"You've come to me," she whispered.

A hand touched her forehead, and Alicen tilted her head back. She held up her arms to the apparition, her fingers spread wide like a little child's.

"Please hold me tight, mommy," she said.

It was the seven-year-old Alicen asking for affection, the Alicen of all her dreams, where her mother came to love her. But her mother did not embrace her this time. Instead, she pulled her to her feet. Alicen looked at the watery features, wishing she could see them more clearly. She'd waited so long.

"Gina VanBuren made you sad today," the vision said.

"Yes, she made me think of you, mommy."

"That was bad of her," was the reply. "She must be made to pay for it, right?"

"Yes, mommy."

"Then do as I say," the vision ordered. "Tomorrow there is a bus trip."

"Yes."

"Gina must sit directly behind the driver of the bus. Then she will die."

"Die," Alicen breathed.

"And when we are rid of her," the vision said, "I will give you this."

Smoke billowed around the apparition's hand as she raised it to Alicen's face. In the white cloud sat the huge, brilliant diamond that had once been on Sarah Kaufman's hand. Alicen reached for it, mesmerized. She saw it not as Sarah's ring, but as the ring her mother had always worn.

"She must sit up front," the vision said, snatching her hand away.

"She will," Alicen promised. "Oh, mommy, I'll be so happy to wear your beautiful ring!"

The next morning, Alicen woke up in her bed. She went down to the kitchen for breakfast, completely unaware that she had been sitting on its floor just a few hours earlier.

"Look at that bus, Alicen!" Gina cried as they stood together in the school yard. "Isn't it beautiful?"

"Yeah, it sure is," Alicen said, yawning. She was exhausted but didn't know why.

It was an enormous touring bus, one with a completely flat front covered with shining glass. The two girls climbed up inside of it and looked down the narrow aisle at the rows of high, upholstered seats.

"Hey, there's Doreen and Beverly," Gina cried, pointing.

Her friends had taken over the seat under the back window. Gina waved and started to go to them, but Alicen grabbed her arm.

"Can't we sit up front?" she asked.

"Why?" Gina responded. "Everyone else is in the back."

"I'd rather sit up here," Alicen said, indicating the seat behind the driver's.

"What difference does it make?"

Alicen shrugged. "I don't know. Uh—I sort of get sick sitting in the back."

Gina still felt guilty about mentioning Alicen's mother. Maybe she could make up for that by humoring her friend. She nodded.

"Okay," she said, "but I think you're weird. A seat's a seat!"

Alicen slid into the seat. Gina followed, then leaned out in the aisle to talk to Doreen and Beverly, moving back every few seconds to let other children walk past.

Alicen leaned forward and pressed her hands against the glass partition behind the driver's seat. Suddenly she felt sleepy. She yawned, and all at once her yawn became a groan. Gina looked at her.

"What's the matter?"

"Percy's the bus monitor," Alicen said. "And Jamie Hutchinson's coming in right behind him."

"We could have sat in the back," Gina said. "The bus is full now."

"I guess it's okay." Alicen groaned. She turned to look out the window, hoping neither Percy nor Jamie would see her. She was still mad at the boy for telling her stories of murders and making her look like a fool in front of her father and Melanie. But Jamie was too busy reading. Mr. Percy, after a few orders to the children about behavior and staying in groups, sat down and opened up a copy of the *Wall Street Journal*.

The driver came in next, her face hidden behind a curtain of stringy blond hair. Percy scoffed at her, then turned his eyes back down to the paper, wondering why the bus company would hire such an unkempt woman. The driver climbed behind the wheel of the bus without a word to anyone and started the engine.

Just then, Alicen felt a tap on her shoulder. "Hi, Alicen!"

"I'm not talking to you," Alicen said plainly, recognizing Jamie's voice.

"Oh, come on," Jamie said. "Are you still mad at me? Don't you want to look at my book? It tells you all about the planetarium."

"No."

"It's real neat," Jamie said. "Don't you want to see the pictures?"

"No!"

Jamie shook his head at her and sank back down into his seat. Now Gina turned and pinched Alicen's arm.

"Are you crazy?" she asked. "He's trying to be nice to you, and you're acting stuck-up. Why are you mad at him?"

"It's none of your business," Alicen said, not wanting to mention the incident that had so embarrassed her. "He's stupid, and I don't like him any more."

Alicen gazed out at the passing highway. She saw a station wagon with several black dogs in the back, a van driven by a young man with long hair, and a hitchhiking pair of girls. The van stopped to pick them up. This was such a perfect day for a field trip, Alicen thought. The sky was bright blue, and the sun was shining warmly. Why, then, did she feel so uneasy?

She felt a pain in her eyes from the glare of the sun and closed them. Her head dropped against the window, bobbing in rhythm with the vibrations of the engine. She could still hear the children around her talking. Someone started singing, and others joined in. It sounded as if they were singing through a long tunnel. She was far, far at the other end.

"A hundred bottles of beer on the wall, a hundred bottles of beer, if . . ."

Someone was talking inside Alicen's head. She recognized the voice, but couldn't place it. The words made her shudder.

Gina must die, must die, must die.

"Ninety-five bottles of beer, if one of . . ."

Alicen snapped upright and looked through the glass partition at the back of the driver's head. She felt lightheaded, as if she were floating in air and not on board the bus at all. The song the children were singing seemed further and further away. Now the pact she had made in the night came back to her. She knew who the bus driver was. Alicen longed to reach through the glass to touch her mother, but she simply leaned forward and stared. She saw the back of the woman's neck turning from pink to alabaster. Marks of veins began to travel under the skin, like droplets of rain racing on a windowpane. Beyond the woman's shoulder, Alicen could see the soft pink hand twisting as its skin tightened. No one else saw this but her.

She knew the terror had begun.

"Eight-six bottles of beer on the wall, eighty-six . . ."

Suddenly, with a loud growling noise, the bus shot forward.

"Hey!" a boy cried.

"What are you doing?" Percy demanded, leaning forward. "Slow down at once!"

The woman ignored him. The bus picked up speed at such a rate that the trees along the road mashed together in one long, green blur. White lines slipped under its wheels with immeasurable speed.

"Everyone!" Percy shouted, anticipating an accident, "on the floor!"

The children immediately ducked under their seats, too frightened to ask questions. Gina wanted to obey, too; she tried to move but somehow was frozen to her seat. She squeezed her eyes shut, covering them as she screamed.

But no one could hear her cries over the revving of the motor. It spun faster . . .

"Heeelllp!"

. . . and faster . . .

"MOM!"

. . . and faster.

"STOP THIS AT ONCE!" Percy shouted, his old man's voice straining. He grabbed the steel bar in front of his seat, his newspaper flying to the steps below. The old teacher pulled himself to his feet now and stumbled across the rubber-matted floor. His hand shot forward in an effort to grab the driver.

It went right through her.

"What the—?"

Percy backed away in horror, hitting the front window. The driver looked up at him, grinning. Her face was a death mask, grotesquely like blue-veined marble. Percy opened his mouth, but no sound came from it.

Screams jerked him from his dazed state. He looked down the bus at the fifty youngsters crouched on the floor, helpless. He saw a girl with braided brown hair still sitting in the first seat. Her hands were over her face, and she was screaming. Alicen Miller sat next to her, staring at him with hateful eyes.

Percy had the irrelevant thought that she was a disobedient brat. Why wasn't she on the floor?

Alicen smiled slightly and pointed to something beyond Percy's shoulder. He turned and looked out the huge front window of the bus, seeing a sign that read DETOUR and behind it a construction site.

"Oh, dear God," he whispered.

Now a surge of bravery made him lunge again at the driver. But as he touched the steering wheel, ice-cold hands grabbed hard at his wrists. His fingers pulled away in a curling, jerking motion. He whimpered softly as he felt the sickening crunch of his bones under the viselike grip of the phantom driver.

He screamed. The driver roared at him, knocking him back to his seat with breath so foul that Percy felt a wave of nausea. But that pain was cut off by another sharper pain that ripped through his neck like a hot knife. His hand went to his throat, feeling something sharp there. He stumbled toward Gina's seat, blood dripping from his opened mouth.

Screams of the children. The angry motor, honking horns, sirens. These were the last sounds Percy ever heard.

The bus collided at last with the tall wooden fence that surrounded the construction site. It shot over the rim of a pit, rising twelve feet into the air before it dove down into the deep excavation. Small bodies thumped from ceiling to floor as the bus rolled. But somehow, Gina's body didn't move at all. She had not yet opened her eyes, even to see what had knocked her to the floor a second earlier. She could feel Alicen's legs underneath her. Something warm and heavy pinned them on the floor behind the driver's seat.

The bus rolled, bumped, and skidded. It landed nose-first, its entire front crushing, the steering wheel becoming one with the partition. Shards of glass flew like missiles, striking the now-empty upholstered seats.

Though it happened in less than a minute, an eternity passed before the bus finally skidded to a halt and toppled over on its side. Gina at last opened her eyes.

Percy's unseeing eyes stared down at her, inches from her own face. Blood was spurting from a wound that surrounded a shimmering piece of glass in his throat.

"GET HIM OFF OF ME!" she screamed, struggling frantically.

"Gina, you're crushing me!" Alicen cried, the spell broken. She wriggled out from under her friend, grateful that only her legs had been caught. Then she leaned against the top of the bus, now its side, and stared down at Percy's corpse.

"GET HIM OFF! GET HIM OFF!"

Jamie Hutchinson was the first to collect his senses. He pulled himself to his feet, clutching the soft cushion of his seat. Rubbing his temple, where a painful bump was growing larger, he walked ahead to see why Gina was screaming so. In the shock that is the aftermath of a terrible accident, it didn't register in his mind that his teacher was dead. He only thought that Gina was being crushed as he wrapped his fingers around Percy's upper arms. Glass crunched beneath his feet as he pulled hard at the body, to no avail. It was wedged in too tightly, and at thirteen, Jamie wasn't very strong.

72

"Jamie, please," Gina cried. "I can't breathe."

"I'm trying," Jamie answered, desperate. He turned around. "Hey, somebody help me up here!"

No one responded. They were too caught up in their own terror. Jamie saw one boy holding his arm at an odd angle. A piece of raw bone jutted from a rising bruise at his elbow. A girl with blond braids sat on the floor with the back of her hand to her nose, trying to stop the flow of blood. Another girl was crying about her fingers, and a boy was lying on the floor, his eyes closed, blood trickling from his forehead. Jamie turned his head quickly away.

"Gina, push hard when I tell you," he ordered. He tugged at Percy's arms. "Now!"

Gina pushed with all her strength, and still the body did not move. A pounding noise over her head made her look up. There she saw two policemen sawing away at one of the window frames. One shouted through the small opening.

"Stay still, everyone! We'll have you all out in a minute!"

The first cop sawed with all his might, trying to make an exit. The door itself was useless, lost somewhere in the twisted front of the bus. He could barely make out the steering wheel. He knew the bus driver could not have survived. Yet for some reason, there was no sign of a body.

"Where the hell is the driver?"

"Beats me, Tim," the other cop answered.

Gina had started crying again, fighting the pressure of Mr. Percy's corpse. Tim looked down at her as he sawed the metal window frame. Assuming the body on top of her was the driver's, he continued to work. At last the frame gave way, and he jumped down into the bus. Walking carefully along the row of broken windows pressed flat against the ground, he went to Gina and wrenched the body from her. Without a word, he hoisted it up to the opening, where his partner dragged it out. Moments later, it was covered with tarpaulin.

"Easy now," Tim said, sliding his arm under Gina's back. Behind him, two paramedics climbed down into the bus to attend to the injured children.

As he helped Gina to her feet, Tim noticed the seat and realized something like a miracle had just occurred. Three ugly triangles of glass poked out from the vinyl seat, in exactly the place where Gina might have been sitting if the man's body hadn't knocked her to the floor. He looked at her as he held his hand out to help Alicen.

"Are you hurt?"

"No," Gina said softly, not sure of herself. She turned to Alicen, who stood staring at the twisted frame of the partition. There was no expression on her face.

"How about you, honey?" Tim asked, squeezing her hand.

Alicen shook her head mutely. Now Tim led the two of them to the opening in the ceiling, where they waited their turn to be lifted out of the bus. Once outside, the teen-agers blinked at the flashing red lights and bright sunshine. Gina put her arms around Alicen and stood watching as the others were helped out. She was shocked to see one of her classmates, Tommy Jones, on a stretcher with his eyes closed. Someone had bandaged his head.

Hank Emmons, manager of the construction crew, climbed down into the pit to survey the damage. When he reached the bottom, he ran his fingers through his silver hair and looked around in awe. The last of the group were being helped out of the bus. Several of them were put on stretchers and carried to the ambulance waiting at the top of the pit. As far as he could see, these were the only serious injuries.

"This is the kinda thing that makes you believe there's a God," he said to a policeman.

"How do you figure that?"

"Well, no one was killed," Hank said. "And from the looks of that thing"—he indicated the bus—"no one should have lived. Yeah, God was looking out for these kids."

"Not for the driver, though," the cop said. "He was killed."

Hank frowned. "I can't say I'm sorry. I saw that bus coming down the road. Serves the jerk right, speeding down a busy highway with all those kids."

Within the next half hour, all the students had been brought to the top. As they waited for another bus to take them home, they shared a soda and snacks with the construction crew. The food somehow helped them forget the accident.

Gina had had enough time to realize she was all right and to calm down a little. Some of her classmates had also relaxed and were talking together in excited groups. But for the most part they stood silent, numbed by the experience and wanting nothing but to see their mothers. Alicen was one of the silent ones.

Gina offered her a soda, but Alicen shook her head. "Why aren't you afraid?"

"Because I'm all right," Gina said. "Besides, a lot of worse things have happened to me."

Alicen nodded, knowing Gina was right but unable to share her strength. She felt a terrible fear. Why, since they were all right? But that was just it. Something deep inside Alicen made her feel they weren't supposed to be all right, that something was supposed to have happened and didn't.

"I just want to go home," Gina said.

"Me, too," several of her friends who stood nearby agreed in unison.

"But we'll probably have to go back to school and answer a lot of questions," Jamie said. Seeing a cop approaching, he said, "Starting right now."

"All right," Tim said. "I'd like to ask you some questions about your driver."

All the children started to speak at once.

"One of you, I said," Tim interrupted. He pointed to Jamie, who by his height seemed to dominate the group.

"Tell me, son," he said. "Did you get a good look at the driver? Did he seem to be tired, or drunk, or—"

"I don't know, exactly," Jamie said, pushing a lock of red hair from his eyes. "I was reading, so I just kinda glanced up at her."

"Her?" Tim echoed. "The driver was a woman?"

"Yeah, why?"

"Have you seen her since the accident?"

All the teen-agers shook their heads.

"Percy made us all duck under our seats," Jamie said. "After that, we didn't see a thing."

"I heard a scream," Beverly said. "But I sure wasn't going to look."

There was a silence, and then Gina asked, "What did happen to the driver?"

"I don't know," Tim said. "Can anyone tell me what she looked like?"

"I think she was wearing boots," Doreen said. "But I was at the back of the bus."

"Yeah, she was," Jamie agreed. "I remember because I thought it was kinda weird."

"Boots?" Tim said. "In May?"

Doreen and Jamie nodded. Tim could see sincerity in their faces and wondered if the driver might have worn boots to make her foot heavier on the gas pedal. If that was the case, then it probably meant she had planned the entire thing. Was it meant to be a combined suicide-mass murder? Tim's job now would be to find the body—or, judging from the remains of the bus, what was left of it. He thanked the group for their help, then went to find his partner Rick.

He made his way through the clusters of police, construction workers, and students until he found Rick at the edge of the pit, watching a tow truck haul the bus to the surface. Before he could tell him what the children had said, Rick started talking.

"Look at that thing," he said. "Smashed like a beer can. You know, if the driver hadn't been knocked from his seat like that, those two girls would have been killed? I have it figured that when his body wedged between their seats, he acted as a sort of anchor and kept them down on the floor. If they'd have been in that seat when the partition broke—"

Tim cut him off. "Rick, Dwight Percy wasn't the driver. The kids say it was a woman."

"How can that be?" Rick demanded. "There isn't another adult on that bus."

"We couldn't have missed her?"

"Impossible," Rick said. "Miss a full-grown woman in that little package of metal? No way Percy isn't our driver. The kids are suffering from shock. Or else they're lying."

"I don't think they're lying," Tim said.

"There's no one else on that bus," Rick insisted.

Later, back at the school, the children still swore the driver had been a woman. And out of fifty of them, not one remembered her face. Police Chief Bryan Davis asked each individually. They had to know something. And yet they had no answers.

Bryan was surprised to see Gina VanBuren, remembering her from another incident long ago. He asked about her father.

"He's doing okay," Gina said. "He doesn't have casts on any more, and he's learning how to walk again."

"That's great," Bryan said. "You send him my best, okay?"

"Perhaps we should allow them to leave," an elderly nun suggested. "They need their rest. You may return again tomorrow, when their minds are clear."

"Good idea," Bryan answered. "I'll be back after lunch tomorrow."

The children were relieved to hear they were going home. It had been two hours since the accident, and most were still frightened and upset. Originally Bryan had wanted to send them home right away but then decided it was best to get information while the incident was still fresh on their minds. Obviously that hadn't worked. Now he stood in the doorway, watching the children file outside. Their parents had been called, and a number of cars were waiting. Beverly, Doreen, and Jamie, who had working mothers, joined Gina and Alicen.

"Thank God you're all right," Melanie said, putting her arms around her daughter. "I called several times wondering when I could take you home, but they made me wait here. I've been frantic!"

"The police had to ask some questions," Gina said.

"Couldn't it have waited?" Melanie asked as she started the car. "You should have all been sent home at once."

"It wasn't so bad," Gina insisted.

Melanie turned to Alicen. "How about you?"

"I—I'm fine," Alicen said. She fixed her eyes on the road ahead.

Poor kid, Melanie thought. *She must be taking this worse than any of them.*

"Hey, I have an idea," she said aloud, in an effort to cheer everyone. "Why don't you let me treat you all to lunch?"

"That's a great idea," Jamie said.

"Yeah, neat!" cried Beverly.

"Can we go to Nino's pizza place, mom?" Gina asked.

"Sure."

After they had driven for a few minutes, Alicen felt her head growing heavy. She heard a voice inside it, calling to her, commanding that she come home. She looked around, but no one else heard it.

Suddenly she brought one leg up under her body, clutched her stomach, and started to groan.

"Alicen, what's wrong?" Melanie asked with concern.

"My stomach hurts," Alicen wailed. "I want to go home!"

"Maybe you're just hungry," Doreen suggested.

"I want to go home!" Alicen insisted.

"Okay, honey," Melanie cooed. "We'll drop you off. It's on the way, anyway."

She reached behind Gina and touched Alicen's cheek. It felt cool.

"Just lay back," she said.

"I sure hope you're okay, Alicen," Jamie said.

Melanie turned the car around and headed toward the house. On the way, they passed the boarded-up gray mansion that had once belonged to the VanBuren's only neighbor. Jamie leaned over the back of Melanie's seat and asked, "Who lives in that spooky old place?"

"No one now," Melanie said. "But it used to belong to a very old woman named Helen Jennings. She was eighty-four and died of a heart attack."

"Geez," Beverly said. "Eighty-four? That's like a million years."

Melanie laughed, and Jamie asked, "Is anything inside there?"

"No, it's been empty for months," Melanie said.

She sighed, remembering Helen Jennings, who had tried to help her family when they were in trouble, during the months leading to Gary's accident. Helen had been a little eccentric, watching their house from her bedroom through a pair of binoculars. But Helen had paid a price for helping them. She had died not of a heart attack, but of a broken neck—murdered by the same intruder who had crippled Gary.

But Melanie didn't want to think about that. She drove up to the front door of her house and let Alicen out. The girl left them without saying goodbye or thanks. Melanie watched her climb the porch steps with her head hung low, like a dog anticipating a beating.

"Everything scares her," Gina said.

"Maybe she really is sick," Doreen said.

"She'll be all right," Melanie said.

A little voice inside her added, *I hope.*

10

Alicen laid her white purse on a table in the foyer and walked down the long hallway. She passed several doors before finally opening the one that led to the library. For some reason she wanted to look at the picture of Scrooge in Gina's book, the one that looked so much like Mr. Percy. She heaved it down from its shelf and lugged it to the sofa.

Scrooge was shaking his fist at someone. (Mr. Percy was

wagging his finger at Alicen.) Scrooge was running scared from a ghost. (Mr. Percy was running scared from a . . .)

A what?

Alicen stared at the ink drawing and wondered what she was doing in here. She hadn't felt right since the accident. It was a feeling of failure, as if she were supposed to have made something happen and hadn't. She sighed and looked up at the carved angels that watched the room from atop the bookshelves.

She shivered. The room had suddenly grown cold, even though the sun was shining warmly through the windows. Alicen placed the book on the library table in front of her and stretched out on the sofa. She pressed a finger to one of the buttons in the upholstery and started to twist it. She could hear the squeak of metal on metal upstairs as Gary worked out in his therapy room. Outside in the yard, Lad barked at something. Birds sang, someone laughed—

Alicen sat up abruptly. It had sounded as if the laughter were right there in the room, and yet she was alone. She looked around. It was the same high-pitched laughter she had heard in her bedroom. Now she found its source. It was one of the angels that were carved in the shelves, its mouth opened wide, emitting short, cackling guffaws. Alicen looked up at it, mesmerized, watching its head loll back and forth as it screamed. She sat up straighter.

The other angels joined in the laughter. Alicen looked from one to the other, seeing angels no longer, but demons. Hideous demons with sharp teeth and bats' wings and blood dripping from the vines that hung around their necks.

"Ohhh," Alicen moaned, trying to stand.

Something pushed her back down on the couch.

"You defied me today," a voice said angrily. "Gina is still alive!"

Something snapped inside Alicen's head, and she was reminded of the pact she had made the night before. She bit her knuckles hard and stared up at the filmy mass before her. Though she could not see them, she could feel cold hands around her wrists.

"I tried, mother," she whispered. "I made Gina sit up front, but—"

"Shut up!" the vision snapped. "The VanBuren brat is still alive. Do you want to see your mother again?"

"Yes!"

"I don't think you do—"

79

"Yes, I do," Alicen cried, tears streaming down her face. "Oh, mommy. Why don't you show me your face?"

There was a long silence.

"You must make them go away from here," the apparition said at last, ignoring Alicen's plea. "They must all die."

"Mommy, why must they all die?"

But the vision was gone. Alicen looked around the room. The angels were still. Her head felt very heavy, and, unable to stop herself, she let it flop back as she fell asleep.

"I'm telling you, I never saw the driver of that bus," Hank Emmons insisted. It had been just a few hours since the accident, and he was sitting in Bryan Davis's office.

"You must have seen it coming," Bryan said. "You could hardly have missed a huge vehicle like that, heading right for the fence."

"Hey, look," Hank said, waving his hands, "I was busy. The union just ended a strike, and there's lots of work to do, you know? I don't waste my time running to investigate every car that comes speeding down that busy highway. Sure, I heard the thing. I think everyone from here to Montauk heard it. But I didn't see the bus till it came crashing through the fence. Geez! Everything happened so fast after that."

"What about your men?"

"What about them?" Hank asked. "Oh, I get it. No, they didn't see any more than I did. My guys pay attention to their work, you know? They'd better, at least, for what I pay them."

Bryan ran his fingers through his hair and sighed. He was getting nowhere and wished the case had been left entirely to the Suffolk County police. He shouldn't have volunteered to ask questions. Sure the kids were from his town, and he owed it to them, but where was all this getting him? Nowhere. He had no answers after hours of questioning, and doubted he'd get any more in the days to come.

"Listen," Hank said then, "I want to find this driver as much as you do. I want to know who she is when I sue the bus company for damages. Say, why haven't you called the depot? They'd have her name on a sign-out sheet, wouldn't they?"

"One of my men is seeing to that," Bryan said, a little resentful that this other man should tell him his business. "The office was closed for lunch, but we ought to be hearing from him shortly."

The phone rang.

"That's him," Bryan said, lifting the receiver. "Belle Bay Police. Well, no ma'am, we're working on it." He shook his head at Hank. "I'm sorry about your boy. How is he? Gonna be okay? That's good. Yes, ma'am. It is a shame, ma'am. We'll let you know. . . . Yes, yes. Goodbye now, ma'am."

He hung up. "Damn! That was the mother of the boy who broke his arm. I wish I had answers for her."

"You've been getting a lot of calls," Hank commented.

"People are angry," Bryan answered. "They want to know who this driver is. I've got a lynch mob out there, Mr. Emmons."

The phone rang again. Bryan shifted a little before answering it, bracing himself for another barrage of unanswerable questions. This time, it was the cop at the bus depot.

"What can you tell me, Mike?" Bryan asked. "Who's the driver?"

"Nobody," Mike said, his tone serious.

"What?!"

"I mean it," Mike said. "There isn't any name next to the bus number on the morning register. The supervisor says he saw her writing in the book, but there's nothing on the page. Not even an indentation from an empty pen."

"Damn," Bryan whispered. "Mike, did the supervisor get a good look at her?"

"I asked," Mike said. "He was too busy to notice her. All he remembered was her blond hair. And get this—she was wearing fur boots."

"Must have been on drugs or something," Bryan said, "dressing like that. Okay, Mike, that's all. Why don't you go to lunch now?"

"I'll do that," Mike said, hanging up.

Bryan put down his own phone and looked at Hank Emmons. The man was sitting across the desk with his chin in his hands, studying Bryan's face. Now he sat a little straighter, ran his palms over the front of his shirt, and said, "You haven't got the slightest idea what do do about all this, do you?"

"No," Bryan admitted. He started to bounce a pencil on his desk.

"Say, I have to get back to work."

Bryan looked up. "Huh? Oh, sure. Sure. I'm finished with you."

With a wave of his hand, Hank indicated a piece of paper.

"You have my number if you need me again," he said.

"I know," Bryan answered.

He stood up and walked from the room with Hank. The two men parted company out in the hall, Hank heading for the front door and Bryan for the men's room. When he returned to his office, he was surprised to see a girl sitting in a wooden chair near his desk. He looked over her long black hair and chubby face and remembered her from the school. He smiled at her.

"Alicen, right?" he asked.

"Right," the girl said, not smiling.

"My memory's pretty good, isn't it?" Bryan said, sitting behind his desk. "So, what can I do for you?"

"I came to tell you what happened on the bus," Alicen said. "I saw everything."

"Yeah?" Bryan asked, a little skeptical. "Why didn't you tell me before?"

"Everything happened too fast, and I was scared," Alicen cried, her expression becoming frantic for a moment. Then it quickly dissolved again into blankness. "Now I remember things. Just before the bus hit the fence, the driver opened the door and jumped out."

"She did, huh?"

"You have to believe me!"

"Okay, okay," Bryan said, waving a hand. "So what happened after she jumped out?"

"I saw her roll down a slope," Alicen said. "I don't remember anything else."

Bryan picked up a pencil and started to bounce it again, his habit when thinking. This was possible, he thought. Anyone crazy enough to drive a bus at over eighty miles an hour might be crazy enough to jump from it. That would explain why Hank hadn't seen her. But then again, none of the other children had witnessed this feat.

"I think I remember some of the kids saying Mr. Percy made you all lie down on the floor?"

"Yeah."

"Then how could you have seen what the driver was doing?"

"I wasn't on the floor," Alicen said. "My friend Gina was too scared to move, and I was supposed to hold her— I mean, she was holding onto me, and I couldn't move, either."

"But Gina didn't tell me she saw the driver jump," Bryan said.

"She had her hands over her eyes," Alicen said. "She was scared, but I wasn't."

"I'm just glad she wasn't hurt," Bryan said. "I like Gina."

"You know her?"

"Yeah, from some work I did with her family last year," Bryan said. "Nothing that concerns you."

"Were people really murdered in her house?"

Bryan's eyes widened. "Who told you that?"

"People," Alicen said, shrugging.

"Well, it's not true," Bryan insisted, his tone a little uneasy. "Listen, honey. I appreciate you coming here, and I'll call the Suffolk police. They'll take a look along the roadside."

Alicen nodded. To Bryan, her expression looked a little smug. He was suspicious of her, and yet her explanation was the only one he had to go on right now.

Half an hour later, Derek found his daughter sitting on the porch swing, tickling Lad's fur with her bare toes. He sat down next to her, putting an arm along the edge of the seat back.

"I saw your purse in the hallway," he said. "Why didn't you tell me you were home?"

"You were busy," Alicen said. "I didn't want to bother you."

"You wouldn't have bothered me."

"You always tell me to work out my problems for myself," Alicen replied.

"But this is different. This is not one of your nightmares. It was a serious accident, and I'm concerned about you. I heard what happened to Mr. Percy. You must have been terribly frightened."

"I wasn't," Alicen said.

"I don't believe you."

"I'm glad he died," Alicen said, staring at a ladybug that crept along the white railing. "I hate him."

"Alicen," Derek said gently, "you shouldn't ever hate anyone."

Alicen looked up at him, her brown eyes deep. "Don't you hate anyone?"

"No one," Derek said.

"Not even the man who killed my mother?"

Derek sighed deeply and put his arms around his daughter. Unaccustomed to such affection, she stiffened. Derek drew his arms away.

83

"Alicen, of course I hate what that man did," he said, "and I'll never get over losing your mother. But I can't hate the man himself. He'll have to live with his guilt, and that's enough without my hatred, too."

Alicen closed her eyes. "Sometimes I talk to mommy, and it feels like she's really here."

"Alicen," Derek said patiently, "you know what I told you about those dreams. It's nice to wish your mother was alive again—God knows I do—but you have to accept the fact that she just isn't coming back."

"She's coming back for me," Alicen said, opening her eyes to glare into her father's. "We're going to be together again."

Derek wasn't about to encourage Alicen's fantasies by arguing with her. Ignoring her bizarre words, he stood up and walked to the porch railing. The azaleas were starting to wither now, but their fragrance was still sweet. Derek watched a flock of birds shoot up from the nearby woods and heard the swing creak behind him as Alicen rocked it.

She didn't seem upset by any of this, and that bothered him. Had he scolded her so many times for being overly emotional that she was now afraid to let him know her feelings? He didn't like her having nightmares or pretending to talk with her mother. But he had never meant for her to hide her fears when those fears were justified. He had to make her understand she could trust him.

"Say, Alicen," he said, turning around, "would you like to go out to dinner with me?"

It worked. Alicen's dull expression suddenly brightened, and she nodded eagerly. He hadn't taken her to dinner in years. Derek glanced at his watch; it was still early afternoon.

"Well, it's too early for dinner yet," Derek said. "We can go in a few hours."

The look on his daughter's face was one of such disappointment that Derek tried to think of a quick remedy. He ran his fingers through his dark hair and said, "I know. We'll spend the afternoon in the city. Would you like that?"

"Okay," Alicen said, sounding genuinely eager.

"Then get your shoes and raincoat," Derek said. "And I'll meet you down here in fifteen minutes. I just have to let Gary know we're going out."

After changing his clothes, Derek walked out into the hall. He heard Alicen talking in her room. Knocking at her door, he asked if she was ready. When she didn't answer, he pushed

84

the door open a little. Alicen was sitting on the edge of her bed with one foot propped up and her fingers wrapped around her shoelaces. She was not moving and had a frightened look on her face. She seemed to be staring at something. Derek followed her gaze and saw a milky cloud hovering near the window.

"What the hell is that?" he demanded.

"Dad!"

Alicen jumped, pulling her hands away from her shoe. The cloud disintegrated and became a beam of sunlight. *Just sunlight,* Derek thought. *My eyes must be playing tricks on me.*

"Sorry if I startled you," he said, "but you didn't answer when I knocked at the door. Are you ready yet?"

"Yea," Alicen said, resuming her tying. She got up at last and pulled her raincoat from the closet. Derek noticed her hands trembling a bit but thought it was because he had startled her.

It was hard to believe the day had gone from brilliantly sunny to gloomy gray. But the air was heavy with moisture, and rain would be welcome. The breeze blowing now made the drive to Manhattan more pleasant, and the Volvo rode smoothly along. Derek turned on the radio and hummed with the music. Alicen rested her head on the window ledge and let the breeze blow her hair back.

"Hey, that's it for today for the Charlie Grinn show. I'll be back tomorrow with more hits, old and new."

An interlude of music led to the news.

"Good afternoon. In Washington today, President Carter . . ."

Derek looked across the seat at his daughter. She seemed lost in a dream world, her eyes squinted against the wind. He returned his own eyes to the road and said, "Alicen, do you want to talk about the accident?"

"I've been talking about it all day," Alicen said. "That cop Bryan Davis asked so many questions."

"Talking might make you feel better," Derek said. "You can't face your problems until they're out in the open."

"I don't have any problems!" Alicen snapped.

"Don't use that tone of voice with me," Derek cautioned.

Alicen clicked her tongue. "Oh, dad! Can't we just have a nice time tonight without talking about dumb things like that accident?"

"I don't think it's so dumb, Alicen," Derek said. He

glanced at her again. "Stop pouting. We won't talk about the accident if you don't want to."

"I don't," Alicen said.

They sat in silence for a while longer, listening to the news broadcast. There was a report on the bus accident.

"Here on Long Island, police are baffled over a bus accident involving fifty children from Saint Anne's school in Belle Bay. The bus, en route to the Vanderbilt Planetarium in Centerport, collided head-on with the fence surrounding the construction site of the Louis Pasteur Hotel. Speed of the bus was clocked at over eighty miles per hour. The mystery? No driver could be found in the wreckage. Described only as a young woman with long blond hair, she is being sought by police for endangering the lives of minors and for the death of Dwight Percy, the children's teacher. Percy, aged sixty-one, was sitting in the front of the bus at the time of the collision. He had no survivors.

"Miraculously, only four children were seriously injured. A broken arm, nose, and fractured skull were reported. One girl who complained about twisted fingers was treated and released. Police are investigating the incident and request that anyone having information should call . . ."

Derek switched off the radio. "You didn't tell me about the driver," he said.

"You didn't ask," Alicen replied.

"I shouldn't have to," Derek said. "And what do they mean, they couldn't find her?"

Alicen shrugged, not turning her head from the window.

"She sort of disappeared, I guess."

"How does anyone 'sort of disappear' from a speeding bus?" Derek wanted to know. When Alicen didn't reply, Derek tapped her impatiently. "Will you please answer me?"

"I don't know!" Alicen cried. "It happened too fast! Everyone's asking me so many questions." She sniffled, fighting tears.

"I'm sorry," Derek said. "I promised you we wouldn't talk about the accident, didn't I?"

From the corner of his eye he saw Alicen nod.

"Then we'll drop it," he said. "So, what do you want to do today?"

"I want to see the Central Park Zoo," Alicen said, cheering up again.

"That's the girl," Derek encouraged.

As she tried to forget the accident, Alicen told her father

all the things she wanted to see in the city. She didn't tell him that she dreaded coming home again.

11

Balancing himself with outstretched arms, the policeman named Tim hurried down the steep slope that led from the roadside. Under orders from their captain, he and his partner Rick were investigating the scene of that morning's bus accident. Rick walked up ahead, holding fast to the leashes of a pair of German shepherds. The animals whined and looked about in bewilderment, not picking up a scent. Tim kept his eyes to the ground, looking for footprints, pieces of clothing, or anything to indicate someone had been there. He was becoming as frustrated as the dogs; they had been walking for a mile and had yet to find a thing.

"I don't know why Davis took the word of some kid," he said, kicking aside a rusted can.

"I'm telling you," Rick answered, "that guy named Percy must have been the driver. I don't know why we're looking for some woman who doesn't even exist."

"Fifty kids can't all be lying," Tim pointed out.

"Well, the kid who talked to Davis was," Rick said. "You can't tell me a woman jumped from a speeding bus and just got up and walked away."

"I'm not telling you that," Tim said quietly.

They moved on in silence, walking further and further from the construction site. The sun was starting to go down now, and the air was growing pleasantly cool. Every once in a while, Tim would look up at the cars passing on the road, squinting against the brilliance of their lights. He laughed a little to see them slow down at the sight of the police car's flashing red light. Then he looked down at the ground again.

"It's six, Tim," Rick said some time later. "Let's call it quits."

"Yeah," Tim said. "We aren't going to find anything here."

Back at the police station, they turned the dogs over to the kennel master, made their report, and went home. Chief Morris contacted Bryan Davis, telling him no body had been found, let alone evidence there had been one at all.

Several miles away, Bryan hung up the receiver and got up from behind his desk. A while ago, he had been looking forward to the end of a long day. But now that his only lead to the driver's whereabouts was gone, he knew he wouldn't be able to rest until he had some answers. That Miller kid had to know something more. She'd looked so spaced-out that afternoon, and she had been overly adamant that he should believe her story. There had to be more to it.

Was it possible, Bryan thought, that she had been told to bring that story to him? An innocent kid doing someone's dirty work? Bryan decided the best way to find out would be to talk to her at home. It was only eight o'clock, not too late to make a call on the Miller house. Pulling the folder on the accident from the file, Bryan looked up Alicen's address in the list of children. His eyebrows went up when he read it.

"Three twenty-eight Starbine Court Road," he said aloud. "What's that kid doing in the VanBuren house?"

He'd find out soon enough, he thought. Thinking the girl might be more relaxed if he was out of uniform, he changed into jeans and a plaid shirt in the locker room. Then he went out to his car. As he drove through town, he recalled the night he had last been at the VanBurens' some six months ago. He remembered comforting Melanie after her husband's accident. Even now, Bryan shuddered to think of it.

"This has nothing to do with what happened last year," he told himself firmly.

But tonight it was too clearly stamped on his mind. He reluctantly recalled the events that had taken place at the house, when a "maniac" had tried to destroy the VanBuren family. It had been so terrifying, so unbelievable, the things that had happened that snowy November night. And he and the five other cops with him had vowed never to talk about it again.

The main street of Belle Bay was active right now, filled with teen-agers hanging out in front of well-lit stores, young couples shopping, and elderly people out for strolls. Bryan looked up at the trees that lined the street, seeing rich foliage of late spring silhouetted against the moonlit sky. As the stores and people faded out, the homes became more numerous, old Colonials mixed in with modern brick and aluminum-sided houses. Bryan noted the finely trimmed lawns and painted picket fences. People took care of their homes in Belle Bay. That was one reason why he loved this town. He didn't need any trouble here.

Now the houses thinned out, and Bryan found himself on Houston Street. From here, he could see the huge VanBuren mansion, sitting regally upon a hill. Though only one upstairs light was on, the entire house seemed to glow. Bryan was surprised to feel himself shudder.

No cars passed him on the road as he neared Starbine Court. He swung onto it, driving close to the beach for several hundred yards. He could just barely make out a couple sharing a blanket at the water's edge. In a few weeks, he thought, it would be beach season.

Just before he reached the hill that led to the mansion, he passed another house, huge and gray. It was empty now, ever since its elderly owner's death a year earlier. The house made Bryan think of hell, as if one could enter the eternal darkness by stepping behind one of the boarded-up windows.

He shook that ridiculous thought from his mind and drove up the hill. Parking his car in the driveway, he went to the front of the house, climbed the wooden stairs, and rang the bell. Seconds later, the porch was flooded with light. Melanie VanBuren opened the door, dressed in a robe. Recognizing him, she stepped back and smiled a little.

"Captain Davis," she said pleasantly, running her hand over her just-washed hair. "Come on in."

"It looks like I've come at a bad time," Bryan said. He saw Gary behind his wife, leaning on crutches. "But I had the idea to ask some questions about the accident."

"Is this official?" Gary asked, leading the police chief into the living room. "You aren't in uniform."

"I thought this was a little less intimidating," Bryan said. He sat down on the couch, sinking comfortably into the overstuffed cushions. "I'd like to talk with Alicen Miller—I understand she lives with you?"

"Yes, she does," Melanie said. "But she's not here right now. She's out with her father."

"I thought you asked questions at the school today," Gary said.

"I did," Bryan answered. "But I got nowhere." He thought for a moment, toeing the ball-and-claw feet of the coffee table, then said, "I thought the children would be more comfortable if I spoke to them in their homes, with their parents there beside them. I'm hoping to get more information this way."

"It's a good idea," Melanie said. "But why did you choose to start with Alicen?"

"She came to see me today," Bryan said.

Gary rocked a bit on his crutches. "Alicen didn't tell anyone she went out," he said.

"Well, she came to the station around twelve-thirty," Bryan reported.

"Oh, that's impossible," Melanie said, leaning forward in her chair. "I dropped her off here at noon. She couldn't have had time to walk back into town!"

"Then she managed to hitch a ride," Bryan suggested. "But she was there, and she had quite a story to tell me. I want to hear it from her again."

"A story?" Melanie echoed. "Alicen hardly seems the type to tell stories. She's a very shy girl."

"Didn't seem that way to me," Bryan answered. He stood up. "Well, if she's not here, I'll see her tomorrow. Sorry if I disturbed you."

Gary called to him before he reached the door. "I thought you wanted to talk to all of the children?"

"Huh?" Bryan answered, turning. "Oh, yeah. I said that, didn't I?"

"Let me get Gina," Melanie said. "She's still up."

She had left the room before Bryan could protest. Sighing, he returned to the couch and sat down again.

"How did she take the accident?" he asked.

"Not too badly," Gary answered. "My kids are pretty tough. They've been through worse, remember."

"I remember," Bryan said quietly. "It just seems wrong that one girl should suffer so much. I mean, after what happened last year. . . ."

"We don't talk about that," Gary said.

Bryan nodded. "Smart thing." He shifted on the couch, making himself more comfortable, then indicated Gary's crutches. "You look like you're doing well, though," he said. "Am I right?"

"I do the best I can," Gary answered. "I've been on crutches for a few weeks now. My next challenge is the stairs."

"You have to go to some clinic for that?"

"No, I've got a private therapist," Gary said. "He—Derek—is Alicen's father."

"That explains why she lives with you," Bryan said.

"You were wondering what a kid is doing in this spooky house, huh?"

"Sort of," Bryan said. "It surprised me to see she had the same address as Gina. Does her mother live here, too?"

"Alicen's mother is dead," he heard Melanie say. He turned and saw her enter the room with Gina, who was dressed in chinos and a T-shirt with a rainbow painted on it. She looked at him with questioning brown eyes, then went to sit on the armchair across from the couch.

"Hello," she said.

"Hey, there," Bryan said, smiling. "How're you?"

"Fine," Gina said. "Do you want to ask me some questions?"

"That's right," Bryan answered. "I was hoping you could remember something new."

Without hesitation, Gina shook her head. "I told you everything this morning."

"Tell me again," Bryan said. "And take your time. I'm not going anywhere."

Gina brought her legs up under her and folded her hands in her lap. She looked around the room, her brow furrowed as she tried to remember the morning's events. At last she fixed her gaze on the bronze fireplace screen and started to speak.

"We were supposed to go to the planetarium," she said. "I wanted to sit in the back, but Alicen said she'd get sick. So we sat right behind the driver."

"Did you see her?"

"Sure," Gina said.

Bryan straightened. "You did? What did she look like?"

"Well, I didn't see her face," Gina admitted. "I just saw the back of her. I was turned around when she got on. I was talking to Doreen—she's my friend. Anyway, all I know is that the driver had blond hair."

"Did she talk to you kids at all?"

"No, she didn't say anything. We told you that this morning, remember?"

Bryan smiled, nodding, then let her go on.

"We were all talking and fooling around," Gina continued. "Then one of the boys yelled something, and all of a sudden the bus started going faster and faster. Mr. Percy yelled at everybody to get on the floor. That's Alicen's teacher."

"You did that?"

"I couldn't!" Gina cried, looking at him with huge eyes. "I was so scared that I couldn't move at all. I just hung on to Alicen and covered my eyes. You know, like you do when you're on a scary roller coaster?"

"Calm down, honey," Gary said.

Bryan said nothing, thinking. It was exactly the same story Alicen had told him, yet . . .

"Gina, did you see the driver fighting with Mr. Percy?"

Gina shook her head. "I didn't see *anything*. I didn't even open my eyes when Mr. Percy—uh, when he knocked me from my seat."

She turned to gaze back at the fireplace. Melanie went to the chair and sat on the arm, taking her daughter's hand.

"Are these questions absolutely necessary?" she asked.

"Yes," Bryan insisted. "But they can wait until tomorrow if—"

"It's okay," Gina said. "What else do you want to know?"

"Did you see anything the driver did before the bus crashed?"

"I said I had my eyes closed."

"You didn't see her jump from the bus?"

"Is that what she did?" Gina asked. "Is that how she disappeared?"

"We don't know," Bryan said, standing. "That's enough for tonight, I think. If you remember anything more, you can tell me at school tomorrow. I'll be there again."

"Sure," Gina said.

Gary walked Bryan to the front door while Melanie sat in the living room with her daughter.

"Are you really going to all the children's homes?" Gary asked.

Bryan shook his head. "No. I really just wanted to talk to Alicen. She told me she saw the driver jump from the bus, but now I'm beginning to think I'm wasting my time following that lead. The Suffolk police couldn't locate a body near the construction site."

"Why would Alicen lie to you?" Gary asked.

"Beats me," Bryan said. "Maybe she's got an overactive imagination."

"Do you want me to have her father contact you?"

"Nah," Bryan said. "I've got enough parents breathing down my neck." He opened the door. "Call me if you learn anything new."

"I'll do that," Gary promised.

He stood unmoving as Bryan left the house, listening until his car started and drove away. Then he locked the front door and returned to the living room. Melanie and Gina were sharing an armchair, Gina's head on her mother's shoulder. Melanie looked up at her husband.

"Gina says he made her think of the night you were hurt," she said. "Don't you think he could have shown a little more tact?"

"He's just doing his job," Gary said gently. "Gina, you know this has nothing to do with that time."

"I know, daddy," Gina said. She climbed out of the chair. "I'm tired. I think I'll go to bed."

"Don't think about it," Melanie said. "Just get a good night's sleep."

But Gina did think about it, lying alone in the darkness of her room. Over and over she heard Bryan Davis asking, "Did you see the driver?" Gina rolled over and clutched at her pillow, trying to relax. The last thing she saw before falling asleep was Davis, standing over her in his blue uniform.

Minutes ticked by, and Gina sank deeper and deeper into sleep. She was warm and safe in her bed, under a cotton comforter that surrounded her with gentle softness.

And then something made that softness disappear, ripping it from her body. She bolted upright, her bare legs sprawled out in front of her. She couldn't move her arms to cover them.

"Hey, there," she heard Bryan Davis say.

She looked around. The room was empty, and yet someone had to be in there because the light was on. She leaned forward, her eyes darting. Everything seemed okay. But her clock radio was playing music, and she couldn't remember having turned it on.

"Did you see the driver?"

"I'm cold," Gina heard herself say.

"Did you see the driver?"

Next thing, Gina was leaning over the side of her bed, face down into a black pit. Two eyes glared up at her through the darkness, pinpoints of red light. Her stuffed kangaroo suddenly came into view, floating up toward her. No, just its severed head. Gina's hand dropped into the pit, grabbing for it. It turned into a piece of glass.

"Did you see the driver!"

"No!"

The glass dropped, down and down. The pit closed up, but it was not her floor she saw next. It was the sand of the beach, flecked with snow. Everything was icy cold in her room.

Bryan Davis was leaning over her, smiling. He looked so nice, and yet there was an evil glimmer in his eyes when he said, "Hey, there. Did you see the driver?"

"Go away!"

Bryan grinned more broadly and grabbed hold of her wrist. His features began to change, his graying hair turned darker, thicker. The blue uniform swirled and became a cape. The round face became more chiseled. Something flashed in Gina's dream consciousness, making her remember this face against her will. She wanted to get away, and yet she could only lay helplessly as cold fingers wrapped around her neck.

"Did you see the driver?"

"No!"

The fingers tightened.

"You must die, you know," the man said.

"Nnnnnoooo!"

The man smiled.

Gina screamed and bolted upright, alone in her room but unable to realize yet that it had all been a terrible dream. She screamed and screamed, terror churning in her stomach. The door opened; Derek was there with Alicen at his side. They were walking toward her bed, eyeing her strangely.

"Go away!" Gina shouted at them.

"It's only me," Derek said. "Derek. You're dreaming."

Gina simply stared at him, tears falling from her huge eyes. Her mother burst into the room just then and said in a soft voice, "Oh, my God."

She climbed onto the bed and took Gina into her arms. The girl was trembling all over. Melanie could feel her heart beating. She stroked her hair and rocked her.

"It's all right," she whispered. "I'm here, my baby. It's okay."

Gary came into the room, Kyle and Nancy behind him, sleepy-eyed. He glanced briefly at Derek, then hobbled to his daughter's bed.

"Were you having a dream about the accident?" he asked, taking Gina's hand.

Gina shook her head. "That man was here."

"What man?"

"The man with the cape," Gina said hoarsely. She stared down at her blanket with round eyes. "The man from the beach last year, who tried to hurt me. He was here!"

Alicen gasped. Derek quickly hushed her.

"Daddy—" Nancy said.

Gary looked over his shoulder at the two younger children. "Kyle, take your sister back to bed," he ordered.

"I wanna hear about Gina's dream," Kyle whined.

"You want a kick in the pants?" Gary snapped. "Get back into bed!"

Kyle took Nancy by the wrist, not daring to question his father when he acted that angrily. Once he was gone, Gary turned back to Gina and said, "Honey, you know that man will never come back."

Gina looked at her mother.

"Aren't you worried that he will, maybe?"

Melanie didn't answer at first. She thought of the day she had found the bloodstain on her painting, and then of the ransacked studio. Sarah Kaufman's face tried to creep into her mind, but she forced it away.

"No, of course I'm not," she insisted.

"Gina, why don't you try to go to sleep again?" Gary suggested. "You'll probably feel better."

Gina lay back down and held fast to her mother's hand. The room was silent, and soon she was sleeping again. Carefully, Melanie let go of her and left the room with the others.

"It's that cop's fault," she whispered. "Asking her all those questions!"

"I thought Gina didn't care about the accident," Alicen said.

"Go to bed, Alicen," Derek ordered. "It's late."

"Is Gina okay?"

"She's fine, I'm sure," Gary said, not believing it.

Alicen tapped Melanie on the arm. "Did someone try to kill her last year?"

"Alicen, did you hear me?" Derek said. "I told you to go to bed!"

"I'm going," Alicen said, walking away, pouting.

After she turned the corner, Derek looked at Gary and said, "Is there really no chance that the man who hurt you might come back again?"

"None at all," Melanie said. "He was a prowler, and the police took care of him."

"I just want to be sure my daughter is safe here," Derek said.

"She is," Melanie insisted. "There's nothing for you to worry about."

"No, wait a minute," Gary said. "Derek's got a right to know the truth."

"Are you sure you want to tell him?"

"Of course I am," Gary said. "Derek, remember the day

you moved in, when I told you the owner of our house had been a captain in the eighteenth-century British navy?"

"What's he got to do with this?"

"Take off your coat and come into my study," Gary said. "It's time you heard about him."

12

Derek had always liked Gary's office. It was a decidedly masculine room, with dark paneling and leather-covered furniture. A huge antique map hung on one wall, and near the window stood a brass stand that had once held a telescope. Now, as promised weeks earlier, Derek was about to learn of the man who had put them in here. He couldn't see the connection with Gina's dream, but curiosity made him anticipate the upcoming story with interest. He hung his raincoat up on a brass coat rack and sat in a chair. Melanie and Gary shared a small couch across from him.

"To begin with," Gary said, "our 'hero's' name was Jacob Armand, a British naval captain who came to America during the early 1790s."

"The colonists, of course, didn't care much for the British at that time," Melanie put in. "Which made life rather difficult for him, added to the fact that he was in the enemy's militia."

"So he built a house far away from the town," said Gary, tightening the belt on his robe. "He hoped they'd leave him alone. It turns out he had to pay a sort of protection fee to keep them from stoning his windows out."

"It didn't hurt him to pay it," Melanie said. "Jacob Armand was a very wealthy man."

"I can see that by this house," Derek answered.

"One day," Gary went on, "Jacob met a beautiful young woman named Lydia Browning. They fell in love, and everything was fine and dandy. But there was a hitch—Lydia was married."

"Her husband detested the British with a passion," Melanie said. "When he found out her lover's nationality, he became enraged. It wasn't enough to have Lydia punished for adultery. He had to throw in a charge of witchcraft, too. And to make matters worse, he forced his two young children to testify against their mother."

Gary pointed out the window. "So Lydia was dragged down to the beach and burned at the stake. Jacob Armand saw all of it but couldn't do a thing. When his beloved Lydia died, he vowed to avenge her death."

"Wait a minute," Derek said. "Why wasn't he executed with her?"

"Don't forget he was putting a lot of money into the town with his protection fee," Gary reminded him. "They were willing to forget his part in the 'crime' just to keep getting the money."

"Jacob himself died just a few months later," Melanie said. "Literally of a broken heart. He carried his vow to avenge Lydia's death to the grave."

"That was the end of him, then," Derek said. "So why the history lesson?"

Gary and Melanie exchanged glances.

"It wasn't the end of him," Gary said in a low voice. "We bought this house last year without knowing his spirit still walked its grounds."

"Whoa!" Derek cried. "Hold on a minute. Spirit? As in haunted? You're trying to tell me this place is haunted?"

He was looking at them as if they were crazy, but Gary was undaunted.

"*Was* haunted," he corrected. "We drove Jacob Armand out last November. He had become attached to my wife and tried to kill the rest of us to have her."

Melanie took Gary's hand and looked at him with sad eyes. Remembering the events that led to this story, she spoke in a soft, choked voice.

"He saw me as his Lydia," Melanie said. "And Gary and the children as the husband and children who led her to her death. In order to save me—Lydia—he first had to get rid of them. And he almost succeeded."

She shuddered and turned to put her head on Gary's shoulder. Gary put his arms around her and kneaded the hair at the back of her neck.

"On the night it ended," he said, "he pushed me from a window upstairs." He motioned toward his legs. "That's why I'm like this."

"You said it was a prowler," Derek said quietly, a little overwhelmed.

"Would you have believed the truth?" Gary asked. "We hardly believe it ourselves. In fact, we promised each other not to talk about it ever again. But, considering Gina's dream, we might have made a mistake. It was wrong to expect the children to forget that night."

"The bus accident made Gina remember what had happened," Melanie put in. "And she was tormented as horribly as any of us that night. I don't think I'll ever forget—" She began to cry now. "Oh, God, Gary!"

"Jacob Armand tried to murder my daughter on the beach," Gary said. "In the same spot where Lydia had been executed. Fortunately, Melanie got to him in time to prevent him from taking another life."

There was silence for a while. Derek considered all this, wanting not to believe it, and yet unable to think of a reason why they would be telling him such a fantastic yarn. Were they hiding something behind the fantasy? A thought came into his head.

"Those murders Alicen mentioned," he said quietly. "They really happened, didn't they? Is that what you meant by his taking another life?"

"Yes," Gary said. "In his pursuit of Melanie, he murdered three people. The first was an old woman named Helen Jennings, who used to own that house down the road. Then there was a young cop, Tony DiMagi. And last of all, Melanie's best—"

"Gary, please," Melanie begged. "Don't talk about her."

"It's okay," Derek said. "I know about your friend Janice. Gary told me the day you got so upset when I mentioned that name."

Melanie looked at him through tears. "He told you what happened to her?"

"Not that Jacob Armand murdered her," Derek said.

"Well, he did," Melanie answered. "He hit her across the head and killed her."

She said that in the tormented way of someone who wants the truth to be known. It was as if she were afraid he wouldn't believe her. In truth, he wasn't quite sure what to believe. His loyalty to Gary made him want to buy the story, and yet his own common sense told him it couldn't be true. Ghosts! But Melanie looked so upset and Gary so solemn that he figured it was best to humor them right now.

"So Gina was reliving that night?" he asked. "Just because of the bus accident? I know it was a horrible experience, but Gina seemed so calm at dinner tonight."

"Well, it was more than the accident," Melanie said, sniffling back the last of her tears. "Bryan Davis—the police chief—came to talk to her tonight. He'd been here the night of Gary's accident."

"Why did he come here at night?" Derek asked. "Didn't he spend enough time questioning the kids at school? At least that's the impression I got from talking to Alicen."

"Actually, your daughter was his reason for coming," Gary said. "He said she'd been down at the station telling him she'd seen the driver jump from the bus."

"I don't see how it was possible," Melanie put in. "He said she was in his office at twelve-thirty, but I only left her here at noon. It takes longer than half an hour to get into town. So Bryan hinks she might have hitchhiked."

"Oh, brother," Derek said, recalling the woman who had hidden in his car. What if Alicen had met with that evil woman named Janice? He shook the thought from his mind.

"I find the fact that Alicen went at all even more unbelievable," he said. "Funny she didn't tell me about the driver. She didn't seem to know anything at all."

"Maybe Bryan mistook her for another child," Melanie said.

"There isn't anyone like Alicen," Derek answered. He clapped his hands together. "Well, if she did go, I'm glad. It just means she's starting to come out of that shell of hers. It's about time she started taking things into her own hands."

"Thirteen seems a little early to start taking things into your own hands," Melanie said softly.

"What did you say?"

"Nothing, Derek," Melanie said in a clearer voice. "I didn't say a thing. Gary, finish the story for him."

"Just tell me how you finally got rid of your ghost," Derek said, running a finger under his lip.

"We weren't the ones who did it," Gary said. "It seems he'd been tormenting other families who had lived in this house. All their spirits came to fight him, and they sent him to hell. In the process Lydia herself showed up. Now that Jacob had her again, his spirit was put to rest."

"Where was Lydia before this?"

"Waiting for him to come to her," Melanie said. "Remember, in her day women would wait for months, even years, for their men to return from the sea. I—uh—suppose that in the afterlife, two hundred years is like six months."

"It sounds interesting," Derek said.

Gary eyed him. "But you don't believe it."

"How can I!" Derek asked. "I hardly believe there's a God, and I'm not quite sure there's an afterlife. I never believed in supernatural powers, and I'm not about to start."

"Then you must think we're a pair of fools," Melanie said bitterly.

"Not at all," Derek said. "I'm sure you have your reasons for telling me this story. Hey, look, what do I know, right? Just because I don't believe it doesn't make it untrue."

He stood up. "I'm very tired. Sorry to run out on you, but I'd like to hit the sack."

"We didn't lie to you," Melanie said darkly.

Derek didn't answer her. He opened the door, then turned and said, "My daughter's a hysterical type. Make sure she doesn't hear about this, okay? Her nightmares are frequent enough."

With that, he was gone. Melanie stared at the closed door for a long time without speaking. And then she said, in a quiet voice, "You didn't have to tell him about Janice."

"Honey, he was bound to find out," Gary said. "Why let it bother you so much?"

"My best friend is dead," Melanie snapped, "and I'm not supposed to let it bother me?"

Gary waved his hand at her. "Of course you are. But why do you single Janice's death out in particular? Why didn't you stop me from mentioning Helen Jennings and Tony DiMagi?"

"That's different," Melanie said.

She stood up and headed for the door, not waiting for her husband. The hallway was dark, in spite of the light pouring into it from the study. Melanie's nerves were on edge, as if anticipating that cold fingers would reach out through the blackness to grab her. But whose fingers?

At the end of the hallway, the small stained-glass window burst open, crashing against the wall.

"What?" Melanie cried out, turning around. She saw Gary in the doorway of his office.

"Just the wind, Melanie," he said, hobbling to the window to shut it. When he looked out, he noticed the trees were perfectly still.

"Wait for me," he said as he latched the window. "I'll walk back to our room with you."

He thought he heard someone laughing in the distance. But he blocked the sound from his ears and went to his wife. He wasn't about to join her in thinking every little noise was the herald of something evil.

* * *

100

The next day Gary called his family together. After what had happened last night, he knew it was very important to talk to his children. He and Melanie shared a loveseat, while the children sat on the couch. Nancy bounced up and down playfully, until Gina stopped her. Gary noticed the dark circles under his oldest daughter's eyes.

"I have to ask you kids something," Gary said. "Kyle, Gina, Nancy—do any of you ever have dreams like Gina had?"

Kyle looked at the fireplace, as if in deep thought. Nancy brought her thumbs to her mouth. Melanie frowned as she noted Nancy's gesture. It had been two months since Nancy had sucked her thumbs, and all it took was this suggestion of Gary's to start her again. Maybe the children had the incident with Jacob Armand more deeply rooted in their minds than she thought?

"I had a lots of dreams right after the accident," Kyle said. "But you knew about them, 'cause I came into your room a couple of times, remember?"

"I remember," Gary said. "And that was to be expected so soon after what happened. But I'm asking if you've been having dreams lately?"

"No, dad," Kyle said. "You told us not to think about those things."

"How about you, Nancy?"

The little girl shrugged.

Melanie looked out the window and saw the bus coming. "Hey, you'd better get going," she said.

Gary hoisted himself up from the chair and said, "Now, listen. If you ever want to discuss what happened that night, you just come to your mother or me, okay? Don't bottle your feelings inside."

"We won't, dad," Kyle said, heading out into the hall.

"They'll be okay," he said, putting his arm around Melanie. "I just wanted to let them know we won't make fun of them if they're still afraid. Now listen," he said, abruptly changing the subject, "I've got news for you that'll take your mind off of all this."

"What's that?"

"Guess where I'm going tomorrow?"

Melanie shrugged.

"To the medical center for tests. Melanie, if I do okay, I may be able to go back to work."

Melanie's smile broadened and became genuine. "Gary, that's wonderful! It'll be just like it was when we first moved here! The way it was supposed to be—with you going to work and me doing my painting."

She threw her arms around him. She wanted so much to be happy, to believe that nothing but good could happen to her family from now on.

13

"Hey, Alicen, wait up!"

Alicen recognized Jamie Hutchinson's voice and quickened her pace toward home. She had been made to stay after school that day. The accident had been heavy on her mind, and she had been caught daydreaming—*again*. This new teacher was worse than Mr. Percy had ever been. She had yelled at Alicen, humiliating her in front of the whole class. Oh, God, the girl thought, isn't this day bad enough? All I need now is Jamie Hutchinson teasing me.

"Alicen, I know you can hear me," Jamie said, his voice right behind her. "Why don't you stop?"

"Why don't you go away?" Alicen replied.

"You want a ride home?" Jamie asked, ignoring her remark. He came up alongside her on a bicycle.

"No," Alicen said plainly.

"It's a long walk," Jamie coaxed. "Come on, will you? I rode all the way back to school just 'cause I thought you'd want a ride home."

Alicen stopped, considering this. "Really?" she asked. "You really came back for me?"

"Sure," Jamie said. "Now, hop on, will you?"

He stopped the bicycle and patted the fender behind him. Alicen studied it doubtfully.

"I think I'm too heavy for that," she said.

"It's stronger than it looks," Jamie said. "And besides, I already told you, you aren't that fat. Get on."

Alicen sighed with defeat and climbed behind him. She hoped none of her classmates would see them riding together.

They rode on in silence, until they reached the bottom of the hill that led to the VanBuren property. Alicen jumped off the bike, knowing it wouldn't make it up the hill under their combined weight. She adjusted her skirt and books.

"Thanks, Jamie," she said. "I'm sorry I acted so stuck-up before."

But Jamie wasn't listening. Straddling his bike, his sneakers toeing the asphalt, he was staring at the big gray house. It fascinated him, with its boarded-up windows and brown, overgrown grass. He turned back to Alicen.

"I want to look inside there," he said.

"You can't," Alicen replied. "It's private property. And besides, how would you get in?"

"I'll find a way," Jamie said.

He jumped off his bike and walked it toward the house, dried weeds and crab grass crunching beneath his feet. Alicen ran after him.

"Jamie, you can't go in there!" she cried. "You'll get in trouble."

Jamie stopped and turned to her. "If no one tells on me," he said, a warning tone in his voice, "I won't get in trouble. Besides, I'm just looking."

He found a place to hide his bicycle in the bushes that surrounded the house. To his dismay all the windows and doors were tightly boarded over. Alicen hoped it would discourage him.

"Ah-ha!" Jamie cried. He had discovered an entrance to the basement. An empty, rusted milk can rested against the slanted doors.

"Help me tear some of this up," he said, pulling at the weeds. Alicen joined him, somewhat reluctantly. "See? They forgot to secure this lock."

Jamie removed it and set it on top of the milk can. With a heave, he jerked one big door open. The basement below was a black pit, silent and frightening. But this only sharpened Jamie's curiosity. He hurried down the stone steps. Alicen hesitated but decided she didn't want to be alone out here and ran after him.

"Brr!" she mumbled. "It's so cold!"

"Shh," Jamie said, as if the house had ears. "Help me find the stairs."

They groped through the darkness, Alicen holding fast to Jamie's belt. She was struck by a mixture of smells. Cats, rusting metal, old wood. Her hands felt the stucco of a wall, then pulled back when cobwebs brushed her fingers.

"I don't like this," she said.

"Here're the stairs," Jamie said. "Follow me up."

103

Unused for months, the wooden stairs creaked in protest under this new weight. Alicen felt the banister wobbling and tightened her grip on Jamie's belt. At last he opened the door. They were in the kitchen. A beam of light shining through a crack in the window illuminated the empty floor. Jamie and Alicen stepped further inside.

"I'll bet she's watching us," Jamie said.

"Who?"

"The old lady," Jamie said. "Helen Jennings. You know she died out on that hill last year?"

"Mrs. VanBuren said she had a heart attack."

"Uh-uh," Jamie said. In the half-light, Alicen saw his head shake back and forth. "I'll bet she was one of the murder victims I told you about."

"That was a lie!" Alicen cried.

Jamie didn't reply. He opened a door and walked out of the kitchen. His sneakers made squeaking noises as he moved across the bare wooden floors, investigating each empty room. Their barrenness made them very cold, and Alicen wished she hadn't come in here after all. Jamie poked around a fireplace in the living room, hoping to discover some treasure the movers had left behind. Alicen looked around the big room but didn't move from Jamie's side.

Suddenly something moved in the entranceway to the dining room. Alicen took a step toward it but quickly found herself unable to move. A woman was staring at her. She pointed at Alicen, her long arm glowingly white.

"Leave this place!" she cried. "There is danger, child!"

Alicen was frozen to the floor. The vision continued to point at her, a frothy light in the darkness of the dining room. Alicen wondered what was hidden in that darkness.

"Alicen, let's look up—"

Jamie turned to see Alicen staring across the room. He snapped his fingers in front of her eyes.

"Alicen!" he cried. "What's the matter?"

His cries broke her spell, and giving a gasp, Alicen turned to face him. She pointed to the entranceway. "There's someone standing there!" she hissed.

Jamie squinted his eyes and looked through the darkness. He saw a shimmer of white where Alicen pointed. Someone was standing there, all right, blocking their only exit! For the first time since entering the house, Jamie was scared. Slowly he unbuckled his belt and pulled it through the loops of his jeans. Winding an end around his hand, leaving the buckle free, he walked carefully toward the white light. It did not move.

He raised it in the air, ready to swing it forward with all his might.

"Go away!" Alicen cried. "Leave us alone!"

Jamie gave a cry then and let the buckle of his belt swirl through the air at the unmoving form. It made a loud sound as it struck wood. The sound reverberated through the house like mocking laughter. There was no one there at all.

"Alicen, it's only a curtain," Jamie cried. "I just made a fool of myself over a dumb curtain."

"I know I saw someone there," Alicen insisted. "She pointed right at me and said, 'Leave this place. There is danger, child!' "

"I think your brain is in danger," Jamie scoffed. "I didn't hear a thing."

"It's true," Alicen said.

"Oh, you're seeing things," Jamie said. "If you're so scared to be in this house, I'll leave."

He took her by the hand and walked through the darkness to the kitchen. Alicen didn't protest, only too happy to be getting out of there. But she had seen something. It had spoken to her.

They cut across the dark basement, heading toward the light of the doorway. Once outside, Jamie closed the doors. Then he turned to Alicen, and squinting in the bright sunlight, he said, "If you tell anyone what happened in there, I'll kill you. I feel like such a jerk—hitting a curtain with a belt!"

"I won't tell a soul," Alicen promised. She pulled her hand from his and ran across the lawn, wanting to get as far away from the house as possible. Jamie went to fetch his bicycle, pondering over Alicen's overactive imagination.

"She's nuts," he said, then sighed. Climbing onto his bike, he rode back to the road and headed home.

He didn't know he was being watched.

I try so hard to warn them, the dark-haired woman thought. *I have spoken to Melanie many times, but she ignores me. They all ignore me.*

I don't know that I can save them.

After shepherding Gary through a number of tests and X-rays, Doctor Norton announced that he could go back to

105

work on a three-day-a-week schedule. Derek readily agreed to drive Gary into the city, provided he promise that the remaining days be dedicated to therapy.

"After the bus accident, I knew something good had to happen to this family," Melanie said when she heard the news. Thoughts of the mysterious dark-haired woman flashed in her mind, but she shook them away. This was a happy occasion, and nothing would mar it.

"You've waited so long for this," she went on, "and now it's here."

The next morning, all the children gave Gary kisses of encouragement before they left for school. Around ten, Derek helped Gary put his things in order, then carried the briefcase and crutches downstairs while Gary rode the lift. Derek made a mental note to begin stairs therapy that week.

Gary took the crutches from him at the bottom, then hobbled into the kitchen to say goodbye to Melanie. There were tears in her blue eyes. He laughed and ran a thumb under one of them.

"Hey, this is a happy occasion," he said.

"Why do you think I'm crying?" Melanie blubbered.

"Well, I'll see you later tonight," Gary said, kissing her. "Stop crying and wish me luck."

"Good luck, Gary," Melanie said, smiling.

The sun was shining brightly as the two men got into Derek's car. There was a low hum in the air, the buzz of insects heralding summer. Gary opened his window and breathed in the aroma of flowers on the warm, soft breeze.

"Summer's so close you can smell it," he said.

"I love this time of the year," Derek replied, turning his key. "I met Elaine on a day just like this."

He looked up at the blue, cloudless sky and pressed his foot on the gas pedal. "Funny how a certain kind of day can make you remember things," he said.

"For sure," Gary agreed, wondering if Derek wanted to talk about his wife.

"I don't think I could ever forget the way Elaine looked that day," Derek said wistfully. "She was so beautiful." But he forced his voice into a more cheerful tone. "I'm happy that I met Liza Crewe. She's giving me something to look forward to in life. I'm hoping to marry her."

"Hey, that's great," Gary said. "Any idea when?"

"I haven't asked her yet," Derek said. "I don't think the time is right, since we've only known each other a few weeks. I don't want to scare her off."

"It's usually smart to take it easy," Gary said. "Although Melanie and I only knew each other for a few months before we tied the knot."

"Those kind of marriages usually don't work," Derek said. "Which is why I hesitate to ask Liza this early on. You and Melanie were lucky."

"We've had our problems," Gary said.

"So I gathered from what you told me the other night," Derek said. "Hey, listen. I wanted to apologize for laughing at you."

"Don't worry about it," Gary said. "It is an unbelievable story."

"Are you taking it back?"

"No," Gary said. "It's true. I just hope nothing ever happens again to prove it."

Derek put on his signal as he headed for the exit ramp. He thought about the things Gary and Melanie had told him and wondered if there wasn't a germ of truth in them. Not ghosts, of course. Derek firmly believed those things didn't exist. But he knew some crazy people practiced the occult. Could the prowler who murdered those three people have been one of those?

Whatever, it didn't concern him. He looked up into his rear-view mirror to be sure no one was tailgating him. Then he returned his eyes to the road. Seconds later, he did a double take.

"Damn!" he cried. "She's back again."

"Who?" Gary asked, trying to look out the back window.

"The hitchhiker I told you about," Derek said, looking in his mirror at her. She was waving slowly. "I was hoping that bitch had decided to leave me alone."

Gary hadn't seen anything on the road but thought perhaps that the woman had moved out of his line of vision. He noticed that Derek's forehead had broken out in a sweat and that his usually calm therapist was chewing at his lips.

"Hey, she's really gotten to you, hasn't she?"

"Huh?" Derek jumped a little. "Oh, Jesus in Heaven. I guess so. I had forgotten about her, but it looks as if she's moving in on me again."

"Somebody ought to call the police about her," Gary suggested.

Derek reached the parkway exit, and he sped onto it, glad to be getting away from the woman. He didn't understand why she frightened him so much. But he had seen something in her eyes a moment ago—the look one sometimes sees in the faces of killers pictured in the newspapers. If Jacob Armand—or whoever the prowler was—had belonged to some occult group, could she have also been a member? Was that why she was hanging around the VanBuren house?

WELCOME BACK, GARY!

The sign was stretched across the waiting room, from a translucent glass door that read Warren Lee to one that read Gary VanBuren. Gary rocked on his crutches, grinning up at it. The secretary, who had been hired during his absence, asked politely if he needed help.

"I work here," he said, grinning at the sound of those words. "I'm Gary VanBuren."

"Oh!" the young woman said, standing. She rounded the desk, a petite redhead with a broad smile. She held out a hand, and Gary shook it. "I'm Judy Palance. Mr. Lee's told me so much about you! Can I help you sit down? Then I'll go get—"

Gary assured her that he was fine. The door to Warren Lee's offce opened then, and a handsome young Oriental stepped out. Seeing Gary, he smiled and went to put his arms around his partner. Then he stepped back and looked him over.

"It's been a long time," he said. He gave him a slight punch. "You look terrific. Are those muscles I see under that suit?"

Gary looked from one arm to the other. "I guess that's from lifting weights. The way my therapist pushes me, you'd think I was training for the fight of the century."

"At least he's got you walking again," Warren said. He turned to Judy. "Get the champagne out, okay? We're going to have a party."

"You bought champagne?" Gary asked. Warren nodded, smiling. "And what about my appointments?"

"I set the first one up for one o'clock, so we'd have time to talk. And you're only getting one today. You don't need to overburden yourself."

"Yes, doctor," said Gary.

Gary, Warren, and Judy shared champagne, joking together so joyfully that they barely heard the phone ringing over their laughter. Judy leaned over her desk to grab the phone. "Mr. VanBuren? Yes, he's in. Hold on."

Gary looked at Warren. "I didn't think anyone knew I was coming back today."

Warren shrugged his shoulders in response. Gary turned and went into his office. For a moment he stopped to admire it. It looked exactly as it had when he had left it last November. Even the calendar hadn't been changed. He flipped through it to the right date and settled down in his leather chair. God, that felt good! It was wonderful to be back on familiar territory. Propping his crutches against the window behind him, he paused for a moment to look out at the city. Then he finally answered the phone.

"Mr. VanBuren?" a voice asked. It was vaguely familiar.

"Yes?"

"It's Marc Kaufman," the man said.

Gary leaned back in his chair. "Oh, yes. How are you, mayor?"

"Under the circumstances—" Marc began. Gary could hear him sigh. "Well, I should get right to the point. It's about Sarah's diamond ring. I don't want to seem as if I'm making accusations, but it was missing from her hand when . . ."

"The heirloom she was wearing that night?"

"Yes," said Marc. "Mr. VanBuren, I was wondering if you might have seen it? Perhaps she dropped it in your house."

"Did you call my wife?" Gary asked.

"I tried," said Marc. "No one answered the phone."

"Then she's probably out shopping," Gary said. "How about the people at the hospital? Or in the ambulance?"

"I've talked to them," Marc said. "And to the police. Please don't think I'm saying anyone at your house took it. But it was the last place Sarah wore the ring."

Gary thought a moment, then said, "When I get home tonight, I promise I'll have the whole family look for it. Come to think of it, we gave you two a tour of the house that day. It could be anywhere."

"I'd really appreciate it if you'd look," Marc said.

As soon as he hung up, Gary's door opened. Into the room walked his partner, carrying a pile of folders. He dumped them on Gary's desk and told him they were backlogged files that needed to be gone through.

"Hey," Gary said. "I thought you weren't going to overburden me today?"

"Admit it," Warren said. "You love every minute of this."

Gary smiled crookedly and opened the top folder. At last he was back at work again.

While Gary readjusted himself to the working world, Derek Miller waited outside Madame Martin's Dance Studio for Liza to finish her class. He sat on a cushion-covered bench in the waiting room, looking at the pictures of a magazine written in French. He heard a French voice from behind a door.

"Un et deux, un et deux," it repeated over and over to the beat of the piano music. "Et c'est assez, mesdames. À demain!"

Seconds later, the door opened, and a thin woman with hair pulled back in a bun came out. Derek looked past her at the small group of students and signaled to Liza. She waved and indicated the locker room. Derek went back to his seat and waited.

Liza came out at last and in front of several other dance students, threw her arms around him and kissed him.

"That's the kind of greeting I like," Derek said.

"Have you been waiting long?"

"Not really," Derek answered. "But I'm ready for lunch if you are."

"I'm famished!" Liza cried, patting her flat stomach. "And I know a terrific Chinese restaurant."

It was only three blocks away, but Derek insisted upon carrying Liza's case. It wasn't heavy at all, and Liza was a little embarrassed when a few classmates saw her handing it to him. But Derek wasn't worried about their opinion.

"Women shouldn't have to burden themselves," he said.

"You're such a chauvinist," Liza teased, "but I guess I love you, anyway." At the restaurant Liza opened the door before Derek could get to it.

The restaurant was crowded, but recognizing Liza, the maitre d' led them quickly to a table. In silence Derek and Liza ran over the menu, then placed their orders. When the waiter left, Liza folded her hands together and leaned forward.

"How's your daughter?" she asked. "You told me about the accident over the phone but no details. Did it upset her very much?"

"I wouldn't know," Derek admitted. "I took her out to dinner that day, but she didn't want to talk about it. Alicen has a habit of clamming up like that."

"I can't blame her," Liza said. "I saw the picture in the paper. What a horrible mess!"

"Thank God none of the children were seriously hurt," Derek said. "But that poor teacher . . ."

Alicen's words came back to him: *I'm glad he died. I hate him!*

Derek shook his head roughly.

"What's wrong?"

"Nothing," Derek said. "Dwight Percy was Alicen's teacher. I understand, though, that they weren't too fond of each other. Alicen has a tendency to daydream, and Percy was a no-nonsense type."

Liza laughed, a bell-like sound that relaxed Derek at once.

"Oh, I used to daydream all the time," she said. "I used to pretend I was a prima ballerina when I was supposed to be doing equations. I think all girls go through a time like that. How old did you say Alicen was?"

"Thirteen," Derek said. "And I don't think this is a passing phase. She's been having these dreams for six years." He lifted his fork and dropped it. "Ever since Elaine died."

"Oh . . ."

Looking up at Liza, Derek realized his mistake.

"Oh, hey, I'm sorry," he said, reaching across the table to take her hand. "I shouldn't have said that."

"You're just upset because of the accident," Liza said. "I understand."

"I don't want to spoil our lunch," Derek replied. "Let me think of something better to talk about. Do you like ghost stories?"

"Sure," Liza said.

"Then listen to this one," Derek answered. "You'll love it."

He proceeded to relate the story of the VanBuren hauntings. Liza listened intently, her almond eyes as bright as a child's. When Derek finished, she stabbed a shrimp on her plate with a fork and said, "That's interesting, but a little unbelieveable, don't you think? I mean, haunted houses?"

"I don't believe it," Derek said, "and yet I don't disbelieve that something went on in that house last year. I think the VanBurens made up that story to push the truth from their minds. But one thing that is true is the fact that three people died at the house. One of them was a young woman named

111

Janice. She was Melanie's best friend, and needless to say, my patient's wife gets rather upset at the mention of her name."

"The poor thing," Liza said. "It must have been a horrible experience for her."

"Melanie tends to get emotional about it," Derek said. "But who can blame her?"

Liza ate a few bites of food, then said, "I'd sure like to see that house. I'll bet it's eerie."

"You wouldn't be disappointed," Derek answered. "But the VanBurens do keep the cobwebs swept."

Liza laughed. "Do you suppose I could come there one night?" she asked. "I mean, after giving Alicen time to adjust after the accident? I think meeting her father's new girlfriend would be too much for her right now."

"You missed your calling," Derek said. "You should have been a child psychologist."

"I worked with one for eight years," Liza said. "That's how I saved money to come to New York."

Derek lifted her hand and kissed it. "You're a very kind woman," he said.

"I was just thinking about Alicen."

"Shh," Derek said. "Enough about Alicen. You'll meet her soon, I promise."

Making his nightly rounds of the bay area, Harold Kent, a security guard for one of Belle Bay's prestigious private communities, drove his dune buggy along the water line. His headlights danced off the little ripples made by the wind, competing with the golden reflections of the moon. The bay was so peaceful at this hour, just before dawn. Harold began to whistle.

But something caught his eye, an interruption in the golden ripples of the bay that made him stop whistling. He stopped his truck and went to investigate.

It was a woman's body. Harold bent closer to it, waving his flashlight over the wet, sand-covered flesh. In the moonlight the bloated face seemed to be grinning with evil pleasure. Blond hair was braided with seaweed. Some of it had wrapped around the woman's throat.

Harold rushed back to his truck and drove up to the guard house. There, he phoned his discovery into the Belle Bay police. Within two hours the body, named Jane Doe for lack of identification, was taken to the Belle Bay funeral home for

112

storage. There it would wait until someone came to identify it.

14

"As soon as you kids are through with your homework," Gary said at dinner that night, "come downstairs. I have a chore for you."

"What is it, dad?" Kyle asked.

"Well, Mayor Kaufman gave me a call today," Gary explained. "It seems Sarah lost that big diamond ring of hers, and he wondered if it might be in this house somewhere. So we're going to look for it."

"Gary, I've cleaned this house since then," Melanie said, serving beets to a grimacing Nancy. "I didn't see it."

"Well, it wouldn't hurt to look," Gary said.

"Alicen and I will help you," Derek said.

Alicen, picking listlessly at her food, didn't hear her father say that. She was thinking of the old house down the road. Jamie hadn't mentioned a word of what had happened in school the next day. And true to her promise, Alicen had kept her own mouth shut. She wasn't quite sure what she'd say, anyway. That she had seen a ghost that turned out to be a curtain? Having had time to decide the whole scene just had to be her imagination, she felt as silly now as Jamie had. Still, she wished her mother were there. Her mother would make her feel better about all the crazy things that had been happening.

Her head felt funny tonight, the way it had just before the bus accident. She stabbed a beet and saw red juice flow over her plate like blood.

"Nancy!" Gina cried then. "Stop feeding beets to Lad!"

"Yeah, little girl." Gary said. "You eat those. They're good."

"Alicen isn't eating hers," Nancy said, pouting.

Melanie looked across the table at her young house guest. She frowned to see Alicen staring dully at her plate, pushing her food around. The fork looked ready to drop from her fingers.

"Are you all right, Alicen?"

No answer.

"Alicen!" Derek shouted.

She jumped. "Huh?"

"Mrs. VanBuren asked if you're all right," Derek said, studying her face.

"I'm just real tired," Alicen said. "Can I go to my room?"

"Eat first," Derek insisted. "It'll make you feel better."

"Please?"

"Alicen, just eat dinner," Derek snapped.

Alicen obeyed him. She ate as quickly as possible without making herself obvious, wanting only to get upstairs. She had heard a voice in her head, a voice calling her to her room. When at last her plate was empty, she excused herself and all but ran from the dining room.

"I'll never understand that kid," Derek said, looking over his shoulder.

"You don't try very hard," Melanie mumbled.

Derek ignored the remark.

Upstairs, Alicen sat down at her desk and waited. Her head was light as a cloud now, her ears deaf to the noises around her. Only her mind listened, waiting for the voice that would mean her mother had come once more to talk with her. The conscious Alicen was suppressed now, and she waited in a trance.

"Alicen," she heard.

"I'm here, mommy. Why did you wait so long to talk to me, mommy?"

"Selfish brat!" the apparition hissed. "Do you think I have nothing better to do than talk with you?"

"Mommy, please don't be mad," Alicen begged. She squinted at the cloud of smoke, shaped like a human body one moment, then unidentifiable the next, and tried to see her mother's features.

"Tell me of the man Davis," she heard.

"He came back to school a couple of times," Alicen reported. "I told him about the driver jumping from the bus, like you wanted. But he didn't believe me 'cause none of the other kids said they saw it." Alicen looked down at her hands. "They didn't find a body."

"If they want a body," the vision said, "I will give them one. Then they'll be satisfied. But you must help me. You'll know what to do."

There was a deep silence for a few moments. Alicen felt something cold press against her forehead, but she didn't move away from its stinging touch. Then the vision spoke again.

"You will know what to do. Succeed, and I will give you this."

Alicen saw the diamond ring floating before her. She reached for it, taking it in her hands. It glowed in an almost unnatural way, as if possessed by the very soul of the apparition. Alicen gazed into it.

Someone knocked at the door. "Alicen?"

The girl turned around at the sound of her father's voice, the spell that held her breaking. She became her own person in a split second, in the same time that the cloud of smoke disappeared and left her holding the ring. Momentarily confused, Alicen didn't think to hide it when her father opened her door.

"Are you okay?" Derek asked. "I want you to come downstairs and help look for the—"

Alicen realized that her father had seen the ring. Not knowing how she'd come to have it and afraid her father would think she'd stolen it, she dropped the ring in the pocket of the cardigan that hung over the back of the desk chair. Derek waited for his daughter to tell him about the ring, but she said nothing.

"I was just putting on a sweater," she said quietly, standing. "It's cold in this house."

"I was rather warm myself," Derek said. He debated whether or not to take the ring forcefully but decided against it. Why create a scene in front of the VanBurens?

"Get busy looking for that ring," he said. "It's very important that we find it."

He left the room and went to the staircase, pretending to look for it. As he poked around the carpeting, knowing there was nothing to be found, Derek tried to understand what he had just seen. *Jesus,* he thought, *my daughter's a klepto! How'd she get the ring? And what the hell am I going to tell the VanBurens?*

"Nothing," he said out loud. With three kids of their own, they wouldn't want a little thief around. They would call her a bad influence and kick her out—and him with her.

He sank down on the step and punched one of the balusters. "Damn you, Alicen," he whispered. "I've waited too long for a job like this to have you ruin it for me."

He'd have to get the ring from her and plant it somewhere in the house where Sarah could have dropped it.

Hearing soft steps on the carpeting behind him, he turned to see Alicen coming down the stairs. She barely glanced at him when she said, "I'm going to look in the dining room."

Derek said nothing. He clutched hard at the baluster, resisting an urge to grab and shake her. When she disappeared into the dining room, he got up and hurried back to her room.

It looked so innocent, with its yellow curtains and white furniture. Derek went first to the desk, pulling open all the drawers. He found stationery, pencils, and a roll of tape, but no ring. Next he went to the bed and pulled back the yellow coverlet. The ring wasn't under the pillow, nor was it between the mattress and box spring. And it wasn't anywhere else in the room.

"She's still got it in her pocket," he guessed. He left the room and walked down the hall, meeting Melanie.

"Is Alicen still in the dining room?"

"I sent her to help Gina look in the living room," Melanie replied. "Honestly, I don't think any of us will find that ring. One of those hospital people probably took it."

"It—uh—doesn't hurt to check," Derek said, moving down the stairs.

He stood in the doorway of the living room for a few minutes, wondering how he could get the ring from his daughter. He couldn't tell her to give it to him—not with Gina standing right there. He watched Alicen make a big production of the search, masking her guilt. She poked around the fireplace, looking like such a little girl in front of the huge structure that Derek momentarily forgot his anger. Could he have made a mistake? Maybe he hadn't seen the ring at all but had imagined it. Alicen had never stolen anything in her life!

Still, he had to be certain. He walked into the room and reached to touch the pocket of her sweater, in a gesture that would appear to be an embrace. Alicen jumped away from him.

"Dad!" she cried. "You startled me!"

"Me, too," Gina said. "I didn't hear you come into the room."

"I walk softly," Derek said.

His smile was a false one—he had felt the ring. Nervously, his daughter had resumed her search, moving to the window seat. She would not look her father in the eye. Derek saw

116

that her hands were trembling. That was good. Let her suffer a little. He'd get the ring tonight.

By midnight, Derek decided it was safe to enter Alicen's room. To be certain, he listened carefully at her door until he heard her even breathing. Then he pushed it open and groped his way inside. His hands touched the sweater, hanging on the desk chair again, but found that the pockets were empty. Holding his breath, he carefully searched the desk. When it came to nothing, he turned and crept to the bed.

Derek stood over his daughter for a long time, wondering why she had done this thing. She looked so innocent, lying there breathing softly. Her hair was spread out on her pillow, her lower lip jutted out in a slight pout. She looked more than innocent. She was like a little child, the way Derek remembered her being before Elaine's death. My God, she had been a pretty little girl. What the hell had happened these past six years? Was Alicen's crime the result of their struggles to get by on catch-as-catch-can jobs, living in motels or basement apartments? Or was it the fact that Derek had been just a little ignorant of a growing girl's needs?

He had never admitted that possibility to himself. But now, seeing the trouble his daughter was in, he wondered if he should have been a little more understanding. After all, she was a child, and—

No, Derek told himself firmly, *I did the right thing when I tried to make her independent. You have to control your emotions to get by in this world.*

And right now, I have to get that ring.

Derek snaked his hand under her pillow. His daughter turned in her sleep, mumbling something. Thinking he had awakened her, he stepped back into the shadows. Alicen moved again, and in the thin shaft of moonlight, Derek saw the glistening facets of the diamond in her opened palm. Carefully he took it.

He could barely make out the banister and wheelchair lift as he reached the stairs, and he touched them both as he walked down. The dining room was dimly lit by moonlight shining through the bay windows. By contrast, the kitchen was almost blinding. Someone had left the light on, and he squeezed his eyes shut until they could adjust. At last, removing the ring from his bathrobe pocket, he walked to the oven. If he hid the ring there, it would look as if Sarah had dropped it when she fell.

117

Derek bent toward the floor but stopped when he heard a noise behind him, a dull thud, like a heavy footstep. He looked over his shoulder. There was no one behind him, and when he turned back to the oven, he saw only his reflection in its glass door. He laughed at his fears, then proceeded with his task.

All at once there was another thud, and he felt a flash of pain. This noise had sounded from his own back, something knocking against it and sending him flying forward. His face came down hard on the oven door handle, a pain shot up through his forehead. He dropped to the floor in a flurry of gray mists and twinkling lights.

He was too stunned to react when he heard laughter. Then, as if through water, he saw a young woman standing over him, her smile a familiar one. He wanted to scream, but he couldn't. He couldn't even open his mouth.

She bent closer to him, smiling all the while, and ran her fingernails over his stomach as if to rip it open. From far away, Derek heard the sound of cloth tearing, and he thought it was his flesh. *No, no, no!* His mind echoed the plea over and over.

"I wanted you," he heard her say, in an eerily seductive way. "I've wanted you for so long, Derek Miller."

"No," Derek said aloud, barely hearing his voice.

She was on top of him, her small frame somehow crushing his muscular body. He closed his eyes tightly, something deep inside his will making him do so. He would open them again, and she wouldn't be there. She didn't exist. She was his imagination.

She was still there.

"My Derek, my handsome lover Derek," she breathed.

Her face came closer and closer to his. He could see the repulsive veins, the thin blue lips, the filmy eyes. He couldn't turn from her, for when he did, he felt something rip at the sides of his head. She had him by two handfuls of hair.

"Give me what you would give a woman," she whispered, pressing her lips to his.

It was cold. My God, it was so cold! Something like a fish was pushing into Derek's mouth. He realized with horror that it was the woman's tongue. Her hands left his hair and slid down his chest, kneading the matted black hair. Mercifully, her lips left his.

Why can't I move? I'm stronger than her! I'm str—

She bit him hard on the stomach, then kissed him over and over as if to make up for the wound. It was impossible, crazy.

Derek didn't want this. Not from her repulsive lips, her cold hands. He tried to push her away, but it was like moving lead.

But for a moment her touch shattered him so that he had no thoughts. His arms dropped weakly to his sides. He felt himself floating, higher and higher. Only when he was still again did he dare to open his eyes. She was sitting up, straddling him, her smile red. He wanted to kill her for using him this way, and yet something told him that that was impossible.

Something told him she was already dead.

"No," he whispered, falling at last into blackness.

The woman stood up, holding the ring in her hand. This was good, but it didn't satisfy her lustful needs. She wanted him through his own free will, not forcefully as tonight. And she would have him, soon. She smiled to think of owning that handsome man, of having him as her lover. And her anticipations made her desire to destroy the VanBuren family all the stronger.

She found Alicen waiting for her in the upstairs hallway. She handed the child the ring, then stepped back into the shadows. There was no need for words. Alicen knew exactly what to do. She entered her father's room, barely seeing the bed and dresser there. Walking to the floor grating, she knelt down and pushed her fingers between the woven strips of iron. It creaked softly. She felt pain where the iron pinched the soft underside of her hands, but she did not stop.

At last, the grating gave way, and she lifted it out. Alicen reached deep inside the cavity and dropped the ring. It made a soft tap against the floor. Then she replaced the grating, pushing it down hard so that it would not come loose again. Less than five minutes later, she was in her own bed. The smile on her face as she fell asleep was a triumphant one.

The night watchman at the Belle Bay Funeral Parlor sat up a little straighter in his chair when he felt a cold breeze brush past him. He looked behind him, saw that the back entrance was tightly closed, and shrugged. It was an old building, and drafts like that weren't uncommon. He checked his watch: 5 A.M. Two more hours and his shift would be over.

He was flipping through the pages of a girlie magazine when he heard a dull thud from one of the other rooms. He stood up, fingering the nightstick in his belt, and walked carefully toward the noise.

119

"Who's in there?" he asked.

Across the icy, refrigerated room, he could see the sheet-wrapped body of the latest Jane Doe to enter the morgue. A young blonde who had been found rotting on the nearby beach. The autopsy said it was a drug overdose but that the actual cause of death was probably drowning.

"Too many low-lifes in this town," the guard said with a quick glimpse at the shrouded corpse. The bump made by its nose under the sheets cast a long, grotesque shadow in the lamplight. The guard saw now that an ashtray, left here by the coroner, had fallen to the floor. He put it back up on a table and left the room. The night was silent once more.

Bored, he decided to put his head down and rest—for just a few minutes. He didn't feel the touch on his arm that turned that rest into a deep, deep sleep. Nor did he see the back door opening. He was snoring when the body of Jane Doe was dragged feet-first through the door into a back alley, pulled by unseen hands.

15

Melanie entered the kitchen the next morning to find Derek slumped in a chair, an icepack to his swollen mouth. A thin bruise covered the bridge of his nose and spread out under each closed eye.

"Derek?"

He opened his eyes. "Good morning," he said groggily.

"It certainly doesn't look like it's been a good morning for you," Melanie said. "What on earth happened?"

Conscious for about an hour, Derek had prepared himself for the questions he knew would come. He shifted in his seat and adjusted the icepack to speak more easily.

"I was up in the night to get a cup of tea," he said. "I slipped on the floor and hit the oven handle."

Melanie shook her head in sympathy, then went to the cupboard to find a bottle of aspirin. She shook two of the tablets into her palm and handed them to Derek with a glass of water.

The cold glass felt strange against his teeth, and Derek grimaced when he put it down on the table. Melanie gasped.

"Derek, you've broken your teeth!" she cried.

Not for the first time that morning, Derek ran his tongue around his mouth. It scraped over the remains of one front tooth and the thread of the tooth beside it. He tasted blood. Then he pointed to the oven door handle in explanation.

Melanie took the sponge from the sink and tried to scrub the stains from the chrome. She looked over her shoulder at him. For the first time, Melanie felt sorry for Derek. He looked so vulnerable, obviously hiding a good deal of pain. But sorrow turned to shock when she noticed a circle of red dots on his stomach, where his robe had fallen open.

Teeth marks?

She turned from the sight. It was just a love bite, of course. Derek did have a girlfriend, after all. It had nothing to do with his accident and was none of her business.

"Melanie?"

"Hmm?"

"Would you do me a big favor?" Derek asked. "Would you drive Gary into work today? I couldn't make it, and I don't want him to miss a day because of me."

"Sure," Melanie said. She rinsed out the sponge, then thought better of using it again and dropped it in the trash can.

"Derek," she said, "you should really see a dentist today. Why don't you let me call ours after breakfast? Then I could drop you off on the way to the city."

"I can call a taxi," Derek said.

"Never mind," Melanie answered. "It isn't out of the way. And don't worry, you'll feel better soon."

He didn't feel better. Not now, several hours into the morning with a numb upper lip. He rested on the couch in the library, two temporary teeth in his mouth. It was more than the physical hurting that fatigued him. It was the mental anguish, the trying to remember. Derek needed to recall what had happened the night before so much that all thoughts of Alicen and the ring were obliterated. Maybe he had gone to get tea and had fallen, just like he told Melanie. But bits and pieces of a nightmare kept coming back to him, making him think there was much more to it than that.

It must have been an erotic dream. Derek figured that much out by the dull ache he had felt in his groin when he had picked himself up off the floor early that morning. In his patchy memory, he saw a blond woman straddling him, laughing at him. She looked like that woman Janice, that crazy hitchhiker. Yet Derek knew she couldn't have been in the house. The door had been locked all night.

How, then, could he explain the teeth marks?

He looked down at his stomach and pulled his shirt out of his jeans. He ran his finger over the red bumps, as he had done many times that morning, trying to tell himself they weren't what they seemed. He knew they looked like a human bite, but he wanted another, saner explanation, something to tell him the terror he remembered so vaguely was nothing more than a dream.

Suddenly the phone rang. Derek considered ignoring it, then thought that it might be Gary, or even Liza. He crawled off the couch and stumbled out into the hall, the phone's high-pitched ringing hurting his ears. He lifted the receiver and mumbled a greeting. There was no reply.

"Hello?" he repeated, his voice sounding slurred because of the Novocain. He started to hang up but heard his name. "Yes, this is Derek," he said, putting the phone to his ear again. "Who's this?"

"The woman who craves you," a voice said, teasingly passionate.

Derek laughed. "Liza, you're pretty fun—"

A loud, ear-shattering screech made him drop the receiver. It wasn't Liza on the phone at all, but some crank. Wisely, Derek hung up. When the phone rang again a moment later, however, he picked it up against his better judgment.

"Hello?"

"Don't hang up."

"I won't," Derek promised. "Is this the woman from the roadside? Janice?"

"Yes."

Derek sighed. "I thought I had made it clear that you weren't to bother me any more. What is it you want?"

"You, Derek Miller," she said. "I want you."

Derek swung the cord of the phone over the banister, then went to sit on the stairs. Leaning against the double-twisted rungs, he answered, "I'm flattered. But you see, kid, you're wasting your time. Why don't you find another fellow, someone your own age? I already have a girlfriend."

"EEEEEYYYYYYAAAA!"

"Don't do that!" Derek ordered. "Stop screaming."

"I want you!" the woman shouted. "And I'll make you want me!"

"Just leave me alone," Derek said in an angry tone.

"I'll never leave you alone," Janice hissed. There was a silence, and then suddenly her voice took on the pleading quality of a little girl's. "Please, Derek! We can have so much fun together. Once I get rid of those people in that house."

"Wait a minute," Derek interrupted. " 'Those people'?"

"The VanBurens," Janice said with a click of her tongue, as if Derek should have known. "I want them out of there. I want them *dead!*"

Derek resisted an urge to hang up and asked with forced calm, "Why? What did they do to you?"

"I'll tell you," the woman said. "One night, I came to this house to visit Melanie. But first I met the spirit of the house's original owner. He sought my aid in his getting revenge against the VanBurens. But not Melanie! He *loved* Melanie. He'd been following her for nearly two hundred years, and that night I was going to help him have her, at last."

Derek recalled the story of Jacob Armand and Lydia Browning. Was this some lunatic who had also heard that tale? Someone making fun of the VanBurens' troubles?

"But those evil children tried to stand in my way," Janice said. "When I tried to rid myself of Kyle, Melanie came to his defense. She defended a devil-child by striking me across the head with a pistol! And now"—she paused—"I will walk in this limbo until I have vengeance!"

Struck in the head? Derek thought. She must be brain damaged! That would explain it. And Derek would bet all his money that Melanie had nothing at all to do with it. This woman was just plain nuts!

"I don't think this is very amusing," Derek said soberly.

"I'm serious," the woman said. "I'll get rid of them, one by one. Melanie goes today."

"What?" Derek cried. "What does that mean?"

But she had hung up on him. For a long time Derek sat holding the receiver on his lap, not believing what he had just heard. This woman was deranged, no doubt. What reason could she possibly have for hating the VanBurens?

He got up and returned the phone to its stand. Whatever that lunatic tried to do, she wouldn't frighten him into giving in to her!

Bryan Davis stopped working on his report and reached across his desk to answer the telephone. "Belle Bay Police," he said. "Bryan Davis speaking."

"Captain Davis?" a woman asked. "It's Joan Mead, from the funeral parlor. I'm afraid we have a problem."

"What can I do for you, Mrs. Mead?" Bryan asked.

"It seems someone stole one of our residents," Joan said. "Do you remember the Jane Doe brought in a few nights ago?"

"Yes," Bryan said. "The one found on the beach. Are you certain she's missing?"

"Definitely," Joan said. "As a matter of good business policy, I always have my employees check each room before we officially open. People so need to be catered to at times like these."

"Of course," Bryan said.

"But when we entered the morgue," Joan continued, "Jane Doe was gone."

There was a pause, and Bryan heard the old woman sigh. "To think I found the security guard sleeping," she said. "Of course, I fired him. But he's still waiting here if you need to question him."

"Thanks," Bryan said. "I will. I'll send someone down there right away."

He hung up the phone. Wasn't it bad enough that he hadn't yet found the bus driver? Now there was another mystery to solve.

"Oh, God," Bryan sighed. "Who'd guess what a peaceful town this was, just a year ago?"

Derek waited all morning for the phone to ring again. At lunchtime, while he sat on the steps with a sandwich, his daughter was making a call of her own. She had told the cafeteria monitor that her father had been sick that morning and that she wanted to have flowers delivered to him.

"That's sweet of you," the monitor had said.

"I'll have to use my whole allowance," Alicen said. "But I don't care. I love my father."

Now she stood up in the little hallway just outside the cafeteria, thumbing the phone book for a number she never intended to call. With the pages opened to "Florists," she instead dialed the police.

"Belle Bay Police," a voice said. "Bryan Davis."

"Yeah, hi," Alicen mumbled, turning her back to the cafeteria doors. She covered the receiver with a napkin. "Listen, I read in the papers that you guys are looking for a body? Some bus driver?"

"What about it?"

He sounded eager. That was good.

"I sorta saw one," Alicen replied. "At that construction place, you know? I was driving by, and I saw this big dude dump this thing in a green trash container. Looked like a body, but I can't be sure, you know? I just figured I should call."

"We appreciate it," Bryan said. "Would you tell me your name?"

"Never mind," Alicen said. "Just go—"

Alicen heard a tap at the door and nearly dropped the receiver. Hanging up, she stuffed the napkin into her pocket. Then she opened the door and smiled at the monitor.

"I had to call three florists," she said.

"Had a hard time of it, huh?"

"Everything's just fine now," Alicen said, smiling.

Tim and Rick were certain they were being sent on another wild goose chase, but they couldn't question their captain's orders. So now they stood banging on the newly repaired fence of the construction site, their shirts sticking to them under the merciless sun. The crane above them drowned out the sound of their knocking, and Rick was inclined to give up until the machine stopped. He removed his cap and wiped his forehead.

"Damned hot, ain't it?" someone said. A broad-shouldered, shirtless man had opened the gate. Hank Emmons tilted his helmet back. "Are you guys back again?"

"We received a call this morning pertaining to the case," Rick said. He stepped inside the fence, followed by his partner. Over the din of the crane, he said, "Do you have any trash bins around here?"

"Of course we do," Hank said. "What do you think? But you can't come in without a helmet. Wait a second."

He left and returned a moment later with two hard hats. Rick and Tim donned them, then followed Hank past work crews and machinery. Along the back fence of the site, they found two five-yard containers.

Rick went close to one and asked, "How long has it been since you opened these?"

"That one was emptied yesterday," Hank said. "But this one here hasn't been opened in a few days. Since the accident, I guess. We use it for dry rubbish—wood scraps, you know? Stuff that keeps for a while."

Rick turned to his partner. "You brought the body bag, didn't you?"

"Right here," Tim replied, holding it up.

Hank looked around at his work crew and saw they were still busy. Then he said in a low voice, "What in the hell is the body bag for?"

"What do you think?" Rick asked, almost sarcastically.

Now Hank laughed at him. "Oh, hell! There ain't nothing in there but trash. Just get out of my way and I'll prove it."

Before Rick could stop him, the foreman climbed up the side of the container and threw it open. The smell that shot up from it was so horrendous that tears welled in his eyes. He backed away, choking.

"Shit! That's like rotten meat!"

"She's in there, then," Tim said.

"Damn right she is," Hank growled. "And you'd better get her out."

Tim and Rick had brought special masks with them, and they tied them around their mouths and noses. Rick was first to climb to the top of the bin, and what he saw made his heart skip a beat. The young woman's twisted body had been thrown on top of the trash, a broken two-by-four pushed into her stomach. One arm reached for the side of the container, the fingers at its end clawing as if the woman had tried to climb out. Tiny worms made a feast of her flesh, or what was left of it.

"She looks like she's been dead for six months," he said.

Tim was looking at her now, too, a grimace on his face. At last, wearing canvas gloves, he jumped down into the container. He had to fight a wave of nausea as he knelt down on the floor, feeling the wet, bloated flesh through his gloves. He pulled the heavy-weight bag over her head-first, glad her face was down. When he reached her feet, he stopped to study them for a moment.

"Want me to come in?" Rick shouted.

"I can do this," Tim said, resuming his work. "Just be ready to lift her out."

Something about her feet bothered him. They had been white and bloated, cut by the thin straps of her sandals. It was horrible, horrible. But why did he single out that one feature?

At last he tied the end of the bag, stood up, and lifted the gruesome parcel to Rick. He climbed from the container as his partner laid the body on the ground. The work crew stood at a distance, curiosity taking precedence over their duties.

Suddenly Tim understood what bothered him about the victim's sandals. Determining that Hank had kept the crew far enough away so as not to hear him, he turned to Rick and asked, "Didn't the kids say their driver was wearing boots?"

"I think I remember that."

"This one's in sandals," Tim said quietly.

Rick shook his head at his partner.

"Do you want to spend the rest of your life looking for a body?" he asked. "Who the hell else would she be?"

"But the kids said—"

"The kids were lying," Rick interrupted.

"You said that before," Tim reminded him.

Rick didn't answer. He stooped down and grabbed an end of the bag. Tim picked up the other, and in silence they carried the body to the car. Rick made it clear that he didn't want to discuss this any further. He had his body, and he didn't care what she was wearing.

Bryan Davis's emotions were mixed when he heard the news. He was sad that a woman had died but happy that he at last had something to say to the irate parents who called all day long. Horrifying as all this had been, it was at last over. Bryan could return to keeping the peace in Belle Bay while the county worried about finding the woman's next of kin.

Melanie glanced at her watch and saw it was time to meet Gary. She walked toward the exit of the art gallery she had been visiting. The street outside was filled with people and cars that seemed to glow in the hot sunlight. Melanie could see ripples of heat rising from the cracked sidewalk as she opened the door to her car and climbed behind the wheel.

The engine turned over easily, as it had done every day since she had had it overhauled. Looking behind her, she turned the front of the car just slightly into the street. A taxi came speeding down it, forcing her to stop. Another followed, then a bus and a few cars. It was five minutes before Melanie was able to pull out.

"Nice way to waste gasoline," she mumbled, zooming into the road while she had the chance. Following traffic, she crossed Sixth, then Fifth Avenue. Except for the stops and starts expected of New York City traffic, the going was smooth. And then, just as Melanie turned onto Madison, the car began to choke. It slowed down to a complete stop.

Angered, Melanie pumped the gas pedal and tried to start it again. How could this be happening now? She was embarrassed to hear a dozen horns honking behind her. Angry drivers cursed loudly. Melanie was about to answer them in kind when a loud thud cut off her words. Someone had hit the car, sending it spinning. Melanie heard herself cry out and felt her body stiffening in reaction to the impact.

The car skidded across the road and sideswiped a lamp-post. Melanie never saw it coming.

A moment of stunned silence followed, and then suddenly a dozen people were swarming about the wreck.

"Did you see that guy? Hit and run!"

"She's bleeding!"

"Of course she's bleeding, you idiot! Someone call an ambulance!"

The proprietor of a nearby men's store had already taken care of that, and even now the group could hear sirens wailing. More curious than helpful, they didn't move when the ambulance turned the corner. A police car followed, and two policemen jumped out to push the crowd back as the paramedics tended to Melanie. They carefully pulled her from the wreck and laid her on a stretcher. Twenty minutes later, she was wheeled into the emergency room of nearby Saint Joan's Hospital.

In the meantime, Gary was waiting patiently in his office for Melanie's arrival. It didn't surprise him that she was late, since traffic was always heavy at this hour.

The secretary announced that Derek Miller was on the line. Wondering what he wanted, Gary picked up the phone.

"Saint Joan's Hospital just called," Derek said. "Gary, your wife was in an accident just a short while ago."

"What?!" Gary cried. "When did this happen? Where is she?"

"At Saint Joan's," Derek repeated. "They found this number in her handbag and called here. But they wouldn't tell me anything."

"I'll go there at once," Gary said, reaching behind him for his crutches.

"Don't go by yourself, okay?" Derek said.

"My partner will take me," Gary assured him.

It only took twenty minutes to get to the hospital, but to Gary it might have been two hours. Warren opened the glass door for him, and the two men walked up to the reception desk.

"Can you tell me where my wife is?" Gary asked.

"Melanie VanBuren," Warren explained.

The nurse flipped through a file. "She was admitted just a short while ago," she said. "Would you please wait over there while I call the doctor?"

She indicated a small gathering of orange vinyl couches in a corner of the lobby. An elderly woman frowned at Gary over the top of *Reader's Digest.*

"What about my wife?" Gary asked, turning back to the nurse. "Is she all right?"

"The doctor will tell you everything, sir," the nurse said politely. "Please sit down."

"But is she—"

"Gary, come on and sit," Warren said. "The doctor will be out in a minute."

Half an hour, then an hour passed with no word, and Gary found himself knocking his crutches together in frustration. At last, though, the doctor appeared.

"Your wife had a bad blow to the head," he said quietly. "She's suffering from a concussion."

Gary closed his eyes and steeled himself. "What else is wrong?"

"Nothing," the doctor said. "She has a nasty cut on her forehead, of course. But there's no internal bleeding. She'll be able to go home after a few days of rest."

"How did the accident happen?" Warren asked.

"It seems Mrs. VanBuren's car had stalled," the doctor said, "and was struck by a speeding car. She hit a lamppost, but luckily there wasn't much damage done to her."

"Not much!" Gary cried. "You just said she had a concussion, and—"

"Relax," the doctor said. "Would you like to see her?"

Gary nodded. The doctor led him down a long hallway and opened a door at its end. Gary felt his stomach twist to see his wife lying in that bed, her face swollen beneath a gauze bandage. Her hair was in disarray, some of it plastered to her cheeks. Gary leaned awkwardly on his crutches and brushed it gently away.

"God," he whispered, "can we ever live in peace?"

16

Kyle was at first delighted to find pizza on the table for dinner, until he realized his mother wasn't there to serve it. When he and his sisters had come home from school to find her studio empty, they had assumed she was still in the city with their father. But why wasn't she home yet? Why was Derek taking care of dinner?

"I'm afraid your mother isn't coming home tonight," Derek said, tearing the top off of one of the boxes. "There was an accident today."

"Oh, no!" Kyle cried.

"Hey, it wasn't that bad," Derek said, realizing he had spoken too bluntly. "Another car hit hers. All she has is a little concussion, and she'll be home in a few days. Nothing serious."

"What's a ca-cussion?" Nancy asked.

"Concussion," Derek corrected. "It—uh—it just means her head hurts a little bit. But everything else is okay."

"Are you sure my mom's okay?" Gina asked, concerned.

"That's what your father said. He'll be spending the night with her. Hey, start eating this food before it gets cold."

"I'm not hungry," Kyle said.

"I sure am," Alicen said.

Derek put out the pizza. "Please eat at least one slice," he said. "What would your father do to me if he came home and found you starved? I promise you, your mother's okay."

"Then why does she have to stay in the hospital a few days?" Gina asked. "Why can't she come home now?"

"Because the doctors want to keep her under surveillance," Derek said, not quite sure how to handle this. "It's just routine. Now, eat!"

He said that in such an authoritative way that the children obeyed, though they didn't taste their food. The room became silent, each person busy with his or her own thoughts. Derek's mind was filled with the sound of that voice over the telephone that morning, the one telling him "Melanie goes today." What did it mean? That it was no accident that Melanie was in a hospital right now? Derek had thought of phoning the police about the call—especially now that the threat had come true. But having no idea where to find the woman who'd called him, he changed his mind. It had to be coincidence, of course. Melanie was miles and miles away at the time of the call. The woman named Janice didn't know she was going to be in the city today.

Besides, the VanBurens had enough worries without him bringing up a new one. That was why he decided to keep the call a secret. And it was also why he hadn't yet brought up Sarah's ring. Even though he knew Alicen must have taken it when he passed out last night (he tried not to think of it in any more detail than that), he didn't want to confront her in front of the children. But later . . .

Just then, his thoughts were interrupted by small, squeaking noises. He looked up from his plate and saw Nancy's shoulders quivering. He reached across the table and patted her hair.

"Nancy, everything's all right," he said. "Your mommy'll be home before the weekend."

"I want my mommy now!" the little girl wailed. The word accident had frightened her terribly, making her remember the accident that had hurt her father. Would her mother be a cripple, too?

"Nancy, it's just a *little* accident," Gina said firmly, as if trying to convince herself. "Derek said mom was fine—didn't you, Derek?"

"I sure did," Derek said, grateful that she was backing him. "And I wouldn't lie to you."

He thought for a moment, trying to change the subject. "Hey, guess what?" he said at last.

"What?" Nancy asked, looking at him through tearful blue eyes.

"We're having company tonight," Derek said. "I called a friend of mine to come over and help me out. Her name is Liza, and she loves kids. I think you'll like her."

Alicen's eyes became wide. She put her glass of milk down and raised her head to glare at her father. Liza? He had a girlfriend? But how could he do such a thing, when he was supposed to love her mother?

Derek returned the glare with eyes that told Alicen she'd better not ask any questions. Okay, so he had meant to

131

introduce Liza to her at a better time than this. But he needed last-minute help tonight, not knowing how to handle a houseful of children. And it was his life; he wasn't about to let a thirteen-year-old run it.

"When's Liza coming?" Kyle asked.

"Around seven," Derek said. "She's at school right now."

"She goes to school?" Gina asked.

"Dance school," Derek replied, still looking at his daughter. "She'll tell you about it when she gets here."

Alicen finally dropped her gaze to her plate and finished her dinner. When the meal was over, Derek sent the Van-Buren children from the kitchen with the announcement that he and Alicen would take care of cleaning up. He wanted to be alone with his daughter.

He didn't waste any time. "Did you take Sarah Kaufman's ring?"

"Of course not!" Alicen cried. "Why?"

"I found it in your room last night," Derek said. "So don't deny having had it. I was going to put it down here in the kitchen—to make it look as if Sarah had dropped it here when she fell. I was trying to protect you, Alicen. And what do you do? You steal the damned thing again!"

Alicen tore angrily at the empty pizza box and stuffed the pieces into the trash can.

"I didn't take any old ring," she insisted, remembering nothing.

"Alicen," Derek said, forcing himself to be patient, "do you have any idea what would happen to my job if the VanBurens learned you stole that ring?"

"I didn't!" Alicen cried, tears welling in her eyes. "And I don't care about your dumb old job!"

Derek slammed a dish he was washing against the sink, breaking it. "You damned well better care!" he shouted. "This job was a godsend for me, and you know it. Do you want to go back to living in a roach-infested apartment again?"

Alicen was crying openly now, staring down at her feet. She was confused, not understanding why her father was accusing her of this crime. She hadn't done a thing.

"Look, all I ask is that you give it back," Derek said. "I'll mail it to Mayor Kaufman, and no one will ever know where it came from."

"I don't have it," Alicen blubbered.

"Liar!" Derek cried. His head was starting to hurt him, and he rubbed at the bruises under his eyes. "This is a terrible thing you did, Alicen. Give me back that ring, or so help me, I'll—"

"Don't you hit me!"

Derek drew his hand back. He had been so close to slapping her, hating her for all her lies. But no, this wasn't the way to handle her. And the other children didn't need to hear an argument. What was the matter with him? Was he upset because of the mysterious fall he'd taken the night before? Or was it because that crank caller had predicted Melanie's accident? So damned much had happened in the last two days.

"Alicen, you're grounded until that ring shows up again," Derek said. "God knows I'd like to beat the hell out of you, but I can't prove you're guilty. I just hope your conscience takes care of that. Now, get out of here. Go do your homework."

Alicen threw her dish towel on the counter and stormed from the kitchen. How could her father say such terrible things about her? She had never touched Sarah's ring! She heard Gina calling her from the playroom but ignored her and ran upstairs. In her room she threw herself on the bed and started pounding the mattress.

"I hate him!" she seethed. "I hate him!"

The room was growing chilly, and she pulled the bed's coverlet around her like a cocoon. "I wish he was dead."

Something was pressing against her back. Alicen rolled around and looked up. She heard her name called, and she answered very softly. A moment later, a cloud, shaped like a woman, appeared. Alicen's trembling stopped immediately, and the room became very quiet. Slowly she reached up. But no one took her hand.

"Why do you want your father to die?"

"I hate him," Alicen said plainly. Under a spell, there was no emotion in her voice. "He called me a liar."

"It isn't his time to die, you little fool!" the vision cried.

Alicen jerked away as if stunned by her mother's angry words.

"I'm not ready yet for him," the apparition said. "There are things that must be done first. Melanie is still alive—but not for long. They'll all go, one by one. They'll all die!"

"Mommy, why do they have to die?" Alicen asked. "I don't under—"

The loud ringing of the doorbell downstairs shattered the spell like a sledgehammer through glass. Alicen was alone again. She sat up, feeling as if she had just wakened from a

133

deep sleep. She rubbed her eyes and went to her door, opening it. Voices from the downstairs hallway were carried up to her room.

"Hi, Liza," her father was saying. "Come on in."

Alicen heard kissing noises, and her stomach turned.

"How're you, darling?" Liza asked. "Where are the children?"

Alicen closed her door and missed the rest of the conversation. She prayed her father wouldn't make her come downstairs. But a moment later she heard his voice calling her. Alicen thought of ignoring him but remembered his anger and left her room. She walked slowly.

"What's wrong with you?" Derek asked. "Get a move on!"

"Derek, let her be," Liza said quietly.

Alicen stopped at the bottom step and rested a hand on the post. She stared at Liza without speaking. In the soft light, she could see that this woman wasn't at all like her mother. Unlike Elaine, she had dark hair and eyes. And she was much taller than Alicen remembered her mother being. How could her father like a woman who was so different?

"Hi, Alicen," Liza said then.

"Hi," Alicen said perfunctorily.

"Looks like a lot has happened in this house," Liza said, making conversation. "Poor Mrs. VanBuren had an accident, and your daddy fell. Would you like to tell me about that?"

"No," Alicen said plainly, staring at her.

Liza shrugged. "Okay. Then how about taking me around this house? It sure is pretty from the outside, with those towers and the big porch in front. And look at all those doors! What's behind them?"

"I don't know," Alicen said. She turned her eyes to her father. "I have homework to do."

Derek sighed and put his arm around Liza's shoulder. Alicen's eyes narrowed. Her father was doing this to spite her. Without waiting for permission, she turned and ran up the stairs. Derek let her go, leading Liza into the kitchen.

"Derek, I hate to say this," Liza commented, "but if looks could kill . . ."

"Alicen was very rude to you," Derek said. "She'll hear about that."

"Oh, Derek, let it go," Liza said. "I expected her to act that way. Any normal child would! She probably thinks I'm trying to take her mother's place."

"That doesn't give her an excuse to be impolite," Derek

answered, filling the teapot. He set it on the stove, then turned around to Liza. "It isn't just that, anyway. Alicen's being punished for stealing, and she's angry about it."

"What did she steal?"

"A ring," Derek said. He proceeded to explain everything to her, glad he had someone he could trust with his terrible secret.

"Oh, Derek," Liza said when he was finished. She reached across the table and took his hand. "Maybe Alicen really doesn't remember taking the ring. Maybe she's upset about something. Have you considered that?"

"There's nothing wrong with her," Derek insisted.

Something in his eyes told Liza he didn't wish to discuss Alicen any further. So, to get his mind off his troubles, she went to him and sat on his lap. Running her fingers through his thick hair, she bent and kissed him passionately.

"I love you, Derek," she said.

"And I love you, Liza," Derek answered.

The phone began to ring.

"Ignore it," Liza said.

"I can't," Derek replied. "It might be Gary." He stood up. "I'll be right back."

He walked through the dining room and out into the hallway, where the phone sat on its little stand. "Hello?"

"Get rid of her!" someone shouted, the voice high-pitched. "I know you have that woman with you!"

Derek pulled the phone away from his ear, grimacing.

"Get rid of her, or she'll be next."

"Look, I'm getting damned sick of your threats," Derek said angrily. "What are you doing now, following my guests around? How'd you know she was going to be here?"

"I know everything you do, Derek Miller. Just get her out of there!"

"You go to hell," Derek said quietly, hanging up the phone.

He shook his head in exasperation and headed back into the kitchen. Liza had already poured the tea and was setting the cups down on the table. She sat and looked up at him quizzically. Derek realized there was still a look of anger on his face, and he tried to erase it. But Liza's concerned expression didn't fade.

"Is something wrong?"

"No, Liza," Derek said. "Wrong number. I—uh—hate wrong numbers."

Liza could tell that he was lying, but she knew that he'd tell

135

her what had happened if he wanted to do so. She poured a little milk in her tea and began to stir it. Derek, usually strong and self-assured, looked so pitiful right now with his swollen eyes and cut lip that Liza wanted to throw her arms around him. But something made her keep still.

The room was silent, except for the clanking of teaspoons against china cups. Then suddenly Derek blurted out, "Everything's wrong!"

"Derek?" There was encouragement in Liza's voice.

"It isn't just the fact that Alicen stole that ring," Derek said. "Liza, something else happened today. I—I don't think Melanie is in that hospital by accident!"

"What do you mean?"

"I got a phone call this morning. From some crazed woman who apparently hates the VanBurens. She told me Melanie would be in an accident today."

"Derek!"

"Well, not exactly that," Derek corrected himself, "but she made indirect threats toward the family and said, 'Melanie goes first.' Next thing I know, Saint Joan's Hospital in Manhattan was calling me."

"And then you called the police?"

"No. I was going to," Derek said, "then I thought that there was no way I could prove that the woman ever called. I don't know where to find her, or if she even meant what she said about Melanie. Maybe she's just trying to get me upset."

"Why?" Liza asked. "And who is she, anyway?"

"She told me her name is Janice," Derek said. "And that's another reason I don't want to mention this to the VanBurens. Melanie had a best friend named Janice who died violently last year. The similarity in names—"

"I remember you mentioning her at lunch the other day," Liza interrupted. "But surely they wouldn't connect the two! There are a lot of Janices in the world."

"After that story they told me about ghosts the other night," Derek said, "I'm inclined to believe the VanBurens will think anything. This woman is just plain nuts. I met her a few weeks ago, just after I had moved in. She was hitchhiking on Houston Street, and she looked lost and lonely. Like an idiot, I gave her a lift. She's been bothering me ever since."

He searched Liza's almond eyes and found sympathy and deep interest there.

"I should have driven by her," he went on. "But I didn't, and now I'm stuck with her. One night she even hid in my car. It seems she has some sort of crush on me. But, by God, she's the most hideous woman I've ever seen!"

Liza took a sip of tea, then set the cup down again. Her thick lashes seemed to fan out as her eyes widened. *She's so beautiful,* Derek thought as he reached across the table to take her hand and kiss it.

"What does she look like?"

"I might sound like I'm exaggerating," Derek warned. "Her skin looked like a coroner's mistake, it was so pale. You could see her veins right through it. And her eyes—there was no life in them, not even when she was angry. Not to mention hair that probably never saw a comb and the fact that she always wears the same winter clothes."

"She sounds insane," Liza said. "Who would let themselves look like that?"

"Who would threaten to kill off an entire family?"

"Derek, I really think you should go to the police."

"No," Derek insisted. "No police. The VanBurens have enough to worry about."

"But shouldn't they be warned?"

"I don't think this woman was serious," Derek said. "You know crank callers—all talk. The accident today was pure coincidence."

"I find that hard to swallow," Liza said quietly, her mouth turning down a little. She sighed. "But you do what you think is right. And remember I'm here if you need someone to talk to."

"I know that," Derek said. "And I love you for it."

He stood up and walked around the table to put his arms over Liza's shoulders. Her lips felt warm and full against his, and he wanted to take her upstairs with him. But with four children in the house, he knew that was impossible.

"I wish we were alone," he whispered.

"So do I," Liza said. "But there will be other times."

Other times. Across the room, an unseen woman resisted the urge to throw something at Liza. Other times? There would be no other times! The next time Derek made love to a woman, it would be with her, not with this Liza!

She would get rid of that beautiful bitch, she vowed, when Derek was least expecting trouble . . . .

17

"Melanie?" Gary kissed his wife's hand. "Honey, come on. Open your eyes. It's morning."

Melanie stirred a little bit, her lashes fluttering. "Gary, where am I?" she asked weakly. The sheets on her bed felt cool beneath her fingers.

"In the hospital," Gary said. "You had a little accident, but you're going to be okay. How do you feel?"

"My head hurts." She breathed deeply as if to fall asleep again. Then she opened her eyes and blinked at the glow of the track lights overhead. She turned to look at Gary.

"What do I look like?" she asked, her voice only slightly clearer.

"You always look beautiful to me," Gary answered.

"You're evading my question," Melanie said, raising a hand to touch the bandage on her forehead. It was a small one, yet she couldn't be sure there was nothing more wrong with her. Or else, why would she be in this room with an i.v. in her arm and all sorts of unfamiliar machinery near her bed?

"Trust me," Gary said. "It's just a small cut. The worse thing is that you've had a concussion. Your head is going to ache quite a bit for a few days."

"Right now," Melanie said, "it feels as if someone's using it for target practice. How long am I going to be in here, anyway?"

"Just a few days," Gary said. "You need to rest, and they want to run some more tests."

He lifted her hand again and kissed it. "I wish someone had seen the accident. Two dozen people, and not one of them could tell the police anything about the car that hit you."

"You called the police?"

"Warren did," Gary said. "But I doubt it did any good."

Melanie thought for a moment, trying to remember something that had been in her mind before the car was hit. But it evaded her, and Gary was talking again.

"You'll be home before you know it," he said.

Melanie nodded slightly. She stared up into the light, squeezing Gary's hand. What was it she was trying to remember?

"Oh, my God, Gary!"

It had come to her, and now she looked up at her husband with panic widening her eyes.

"Gary, the car stalled," she said frantically. "The car stalled, and I didn't even have the brakes on. And we just had that engine overhauled last month."

"It's an old car," Gary reminded her. "I told you I wanted to buy you a new one, and that's just what I'm going to do when we go home."

"N-no," Melanie stammered. "No, it isn't as simple as that. Gary, that car shouldn't have stalled. There was no reason. Someone must have tampered with it. Somebody wanted to kill me!"

"Nobody wanted to kill you," Gary said. "Why would you think such a thing?"

Melanie was crying loudly now. "Those dreams. That woman trying to warn me. She tried to tell me to get out of the house, but I didn't listen to her. Oh, Gary, something's wrong at the house again. I know it. It's Sarah's death and the bottle that broke in my hand, and now this! And the bus accident and—"

"Melanie, please calm down," Gary ordered. "Nothing is going on in Belle Bay. It's just coincidences."

"Coincidences?" Melanie said. "Oh, Gary! After what happened last year? How can you stand there, crippled by something no one would believe in, and not see that it's starting all over again?"

"Melanie, for God's sake," Gary said. "Jacob Armand is *gone*. He got his Lydia, didn't he? What the hell would he want to come back for? Now, please quiet down."

"I can't quiet down!" Melanie screamed.

Just then, a nurse came into the room, alerted by Melanie's cries. Seeing that Melanie was hysterical, she called in a doctor to administer a shot. Gary was then asked to leave the room. Having had no food since the previous morning, he decided he'd better have breakfast to keep his strength up.

As he ate the bland eggs and toast, he felt sorry for Melanie. It was no wonder she was having such fears, considering all that had occurred in the last weeks. But like he said, they weren't connected at all. Didn't every other family on earth have its share of problems?

"She's just sentitive to this sort of thing," he reasoned. "She'll be okay as soon as she gets home."

Derek came in from walking the dog later that afternoon to find Alicen on the phone. Didn't being grounded include use of the telephone? And then Liza's name caught his attention. As he unhooked Lad's leash, he pretended not to be listening.

"Sure, Liza, you can come for dinner," Alicen was saying. "You can help my dad out like you did last night."

A pause.

"I guess about six?"

Alicen looked down the hall at her father. Derek nodded without emotion. "Six is fine, Liza. See you then!"

She hung up and smiled down the hall at her father. Derek approached her, eyeing her warily. Why this sudden friendliness toward Liza? Especially now, when she and Derek were having differences? It didn't make sense that she should invite his girlfriend for dinner. Unless—

"This isn't going to change anything, Alicen," he said. "You're still grounded."

"I know that," Alicen said, smiling. "Can't I invite a guest for dinner?"

"I didn't think you liked her."

"I never said that," Alicen replied. "I only just met her." She shifted a little. "Dad, I have homework to do—"

"Go ahead," Derek said, wondering what Alicen's game was. No matter. He liked the idea that Liza was coming for dinner.

As promised, she arrived at six on the dot, bearing four giant cookies, one for each child. Alicen was all smiles and thank-yous, which sharpened Derek's suspicions. She ran to her room to put the cookie away for safekeeping.

"Is that the girl who shot daggers at me last night?" Liza asked with disbelief.

"She's up to something, I'm sure," Derek said. "I wonder why she called you? I can't believe she wants to be friends."

"Give the kid a chance, Derek," Liza said as they entered the kitchen. "Maybe she really does want to make amends. Did she tell you anything about the ring?"

"Of course not," Derek said.

At dinner that night Alicen surprised everyone by talking to Liza as if they were good friends. Derek knew he should be happy about that, but there was something in the glistening of Alicen's eyes that made him uneasy. Her words were polite enough, but there was an underlying sharpness to them that set him on edge. Not quite sure what to make of it all, Derek ate in silence and listened.

"Do you like the beach?" Alicen asked.

"Sure, I love it," Liza answered.

"Well, why don't you ask my father to take you down there after dinner?" Alicen suggested. "It sure is pretty when the sun goes down."

"Alicen, it looks like rain out there," Derek said. Why would his daughter want him out of the house?

"It's a beautiful night," Alicen insisted.

"Oh, let's go down!" Liza cried eagerly. "It probably won't rain for a few hours."

"There are umbrellas in the hall closet if it does," Gina said. "Want me to get two for you, Derek?"

"That's okay," Derek said. He smiled at Liza. "If Liza really wants to go, I don't think we'll mind getting wet."

"You'll like the beach at night," Alicen drawled. "It's so pretty."

An hour later Liza and Derek were headed toward the bay. They walked hand in hand, forgetting the events of the past few days. Impulsively, Derek swung Liza around and kissed her.

"You know I love you?"

"Yes," Liza said. "And I love you, Derek."

He kissed her again.

"I was going to wait," he said, "but I can't. All this nature is turning me into some kind of romantic. Liza, will you marry me?"

A beautiful smile spread across Liza's face. Leave it to Derek to be this abrupt! She nodded enthusiastically, letting him pull her close. "Of course I'll marry you," she said.

They held each other tightly, then Liza said, "Derek, let's spend a long time on the beach. I don't care if it is raining."

"Well, let me run back to the house for an umbrella," Derek said. "I don't want you to catch cold."

"Hurry back," Liza said.

She settled down on a log and watched him run back to the house. The rain increased in intensity, and she was grateful

141

for the thick evergreen above her. Breathing in the damp, pine-scented air, she bent forward to pick one of the tiny white flowers. Something crackled behind her.

She turned abruptly, startled. There in the thick undergrowth stood a young woman, a patch of blood matting the blond tendrils at her forehead. The woman's face was corpselike, her smile blue and thin. Liza found herself standing up, staring at her. She knew this was the woman Derek had spoken of, and yet she was too stunned to scream for help. That moment of hesitation was the last mistake she would ever make.

The woman jerked her to the ground, pulling Liza's face close to her own. Frantically Liza tried to turn away from the horrible, putrefactive flesh. But this woman was too strong. She had a gleam in her eyes that burned into her victim's, draining the fight in her. Something twisted Liza's hand, and a cold line of metals slipped over her wrist as the bracelet she was wearing broke off and fell to the ground. Her sanity slowly drained by the piercing, evil eyes above her, Liza stopped thinking she was going to die and saw only blackness.

Her spirit had given up her body to the malevolence that longed to possess it.

A few minutes later, the body that was once Liza Crewe's heard the sound of Derek's whistling. He appeared in the clearing with an umbrella, a smile on his face. She smiled back at him, giving no clue to the evil that had just taken place here.

"Ready?" Derek said.

"Quite ready, Derek," 'Liza' said.

She smiled slyly at him and hooked her hand around his elbow. She liked the hardness of his biceps. They didn't speak until they reached the bay, where they kicked off their shoes and walked barefoot in the sand. The light rain had stopped, the sky was growing pink, and the salty wind was cool. Derek took Liza's hand and squeezed it hard.

"Melanie's going to be all right, isn't she?" Liza asked.

"That's a funny thing to bring up now," Derek answered. "Well, yes. She's going to be fine."

Liza nodded. "That's too bad."

"You sound as if you *wanted* her to be hurt," Derek said.

They caught each other's eyes, and Derek noticed there was no light in Liza's eyes. Her voice sounded dull when she said, "I meant it was too bad about the accident."

"I know," Derek said, toeing the water that rippled along the beach. "I was only kidding."

He had brought a blanket with him, and when they found a huge pile of rocks, they sat down together and wrapped themselves in it. Derek kissed Liza gently.

"You're trembling," he said. "Do you want more of the blanket?"

"I only want you, Derek Miller," Liza said.

She began to pull him down, pressing her lips to his as they sank into the pit of sand in the center of the rocks. It was their own private shelter, where no one else could see them. As Derek kissed Liza, his desires grew. So did hers, and she was suddenly sitting up and unbuttoning her blouse.

He watched her, tucking his hands behind his head, until she was kneeling over him wearing nothing but a necklace. This Derek fingered gently and then let his hand travel down the length of her body. She undressed him, and he stared into her eyes, his head filling with the mixed scents of her perfume and the wet, briny air.

"Funny," he said.

"What?"

"In the twilight," he said, "your eyes look blue."

"Yes, Derek," she said, leaning toward him.

She felt so warm to his touch. He covered her with kisses, not missing an inch of her dark, soft skin. Liza pressed herself hard against him. Derek was in ecstasy, never remembering a time when their lovemaking had been this intensely pleasurable.

When it was over, he opened his eyes and looked again into hers. Their blue had become lighter, but Derek was too filled with passion to really notice. Liza smiled up at him, digging her nails into the taut muscles of his arms.

"I knew I could have you, Derek Miller," she said. Her smile revealed pointed teeth.

Liza had always had perfect teeth.

"What?"

Stunned, Derek rolled off of her. He gazed down at the nude woman lying on the sand, studying her face. It was Liza's face, and yet the eyes and smile . . .

"Liza, what's wrong with you?" he whispered.

She threw back her head and let out an ear-shattering screech. All at once, Derek felt himself being flipped over, his back crashing down against the flat rocks. Before he could right himself, the woman knelt over him, pinning his arms to the ground with superhuman strength. Her face twisted and stretched and became the hitchhiker's. She grinned at him, knowing he was now in her power and that she could do anything to him that she desired. But there was still a flicker of defiance in Derek's eyes, and he dared to lean his head back and spit at her.

"AAAAAUUUUGGGH!"

The cry was deep and guttural, not a woman's cry at all. Angered, Janice-Liza willed her face to change once more. What Derek witnessed now tore away the last shreds of his resistance. For looming above him were the horrid remains of his wife Elaine's face, just as she had looked after her terrible accident. Derek screamed, reliving that long-ago afternoon. Elaine's car had gone up in flames, her body melting in an inferno. Her face, once beautiful, had become so twisted and ugly that Derek had passed out after identifying her at the morgue.

And now she was back again . . . .

"NNNOOOO!"

He tried desperately to turn away from the sickening vision. He screamed and kicked and pleaded, and yet the hideous face still hovered over him.

"Please, oh, dear God," Derek cried. "I'll do anything! Just get her away. Please!"

The face drained away and became the hitchhiker's, smiling at him. He had said exactly what she wanted to hear.

"You'll remember that face from now on, won't you?" she said.

Derek nodded.

"And you don't ever want to see it again, do you?"

Derek shook his head.

"Then remember this," she hissed, "if you don't want to suffer again, you'll do everything I say." Her voice took on a sing-song sweetness. "Won't you?"

"Yes," Derek whispered.

"Good," the woman said. "Go back to the house now. You'll go straight to bed, and when you wake in the morning, you'll remember nothing but a pleasant evening with Liza."

"Y-yes," Derek choked.

He did not move when she climbed up the rocks and left him, carrying Liza's clothes in her hands. She padded, naked, across the beach, her feet leaving no marks in the sand. A few moments later, she was behind the wheel of Liza's car. This she started without a key and drove down the hill. When she reached the strip that followed the edge of the beach, she didn't turn onto Houston, but instead found a sand-covered boardwalk, just wide enough to support the vehicle.

She drove on it, without lights, straight for the bay. The car splashed into the water, sending out a series of soft ripples. At first it floated, rocking gently. And then it was drawn down into the murky depths, moving slowly and lazily. When it hit the bottom, Liza's body slumped forward against the steering wheel. The soft sand offered little resistance, and within moments the car had wedged itself in permanently.

On the beach Derek finally stood up and dressed himself. Then he hurried to the house, where, obeying a command, he went straight to bed.

18

"Are you okay?" Gary asked Melanie as they sat in the back of a yellow cab on the way home from the hospital.

"Why wouldn't I be?" Melanie asked, smiling at him. Then she nolded. "I get it. You think I'm nervous to be in a car again."

"It would be understandable."

But Melanie looked calm today. After her outburst about someone tampering with her car, Gary had been afraid for her. Fortunately, she hadn't mentioned it again. Realizing she might have been delirious from the blow to her head, Gary was quick to pass that incident off as hysteria.

Melanie took his hand. "I'm fine. Trust me."

They were home within an hour. Gary paid the driver, then hobbled on his crutches to the front door. He expected Derek to be waiting inside. Instead, it was Lad who gave them a warm welcome-home.

"Hey, puppy," Gary said, rubbing the dog's head. "Where's Derek?"

Lad barked. Gary looked at Melanie. "He's probably right behind us," he said. "Must have gone out for something. He wouldn't let the kids come home to an empty house."

145

"I should think not," Melanie said, feeling a little angry at Derek.

She and Gary walked down the hall to the stairs, then Melanie carried her overnight bag up to her room. By the time she finished unpacking it, she heard the sounds of her children downstairs. Happy to see them again, she hurried down.

"Mom!" Kyle cried, running to her when she reached the bottom landing.

Hugs and kisses were exchanged, and even Alicen managed an embrace for Melanie. She noticed a change in the child. Alicen seemed to be *glowing* today; her smile made her very pretty, as a matter of fact. Melanie wondered what had happened to cause the change.

"You don't look bad at all, mom," Gina said. "It's just a little bandage, like Derek said."

"Derek bought pizza for dinner two nights!" Nancy cried.

"Mom, are you gonna cook for us now?" Kyle wanted to know.

"Of course," Melanie said. "By the way, where is Derek?"

"Maybe he had to go to the dentist again," Alicen suggested.

Well, that's another switch, Melanie thought. *Alicen making excuses for her father?*

"He should have been here when you kids came home," Melanie said. "He didn't know daddy and I were coming today."

Alicen shrugged. "We can take care of ourselves."

"I know that," Melanie said. "But I still don't like the idea of you being alone. Anything could happen here."

Gina's eyes darkened. "Mom, don't talk like that," she said softly.

Melanie smiled at her, realizing she might have frightened her. The dining room door opened now. As if in answer to Melanie's question, Derek stepped into the hallway. There was a shadow of a beard on his face, and underneath his eyes were dark circles. He blinked twice at the group near the front door.

"I thought you were out," Melanie said. "Aren't you feeling well, Derek?"

"I'm fine," Derek said without emotion.

"You look terrible."

Derek yawned and forced a smile that came out like a grimace. "I guess I fell asleep at lunch. I was up late last night."

Melanie looked at him for a few minutes, disturbed to see that he, too, had changed. It was as if he had switched personalities with his daughter. Where she was now cheerful, he was gloomy. And Melanie could tell by his eyes that he was hiding something.

But Nancy was pulling at her arm, and it was more important to enjoy the children than to have worries.

"Where's my daddy?"

"Upstairs in his office," Melanie said. "He had to make a phone call. Why don't you go up and say hi?"

"Come with us, mom," Kyle said, taking her hand.

Melanie had wanted to talk to Derek, but Kyle was insistent. So now Derek leaned against the doorjamb and watched them go up the stairs. He sighed. The slight heaving of his shoulders made his back ache terribly. He felt as if he'd been severely beaten over every inch of his body.

He had been sitting in the kitchen for hours, staring out the back door. Something had happened the night before, Derek knew. He couldn't remember having said goodbye to Liza. He knew they had had a pleasant evening—that much was clear in his head. But when had it ended?

A month, a week ago, Derek would have racked his brains to find a logical explanation for his loss of memory. He was a therapist, after all. He was supposed to always be in perfect physical and mental health. But now his physical being felt like a rat dragged out of a river, and his mental self was frayed to bits.

And for some reason, he didn't give a damn.

He stopped rubbing his arms long enough to go upstairs to the bathroom. He could hear Gary's voice, and he had the vague idea that they should get back to the therapy sessions as soon as possible. Then he reached into the tub and turned on the shower.

The water was like ice, invigorating. Shivering under it, Derek felt the fatigue draining from his body. The pain in his bones lessened a bit, and by the time he dried himself off, he was feeling a little better. Not much—the tiredness was still there. But enough to hide his uneasy feelings from the VanBurens. He wrapped a big towel around himself and hurried down the hall to his bedroom to change. He caught sight of himself in the floor-length mirror. To his shock he saw that his back had a bruise on it from his shoulder blade to the bottom of his ribs.

"Where the hell did that come from?" he asked himself aloud. He couldn't remember falling last night. And his

147

eyes—they weren't like his eyes at all. There were dark circles under them, like a man who hadn't slept in weeks.

What the hell went on here last night?

There was one way to find out: call Liza. Derek wasn't sure if she would be home from school yet, but he'd take a chance. He dialed her number on the downstairs phone and let it ring twenty times before hanging up.

"She must be in school yet," he said sadly.

He tried to call her again after dinner, to no avail. The fact that she wasn't home when he needed her angered him so much that he slammed the phone down with a curse.

"Derek, what's the matter?"

He turned to see Melanie behind him. Her eyes widened, and he knew it was at the sight of his angry face. He closed his eyes and breathed deeply to calm himself, then said, "Sorry. I've been trying to get Liza all day, but she isn't home."

"Well, I'm sure she'll call you when she is," Melanie said, reassuring him. She moved past him and went up the stairs, looking at him over her shoulder. It was as if she couldn't wait to get away from him.

She found Gary in his office upstairs. "Gary, did you notice something funny about Derek today?"

"He looks a little tired," Gary said.

"It's more than that," Melanie said. "Derek usually has energy to spare."

"What are you doing?" Gary asked. "Giving yourself something else to worry about? He's just fatigued after taking care of four kids for two days. He isn't used to that kind of work."

"It looks like more than fatigue, Gary," Melanie said. "The man looks ready to drop."

"Maybe he's coming down with something," Gary suggested. "We've had some damp weather here lately. Even terapists catch cold, you know."

Melanie considered this. "You know, you're probably right," she said. "I'll find some cold capsules and give them to him to take tonight."

That night Derek took the pills, thanked Melanie, then dropped them into his wastebasket as soon as she left his bedroom. She had said they would make him fall asleep, and though he wanted that, a firm voice in his head told him he must stay awake. He sat up reading until midnight, then finally turned off his light and settled back against his pillows.

Suddenly, in the total darkness, he felt himself trembling. His knees turned to jelly, his stomach flipped, his heart pounded. In seconds his pillow was wet with perspiration. All the doubts he'd had earlier drained away, and in their place came a feeling of raw terror. He remembered everything of the previous night now. Liza's face loomed over him, then the hitchhiker's, and then, oh, my God, Elaine's. Derek started to scream, but lips pressed hard against his to stifle it. A tongue pressed between his lips and sought his. Derek gave in weakly and wrapped his arms around the ghostly body above him. It felt strangely warm, not what he had expected. When she pulled away from him, he saw Liza's face.

"I want you, Derek Miller."

It was Janice's voice.

"Yes," Derek said.

He knew he would have to give in to her. He knew she would show him Elaine's face again, if he protested. So tonight, he didn't try to get away from her. He didn't dare.

She stood up now, pulling him onto his feet. When they passed through the beam of moonlight, he saw to his surprise that she was completely nude. It was Liza's body, beautiful and firm. Derek reached out to touch it and heard Janice's laugh. His hand shot through her.

"Please," he whispered. "I want you, Liza."

"Janice," he heard.

They left the room, Derek following Liza-Janice like a little boy. He could feel his heart beating with anticipation, and did not try to fight it. He wanted her! He wasn't afraid! He craved her more than he had ever craved anyone or anything in his life. And so he let her lead him down to the kitchen, to where Lad slept soundly under the table. As if they weren't there at all, the dog didn't stir.

Derek sank down to the floor, pulling Liza-Janice with him. His organ was stiff, his veins throbbing all through his body.

"I want you now," he breathed. *"Now."*

Janice fell on top of him, kissing him passionately. Then she sat up and smiled down at him. This was *perfect.* He was completely under her spell. This was exactly what she wanted.

"Make me feel like a woman," she ordered.

Derek tightened his arms around her, crushing her. This time, there was substance there, warm flesh like a living mortal's. And under Janice's spell, he saw her only as Liza. She was good, pure, beautiful. She was not a thing of evil.

* * *

If Derek had been listening, he would have heard the sound of Melanie's door opening. She had wakened up in the middle of the night with a splitting headache and was shuffling down the hallway to the bathroom. The bright light made her head ache all the more, and she clutched at the sink as she opened the medicine cabinet. To her anger, she remembered that she had left her painkillers in the kitchen.

She couldn't stand the pain enough to go back to bed, so she decided to brave the dark house and go get her medicine.

Liza-Janice suddenly looked up with a start. She and Derek were embracing on the kitchen floor, completely naked. Derek's underwear and robe were scattered on the floor near where the dog still slept, undisturbed.

"She's coming," Janice hissed. "That bitch Melanie is coming."

"Keep her out of here," Derek said.

"I'll kill her."

There was a coldness in Janice's voice that made Derek shudder. He grabbed her wrist.

"Don't go away," he begged.

Janice looked at him. His eyes were so beautiful in the moonlight that she felt her evil passions growing again. She smiled crookedly. "I'll get rid of her," she said.

Melanie was halfway into the dining room when a loud noise behind her made her turn around with a yelp. It was the sound of a motor revving. Melanie listened, not knowing which way to turn. Something was drawing her away from the kitchen door.

Come out to the stairs, Melanie. Come out to the stairs.

She ran into the hallway. To her shock she saw that the lift had somehow started up by itself. Its pulleys and gears whirred wildly, but it wasn't moving. Melanie switched on the hall light and stared up at it in confusion. A moment later, Gina appeared on the top landing. Kyle came up behind her, rubbing his eyes.

"Mommy?" he whimpered. The yellow hall light made his mother's face look all distorted, and he moved closer to Gina.

"Mom, turn that off," Gina ordered. "It woke us up."

"I don't want to touch it!' Melanie screamed. "Just go back to bed."

"I don't want to," Kyle said. "I'm afraid."

Gary was here now. "Kyle, listen to your mother. I'll fix it."

Reluctantly, the children obeyed him. Gary glanced at Melanie, then grabbed the banister to try to get to the lift. It had stopped halfway down the stairs. Melanie, realizing Gary didn't know how to walk on steps, suddenly shot up the stairs after him.

"Let me get Derek—please," she begged.

"Derek isn't in his room," Gary said. "I want that thing off before it wakes Nancy."

"Gary, *please*," Melanie said. She was terrified that he might fall and hurt himself again. She began to cry.

Gary frowned at her, then turned his gaze to something over her shoulder. He watched a shadow move across the floor as the dining room door opened wider. Melanie turned and saw Derek.

"What are you doing down there?" she demanded. "Why—"

Gary interrupted her. "Could you please turn that thing off for us?"

Nodding, Derek walked up the stairs. Pulling a wire, he at last silenced the machine. Then he took something soft and warm into his hand and held it up. It was a dead rat.

Melanie groaned.

"He must have gotten caught in the gears," Derek said calmly.

"Oh, get it out of here!" Melanie ordered, unable to take her eyes off the tangled mass of fur and blood. The rodent's teeth glistened viciously in the light. Derek turned back down the stairs to dispose of it.

"See that?" Gary said. "It was only a mouse."

"Rat," Melanie corrected.

"A mouse," Gary insisted. "Like you always find in big old houses."

Melanie stared down the stairs in silence.

"It really is happening again, Gary," she said quietly.

"No," Gary said.

"Someone's coming for us," she said.

"Oh, damn it, Melanie!" Gary cried. "You're supposed to be the strong one in this family, remember? Stop being ridiculous."

151

Melanie glared at him. Suddenly she wanted to get away from him. She hated him for mocking her fears.

"I think I hear one of the kids up," she said, hurrying past him.

"Oh, Melanie," Gary whispered. "Don't you see it can't be happening again? It just can't be."

He didn't hear strange, feminine laughter. He didn't hear a voice saying:

It is happening again, you fool. And nothing is going to stop it.

Derek returned to his room after dumping the rat in the trash. Now he lay in his bed on his stomach, his face buried in his arms, trying to breathe deeply and fall asleep.

But sleep wouldn't come to him. He felt too dirty, too shamed to allow himself the peace of sleep. Too scared. How could he have let himself fall into her trap? He should have seen this coming when Janice called him by name that day in his car. He should have known there was something different about her by the insane look in her eyes and the crazy way she talked.

Shame was a painful thing for him. It twisted at his muscles and made his stomach burn. He claimed to love Liza Crewe, had even asked her to marry him. Yet he had been unfaithful to her, with the woman he hated most. Janice had lured him from Liza's arms into her own evil embrace.

But he was a man, after all. A man deprived of sexual love for many years. Janice's lustful embraces had awakened some sort of animal feelings in him, and he had been unable to control himself.

He was making excuses. Wasn't he always the one who claimed to be strong? Why couldn't he fight this woman?

"What is it you're ashamed of, Derek?" he asked himself out loud. "That you cheated on Liza or that you fell under that bitch Janice's powers?"

But what kind of powers were they? How could she change her face to Elaine's—God, don't let me think of that, he prayed—to Liza's, to any face she knew would control him? How could she have such a hold on him, so much so that he couldn't get up right now, pack his bags, and leave?

What was she?

He felt panic-stricken. How could he explain this to anyone? How could he explain it to himself? It was crazy. If he ever told anyone, they'd think he was crazy.

He was trembling and wished Liza were there by his side. She would hold him in her arms, tell him everything was all right, protect him. She would understand.

Derek had never thought he would need to be protected by a woman. But where was Liza now? He'd been unable to get in touch with her since the night he asked her to marry him. Had something happened to her? He had the sick feeling Janice had something to do with that. And the only way to find out would be to stay here and give in to her. If it meant finding Liza again, Derek would do anything.

But he knew he would hate himself for his weakness . . . .

19

At breakfast the next morning, Melanie explained to Kyle and Gina how the lift had started. Not wanting to frighten them, she changed the rat into a little field mouse. She related the events less to ease their fears than to make herself believe her own had been unjustified. In the darkness she had been terrified. But somehow, the daylight made her strong again. She was willing to believe it had been "just one of those things."

"Poor mouse," Gina said. "How do you suppose it got in here?"

"Probably crawled through a hole under the house," Derek suggested, shifting a little to ease the aching in his muscles. He knew exactly where the animal had come from. Janice had lured it into the house and had planted it in the gears of the machine.

"I'll have to have that checked out," Gary said. "And God knows what else we'll have to have fixed this summer. We'll have to have the roof repaired, too, before we have floods."

"That's to be expected of an old house," Melanie said.

Gary looked at her.

"So are a lot of other things, darling," he said.

Melanie smiled at him and got up. She wasn't completely convinced that he was right. But what good would it do to mope around, waiting for something to happen? Wouldn't it be better to fight her terrors? The best way to do that, she knew, would be to throw herself completely into her work.

She went up to her studio, and Gary and Derek headed up to the therapy room. Derek wasn't really in the mood for a workout, but what excuse could he give? So he motioned toward the mock stairs and said, "We're going to start on them today."

Gary studied the four steps. "It doesn't look difficult."

"That's what you said about getting out of the wheelchair," Derek reminded him.

Gary looked over his shoulder. "Thanks for the vote of confidence," he said.

Without answering, Derek proceeded to show Gary the right way to use crutches on stairs. Then, yawning, he told him to practice. He was supposed to stand and watch Gary, to support him if he fell. But instead, he went to look out the window. He thought he saw Janice walking through the woods—but then there was no one there.

"How long do you think it'll take me to get used to this?" Gary asked.

Derek ran his fingers through his dark hair, but didn't say anything. The previous night still weighed too heavily on his mind, and the shame and sickness he felt were competing too strongly with his work.

"Derek, come see if I'm doing this right," Gary requested, loudly. Still, his therapist was silent. "Hey, what's the matter with you?"

"I—I'm sorry," Derek said, turning. "Hey, look. You're almost at the top. One step to go."

Gary frowned at him and continued up the stairs. His legs ached only a little from the effort, since months of lifting weights had made them strong. Still, he hesitated a little as he turned and looked down the stairs. One slip of the crutch . . .

Cut it out, he said to himself. *You aren't going to fall.*

Five minutes later, he reached the bottom step. Five minutes! Gary sighed with frustration.

"Tired?" Derek asked.

"A little," Gary admitted. "But I suppose you want me to try again."

"I don't care—" Derek cut himself off. "Sure, sure go ahead."

Once more, Gary ascended the stairs. He was nervous about coming down. He moved slowly and held fast to the railing.

"I hope this gets easier," he said. Derek didn't answer. "I mean, I don't know what to put down first sometimes."

Derek cleared his throat and realized he had let his mind wander. "You'll get the hang of it," he said, catching the last of Gary's sentence. "By the time your wife comes back home, you'll be an old pro."

With all his strength, Derek tried to drive away the memory of the previous night. It was daylight, and he wasn't alone. Why should he be afraid now?

He knew, though, that he dreaded the fall of darkness. And worse than that, he knew he couldn't run away from it.

"Do you feel any better today?" Gary asked his wife as they sat together on the living room couch after dinner.

"A lot," Melanie said. "Getting into a new painting was a smart move."

"You're not afraid any more?"

"No," Melanie said slowly.

"Nothing should scare you," Gary said, kissing her. "We're safe here, I promise."

Across the room an unseen being sat in the huge rocking chair, watching them. So they thought everything was all right? The idiots! They had escaped her wrath up to now, but no more. She wouldn't rest until they were punished for what they had done to her. Tonight, she would move in first on the easiest victim.

Later in the night, when all the house was sleeping, she went to Alicen. The little girl had been dreaming of her mother. Elaine looked so beautiful, not mysterious or cloudy at all. Alicen reached up for her.

"Hold me, mommy," she cried.

Something cold took her hands, and her dream mother faded away. Alicen's eyes fluttered open, and she sat up slowly.

"Mommy?"

"I have something for you to do, Alicen," her vision said, pressing a small, hard object into the girl's palm. Alicen looked down at a tiny black vial, then back up at the vision.

"I want you to put that in the dog's dish."

"Why?"

"Don't question me," the apparition said firmly. "Do as you're told."

"Okay, mommy," Alicen said quietly.

Wanting to make her mother happy, she walked silently, hardly seeing the long stretch of doors or the darkened rooms downstairs, and went into the kitchen. She found Lad's dish in a corner and emptied the bottle into it.

Lad, disturbed by the sound of her footsteps, sat up with his ears perked. He got on his feet and went to his dog dish, where he sniffed the strange new scent . . . .

At the same time Gary was learning to walk on stairs that Saturday morning, a plane touched down on the runway at LaGuardia Airport, just in from Fort Lauderdale, Florida. It taxied to its final destination, where a collapsible tunnel was fixed to its door. Bearing garment bags and overnight suitcases, the passengers filed out. Children wearing Mickey Mouse hats held fast to their parents' tanned hands, while old couples discussed moving to Florida for good. A blond, tan young man burdened with an overnight bag filled with books exited, pleased to be in New York. He was here on business, with the hopes of seeing his sister Liza during his visit.

Owen Crewe shifted his bag from one muscular shoulder to the other and brushed a strand of mustache from his lip. Liza would be surprised to see it; he hoped she'd like it.

Walking through the tunnel, Owen headed first for the phone booth. To his disappointment Liza didn't answer his call. She hadn't answered the night before, either. But then she had no idea that he was coming to visit. He had had no idea until yesterday that he'd be assigned to a psychiatrist's forum here in Manhattan. It had been a last-minute decision by his superiors to let him sub for one of their sick colleagues.

Owen had ordered a car for himself and was pleased to find it was air-conditioned. He climbed behind the wheel and took out a map of Long Island. He located Belle Bay on the Nassau-Suffolk border, then switched on the ignition.

Traffic was heavy this Saturday morning, and it took him nearly an hour. Owen was almost convinced he had passed the town when he saw a sign showing Belle Bay at the next exit. Guiding his car onto the ramp, he found himself on Houston Street, a long, barren stretch of road that skirted the edge of the town.

With Liza's address memorized, he drove up to the first person he saw and asked for directions to her street. Liza's apartment, he found, was on the top floor of a comfortable-looking house. He went up to the door and rang the bell.

"Can I help you?" a middle-aged Italian woman asked, opening her window.

"I'm Owen Crewe," he replied. "Liza's brother. Is my sister home?"

"Wait a minute," the woman said. She shut the window and came out to the steps. "Liza didn't tell me you were coming. Besides, I haven't seen her today. She didn't come home last night."

"No?"

"You don't see her car, do you?"

Owen looked past the newly mowed lawn.

"I wouldn't know it, anyway," he said. "Look, could I wait in her apartment until she arrives?"

The woman eyed him suspiciously. "How do I know you're really her brother? She's a young woman alone, you know."

"I'm glad you're so protective," Owen said, smiling. "Here's my driver's license—it has my name on it, see? And here's a family picture of us."

The woman nodded, convinced. She unlocked the upstairs door for him and held it open while he carried his suitcases upstairs. After setting them in the living room, Owen went to the kitchen. He'd have a beer and watch TV until his sister came home.

20

Nancy, her blond curls catching the early morning sunlight, tugged on her mother's sleeve as she walked with her family to the bay. It was Sunday, and they were going to have a picnic.

"I forgot my yellow rabbit, mommy," she said. "I want to bring him with me."

"Can't you live without that dumb rabbit?" Kyle asked.

"I want it!" Nancy wailed.

"Yeah, well I wish Lad was coming with us," Kyle said. He

was in a bad mood because the dog had disappeared in the night.

"Don't worry about Lad," Gary said. "He'll probably show up on the beach in a while."

"Mommy, my rabbit!" Nancy cried.

"Okay, okay," Melanie said, handing Gina the basket she was carrying. "I'll go up and get it. Wait here for me."

"He's on my bed," Nancy told her.

Melanie unlocked the door, smiling at the idea her daughter needed her toy so badly. *Oh, to be a child again,* she thought. *If only a simple toy could make me feel secure!*

Well, that was what this picnic was all about. It had been Gary's idea—something to prove they were nothing but an average American family. Mother, father, and kids. All they needed was the dog, but no one had seen Lad that morning. He wasn't at the breakfast table looking for handouts.

"He's probably digging up the garden," Melanie had reassured the children.

Melanie pushed open the door to Nancy's room. She hardly took a step inside before she started choking. A horrible stench filled the air, permeating her nostrils even when she tried to hold her breath. Holding her hand over her mouth and nose, Melanie walked carefully into the room. What the hell was that?

She found it in Nancy's doll carriage.

Don't scream, she thought. *Don't get the kids up here.*

It was Lad's body, stuffed somehow into the little carriage. One paw was pushed up against the cover, making a dent. Lad's head was bent into his chest.

"Not again," Melanie whispered, unable to take her eyes from the hideous sight.

Pictures flashed in her mind: Sarah's face, a crashing bus, her own car spinning in circles. And through these, she saw Lad's body. Was she justified in her fears that evil had descended once more upon their home?

"Oh, dear God," she prayed. "Don't let that be happening again."

She ran from the room and down the stairs, her heart pounding. In the kitchen she stopped and leaned heavily against the refrigerator. She had fought tears until now, and though her head ached, she didn't want the children to see her crying. They were so happy today—nothing would spoil that. She heard Kyle's laughter, high and sweet. *Hold onto that,* she told herself. *There are good things in this house, too.*

She took a very deep breath, then let it out slowly before opening the back door. Her calm voice belied the pounding of her heart as she called, "Derek, could you come in here?"

"Is anything wrong, honey?" Gary wanted to know.

"Nothing," Melanie insisted. "I—I just want Derek to help me with something."

Derek hurried up to the house. He couldn't help staring at Melanie, wondering why her face was so pale. Silently she motioned him toward Nancy's room. The color drained from Derek's face when he saw Lad's corpse. He looked up into her blue eyes, his own very wide. Melanie returned the gaze, wondering how he could ignore the terrible stench. She didn't know it was meant for her alone and that Derek was unaware of it.

"How did this happen?" he asked, returning his gaze to Lad.

"I don't know," Melanie said. She blinked away tears. "I called you in because there isn't anything Gary can do about it. Please, Derek, can you get ri—put him somewhere? If the children saw him . . ."

"Of course," Derek said gently. "Can you get me a sheet?"

Melanie nodded and went to the linen closet. It was all she could do not to burst into tears.

"You'll have to tell them," Derek said, taking the sheet from her.

"Tell them what?" Melanie asked. "That their pet was murdered?"

"Somebody killed him," Derek said, feeling a twist in his stomach. He recalled the pleasure he'd had with Janice and was sickened. *She* was responsible for this.

"I know that," Melanie said. "And I'm frightened, Derek. But I don't want to spoil this day for the kids. They don't need to know he's dead. I—I'll tell them tomorrow that he ran away."

"Thank you," Melanie said. "For taking care of Lad."

Derek walked downstairs, carrying the wrapped body. Melanie waited a few moments at the top of the stairs, until she heard the front door open and close. Then, forcing a smile on her face, she hurried down and went out the back door. By the time she crossed the vast lawn to her waiting family, she had relaxed, if only a little.

"Is everything okay?" Gary asked.

"Sure," Melanie said, handing Nancy her rabbit.

"Where's Derek?"

"He'll be out in a minute," Melanie said. She looked up to where the children were racing ahead.

"Lad's dead, Gary."

Gary's head snapped around. "What?"

"Someone killed him," Melanie went on, still fighting tears. "I—I asked Derek to hide the body from the kids."

"Melanie, what do you mean?" Gary asked. "Who killed Lad?"

"I don't know," Melanie answered. "I found him in Nancy's room, in her doll carriage." The horror of it finally struck her, and tears began to fall. "Oh, my God, Gary! If Nancy had found him!"

"She didn't," Gary said soothingly, his own grief taking second place to shock. "It's okay."

"It's not okay," Melanie cried. "Nothing's been okay for the past month! It's starting again, Gary. I know it is!"

Gary looked past the trees to the house. Huge and white, it looked beautiful to him. How could it harbor so much evil? How could it be responsible for so much sorrow? Lad dead? But he was just a puppy—bought for the children when Gary came home from the hospital a few months earlier. He was barely eight months old.

"Gary, we have to do something," Melanie said.

"No," Gary said. "We'll tell the children he ran away, and leave it at that."

"I already figured that out," Melanie said. "I mean, I don't know what to do about the house."

"Melanie," Gary said stiffly, "there is nothing going on there. Not again. We've discussed this before, and my beliefs are unchanged."

"Damn, you're stubborn!" Melanie hissed. "After all that's happened—"

Gary cut her off. "You know what I think? I think the culprit behind all this is mortal. Someone so filled with hatred that she'll do anything to hurt others."

"Who are you talking about?" Melanie asked quietly.

"Alicen," Gary said simply.

"Oh!" Melanie cried. "Gary, that's just ridiculous! She's a little girl. I won't have you accusing—"

"Listen to me," Gary interrupted. "You can't deny Alicen isn't like normal children. She keeps to herself for hours, and her mind always seems to be off somewhere when anyone tries to talk to her. Haven't you ever noticed that?"

"Why does it make her a murderer?"

"She's trying to get back at her father," Gary said. "Derek ignores her too much, and she's rebelling."

"I can't say I blame her," Melanie said. "But I refuse to believe she'd do all these things. Sabotage my car? Murder a dog? Damn it, Gary, she's thirteen years old!"

"That doesn't matter," Gary said. "And in spite of your doubts, I think our problems will be over once we get rid of her."

"Gary, we're not sending that child away," Melanie said. How could he be so stubborn? Couldn't he see what was happening? He of all people, who stood there a cripple because of supernatural evil?

Before Gary could answer her, the sound of running feet silenced him. Kyle came up to them and tugged Melanie's arm.

"Aren't you coming?" he asked.

When Melanie turned, Kyle backed away at the sight of her bloodshot eyes.

"What's the matter, mommy?" he asked.

Melanie forced a smile. "I got something in my eye, and we had to stop a minute. But I'm all right now."

"Oh?" Kyle sounded unconvinced. But his excitement about the picnic soon overcame his doubts, and he cried, "Come on!"

He took his mother's hand and pulled her forward. Hating to leave things unfinished, Melanie looked over her shoulder and shook her head a little at Gary. Then she saw Derek coming up behind him. Seeing him made her think of Lad, and she had to turn away to keep from crying again.

"Melanie told you?" Derek asked Gary.

"Yeah," Gary said.

"I wish I had some explanation," Derek answered.

I'll bet you do, Gary thought.

Derek did have one, but he kept silent, even though the urge to tell Gary was strong. Poor Lad. Derek had found a pit in the grounds of the gray mansion that might have once been a duck pond. Thick with ivy and weeds, it was a perfect place to hide the dog. Infuriated that such a thing could happen, and at the same time moved with sorrow, he had dumped the body and marked the grave with Lad's chain.

Melanie had been wise to keep the truth from them, Derek realized as he sat on a rock and watched the children playing in the water. Even Alicen looked happy today. Derek was surprised to find himself admiring her. She had grown prettier. Her hair was neatly combed, and even in her bathing suit, she was no longer fat. But at such a cost . . .

"Aren't they wonderful?" he heard Melanie say. "They make you think everything's going to be all right."

"They're having a great time," Gary agreed. "Look, even Alicen's laughing."

Melanie shot him a glare, embarrassed. But Derek said, "Yeah, isn't that something?"

He stood up, curling his toes in the sand. "I'd like to take a walk with her. How long until lunch?"

"At least half an hour," Gary said. "Although I'm not very hungry."

Derek nodded, then went to his daughter. Gary, keeping his eyes on the therapist, said, "He knows something."

"Gary, please."

To make her happy, Gary said nothing more. He kissed her lightly on the cheek and went back to the barbecue.

Derek tapped Alicen on the shoulder. She turned and smiled at him.

"Want to go for a walk?" he asked.

"Sure!" Alicen cried. She took his hand. "Just me and you?"

"If the other kids don't mind," Derek said.

Gina shook her wet head. "Go on."

"I'll see you at lunch," Alicen said.

When they were a few dozen yards away, Derek spoke to his daughter. "Alicen, do you know anything about the VanBuren's dog?"

"No," Alicen said. "I told Mrs. VanBuren that at breakfast. Why?"

"He's dead, Alicen," Derek said softly.

He heard the choking sound of her breath stopping.

"What do you know about that?" Derek asked.

Alicen was wide-eyed. "Nothing!"

"Don't start crying, please," Derek said. "The other kids don't know about it, and we're going to tell them he ran away."

"I didn't kill him," Alicen said.

"I know."

She looked up at him, surprised. "You do?"

"Yes," Derek said. "Alicen, did you hear anyone talking about hurting Lad? I mean, not one of the VanBurens—but someone no one else knows but you?"

Alicen gazed into his eyes for a long time, not speaking. They had stopped at a jetty, the dividing line between the

VanBuren's private beach and the public one. Alicen climbed up on the rocks and sat down. She brought her knees up under her chin and gazed at a boat passing on the bay.

"Mommy told me to kill him," she said finally, distantly.

Derek stiffened. "Mommy told you?"

"She told me to put this funny-smelling stuff in his dish," Alicen said. There was no trace of remorse in her voice. She was simply reporting an order obeyed. "She said she wouldn't come see me any more if I didn't do it." Alicen looked up at her father, all innocence. "Mommy went away once. I don't want her to go away again."

Derek nodded slowly. He understood now why he had heard Alicen talking in her sleep so many times in the past weeks. She hadn't been dreaming at all; she, too, was under the spell of the woman who controlled him. Innocent little Alicen, who sought in her dead mother the love she lacked from her father.

A pang of guilt made Derek's throat tighten. Would it have been so hard to be kind to the child? It might be too late, but—

Suddenly he turned and pulled Alicen very close to him. Alicen returned the embrace, resting her head against her father's warm chest.

"Isn't it wonderful, daddy?" she asked. "Mommy's back, and we can be a real family again."

"Yeah, it's wonderful," Derek said quietly. He couldn't tell her this woman wasn't her mother.

"Daddy," Alicen said, rubbing her bare feet up and down the moss-covered rock. "You'd rather have mommy than old Liza, wouldn't you?"

What did Alicen know of Liza? Could she tell him why Liza never answered his calls? But something in Alicen's expression told Derek she would never answer his questions, so he ignored hers and stood up. Alicen followed him down the rocks and took his hand as they headed back to the picnic.

"Listen," Derek said, "this conversation is our secret, okay?"

"Sure," Alicen said.

"No one has to know about Lad," he said. "Or your mother."

"Mommy told me that already," Alicen said.

"If you ever need to talk," Derek said, squeezing her hand, "come to me, okay?"

"Okay."

Alicen ran to catch up to the VanBuren children. Derek

163

walked slowly, planning. He'd give Gary his notice tomorrow and would hopefully be out of the house within a week's time. Gary had made great progress and would get along fine with another therapist.

Derek looked at his patient. He didn't really want to leave him. Gary was more a friend than a patient now. But that gave Derek all the more reason to believe he should get away from the house before it was too late.

He knew he should warn them. He should tell them about her, about the things she'd done. It was no accident that Melanie's car was now in a junk yard. Her studio had not been torn apart by a mischievous puppy. And there was so much more. Lad's death was only the beginning.

But for the first time in his life, Derek was afraid. All he wanted to do was run away from his problems. God knew he couldn't face them much longer. Not when she drained his resistance each time he saw her. Or she saw him—was she watching him right now?

Derek wished to God he could forget.

But that wasn't going to happen. Late that Sunday night, he was lying with his face buried in his arms when he felt a cold touch on his back. He didn't move, but breathed more evenly as if in sleep. The touch stayed on him, moving up and down. It should have made him feel good, but instead a chill rushed through him.

"Look at me, Derek Miller," he heard.

Derek refused to move. He didn't want to see who shared his bed. But the pain of her nails in his flesh was so great that he was forced to roll over. He glared up at her. Even in the dim light of the moon, she was hideous. Derek fought to keep his eyes on hers, afraid to turn away.

"Good," she said. "You should know by now that you can't defy me, Derek. I own you."

"No one owns me," Derek said.

"I'll make you happy," Janice said. She leaned down and kissed his lips.

"What are you?" Derek asked. "How can you do these things?"

She didn't answer.

"Why are you doing this?" Derek persisted. "Why are you trying to hurt the VanBurens?"

"I was murdered," the vision said. "And I was only twenty-eight."

164

"Murdered?" Derek asked, confused.

"Silence!"

Before Derek could protest, she pressed her mouth to his and pried his lips open with her tongue. Derek had learned to give in to her. She became violent when he showed his repugnance. But God, how he hated this! How he wished he could throw her away from him, smash her hideous face, drive her away forever. But that was impossible.

At last, satisfied for the time, she rolled away from him. Derek knew what would happen now. He would fall asleep and remember this only vaguely in the morning. But he needed questions answered. "Why did you say you were murdered? You can't be dead. You're here right now."

She screamed, a scream heard only by him. Throwing her body on top of his, she pulled hard at his hair, making him want to cry out. He foolishly tried to grab her wrists. It was like grabbing water.

"Stop it, please," he said. "I won't ask any more questions."

"You must learn to be submissive," Janice hissed. "You must be taught to obey. Look at me."

Derek resisted.

"Look at me!"

To Derek's horror, she faded away from him and returned as Elaine. He jerked his head away from the sight, feeling nausea rise in his gut. He had prayed never to see that twisted face again.

"Please," he said quietly. "Please go away."

"Remember this face," Janice said.

Derek nodded, his face buried in his pillow. Several moments passed before he dared to turn around. He was alone once more.

21

Because his first meeting was at nine o'clock, Owen Crewe was up very early Monday morning. He sat on the couch in Liza's living room, his blankets tangled up in a knot behind him. Rubbing his eyes, he yawned widely, then looked around. The door to his sister's room was still open, her bed not slept in.

Owen had been certain she'd be home by now, if she was only on a weekend trip. And she couldn't have left for school already—not when the kitchen clock read six o'clock. Owen frowned at it and filled the teakettle. He then walked to the table, where he found the note he had written for her the previous morning. He had explained his presence there and had told her he would be home as soon as orientation was over. But he had returned in the late afternoon to find an empty apartment.

"Easy, Owen," he told himself. "She's a big girl."

Still, anyone seeing him crumble the note and throw it hard across the room to the wastebasket would have known he was more worried than he'd admit. Liza had never been the type to disappear like this. Of course, she hadn't known he was coming. But they had kept a correspondence going over the years, and Liza always told him when she was planning a vacation.

Hearing the kettle whistling, Owen went back to the stove and fixed his coffee. He carried the mug into the living room and sipped it slowly, looking out the window.

Pretty town, he thought, taking in the row of Colonial houses across the street. It was no wonder she had picked this neighborhood to live in. What could possibly happen to her in a town like this?

He finished the last of the coffee, gathered his papers together, then hastily wrote a new note for Liza, propping it up against a vase of dying flowers. Owen checked his pockets for his keys, then left. Surely Liza would be there when he returned.

Gary had spent all the previous night thinking of an excuse to dismiss his therapist. He couldn't accuse Alicen of killing Lad, because Melanie would deny it. But he knew he was right. Alicen was a disturbed child, and he wanted her away from his kids. So now he hobbled up the fake stairs in the therapy room, trying to get up the courage to tell Derek he had to leave. But Derek beat him to the punch.

"I'm afraid I'll be giving you my notice," Derek said.

Gary stopped halfway up the stairs and looked over his shoulder. "Did I hear you right?"

Derek nodded. "I'm leaving. Alicen and I will be moving as soon as I find new work."

Though he was grateful it was out of his hands, Gary had questions. "Why?"

"Don't stop in the middle of your workout," Derek said, waving at the stairs.

Gary continued to the top, then turned and started down again. "You didn't answer my question," he said when he reached the bottom. Would Derek admit the truth?

"I feel it's time Alicen and I were moving on," Derek said. "We're becoming too dependent on you—especially Alicen."

He did know the truth about Alicen—that was why he wanted to leave.

"Then send Alicen to boarding school," Gary suggested. He didn't want to lose his therapist. That would mean going back to the clinic.

"You know I can't do that," Derek said.

"And you can't leave me alone!" Gary snapped. "What happened to the guy who was going to teach me racquet ball?"

What was wrong with him? Why did he argue with Derek, when only moments ago he was looking for reasons to get rid of him?

Gary sighed deeply. "It's your life. You do what you want."

"I'm sorry," Derek said. His voice took on a louder, more authoritative tone when he said, "Let's try the stairs a few more times."

Gary obeyed, not knowing what to think. Well, maybe it would be better to just concentrate on his routine. Their troubles would soon be over, once Alicen was gone. Gary hated that child, not just for tormenting his family, but for taking his best friend away from him.

Melanie had gone to visit some art galleries that morning, needing to do something to forget her fears. On the way home, she glanced at her watch. It was about time now for Nancy to be getting out of kindergarten. Melanie, wishing she could have all her children with her now, decided to drive her youngest home. She pulled the car up alongside the play yard and waited. Minutes later, the lunch bell rang, and hordes of children ran from the brick building. She was surprised to see Alicen coming from the building with Jamie Hutchinson.

"Well, that's a surprise," she thought aloud. Puppy love

167

had claimed Alicen Miller at last. And Gary thought she was abnormal.

Melanie spotted Nancy, walking in a line of children. She got out of the car and called to her. The little girl waved, spoke to her teacher, then ran on chubby legs to her mother. Melanie caught her in her arms and kissed her.

"Mommy, stop!" Nancy giggled. "Everybody's looking!"

"How's my girl?" Melanie asked, opening the door for her.

"Fine," Nancy said. "How come you're here today?"

"I was on my way home," Melanie explained. "And I thought you might like a ride."

"Are you coming back for the other kids?"

Melanie thought for a moment: *it wouldn't be such a bad idea.* Then she told herself to stop being ridiculous.

"No," she said. "They'll come home on the bus."

She started the car. Nancy bounced up and down on the seat a few times, then moved closer to her mother.

"Why do you have such dark circles under your eyes?" she asked.

"I didn't sleep very well last night," Melanie admitted.

"Why?"

"I don't know."

Nancy was silent for a moment. Then: "Mommy, that mean man isn't coming back, is he?"

"Mean man?"

"The man who hurt daddy last year," Nancy cried. "Gina had a dream about him—is he back?"

Melanie was glad she had reached a red light so that she could take the child in her arms. "What makes you say that?"

"Because you're so sad all the time," Nancy said. "And you wanted to know if Kyle and Gina and me wanted to talk about daddy's accident."

"That was just in case you were thinking of it, honey," Melanie said, feeling uneasy.

"He isn't back, is he?"

"No, honey," Melanie insisted, her voice carrying more conviction than her thoughts. "I'm just tired. That's why my eyes have dark circles. You know how busy mommy is with all her work."

"It's okay?"

"Sure it is," Melanie said, kissing her. She drove down the road. She could tell the child was frightened.

168

"How about painting with me today? You could sit at the little table in my studio."

"Sure!" Nancy cried, delighted to share something with her mother.

Melanie was glad Nancy had agreed so readily. She wanted to keep the child in her sight as much as possible. That way, no one could get to her. Nancy would be safe.

After lunch Melanie and Nancy painted and talked until they heard the other children approaching the house. Melanie felt apprehensive; she knew she would have to tell them about Lad without further delay. So she gathered them together in the kitchen, fixing lemonade for everyone.

"There's something I have to tell you," she said as she filled a glass.

"It's about Lad, isn't it?" Kyle asked. "I bet he didn't come home."

"No, he didn't," Melanie said.

"Did you look for him?" Gina asked.

"Yes," Melanie said. It hurt her to lie like this, but what else could she do? "We searched the woodlands, and even Mrs. Jenning's property down the road. I think he wandered off somewhere."

"Maybe you'll never find him," Alicen said darkly.

"Shut up!" Kyle cried angrily. He was more hurt by Lad's disappearance than the others. "Don't talk that way!"

"I'm sure we'll find him," Melanie said, returning Alicen's gaze. When she stared like that, it was almost easy to see why Gary accused her.

Kyle went across the kitchen and opened one of the drawers. He pulled out a colored marker, then fished around a little more.

"What're you doing?" Nancy asked.

"Looking for paper," Kyle replied. "I'm going to make posters and put them all around. Someone will find Lad."

"I'll help," Gina said.

"Me, too!" Nancy cried.

Only Alicen declined. While Melanie was marveling at her optimistic children, Alicen was wondering how they could be so foolish as to think their dog was still alive.

Melanie bent over her sleeping son and gently put his arm under his covers. Kyle had been so excited just a few hours earlier, making the signs for Lad. It seemed impossible that

169

he was so quiet right now. Melanie smiled at his curled-up figure, hidden under a light coverlet. Then she frowned. How could anyone dare to hurt such a beautiful child? Gina and Kyle and Nancy were so precious to her. She had already stopped in the girls' rooms. She didn't want to tell herself it was because she wanted to be certain they were safe. Earlier, she had been tempted to let them sleep in her room, but she knew that was a ridiculous idea. Gary would never allow it, and besides, it would needlessly frighten the children.

But she had to do something to stop her fears. She was terrified of the night. Though the entire day had been peaceful, Melanie recalled tactics used the last time her house was stalked by an unseen predator. Jacob would let a few days go by, then he'd attack when least expected. Melanie knew her family was being tormented that way again. But if this was Jacob Armand's doing, why hadn't he made contact with her?

Melanie yawned and realized exhaustion was muddling her thoughts. She left Kyle's room, closing the door quietly behind her. When she turned into the dark hallway, she bumped into something.

"What—?"

"Shh," a voice said. "It's Gary. What're you doing up?"

Melanie took a deep breath. "You scared the hell out of me."

"Sorry," Gary said. They walked to their room together. "You don't have to watch them every minute, you know."

"I think I do," Melanie protested.

"It's too late in the night for an argument," Gary said. "So if it makes you feel better, it's all right."

"Of course it's all right," Melanie grumbled. "I don't need your permission to safeguard my children."

"You're really serious, aren't you?"

"You go ahead and make fun of me," Melanie said, "but I'll be the one laughing when you find out I'm right."

"You're wrong," Gary said. "And I have something to prove it. Melanie, Derek gave me his notice today."

"You didn't tell me that before," Melanie said.

"I didn't want to say anything in front of the children. But Derek told me today he and Alicen would be moving as soon as he finds other work."

"That's strange."

"No, it isn't," Gary said. "Not when you consider that he might be running away from something. Melanie, Derek is a top-notch therapist. He just isn't the type to leave so abruptly.

170

Unless he knows something we don't. He knows about Alicen. He knows she's responsible for Lad's death."

"Gary—"

"Melanie, your mother instinct is blinding you," Gary said. "Look at the facts, will you? Why would he be running away if he wasn't afraid we'd learn the truth about Alicen?"

"The truth about Alicen?" Melanie echoed. "It sounds like a cheap porno flick!"

"Derek told me once he had to leave a job because of his daughter," Gary said. "So why not now? Melanie, why would he be leaving so suddenly unless he wants to do so before I fire him?"

Melanie couldn't help but see the logic in Gary's argument. It all fit together, didn't it? Alicen was a strange child. But a murderess? That Melanie found hard to swallow. Still, it was late, and she was tired. It was so much easier to believe in a disturbed little girl than a ghost.

"Maybe you're right," she said. "But I prefer to keep an eye on my children."

Bryan Davis hung up his telephone and started to bounce his pencil nervously. He had just received a call from the county coroner. They had identified the driver; the body was that of one Nora Browne, an eighteen-year-old girl who had run away from home. Her parents had positively identified her and had admitted she was heavily into drugs.

"That's what I thought," Bryan said, "considering how she drove that bus. But eighteen? I can't believe an eighteen-year-old passed for a bus driver!"

The coroner said, "Captain Davis, there's just one problem. According to my autopsy, this can't possibly be your driver."

"What do you mean?" Bryan asked, closing his eyes. He wanted to be through with this.

"We checked her body for traces of drugs," the coroner said, "before we spoke to her parents, that is. We wanted to have something to report in reference to her behavior at the time of the accident. Granted, it was difficult, considering the condition of the deceased. But we found something we weren't looking for—sand and seaweed. It was in her teeth, her throat, and a small piece was found in her hair."

"So?"

"So this woman didn't die of a fall from a bus," the coroner said. "She drowned—probably accidentally."

Bryan thought a moment.

"Maybe she had been swimming before the accident," he said. "It's a long shot, but I'm willing to go for it. Why don't you tell me what she was wearing? Then I'll know for certain if it's our driver."

"Jeans, a white shirt," the coroner said. "And sandals. That's about all. Oh, yes—there was a tortoise-shell comb in her hair."

"What color hair?"

"Blond," the coroner said. "I understand your bus driver had blond hair."

Bryan nodded, as if the coroner could see him. When he hung up a moment later, his mind started to fill with questions. He bounced his pencil more quickly and tried to fit the pieces together. The coroner had just described the Jane Doe missing from the funeral parlor. Was it possible someone had stolen the body, driven it all the way to the site of the accident, and dumped it there? It was obviously done to get the police off a trail. But by whom? It was impossible to think the bus driver was still alive.

Bryan got up and went to the file cabinet near his windows. He found the folder on the bus accident and scrawled across it:

CASE REOPENED.

22

Monday night Owen Crewe returned to an empty apartment. His note was still propped up against the vase on the kitchen table. Owen removed its dead flowers and threw the murky water into the sink. He remembered how much his sister loved plants. It was unusual for her to leave them neglected like this. He filled a pitcher and watered the plants around the apartment.

Water spilled over one of the plantholders in the living room and dripped onto a chrome-and-glass end table. Owen mopped it up, then straightened a pile of mail Liza had left there. On the bottom was a greeting card. A giraffe dressed in a tutu was on the front, and in the blank inside, someone had written: *For my favorite racquet-ball-playing ballerina.*

It was signed "Derek." Owen wondered why his sister had never mentioned anyone by that name in her letters. The date on the card made it two weeks old. Owen wished there was an envelope with it. Maybe this Derek would know where to find his sister. Of course, he shouldn't worry so about her. She was twenty-eight, for heaven's sake. She didn't have to answer to him for everything she did. But Owen was one of those eternal big brothers, and he wouldn't rest until he was sure his sister was all right.

The next day he resolved to try her dance school. It was housed in an ancient brownstone. Owen entered a small, dimly lit hallway. There were no elevators, so he had to walk up three flights. Madame Martin's Dance Studio was written in gold across a black door. Hearing piano music, Owen entered without knocking.

"May I help you, sir?" a young woman asked from behind a desk.

"Yes," Owen said. "I'm looking for my sister. Her name is Liza Crewe—she's a student here."

"Yes, I know Liza," the woman said. "Please sit down until class is over. Madame Martin will speak with you."

"Thank you," Owen said, finding a seat across the room.

He heard French being spoken in the other room, in a lilting rhythm with the music. Finally the music stopped, and there was a shuffle of feet as women headed for the locker room. Madame Martin came out into the lobby for her mail, wiping her neck with a towel. When the receptionist told her of Owen, she turned to him.

"Mr. Crewe? You've come to ask about your sister?"

Owen smiled to hear that she didn't have the slightest accent. Her manner of speech was pure New Yorker.

"Yes," he said, extending his hand. "I came up from Florida for a convention, with the hopes of also seeing my sister. But I've been here since Saturday and haven't heard a word from her."

"I'm afraid I haven't, either," Madame Martin said. "Liza has missed three classes in a row—and it's so unlike her. She may be one of my older students, but she has always been as bright-eyed and dedicated as a young girl."

"You don't have any idea where she might have gone, do you?"

"None whatsoever. I have been expecting her to call me."

"But she hasn't."

"No," said Madame Martin. "I'm sorry, Mr. Crewe. Perhaps you'd like to speak with my other students? Liza had friends in this class."

Owen said he would appreciate that. But as it turned out, none of the other women had any answers, either. After a half hour or so of questioning them, Owen said his thanks and left the building. Now he was determined to find his sister—something was very wrong. When he arrived home, he made a long-distance call to his hospital in Fort Lauderdale. His boss wasn't very happy about his taking a leave of absence so abruptly. But at the moment, Owen didn't care what his boss thought. There was only one more day of the convention, and if Liza didn't show, it wasn't enough time to find her. Still, Owen went to bed that night hoping he would wake to find her home.

Somehow, he wasn't surprised when morning came and Liza wasn't there. This time he didn't bother to write her a note. He dressed and ate breakfast, then left for the Manhattan hotel. Dedicated to his profession, he was able to take notes, look at slides, and listen to speeches without thinking too often of Liza. But as soon as he could, Owen hurried home. Even as he sped along the highway, he knew he'd find nothing there.

He entered the apartment, tossed his briefcase on the couch, and left again. In the foyer downstairs, he knocked on a red door. He could hear an Italian opera playing and someone speaking the language over the music. Moments later, the door was opened by a thin, doe-eyed little girl.

"Is your mother home?"

The child, who couldn't have been more than five, nodded.

"Carmella, who is it?" a woman called.

"Owen from upstairs," he said.

"Owen from upstairs, momma!"

The landlady appeared with a wooden spoon in her hand. She smiled at Owen.

"Hi," he said. "I was wondering if I could talk to you."

"Of course," the woman said. "Has your sister come home yet? I don't see her car."

"No, I'm afraid she hasn't. That's what I want to talk about."

He was led into the apartment and further into the kitchen. Sitting on a barstool, he breathed in the smell of sauce.

"I'll bet you cook all day," he said.

174

"Company tonight," was the reply.

"By the way, I didn't get your name," Owen said now.

"Mrs. Verdino," the woman said. "What can I do for you?"

"I was hoping you could help me find my sister," Owen said, tugging at his mustache.

"Is there trouble?"

"I don't know," Owen answered. "But she hasn't been home since Saturday, and I'm worried. If I knew where she was, I could go home. But I can't leave without being certain she's safe."

"You're a good brother," Mrs. Verdini said. "You have a large family?"

"There are only four of us," Owen said.

"I have three children," Mrs. Verdini said. "Such angels. But we were talking about Liza. Let me think."

She lifted the lid from a pot, stirred her sauce a little, tasted it, and added more spices before speaking again.

"I know she has a new boyfriend," she said. "He was here a few times. I didn't see him very well, but he looked nice and neat. He drives a Volvo."

"I think his name is Derek."

"That's it," Mrs. Verdini said. "They played tennis together. I know because I saw them carrying bags with rackets."

Owen recalled the card he had found the day before, and corrected her.

"Racquet ball," he said. "Do you happen to know where they play?"

"Not really," Mrs. Verdini said. "I don't go in much for sports. But I do know there's a local health club in town. The Hercules Inn. If you want, you can ask my husband how to get there. He gets home at six."

"No, thanks," Owen said, jumping from his stool. "I can look it up in the phone book. I appreciate this, Mrs. Verdini."

"Anytime," she said. "Liza's a lovely woman. I just hope she's all right."

She walked with Owen to the door. "Listen, if she doesn't come home tonight, don't you eat alone. One more person won't make a difference at my table tonight."

Owen grinned. The smell of sauce was making him famished. "Thanks. Maybe I'll see you later."

The club was easy to find. It was in the heart of town, just around the corner from the main road.

"I was wondering if you could help me," he said to the girl behind the horseshoe-shaped desk.

175

"Sure," she answered. She studied his tanned face and sun-bleached hair and smiled. "Sure, what do you want?"

"I'm looking for two people," Owen said. "One is named Liza Crewe, the other is Derek. I don't know his last name."

"Why do you want to know?" the girl asked, tilting her head. "You aren't a cop, are you? I'm not sure you're allowed to ask questions like this."

"Liza's my sister," Owen said. "I've been looking all over town for her. Has she been here in the last few days?"

"I don't know any couple named Liza and Derek."

"Liza has dark hair," Owen said. "And eyes like Ava Gardner."

The girl cut him off. "Who's Ava Gardner?"

"An actress," Owen said patiently. "My sister's a dancer. She plays racquet ball here."

"Oh, I know who you mean!" the girl cried. "I remembered Liza when you said she was a dancer—she has those muscular calves, you know."

"Has she been here recently?"

"I haven't seen her," the girl said. "Or her boyfriend."

"You don't happen to know where he lives, do you?"

The girl shook her head, smiling. "Sorry. Even if I did, I couldn't tell you."

Owen sighed so sadly that she was moved to say, "I'll relay a message to them for you if they come in."

"I'd appreciate that," Owen said. "You have something I can write on?"

The girl pulled a short, eraserless pencil from a red cup and handed it to Owen with a pad. After scribbling his message, he pushed it across the counter and thanked her. He left, feeling no better than he had earlier. He'd found a lead, and it had brought him nowhere.

Well, he thought, he could always come back to the club. Liza had to show up soon.

All that optimism didn't take away the burning in his stomach, a sign Dr. Owen Crewe, psychiatrist, interpreted as fear.

23

That Tuesday Gary had gone back to work. Derek, only too glad to have a chance to get away from the house, drove him to the city. So Melanie spent the entire day alone, keeping very busy with her painting so as not to think about what was happening. Nancy was now sitting at her little table in Melanie's studio, coloring. At last the other children came home from school. Melanie, seeing thick gray clouds in the sky, was glad to see them. She knew now that they were safe.

She thought it was possible that Gary's theory about Alicen might be correct, but she couldn't be absolutely certain. Until there was definite evidence against the child—and Melanie doubted there ever would be—she had to keep herself ready for the worst. No matter how much Gary objected.

The studio door opened wide just then.

"Hi, mom!" Gina cried.

"Hi, honey," Melanie said, taking her in her arms and giving the child a tight hug. For a moment she didn't want to let go.

"Mom, you're squashing me," Gina protested. She pulled away and smoothed her hair.

"I'm just glad to see you, Gina," Melanie said. She noticed her son now. "Hello, Kyle."

"Hi, mom," Kyle said. He kept his distance, having witnessed the bear hug Gina got. He was at an age where gushy affection made him shy.

"What's Nancy doing in here?" Gina asked.

"Well, I just figured she shouldn't be alone in this big house," Melanie said.

"Since when?" Kyle wanted to know.

I'm too protective, Melanie thought. *Even the kids see it.*

"Hey, I don't have to explain myself to you," she said in a warning tone. "Nancy's fine here. By the way, where's Alicen?"

"She went to her room," Gina said.

"She's not ill, is she?"

Gina shrugged. "Who knows? She didn't talk to me at all today. Sometimes she's just weird."

"I told you to be nice to her," Melanie reminded her.

"I am!" Gina cried. "But how can I be nice to her when she doesn't talk to me?"

"I know you do your best, Gina," Melanie said. "But everyone gets into moods. Just let Alicen's pass, and she'll be nice as ever before you know it. Now, why don't you kids go out to play? But stay in the yard where I can see you. It's going to rain soon, and I don't want you caught in a downpour."

The children left the room. In the hall Kyle turned to his sister and said quietly, "Mom sure is acting funny lately."

"Yeah," Gina said. "Just like last year, when daddy was hurt. I hope nothing is going on."

"Oh, it's probably okay," Kyle, the eternal optimist, said. "Say, I know something we can do. We can look for Lad in the woods."

"Good idea," Gina said, forgetting her mother's orders to stay within her sight.

They ran from the house, hand in hand. Melanie watched them cut across the lawn and smiled. They were such nice, normal kids. If only Alicen could be that way, too. Then Gary wouldn't have any cause to be suspicious of her.

But Alicen wasn't normal at all. Normal children didn't become liars, thieves, or murderers just out of obedience to a disembodied voice. And they didn't sit in their rooms, staring at walls, waiting for that voice to come again. That was exactly what Alicen was doing at this moment. All during the bus ride home from school, she had heard her "mother" calling her.

The room grew cold, but Alicen didn't mind. She looked around and saw a cloud hovering near the door. She smiled.

"I wish you'd let me see you just once, mommy," she said.

"No," the vision snapped. "Not yet. There is something I want you to do today. The boy Kyle—he's next."

"Am I going to kill him, too?" Alicen asked, with innocence that would have alarmed a sane person.

"Not today," the vision said. "I want him to suffer first. I want them all to suffer, the way I do."

"What do you want me to do, then?"

"Get him up to the attic."

"The attic?"

"Yes," was the reply. "When you get there, you'll know what to do."

Melanie looked out her window and noticed her two oldest children were nowhere in sight. Thunder sounded in the distance, and a breeze blew up through the trees. Very firmly, she told herself not to panic. But she tore off her smock and threw it across the room. Nancy looked up, startled.

"What's the matter, mommy?"

"Nothing, dear," Melanie said. "You go on coloring. I've got something to do."

"I'm making a picture for daddy," Nancy said.

"That's nice," Melanie said, leaving the room. She saw Alicen coming down the hallway but ignored her. A few moments later she was yelling out the back door: "Kyle! Gina!"

She breathed a sigh of relief to hear their faint reply.

"Come where I can see you!"

Gina and Kyle appeared at the edge of the woods, then ran up to the house. They exchanged confused glances to see the angry look on their mother's face.

"Did we do something wrong?" Gina asked.

"Yes, you did," Melanie said. "Didn't I tell you to stay where I can keep an eye on you?"

"I guess so," Kyle answered, fidgeting. "We forgot. Can't you see in the woods from upstairs?"

"I'm not blessed with X-ray vision," Melanie snapped. She brought her hand to her still-bandaged forehead and rubbed away an oncoming headache. "I can't see through a half acre of fir trees."

"We're sorry," Gina said. "But we were looking for the dog."

"Yeah, don't be mad," Kyle begged.

I must sound like an idiot, Melanie thought. *They're big kids.*

"Sure," she said, smiling weakly. "I'm sorry I yelled. But Lad will come home in his own good time, don't you think?"

"I hope so," Gina said. She turned to her brother. "Kyle, I've got some homework to do."

"See you later," Kyle said.

Alicen was standing in the kitchen. Gina was tempted to

ignore her, but since her mother was at her side, she said hello. Alicen mumbled a greeting as they passed her. She stared at Kyle for a few minutes before speaking.

"Your mother treats you like a baby," she teased.

"She does not!"

"Then how come she has to watch you?"

"What do you care?"

Alicen shrugged. "I don't know. Except that nine is kind of old to be listening to everything your mother says, isn't it?"

"No," Kyle said. "She's my mother."

Alicen turned on him. "I'll bet you can't even cross the street by yourself!"

"I can, too!" Kyle cried.

"Then prove it," Alicen said, her eyes thinning. "Take a dare."

Kyle hesitated. But how could a little boy resist a dare?

"What?"

"Come up to the attic with me," Alicen said.

"Oh, no," Kyle said. "I'm not allowed up there. Some bad things happened there last year. I'm not gonna get myself grounded just when summer starts."

"No one'll know," Alicen said. "Unless, of course, you're afraid."

It was an old trick, but Kyle hadn't been on earth long enough to be wary of it.

"Okay," he sighed. "But let's get it over with. And you gotta promise to stop teasing me if I do."

"Sure," Alicen said.

The two children walked upstairs together. Melanie's studio was not in the same hallway as the linen closet, which led up to the attic, so no one saw Alicen climb its steps. Kyle was close behind her, his heart beating. If his mother caught him ...

Alicen pushed aside the cover and hoisted herself up over the ledge. She had never been in the attic before, and she looked around in awe at its contents. There were chests and toys and old furniture, all covered with a thick layer of dust. Mesmerized, she moved into the room to inspect a full-length mirror. A vision in its glass, of a blond-haired, faceless woman, reminded her of her task.

"Okay, I'm up," Kyle said. "I'm going down again."

"Wait a minute," Alicen replied. "Don't you want to see the neat stuff that's up here?"

"It's just a bunch of furniture," Kyle said, stepping down to

180

the top step. He didn't want to leave Alicen up there, so he stopped for a moment to watch her.

She moved through the room, brushing cobwebs out of her path. She walked as if she had been up there dozens of times. At its other end she found what she was looking for.

"Hey, come here and look," she said. "There's a trapdoor in the ceiling."

Of course there was. Her mother had told her so.

"So?"

"So I'll bet you can see for a million miles if you go on the roof," Alicen said.

"I'm not going on the roof!"

Alicen looked over her shoulder at him. "If you don't, I'll tell your mother you did, anyway. And then you'll get into big trouble."

Kyle considered the threat.

"Maybe she'll ground you for the whole summer."

That was threat enough. Sighing, he walked across the room to Alicen and helped her open the trapdoor. Alicen boosted him through it, then climbed out herself.

The loose tiles made a precarious foothold for them. Alicen sat down, putting herself between Kyle and the door. The little boy clicked his tongue, having hoped to get right back inside before his mother came looking for him. But how could he, with Alicen in the way?

"It's going to rain," he said. "I felt a drop."

"Just look at the bay," Alicen said, ignoring him. "Isn't it neat the way the wind makes it so choppy?"

"Yeah," Kyle said, studying her.

"You're not looking!" Alicen cried.

Kyle turned his head and pretended to be interested in the faroff water. Moments of silence went by, and then suddenly he heard a thud and a click. He turned and saw that the trapdoor had been slammed shut. Alicen had tricked him.

"Hey, open up!" he shouted.

Kyle pounded at the door, unable to pull it open. No reply came.

"Alicen, this is stupid!" he cried. "Let me in!"

No answer.

"ALICEN!"

A clap of thunder made Kyle jump. Crying, he grabbed for the door frame to keep himself from slipping. He held his breath and waited for the downpour. It began to drizzle.

"ALICEN YOU STUPID SHIT-HEAD! OPEN THIS FREAKIN' DOOR!"

He was so frightened that he didn't know what he was saying.

"I'LL KILL YOU, ALICEN! LET ME IN! LET ME IN!"

He pounded on the door, his soft young hands scraping over the shingles. A loose nail caught the side of his fist, opening the skin. Kyle's hand flew to his mouth. Praying someone would find him, he sucked on the wound while rain pelted heavier and heavier against him.

"HELP! HELP!"

His words were so muffled by the downpour that no one heard him. Fighting tears, Kyle lay down and drew himself into a ball. One hand held fast to the door frame while the other remained in his mouth. He could only wait.

"Look at that rain," Melanie said to Nancy as she put the finishing touches on her work. "I hope daddy and Derek get home okay."

"Are they coming soon?"

Melanie looked at her watch.

"In about an hour," she said. "Except this rain may delay them a bit."

She took off her smock and laid it across a stool.

"It sure is loud," Nancy said.

"I can't even hear myself think," Melanie answered.

"What are you thinking about, mommy?"

"Nothing," Melanie said, laughing. And that was true. She had been so ashamed of yelling at Kyle and Gina for no good reason that she had forced herself to stop worrying and concentrate on her painting. For the time, it had worked.

"Well, I've got to start dinner," she said. "You be sure to wash your hands and clean up nice for me."

"Okay."

Melanie went downstairs to the kitchen. She opened the refrigerator and pulled out chopped meat for hamburgers, and a package of fries. Seeing a bag of unshucked corn on the counter, she decided to have that, too. That would show her children she wasn't mad at them.

She could hear all the windows of the house rattling from the terrible storm as she walked out into the hallway and called upstairs for Kyle. Her son didn't answer her. But then, the storm was so loud that he might not have heard. She called again and this time heard a door open upstairs. But it was Gina who appeared on the top landing.

"Find your brother and tell him I need some corn shucked," Melanie said.

"Sure," Gina answered.

Melanie went back to the kitchen. She sat at the wooden table, took some meat, and began molding it into patties. The rain pounded the roof above her, and the wind blew furiously as she worked on dinner. A chill went through her—Melanie hated dark, rainy days.

After she had finished making the hamburgers, Melanie suddenly realized Kyle hadn't yet come downstairs. Melanie felt her heart jump to her throat but controlled herself as she went upstairs. She met Gina in a hallway.

"I can't find him anywhere," she said. "I looked in every room."

"Oh, God," Melanie whispered. "Did you ask Alicen and Nancy?"

"They don't know where he is, either," Gina said.

"He must be downstairs, then."

"I already looked."

"Look again," Melanie ordered. "Then come and get me if you find him."

If you find him . . .

Gina hurried downstairs. Melanie walked down the hallway to Kyle's room. She checked his closet and even under his bed, to no avail. He had to be in here somewhere, though. He couldn't have gone out in that storm.

"Kyle?"

The rain had subsided, so there was no reason he couldn't hear her—unless he was in some kind of trouble.

He has to be okay, Melanie told herself as she rounded a hallway. She passed the linen closet and noticed the door was open. She wouldn't have given it a second thought if she hadn't felt an icy wind rush out of it. Melanie stepped inside and looked up. The trapdoor had been left open.

What's he doing up there? she asked herself. But she didn't stop to think of an answer.

She hurried up the stairs, calling her son's name. The attic was hot, which made Melanie wonder why she had felt such a freezing blast a moment ago. Again, she didn't give herself time for an answer. She moved through the half-light offered by the clouded sun, looking behind the chests and pieces of furniture. She hated this place, with all its cobwebs and dark shadows. Had Kyle come up here on his own, or had someone made him do it?

Every time she looked behind something, only to find he wasn't there, she couldn't help breathing a sigh of relief. Her heart was pounding in anticipation of what she'd find. But at last, after a very thorough search, she realized he wasn't up here. The trapdoor had been left open by accident, of course. She'd find out about that later.

She was on the first step when she heard a small noise. It was a squeaking sound, like a mouse. Melanie remembered the rat that had gotten caught in the wheelchair lift and started to hurry away. But then there was a faint tapping noise from the roof.

"Kyle?"

The child had fainted under the chill of the driving rain, and only now had come to. Shivering, he managed to knock a few times on the trapdoor.

"Oh, my God," Melanie whispered. "Kyle, I'm coming!"

She hurried around the clutter of the attic and unhooked the little door. To her shock, she saw Kyle's pale face and plastered hair. There was blood on his lips from sucking his wounded hand.

"Alicen made me do it," he said weakly.

"Shh," Melanie cooed, hoisting herself up onto the roof to take him in her arms. "Come inside."

Kyle held her very tightly, and Melanie felt the trembling of his body. He coughed a little as she moved back toward the door. Then, suddenly, a loud clap of thunder made him jump. His scream mixed with his mother's as his body was torn from her. He slipped down the roof.

"MMOOMMMMMYY!"

"Kyle, no!"

She couldn't reach out quickly enough to grab him. He fell over the roof, screaming all the while. Melanie crawled out after him and to her relief saw that he had caught hold of the rain gutters.

"Take my hand, Kyle!" she shouted, reaching down. Because of the decorative trim around the roof, the gutters were a foot below her. Kyle was too frightened, however, to reach up.

"I—I can't!" he protested.

"Kyle, it's okay," Melanie insisted. "I'm right here. I'll hold onto you."

"I can't!"

"Kyle, *please*," Melanie begged.

The child began to cry hysterically. Seeing he would never let go of the gutters, Melanie crawled further out, until half her body was hanging over the ledge. She didn't dare think that someone might be behind her, waiting to push her off the wet, steep roof. She didn't think at all, but worked mindlessly in her efforts to save her child. Those gutters were so old they were rotted, and if they should break . . .

"I've got you!" Melanie shouted, feeling Kyle's wrist in her hand. "Let go!"

"No!"

It began to rain again. Without arguing, Melanie gave a heave and tried to pull her son over the ledge. But he was too heavy for her one arm. Blinking in the rain, she reached her other arm down and grabbed his other wrist. At the very moment she managed to at last pull him on the roof, a piece of the gutter gave way and crashed to the gravel driveway below.

Without a word, Melanie held fast to her son and scurried back into the attic. She closed the door above her and locked it, all the time thanking God that Kyle was safe in her arms. He was coughing violently, his wet body shivering against her. She carried him down into the hall.

Gina and Nancy, who had heard all the shouting, were waiting there. Seeing Kyle's wet clothes and hair, Gina reached into the closet for a blanket to wrap around him.

"What happened?" Nancy asked, frightened.

"Kyle was locked up on the roof," Melanie said, hurrying down the hall to his room.

"Alicen did it," Kyle said weakly.

Melanie laid him on his bed and began to remove his soaked clothes, while Gina looked through his drawers for a pair of warm pajamas and handed them to her mother. Melanie dressed her son more violently than she realized, throwing his wet clothes across the room with such force that they made slapping sounds against the furniture. She was furious that such a thing could happen to a nine-year-old.

At last she tucked him under his covers. "You lay still, darling," she said. "I'll call a doctor."

Kyle closed his eyes. Gina and Nancy stood by the bed, watching him with concern. A hand went into Kyle's, and he opened his eyes to smile at Gina. But his smile never happened. He saw Alicen standing beside his sisters.

"GO AWAY! GO AWAY!" He screamed on, stopping only when he doubled over in a coughing fit. Just then, the door opened, and Melanie hurried to his side.

"Get out of here," she said to the girls, who obeyed immediately.

Melanie sat Kyle up to pat his back. "Easy, honey! Mommy's here!"

Kyle quieted at last and fell against her.

"Okay, now?"

His eyelids began to droop, his voice became a whisper. "Alicen. Alicen. Alicen."

Melanie bit her lip and laid her son back down again. He was delirious, the poor child. She kissed his burning forehead and went out into the hall. The three girls were standing there, wide-eyed.

"Alicen," Melanie said, "did you tell Kyle to go up onto the roof?"

Alicen's brown eyes rounded. "No! Why would I do a thing like that?"

"Kyle said you locked him on the roof," Melanie reported.

"He's a liar," Alicen growled.

"Don't you call my brother a liar!" Nancy said angrily.

Alicen," Melanie said, her tone grim, "I'll get the truth when Kyle is better. But right now I have to call a doctor. Stay out of his room."

Gina turned to study her friend's face as her mother walked away. There were tears in Alicen's eyes, tears of a child who couldn't understand why she was being blamed for something she didn't do. Gina said nothing to her. She heard the sound of the front door opening and ran downstairs, Nancy at her heels. Passing her mother at the telephone stand, she raced to throw her arms around her father as he entered the house.

"Well, hello!" Gary said cheerfully. "That's just the kind of greeting I need on a day like this."

"Daddy, Kyle's sick," Nancy said.

Gary's smile faded. "What's wrong with him?"

"He got caught up on the roof," Gina said. Confused, Gary walked down the hall with her, his raincoat dripping on the carpet.

"Please, he's feverish and delirious," Melanie was saying over the phone. "He was caught out in the storm for God knows how long. Couldn't you come here?"

A pause.

186

"Oh, thank you," Melanie said. "You're very kind. I'll see you in a few minutes."

She hung up and looked at Gary. But before she could speak, Derek interrupted her.

"How did Kyle get caught up on the roof?" he asked, thinking the worst.

"I'm not sure," Melanie said. "It seems he climbed out through a trapdoor, and it slammed shut behind him. I didn't hear him calling, because the storm was so loud."

She bowed her head and cried a little. "I didn't hear my child calling me!"

"Melanie, don't blame yourself," Gary said gently. "Let's go upstairs and have a look at him."

"I hope he's all right," Derek said, an uneasy feeling creeping over him.

In Kyle's room Gary bent over his son and brushed back a strand of hair that was plastered to his forehead. Kyle slept fitfully, pulling away at his father's touch and whining a little. Gary straightened up.

"What on earth possessed him to do such a foolish thing?" he asked.

Melanie looked over her shoulder and saw they were alone. But she still kept her voice down. "Gary, he said Alicen made him do it. She must have dared him."

"I believe it," Gary said angrily. "The little—"

"Shh," Melanie said.

"Tell me something," Gary asked. "With Derek leaving us so abruptly and Kyle blaming Alicen for this, do you still think this house is haunted again?"

"I don't know what to think right now," Melanie said.

She put her arms around her husband, her wet hair dampening his shirt. Kyle's room was darkened by the storm outside, and silent but for the wheezing of a little boy in a huge four-poster bed. A short while later, they heard a knock at the door. Melanie let the doctor in, and the young woman came close to the bed. She looked Kyle over carefully and at last stood up.

"It's possibly pneumonia," she said. "I'll take this blood sample in for tests, in case something else is wrong."

"Something else?" Melanie asked.

"Just routine," the doctor said. "All he needs is plenty of rest and fluids. And give him one of these every four hours. I'll leave you a prescription for more."

"Is he going to be all right?" Gary asked.

187

"He'll be fine," the doctor said. "Call me if his fever doesn't break by morning."

"I'll do that," Melanie said.

That night, she sat by Kyle's bed and didn't close her eyes until exhaustion claimed her sometime in the morning.

24

Gary came in sometime the next morning to insist that Melanie come downstairs for breakfast. After all, she hadn't eaten anything for dinner the night before. He had taken care of the children that morning, and now that they were off at school, he had decided it was a good time to get the entire story from his wife.

"Come on, honey," he said, pulling her gently from the chair beside Kyle's bed. "If you don't get food in you, you'll collapse."

Melanie followed him from the room without protest.

Gary poured his wife a cup of hot coffee in the kitchen. She drank it slowly, not tasting it. Gary waited for her to wake up a little more, then said, "While we have the chance, tell me exactly what happened yesterday."

"I'm not quite sure," Melanie said, yawning. "I'll tell you what I think happened. Alicen dared Kyle to go up on the roof—for whatever reason. He knew better, but he couldn't resist a dare."

"Kyle's like that," Gary said. "She probably shamed him into it."

"But Kyle wouldn't have locked himself on the roof," Melanie went on. "And he certainly would have called Alicen right away when he saw it shut. She must have heard him yelling and ignored him. Apparently, she locked him out there on purpose. But when I asked her about it, she denied everything."

"Of course," Gary said.

"I was inclined to believe her," Melanie said, "because she's never been a vicious child. Then I saw the way Kyle reacted when she came to his bedside. Gary, he became completely hysterical!"

"The poor kid," Gary said. "I believe what he said about Alicen. The question is, do you?"

"I still have to force myself," Melanie said, "but I do. I'm not sure she killed Lad—I still can't bring myself to think that. But considering the fact that she did hurt Kyle, I wouldn't put Lad's death past her."

She sipped again at the coffee. "My God," she said. "A thirteen-year-old murderess."

"It's no less believeable than a two-hundred-year-old ghost," Gary said. "Melanie, now that you've seen what Alicen did, are you willing to believe our troubles will be over once we get rid of her?"

"I want to," Melanie said. "I don't want to be afraid, Gary."

"We can handle a child," Gary said "Derek will be gone from here in a week or so, and then everything will be back to normal."

He sighed. "I hate to see him go, though. Derek's a fine therapist. The rest of his life and career are going to be ruined by a disturbed child."

"Alicen should get counseling," Melanie said. "I wish Derek would send her away right now, even if he doesn't leave himself."

"You know he won't do that," Gary said. "In spite of everything, he still feels a sense of responsibility toward her. But don't worry. We'll keep an eye on Alicen. Now that we know who to watch out for, we're perfectly safe."

Across the room an unseen figure began to laugh as she listened to that statement. Perfectly safe! It struck her as so funny that she screamed with delight, a scream heard only by those who dwelt in her own dark world.

Later in the morning, Melanie went to check Kyle's temperature. To her relief it had gone down two degrees. She kissed him and left the room again. With the children at school and Gary busy doing paperwork in his office, she decided to treat herself to a long, warm bath. She had been through such a mental ordeal that even her physical body was taxed.

She and Gary hadn't discussed Alicen with Derek yet. Not because they didn't want to, but because neither of them had

had the chance. He had barely said good morning before he hurried from the house, racquet ball equipment in hand. He had tried to call Liza, needing her, but there had been no answer.

I never really liked you, Derek, Melanie thought to herself, *but I never wished this kind of heartache on you.*

She slipped out of her robe and tested the water with her toe. "But I've been hurt, too," she mused, sinking down into the water.

She closed her eyes and leaned back. The water was so hot that steam rose from it, relaxing every bone and aching muscle in Melanie's body. She heard a squeaking noise but didn't open her eyes to investigate it.

She began to hum lazily. The squeaking continued.

Probably water in the pipes, she thought.

Her arm flung over the side of the tub, then pulled back with a jerk. Something wet had brushed against it. Melanie sat up with a startled cry, staring wide-eyed at a huge brown rat.

It bared its teeth at her, yellow, vicious teeth. Melanie remained perfectly still, too shocked to move. It was one of the beach rats, the filthy animals that lived among the jetty rocks. What the hell was it doing in here?

It wasn't alone. Melanie heard a whimper and slowly turned to see another one running circles around the base of the sink. At that moment Gary pushed the door open.

"Melanie? I heard you cry—" He let out a groan when he saw the rats.

"Gary, get them out of here!"

The rats moved closer together and hissed defiantly. Gary leaned heavily against the doorjamb for support. One crutch raised high in the air and came crashing down full force on one tiny head. Blood squirted across the room. While Melanie clung to the bathtub faucet, Gary made an attempt at the other one. Instead, the rodent made a blood-curdling hissing noise and flew at Gary, it's long teeth sinking into his side.

"AAAAUUUGGG!"

Melanie, forgetting her own fears for the moment, stood up and stepped out of the tub, nearly slipping on the bloody floor. She whipped a towel at the hideous creature that clung so viciously to Gary's side. Gary screamed in pain, his crutches falling from under his arms as he furiously pried at the animal. Unsupported, his legs flew out from under him, and he fell to the floor.

"Gary!"

Grimacing, he at last tore the animal away. His face was red with fury as he smashed the hideous creature against the tile floor, again and again. Melanie watched him, crying loudly, until at last she could stand no more. She pulled the dead rat from his grip and threw it across the room.

"Stop it, please!"

She moved closer to him. Gary clutched at his side, grimacing in pain. "Where d-did they come from?"

"I don't know!" Melanie cried. "Gary, I've got to get you to a doctor."

"I'm okay," Gary insisted, foolishly trying to get on his feet again. Uttering a terrible cry, he fell to the floor. "Damn it!"

Melanie, still naked, stood up now and walked to the medicine cabinet, her body dripping water that mixed with the blood on the floor, making it dangerously slippery. She found a bottle of hydrogen peroxide and a package of gauze. Carrying these in either hand, she walked carefully across the floor and knelt down beside her husband. She sniffled as she helped him get his shirt off. There was a tiny gash in his side, but it was deep, and so much blood gushed out of it that Melanie was forced to use the entire package of gauze to stop it. Although she shook as she worked, she managed to do a good job. At last she stood up and put on her robe.

"That'll hold until the ambulance comes," she said. "Please don't try to move, Gary."

"I'm okay," Gary said weakly.

"That thing could have had rabies," Melanie said firmly.

She hurried downstairs to the phone. Gary protested when the ambulance arrived, but Melanie refused to listen to him. She followed the paramedics from the house as they carried her husband on a stretcher. To her relief, they had placed the rats in a bag for inspection at the hospital.

"Please take care of him," she said.

"You're not coming?"

"I—I can't," Melanie said. "I have a sick child upstairs. Gary, call me when you can?"

"I will," Gary said. "And don't worry."

Don't worry! How many times had he spoken those words? Now, feeling tears rise again, Melanie tightened her robe and watched the ambulance drive away.

"MOMMY?"

Kyle's frantic cry broke her spell. She ran as fast as she

could. Upstairs, to her disgust, she found him staring at the bloodstained bathroom floor. She hurried to him and lifted him away.

"What are you doing out of bed?"

"I had to go," Kyle said.

Gary's cries had wakened him, and now he stood in his bare feet, trembling. Melanie took him in her arms and suddenly felt the seat of his pants becoming wet. He looked at her, embarrassed. But Melanie kissed him and said, "It's okay. You're frightened and sick. Come on back to your room and I'll get you dry pajamas."

She helped the little boy undress. Weakened by his fever, Kyle didn't protest. Melanie then tucked him under his covers and bent to kiss his perspiring forehead. He was sweating— that meant his fever was going down, thank God.

"Go to sleep honey," she said. "You'll be all right."

She wished she could feel that way herself.

Derek had come to the spa to work off his frustrations, only to become more frustrated because he had to wait for a court. At this early hour, it was a marvel to see how many people were playing racquet ball. For a while he sat on a blue vinyl couch, staring at a bad oil painting. Then he stood up and fished a dime out of his pocket. For the tenth time that morning, he would try to get Liza on the phone. She couldn't stay away forever, could she?

Derek tried not to think that something might have happened to her. He was glad when someone answered the phone but disheartened to hear a male voice. Idiot? He'd dialed the wrong number. And now they were calling him onto the court.

It was satisfying to take out his anger on those four walls. The loud, repetitive bouncing marked his fury. BANG! That one was for Alicen. BANG! That was for that bitch Janice and how she controlled his life. BANG! That was for this job. He had once called it a godsend, but for all he cared now, God could send it to hell. BANG! BANG! BANG! He wanted out. Away from Janice, away from Alicen, maybe even away from Liza. Where the hell was she now?

BANG! Liza's name was written on that one.

The ball sped around the court, moving so fast that its echoes were deafening. Derek dove and leaped for it, breathing heavily, sweat marking his T-shirt. It hit a high point

192

above him and bounced to the back wall. But Derek didn't hear it hit.

He turned and saw Janice standing behind him. She was smiling, holding the ball in her hand. Dripping with sweat and panting, Derek frowned at her and held out his hand.

"Give me the ball," he said.

"No," Janice said.

Derek's arm dropped to his side. He closed his eyes and sighed. Then he opened them again.

"What do you want now?" he asked. "Isn't it enough that you forced my daughter to almost kill a little boy?"

Janice smiled. "You shouldn't talk to me like that."

"Why are you here?"

"To ask why you told that slime you aren't going to be his therapist any more."

"Don't call him slime," Derek cautioned.

"He is slime!" Janice hissed. "That whole family is slime, trash, garbage! They murdered me!"

" 'They?' " Derek echoed. "Does that include Kyle and his dog? How about Gina? I suppose you engineered that bus accident—with my daughter's help."

"Alicen is a dreamer," Janice said. "I control her, and I control you. I'll keep you from leaving, Derek. I want you!"

Derek stared defiantly into her blue eyes. Why couldn't he run away from her? Why did he stay here and take this? He had a little money. He could survive until he got a job. Mary Norton would take care of him and Alicen.

What was this power Janice had over him?

"You'd better leave," he said. "My half-hour's up, and someone's bound to come onto the court."

"They won't see me," Janice said. "Only you can see me."

She moved closer to him, putting her arms around him. Derek was surprised to find she smelled like flowers. No, like the beach. And then like the perfume Elaine had always worn. He closed his eyes and gave in to her.

"Court time is over, sir," a voice said.

Derek's eyes snapped open. He was standing alone, his racket hanging at his side.

"I'm sorry," he said, embarrassed. "I played too hard."

"Why don't you relax in the whirlpool?" the man said.

Derek smiled. He went into the locker room, looking around, expecting her to show up. She was making him paranoid. Even the whirlpool didn't help. Derek got out when the memory of Liza came to him—the day they had slipped beneath the water together. Where was Liza now?

What had Janice done to her?

Derek cut off that thought, like he had cut off so many others, and went to the locker room to shower and dress. He was surprised to see it was nearly two o'clock before he left the building. He passed a tanned, blond-haired man on his way out, but didn't even notice him.

Melanie moved slowly back and forth in the antique rocking chair as she stared out the bay windows at the sky. She had been unable to work, nervously waiting for Gary's call. Why was it taking so long?

She thought of Alicen and felt a mixture of pity, anger, and of relief. It was easy to handle a thirteen-year-old mortal, wasn't it?

She felt a hand on her shoulder. Gina, who had come home from school just a half hour earlier, wondered why her mother looked so sad. It had something to do with daddy, of course. She knew her father would never go out with Kyle so sick.

"Where's daddy?" she asked.

Melanie turned her gaze from the window and leaned sideways against the chair's slats. Gina was looking at her with worried eyes, eyes that told Melanie she wanted to know the truth. Yet Melanie couldn't give in to them. How could she tell this beautiful young girl about the rats and rabies?

"He went to the hospital for tests," she said at last.

"He had tests done just a short while ago," Gina said warily.

"I know," Melanie said, building the lie, "but this bad weather made his bones hurt so much that he figured he'd better have them checked out. He'll be staying overnight, but I'm sure he'll be back tomorrow."

"Oh, mom," Gina sighed, putting her arms around Melanie's neck. "Everything is so bad lately, just when we were going to start a nice summer." She pulled away. "How's Kyle?"

"Sleeping," Melanie said. "His fever is broken, but his temperature isn't normal yet. I'll call the doctor if things don't change more drastically by tomorrow."

"Poor Kyle," Gina said. "And damned old Alicen!"

"Gina!"

Gina frowned. "I'm sorry. But she is. She wouldn't talk to me again today. Even when I tried to make her think I'd believe her story about Kyle. I mean, we haven't heard her side yet. It's only fair."

"Alicen won't talk to me, either," Melanie said.

"She's weird," Gina replied. "She didn't talk to anyone today. Not even Jamie Hutchinson, and she's in love with him."

"Jamie Hutchinson?" Melanie repeated. "Is he the red-haired boy I met the day of the bus accident?"

"Yeah."

And the one who got Alicen started on all this, with his stories of murder, Melanie thought.

But she didn't tell Gina this. Instead, she used the opportunity to change the subject. She asked about Jamie, and soon Gina was babbling on about the boys in her school. The mood lightened, and both mother and daughter began to relax. Until the phone rang. It was Gary, at last.

"No rabies," he said.

"Thank God," Melanie whispered. She fought tears of relief and managed to laugh at herself for spending the entire afternoon in that damned rocking chair, expecting the worst and accomplishing nothing.

"When are you coming home?" she asked.

"That's the clincher," Gary said. "The fall I took messed me up a little. I'll be here for the weekend."

"Oh, God!"

"Melanie, Derek is there if you need help," Gary said.

"I know that," Melanie answered. "And I can take care of things myself. I'm worried about you. What's wrong with you?"

"Just a bad sprain in my ankle," Gary said. "It isn't too serious."

"But Gary," Melanie protested, "your legs weren't strong to begin with. Are you sure it isn't serious, or are you just trying to make me feel better?"

"I could put Dr. Norton on the line," Gary suggested.

Melanie sighed. "I believe you."

There was a long silence, in which Melanie heard the distant sound of the hospital P.A. system. Then she said, "What am I going to tell the children?"

"Haven't they asked yet?"

"Gina did," said Melanie. "Nancy's at a birthday party,

195

and of course Kyle is sleeping. I told Gina you were just going in for more tests."

"That's good enough."

"But I told her you'd be coming home tomorrow," Melanie said.

"You can think of some excuse," Gary said. "Our kids know how slow hospitals are."

Melanie nodded, as if Gary could see her. "I love you," she said.

"I love you," Gary answered. "Don't worry. I'll be home before you know it."

At dinner Melanie told Gina and Nancy about slow hospitals. They listened sympathetically, Nancy sad that her daddy was sick again, Gina not believing a word of her mother's story. But she knew better than to push things. It was bad enough that just the three of them were sharing dinner. Kyle, of course, was unable to join them, Alicen refused to eat, and Derek hadn't yet come home.

In the loneliness of the house that night, Melanie was unable to sleep. She decided to go downstairs and read for a little while. She curled herself up on the sofa in the library, her head on a bolster, and flipped lazily through a book.

A few pages blew over in a cold wind that swept through the room. Melanie sat up, looking around. It seemed her heart had stopped beating.

She heard a familiar voice. "Melanie," it said.

"You've come back again," Melanie said when the dark-haired, ragged woman appeared. She didn't shrink away, knowing this woman was her friend.

"I've come to warn you for the last time," the woman said. "You must leave this place, before it is too late."

"I can't leave," Melanie said. "I have a sick child, who can't be moved. But—you said this is your last time? Why?"

"I took great risks coming here," the woman said. "If I return again, she will surely learn of me."

"Who is she?" Melanie asked. "At least tell me that!"

"I dare not speak her name," the woman said.

"Then tell me why you've come to help me. I don't know who you are."

"You know me," the woman said. "It is because of me that evil fell upon this house. His love for me has condemned my lover to eternal suffering in hell. But I am a good Christian woman, and perhaps, by the mercy of God, I can lessen his suffering. I came here to temper tɪ. evil of this house with kindness. But no one listens to me, and she is still strong!"

Melanie reached out a hand to put it on the woman's shoulder. But the woman shrank away from her.

"I must leave now," she said. "My Jacob awaits my return."

She was gone. Melanie stared at the now empty space where the woman had just stood, unmoving. *My Jacob?*

Melanie shot to her feet and cried out: *Lydia?*"

There was no answer. But Melanie knew now who the woman was. It was Lydia Browning—Jacob Armand's lover! The woman who had been burned at the stake for witchcraft while Jacob stood witness. It was the pursuit of her that had brought Jacob's wrath down on Melanie's family the year before.

But why had Lydia come? Did this mean Jacob Armand had nothing to do with all this? Lydia kept talking of a woman. Who? What woman had reason to hate the Van-Burens so?

There were too many questions. And Melanie feared the answers would come all too soon.

25

Alicen could barely make out Kyle's silhouette in the darkness of his room. She stood near his bed, a pillow clutched in her hands, listening to the uneven sounds of his breathing. The doctor had said he had caught pneumonia up on the roof, and they were blaming her for it. As the other Alicen, she had believed in her innocence, but now she remembered the incident on the roof. She smiled. Her mother had been pleased with her.

Now it was time to finish the job . . . .

With her fingers tightening around the pillow, Alicen leaned closer to the sleeping figure. Closer—

Kyle stirred in his sleep, mumbling something. Alicen backed away, her heart pounding. Had she wakened him?

"Do it," a voice commanded.

Alicen nodded. "Okay, mommy."

And the pillow was pressed to Kyle's freckled, angelic face.

Alicen pushed with all her might, hearing her mother's voice. "Kill him, Alicen! Kill the brat!"

Emotionless, Alicen stared down at the little figure. Mommy said kill. Mommy loved her. Mommy made her do the right things—

"AAAUUUGGGHHí"

It was Alicen's own cry. Something had struck her under the chin—a small, bare foot. She regained herself and threw her body on top of Kyle's. Somehow, she had pressed the pillow at the wrong angle, leaving a channel in the folds for Kyle to breathe through. He was fully awake, kicking and screaming.

"Mommy!"

"Shhhh!" Alicen hissed.

"Stop it! Stop!" Kyle yelled hoarsely, his screams torturing his sore throat.

He was like a tiger under Alicen's body, clawing and kicking and biting. Alicen couldn't handle him much longer. Why wasn't her mother helping her?

At that moment Melanie burst into the room to find Alicen straddling Kyle, her fingers around his small neck. Kyle's face was crimson with rage and fear, and his arms and legs seemed to be everywhere. Without a moment's hesitation, Melanie ran to the bed, grabbed Alicen by the hair, and threw her across the room. The girl cried out in pain and ran out. Ignoring her, Melanie climbed onto the bed and took Kyle in her arms.

"Oh, God," she whispered. "Oh, my God."

Over Kyle's blond curls, growing wet with her tears, she saw a blue-and-white-striped pillow. A pillow that didn't belong in Kyle's room.

"Alicen tried to hurt me," Kyle whimpered.

"Shh," Melanie said. "Mommy's here. It's okay."

"Make her go away!" Kyle cried.

"I'll do that," Melanie promised. "Alicen won't hurt anyone again."

She was furious. How could anyone hurt a little boy? Kyle had suffered so much. Alicen had been cruel to lure him onto the roof through that trapdoor. And now the pillow—

Her thoughts skipped backward. Through the trapdoor? But how did Alicen know about it? Melanie herself had only discovered it a few months earlier.

Was she the someone, that mysterious "she" that Lydia had warned about?

She wished Gary was there. Or even Derek. Where the hell was he? He'd been gone all day long, leaving this mess to her. God damn him, Melanie thought. She's his daughter.

"Mom, what's going on?"

Gina was at the door, holding hands with her sister. Both girls were in pink nightgowns, barefoot. Nancy had her thumb in her mouth. Her blue eyes seemed to fill her face.

"Did you see Alicen?" Melanie asked.

"She ran by me," Gina said. "She was crying. What's wrong?"

"She tried to kill your brother," Melanie said, before she could stop herself. She was too angered to smooth things for her children's sake. Gina cried out, and Nancy's face contorted as if she would start crying.

"I hate Alicen!" Gina cried. "She's mean and bad! I *hate* her!"

"Make her go away, mommy," Nancy said.

"I will," Melanie said. She opened her arms, and her daughters ran to her.

"Why is Alicen so mean?" Nancy asked, her round face pressed against Melanie's stomach.

"Alicen's sick," Melanie said. "She's a sick little girl."

Gina's frown deepened, but she didn't say anything. Melanie could almost feel the child's emotions. She crushed her children to her and said, "No one will hurt you. Never again."

She knew she should leave the house at once. If Lydia had been telling the truth, then their unseen enemy could strike at any moment. But how could she leave? How could she move the children, when one was so very sick? More important, where would she go at this hour of the night?

So, Melanie did the next best thing. That night she took the room next to Alicen's, leaving the door open. There was no way she could get past Melanie's room without her knowing. Melanie's eyes didn't close once that night, and her ears were tuned for any unusual noise. The house was deadly silent, except for an occasional mumble from Alicen's room. What was she saying, over and over? *Mommy?*

She thought about the trapdoor, meaning to ask Derek about it when she saw him tomorrow. She prayed he would say he had told Alicen it was up there.

At four in the morning, Melanie heard the front door open. Derek had returned home at last.

Melanie had gotten her daughters off to school the next morning and had gone upstairs to paint. But how could she concentrate? An hour's work had produced a hideous piece of garbage. It was the work of an amateur, not the professional she was supposed to be. The colors were all wrong, the buildings out of proportion. Angrily, Melanie picked it up and threw it across the room.

"Hey!"

It had struck Derek. Well fine, Melanie thought. He deserves it.

"It's about time you're up," she snapped.

Derek bent to pick up the painting without answering her. He propped it on the sofa.

"I was in late last night," he said.

"I know," Melanie said. "Where the hell were you?"

Derek backed away a little. He couldn't tell her where he had been. After leaving Janice, he had driven for miles and miles, clear out to Montauk. He'd driven until he was ready to drop from exhaustion, and then had fallen asleep at a rest stop. He hadn't wanted to come home to that woman or to Alicen. And now Melanie was giving him this.

"I don't think that's any of your business," he said quietly.

Melanie lifted a small can of turpentine and slammed it down on a table.

"It damn well is my business!" she screamed. "That brat of yours tried to murder my son last night!"

Derek fell down to the couch as if Melanie had punched him. His mouth hung open, and he stared up at Melanie in disbelief. Alicen had tried to kill Kyle?

But why was he so surprised? He had known this was coming.

"Oh, don't sit there like an idiot," Melanie growled. "Don't you have anything to say?"

Derek breathed deeply. "Tell me what happened," he said with forced calm.

"I heard Kyle screaming and ran to his room," Melanie said. "I found Alicen in his bed, with her hands around his neck. And there was a pillow on the floor that didn't belong in his room. She had tried to smother him, Derek."

Derek rubbed at his eyes. "Dear God."

He looked up at Melanie. "Where is my daughter?"

"She locked herself in her room," Melanie said. "Derek, I want her out of this house. No later than Monday, even if she has to go without you."

"I'll do what I can," Derek said, knowing he would never be able to get away from the house. "Let me talk to my daughter."

A few moments later, he knocked at Alicen's locked door, but there was no answer.

"What should I do, mommy?" Alicen whispered.

"Let him in."

"Alicen!" Derek called.

Alicen walked across the room and opened the door. Derek entered the room, saw a filmy cloud by the window, and frowned. He knew what that cloud was, even if Alicen didn't. And it was about time Alicen *did* know.

"That isn't your mother," he said abruptly.

In the silence that followed, Derek waited for the consequences. But Alicen merely gave her head a shake, and disembodied laughter filled the room.

"Derek, she's as much in my power as you are," a voice said. "She thinks I'm her mother, the little fool!"

"You bitch!" Derek roared, pushing Alicen aside to lunge at the filmy mass hovering over the floor. His hands slammed hard against the window. The laughter continued.

"Derek!"

Melanie had entered the room just as he fell against the window. She looked at him, then at Alicen. Derek straightened himself, rubbing his wrists.

"Please leave this to me, Melanie," he said, approaching Alicen. "She's my daughter."

"I heard someone yell, and—"

She turned back to Alicen when she heard her speaking. The girl was rocking back and forth on the bed, glaring at Melanie.

"I want you to die," she sneered. "I want *all* of you to die."

It wasn't Alicen's voice at all. Melanie stared wide-eyed at her, terror filling her. Why did she recognize that voice? Where had she heard it before?

"Go away!" Derek yelled, not at Melanie, but at the spirit in Alicen's body.

"Derek, what's wrong with her?" Melanie demanded.

"Die!" Alicen screeched. "Die! Die! Die!"

201

Suddenly Derek burst into tears. His macho, self-assured image was shattered, and he felt no shame when he ran to Melanie's arms.

"Please help me," he sobbed.

"Derek, she'll be okay," Melanie soothed, as much to reassure herself as him. She felt terror creeping inside her. Alicen's voice stayed in her mind, taunting her. She knew that voice. But how? From where?

"Derek, come out of the room," she said. "There's so much to discuss. Alicen will be okay for a while."

And then, as she had done so many times when comforting her children, she kissed him gently.

There was a scream, and suddenly Alicen was on her father's back, pummeling him. "You're mine! You're mine!"

Derek fought her, gathering his strength back together. He knew it wasn't his daughter who reacted so jealously to that simple kiss. And it wasn't his daughter he struck so violently. As Melanie watched in horror, he threw her on the bed and slapped her again and again. Melanie grabbed his arms and tried to pull him away.

"She's out, Derek! Stop it!"

He ignored her, seeing Janice's face.

"Derek, let it go!"

At last she managed to jerk him away from the child before he killed her. Derek stared down at Alicen, his mouth open in shock. What had he done? She was innocent Alicen again, her round face covered with ugly red marks. A bruise grew under one eye.

Ashamed of himself, that he had let himself give in to his emotions, Derek let out a wail. He turned and ran from the room, wanting to get as far away as possible.

"Derek, come back!" Melanie cried, chasing after him.

She caught him just as he reached the front door and raced around him to block his path. Breathing heavily, she pointed to the living room and said, "Please come inside and talk to me. There's something going on here, and I want to know what it is."

"My daughter—"

"I think it's more than your daughter, Derek," Melanie said. "I don't know why, but I do. Please sit down and talk to me!"

Derek nodded slowly, not knowing what he'd say to her. The two entered the living room together and sat on the burgundy sofa. Melanie brushed her hair out of her face and said, "Derek, some things have happened lately that make me wonder if your daughter is simply disturbed, or if she's somehow—say, possessed."

"There's no such thing as possession," Derek said, though no one believed in it more strongly than he.

"Derek, you don't really know the history of this house," Melanie said. "What we told you of Jacob Armand was only the beginning. But there's much more. This is an evil house, Derek. And a young girl like Alicen could easily fall victim to it."

And a full-grown man like me, Derek thought bitterly.

"What—uh—what makes you say this?" he asked.

"Two things," Melanie said, "although I'm sure I could think of a few more. Firstly, the fact that Alicen knew there was a trapdoor to the roof. I never told her that, and as far as I know, neither did Gary. Why would he? And secondly, that voice I heard. I know that voice, Derek! I can't place it, but I've heard it before."

Derek said nothing. He turned and stared into the cold fireplace, trying to come up with an answer. Then he heard a voice in his head, telling him exactly what to say. He turned back to Melanie, his expression serene.

"There are simple answers to those things," he said, repeating the words in his mind. "Gary told me of the trapdoor, and I mentioned it to Alicen, not realizing she'd be foolish enough to investigate it."

"That makes sense," Melanie said. "But the voice?"

"Liza's voice," Derek said very quickly. "Alicen is tremendously jealous of my relationship with Liza. She was tormenting me, using that voice. That's what you recognized."

"Derek, I never met Liza," Melanie said.

"But you did speak to her on the phone once or twice," Derek said. "Which would explain why you didn't recognize the voice right away."

Melanie thought a moment. It made so much sense, and she desperately wanted to believe in Derek's explanations. Why then, did she still feel so uneasy?

"Derek, that child should be put in a hospital," she said. "Not only for her sake, but for my children's safety."

Derek, who on the outside appeared very calm, was being torn apart by guilt and shame. The mention of a hospital for Alicen made him want to scream with rage. He'd beaten his daughter. He'd beaten a little girl.

"No!" he cried. "No, she stays until I leave. Monday—I promise you."

"Derek, she needs a doctor *now,*" Melanie insisted.

"No!" Derek jumped to his feet and ran from the room. Before Melanie could stop him, he was out to his car and climbing behind the wheel. He ignored Melanie's calls and sped down the hill.

As he drove along the beachside, he saw mothers with their children. Their fresh faces and smiles made him think all the more of his hateful deed. He was grateful when he was at last able to turn onto Houston Street. Its steel and asphalt simplicity were soothing to him.

When he reached the intersection of the main street into town, he stopped and caught his breath. He could keep going straight, of course. Houston Street led to an exit ramp for the parkway, and the parkway would take him far, far away. He could forget Alicen, Liza, the VanBurens—

Suddenly he felt a touch on his shoulder. It was Janice.

"Can't you leave me alone for a moment?"

"Not when you try to get away from me," Janice said. Anger flashed in her blue eyes.

"How did you know what I was thinking?"

"I know everything in your mind," she said.

Derek began to drive again. "You made me hurt my daughter."

"You hated her anyway."

"I never hated her!"

Janice ignored the outburst. Keeping his eyes on the road, Derek turned the car into town. He tried to pretend she wasn't there, so hideously close to him.

"Where are you going?" He didn't answer. "Where are you going?" Janice asked again. "You're going to that bitch Liza's house, aren't you? Well, you won't find her! You'll never see her again. She's dead, Derek Miller."

"Leave me alone!" Derek shouted.

He heard her laughter and wanted to strike her with all his might. But when he turned, she was gone. He sped to Liza's house, all the time praying Janice was only taunting him. He wanted to stop and catch his breath but somehow found himself running up the stairs and pounding on Liza's door.

"Hold your horses!" someone yelled from inside—a man's voice. The door jerked open, and Derek found himself looking at a blond-haired man. The two studied each other for a moment before Owen spoke.

"What do you want?" he asked. "You could've broken the door down!"

"I—I'm looking for L-Liza Crewe," Derek said, panting

heavily. The run up the stairs had exhausted him—he wasn't in the shape he used to be.

"You're Derek, right?"

"Yea," Derek said. "Who're you?"

Liza's found someone new.

"Owen Crewe," was the reply. "I'm Liza's brother."

Derek simply nodded. He had almost hoped it was a new lover that kept Liza away from him. That would at least prove she was still alive.

"Come in," Owen said. "I've been looking for you."

Derek sat on a couch he had shared with Liza several weeks earlier, while Owen sat in a leather and chrome chair across the room. He studied his face for so long that Derek felt himself becoming nervous. There again, that was Janice's doing. He'd never been paranoid in his life.

"You seemed in a rush to get in here," Owen said at last. "What's the matter?"

What was the matter? How could Derek answer that? There was no voice in his head to tell him what to say now. So he thought carefully before answering.

"I was driving through town," he said finally, "and I was thinking about Liza. I've been trying to get in contact with her for a week. I thought she was mad at me, but she would have come around with an explanation by now, wouldn't she?"

Owen nodded.

"Anyway," Derek continued, "I decided to come up here and confro—make her listen to me once and for all. If I did something to offend her, I'd like to know what it was. But I know I didn't do anything wrong. I keep wondering, then, why the hell she disappeared."

"That makes two of us," Owen said. "I came up from Florida for a convention last week. I have to say I found it a little unnerving to come here and find my sisters missing. Liza's not one to go wandering off somewhere without letting anyone know."

"No, she isn't," Derek said.

"Why don't we go over that last time you were together?" Owen suggested. Seeing a defensive look in Derek's eyes, he added, "I think it would help, don't you? There may be a clue."

"I've been over it a thousand times," Derek said. "She came to visit me at my home. We went for a walk on the beach, and I asked her to marry me—we've been dating awhile. She said yes and seemed ecstatic. So, after a while, we said goodbye and made plans to see each other again."

That was a lie, since Derek had made no such plans. Or maybe he just didn't remember them, he thought defensively.

"There was no argument, then," Owen said.

"None whatsoever," Derek answered.

He stood up and walked to the window at the back of the room. Staring out at the town, all green and bright with summer, he felt something rise from his stomach. He held his breath for a moment, then said quietly, "I think something happened to her."

Owen stood up now. "I've been trying to keep that thought from my mind," he said. "What makes you say so?"

"I don't know," Derek lied. "There are just too many unanswered questions."

"We could look for her together," Owen said.

Derek's reply was too swift. "No!"

He slowed himself down. "I mean," he said, "it would probably be best to let the police handle this."

He wouldn't admit he was terrified of what he'd find if he looked too hard. Owen was staring at him again, the suspicious bastard. Did he think Derek was responsible for Liza's disappearance?

He made an excuse to leave. "Listen, my daughter is home sick," he said, hating the truth in those words. "I should be with her. What if I come back tomorrow?"

"Please," Owen said, feeling uneasy about Derek's swift goodbye.

Without saying anything more, Derek left the house. He was too busy with his own thoughts to look up in his rear-view mirror a few minutes later to see that Owen was following him.

26

Smiling, Melanie stepped away from Kyle's bed. His fever had gone down considerably and was now only a degree above normal. He'd be his old, energetic self in just a few days. She wished she could say the same about Alicen. Applying lotion to the cuts on her face had brought out the mother instinct in Melanie. Seeing that little girl, all battered and so frail, she couldn't help feeling sorry for her. She was sick and in need of help and understanding. She wasn't responsible for her actions.

But, then, who was?

The voice she had used in her threats stuck in Melanie's mind. She wanted to believe that it was Liza's voice, but something made her think otherwise. She had an uneasy feeling that she had heard that voice before, and not when talking on the phone with Derek's girlfriend. Still, it made sense. Alicen might have mimicked the voice to make her father angry. Melanie knew that Derek had been unable to get in touch with his girlfriend. And, for God's sake, who else would the voice belong to?

Gary would have fits if he heard you now, she told herself. *Stop it! It was Liza's voice you heard.*

She went downstairs to the kitchen. The children would be home soon, and she wanted to fix them a nice dinner. She would do it more to prove to herself than to them that nothing supernatural was going on. A good, ordinary meal on the table would show Gina and Nancy that, in spite of the bad things that had happened in the last few days, everything was going to be all right. Or so Melanie hoped.

But to her frustration, she opened the refrigerator to find it practically empty. In all the confusion of the past week, she had forgotten to stock up on groceries. And the weekend was coming.

Melanie hated to leave Kyle alone with Derek, remembering his angered outburst that morning. But what was she supposed to tell the girls when they came home? That she was too frightened to go out of the house? But she wanted them to see that life would go on as usual, and that meant having dinner with their mother. So Melanie reasoned that Derek had been angered only momentarily at Alicen, and wouldn't harm Kyle. Besides, if she left soon, she would be home before the girls. And Kyle would probably sleep all afternoon.

Just then, she heard the front door open. She left the kitchen and went out in the hallway to meet Derek. He looked tired, his eyes rimmed with red. Melanie went to him.

"I suppose you called a doctor for Alicen," he said.

"I thought I should let you do that," Melanie said.

"Thank you," Derek said, grateful no one else would have to know of his terrible crime.

"Now I have a favor to ask of you," Melanie said. "Would you stay with Kyle for just a little while so I can go to the store? The refrigerator is empty, and I don't want my kids starving on top of everything else."

"I guess it would be all right." Derek sighed.

"Don't worry," Melanie said. "I'll be back before the girls are home."

She left the house.

It was so silent. Derek hated that. He wanted the house to creak and moan, just to let him know it was like any other old house. But it wasn't, was it? Any moment, that heavy silence could fall down on him. She'd be back, for certain, knowing how vulnerable he was right now.

But the house remained silent. Derek opened the door to his room and looked around, expecting to see her. No sign of her. He stretched himself on the bed, putting his hands behind his neck and staring at the ceiling.

He waited.

Hearing the sound of an engine, Owen Crewe ducked behind a tree. He watched the car drive by him on the gravel road, seeing a blond woman behind the wheel. When she passed, he came out of his hiding place and continued up the road. Not wanting Derek to see him, he had parked his car at the public beach and had walked the mile to these woodlands. He could see the huge white house at the top of the hill. How could anyone afford a place like that, he wondered? He thought of Liza's reaction upon seeing the place, with those towers and that porch.

But he was more interested in the woodlands that surrounded it. They were so thick that anything could have happened to Liza in them—and no one would have seen. They led to the beach, no doubt, the last place Derek said he had been with Liza. Owen had a feeling that Derek had been lying when he said he knew nothing of Liza's disappearance.

At last he found a path that cut through the woods. Looking around to be sure no one was watching, he turned onto it.

"I don't see mom's car," Gina said as she and Nancy climbed up the hill, leaving the school bus behind them.

208

"Maybe she went out to a gallery or something?" Nancy suggested.

"Yeah, but she wouldn't have left Kyle alone," Gina said. "Not with crazy Alicen."

She broke into a run, her long legs covering the ground in strides. Nancy protested, unable to keep up with her, and finally let her sister go on alone. She climbed the porch steps and entered through the door Gina had left open.

"Gina!" she cried.

"I'm up in Kyle's room," Gina called back.

Nancy found her sister sitting on Kyle's bed. The little boy was fully awake, propped against his pillow. Nancy, too, jumped on the bed. The three children began to talk.

"Do you think all this stuff is scarier than last year?"

"I don't know, Kyle," Gina said. "Everybody got hurt, like last year. But this time we know why. It wasn't a ghost."

"I don't wanna talk about ghosts," Nancy pouted.

"Okay," Gina said. "But if you ask me, Alicen's scarier. How could she do all this?"

"I hate her," Kyle stated.

"Where is she, anyway?" Gina asked.

"How should I know?" Kyle said. "As long as she stays there."

"And where's mommy?" Nancy asked. "We didn't see her car. Did she go away?"

"No, she had to go to the grocery," Kyle sail. "I started yelling for her, and Derek came in and told me." He brought a hand to his throat. "Boy, that hurt when I yelled."

"Mom left you alone with crazy Alicen?" Gina said.

"Derek said there was no food in the house," Kyle reported. "Gina, can't we stop this? Talking about Alicen gives me the creeps."

"Sure," Gina obliged. She looked around the room for something to do, and underneath Kyle's dresser, she spotted a Monopoly game. She pulled it out and set it up on Kyle's lap.

"Mommy'll be home soon, I bet," she said as she shook the dice.

They tried to concentrate on the game, pushing aside their fears. But Melanie didn't come home soon, and after a while it became too much to wait for her. Nancy started to whine, and Kyle became listless. Trying to cheer them, and herself, Gina put the tiny metal dog inside the little car and pretended it was driving around the board. The trick worked, and soon all the children were laughing. It was nervous laughter, uncontrollable and silly. To the unseen woman who saw it, it was also hateful. Janice went to the bed and knocked the board from it.

"Kyle, you kicked it!" Gina said.

"I guess so," Kyle answered, still laughing. "Isn't it funny?"

Funny! Janice echoed. *When I'm through today, you won't be laughing.*

She willed herself to Derek's room. Gathering herself into her most solid form, she climbed onto the bed. Derek's eyes opened wide when she planted an icy kiss on his lips.

"It's time," she said.

"Time?"

"You know what I mean," Janice replied. "They're alone, aren't they?"

She kissed him again, running her cold fingers through his thick hair. Then she sat back on his hips. The bed did not sag beneath her, but Derek felt pressure. He frowned.

"They're just kids," he said. "What the hell could they have done to you?"

"Don't ask questions," Janice said, rising. "Stand up and come with me."

Derek sat up, pressing his fists into the mattress. But he didn't move. Somehow, the visit with Owen Crewe had strengthened him. He wouldn't listen to anyone who hurt his beloved Liza.

"No," he said.

Janice turned, her eyes surprised.

"What did you say?"

"I said no," Derek repeated. His strong voice belied the weakness in his stomach. But he wouldn't stop now. "If you want to hurt them, I know I can't stop you. But I won't help you."

"You bastard!" Janice screeched. "You'll do as I say!"

She lunged at him, her fingers curled like talons. They sought the flesh of his cheeks and ripped down them. Derek cried out and pulled away.

"You're my slave!" Janice hissed, striking him.

"No!"

He stared into her eyes, and saw them change. The face blurred, widened, became Elaine's face. But this time, Derek was able to look at it. He knew it wasn't his wife's face at all, but a cruel apparition. Janice screamed with rage and struck him again.

210

"You're my slave!" she cried. "My slave and my lover! You'll obey me!"

How could he dare defy her? She would show him. He would learn what terrible things she could do to him, in spite of the fact that she craved his affections almost above vengeance against the VanBurens.

She threw herself at him, pressing her fingers to his throat. He gagged and tried to grab for her wrists. Stupid thing to do, they passed through them as if nothing were there.

"Go away!" Derek cried. "You don't exist!"

Janice laughed and bent to kiss him. He was so handsome. Her tongue pried his lips open, found his tongue, and sucked hard at it, as if to drain his courage. Derek sank down away from her, wishing he could fall through the bed, through the floor. Anything to get away from her passionate kisses!

"Let me alone," he demanded hoarsely.

"Never," Janice said.

She tossed her head back, the lackluster hair falling over her thin, lifeless shoulders. She began to stare at him. The filminess in her eyes began to drain away, and the irises became as sharp and clear as they had ever been when Janice was alive. In those eyes there was a devilish power, a power Derek could not resist. It weakened him more than the sight of Elaine's twisted face, more than the thought that he might never see Liza again. Why? Why did those eyes have such power over him?

After all his resistance, it took only a pair of eyes to turn him inside out. He sat up and put his head against her, not realizing what he was doing. The room began to spin, and her voice sounded as if she were speaking through a long tunnel.

"Take them where their mother won't find them," she said, stroking his thick hair as if he were a child. "I will be there in time to punish them. But first they must suffer in darkness."

"Suffer," Derek said.

Janice kissed him. And then she was gone.

Derek sat up on the bed, his head dropped down to his chest. His heart thudded so loudly that he thought everyone could hear. He tried to quiet it. Otherwise, how could he sneak up on them?

Rubbing his eyes, he stood up and walked from the room. Alicen was waiting in the hallway, dressed in a loose white nightgown.

"Daddy?"

Derek moved past her without answering. Alicen watched his retreating figure, feeling tears rise. She had been lying in bed, knowing he was across the hall, waiting for him to come apologize for beating her that morning. Why did he have to hurt her so, now that mommy was back again? Why couldn't they be a happy family again?

She'd get even with him, that's what she'd do. She'd go into his room and tear it apart and mess up his clothes and use a crayon all over the furniture and . . .

The three VanBuren children, having grown bored with the Monopoly game, were now coloring—even Gina, who was too old for such things. But it made Kyle happy when she shared things with him. They colored the pictures, leaving the game board and all its pieces on the floor. Cleaning up could wait until later.

"Nancy, the sun is yellow," Kyle said. "Why are you making it purple?"

"I like purple."

"Well, I think it's dumb," Kyle said. "Everyone knows—"

His words were cut off when the door swung open. Derek entered the room and stopped to look at them. The three children didn't speak, mesmerized by the coldness in his eyes. He looked so mean.

Gina moved closer to Kyle and pulled Nancy to her. The three children huddled together, watching Derek move to Kyle's closet. He removed a flannel robe and held it out to the boy. At last Gina spoke up.

"What's going on?" she demanded.

"Put this on, Kyle," Derek ordered. "We're going out."

"Out?" Gina echoed. "Are you nuts or something? Kyle can't go out!"

"Don't talk back," Derek said in a warning tone.

"But why do you want us to go out?" Kyle asked. "Mommy'll be home soon, and she'll be so mad."

"If you don't put on the robe and come with me," Derek cautioned, "I'll get my belt and—"

He moved closer to the bed, away from the door. Seeing a chance, Gina jumped from the bed and ran as fast as she could. Derek tried to grab her flying hair, but she was too fast for him. She disappeared around the corner of the hallway, Derek running after her.

I have to get to the stairs! Gina thought.

But someone was standing there. A blond woman. Gina stopped in her tracks. Her mouth dropped open, and she gaped wide-eyed at the woman who blocked her way down. She couldn't be there, she was dead! Crazy Derek was making her so scared she was seeing things.

"You're aren't real," Gina said, her voice trembling. "You're dead!"

But the woman didn't go away. Frozen, Gina stood her ground, not thinking that Derek was coming to find her. She could hear him yelling down one of the hallways. But she was too mesmerized by the vision. The woman smiled wickedly at her. Once Gina had loved her smile. She had been so sweet then. Mommy had met her when they were having all that trouble with Jacob Armand, and she always made them feel better. But Jacob had killed her, mommy said. She was dead.

"Gina, you God-damned brat!"

Derek's shouting broke the spell, and just as he lunged for her, she found her feet. Hardly feeling the floor, she sped down the hallway, reaching its end only to find there was no place to go. She turned, bursting into a bedroom with Derek only a few feet away.

"No!" Gina screamed even as she threw the door shut and locked it. Derek's body fell against it, pounding. The girl could feel vibrations all through her body as she leaned heavily against the door, crying. But after a few terrifying moments, the pounding stopped.

"I'll be back, Gina," Derek said.

Gina listened to the soft thudding of his shoes on the carpet as he retreated. Then, trembling, she turned around. Her breath caught in her throat—the room was in a complete shambles. Someone had torn the covers from the bed, and now they were tossed here and there. So were Derek's clothes, ripped from the room's single dresser and hanging from the bedposts and curtain rods as if they had been thrown around by a madman. Worse than this, the lovely antique bed and dresser were covered with crayon marks.

Gina looked around at all this in a stupor, not believing it. Her eyes fell on a message scrawled across the mirror on the closet door.

MOMMY AND DADDY LOVE ALICEN.

Now she heard a whimpering noise and turned to it. A moment later, Alicen stood up. She had been hiding behind the bed, and now she threw herself on it, oblivious of Gina. The other child felt herself crying again. No! She couldn't be locked here in this room, alone with crazy Alicen!

"I'm sorry, daddy," Alicen whimpered into the bare mattress. "I'm sorry."

Hearing her babbling made Gina all the more nervous, and she burst out sobbing. Alicen sat up, glaring at Gina. What was she doing in here? But then her eyes softened. Gina was her friend. She had made her happy that first day she'd come here. And she needed someone to talk to so much.

If she couldn't have a mother and father right now, a friend would do nicely. Just for now.

"Hi, Gina," she said, as if nothing were wrong.

"H-hi, Alicen," Gina replied, not knowing what else to say. How do you talk to a crazy person?

"I'm sorry I messed up this nice room," Alicen said. "I was mad at my father, 'cause he hurt me."

Gina took in the girl's bruised and bloodied face. For a moment, seeing that Alicen was just as vulnerable as any other girl, Gina forgot her fears. She went to the bed and sat down.

"Your father tried to hurt me, too," she said. "And he's got Kyle and Nancy. What'll he do with them?"

She was afraid of the answer, but didn't get one anyway. Alicen simply nodded.

"My father has a terrible temper," she said. "He's going to beat me for doing this, but I don't care."

"Your father shouldn't beat you," Gina said. "It's wrong."

What was he doing now, with Kyle and Nancy? She should run from the room to rescue them, but she was so afraid. Why didn't her mother come home?

"My mother won't let him hurt me, though," Alicen was saying now.

"Your mother?" Gina replied. "But she's dead."

"She is not!" Alicen cried. "She's right here in this house!"

Gina backed away, suddenly understanding. Janice had made Alicen believe she was her mother.

"Alicen, that isn't your mother at all," she said. "It's a woman named Janice Lors. She was murdered here seven months ago."

"No!"

"You don't have a mother!"

"Yes, I do, yes, I do! Dead people don't give beautiful presents!"

She jumped to the floor, pounding it with her fists and

214

screaming. She grabbed at the heavy floor grating and ripped it up with no effort and threw it across the floor. Her hand thrust into the dark crevice, and when she drew it back, she was holding Sarah's ring. Gina gasped.

"Mommy gave this to me!" she shouted triumphantly.

"Alicen, that's Sarah's ring! Your mother is—"

The door burst open. Derek was standing there, holding a gun.

"You're going to come with me quietly," he said, "or I'll blow your brains out."

Slowly, keeping her eyes on the round hole of the barrel, Gina stood up and went to him.

27

Melanie removed the purchases from her shopping cart and quickly filled the conveyor belt. She was angered at herself for having left the shopping until today, when everyone else was shopping for the weekend. A half-hour trip had turned into more than an hour. And there were still six people ahead of her on line.

She knew the children had been home about an hour now. If only she had sent Derek out to do this. The kids were probably worried about her. But at last she reached the cashier. Two prices had to be checked, slowing her down all the more. She almost ran out to her car when she was finished.

She would be home in a few minutes, she reassured herself.

But that wasn't to be. She turned a corner and found her way blocked by a truck pulling out of a factory driveway. There were four cars in back of her, and no way out.

"Well," she said, sighing, "they've done without me for an hour. They can survive a few minutes longer."

The cellar was cold. It gave no hint of the intense summer heat outside. Kyle coughed violently, the icy air constricting his lungs. Angered at the noise, Derek pressed the gun to the boy's head. Kyle forced himself to stop coughing.

Worse than being cold, the cellar was dark. Nancy began crying loudly. "I want my mommy!"

"Shut up!"

Derek waved the gun. Kyle stared up at him, wondering if the gun was loaded. In the next thought, he prayed his mother would come home soon. What was taking her so long?

Derek pushed them ahead of him. They walked slowly in the darkness, brushing away cobwebs, their shoes making soft noises on the concrete floor. At last, Derek stopped at a door on the back wall. He flung it open and motioned them inside.

"I don't wanna go in there," Nancy protested. "I want my mommy!"

Derek picked her up and threw her into the dark cave. Her little body landed on the sand floor of the storage room like a sack of flour. Before she could right herself, Gina and Kyle were pushed in beside her. Derek stooped down to let himself under the low door and placed a big flashlight on the floor. He turned it on, shining it at the three cowering children, then crawled over to them.

"My mommy'll be home real soon," Kyle said, his voice hoarse. He started coughing again.

"Shut up," Derek said. So much in Janice's power, he didn't know what he was saying. He worked without thinking, tying their small wrists and ankles with pieces of clothesline, and gagging their mouths. Then he went to the door and, lifting the flashlight from the floor, said, "It'll be over soon. Once she's punished you, it'll all be over."

Only Gina knew who "she" was. But why did Janice want to hurt them. Jacob Armand was the one who killed her, not them.

Derek shut the wooden door, sealing the room in total darkness. Nancy started to whimper behind her gag, and Gina moved through the darkness to lie beside her. Soon she felt Kyle's head on her shoulder. All they could do was pray their mother would come home soon.

Owen kicked a stone out of his path and continued on his walk. But he had been searching the woods for over an hour, and his feet ached. Spotting a log, he sat down to rest. No sooner had he stretched his legs out than his eyes were attracted by something glittering in the dirt. He leaned forward and lifted a silver and turquoise bracelet from a pile of wet leaves.

"This is Liza's," he said, recalling that he had given it to her a few Christmases back.

"It's *my* bracelet," he heard someone say.

Owen turned around to see a frail blond woman standing behind him. She looked insane, like the patients at the Fort Lauderdale mental hospital. He backed away from her.

"No," he said calmly. "This is my sister's bracelet. Do you know where she is? Her name is Liza."

"It's my bracelet," the blond screamed. "*Mine.* I knew you were out here. I knew you'd try to steal it."

Suddenly, to Owen's disbelief, she bent down and wrapped her thin arms around the log. She lifted it high in the air, as if it were made of paper.

He didn't wait to see if she could swing it at him. His feet were taking him off at top speed, running for dear life. He ran and ran until he reached the beach, not looking back when he heard her call his name.

"You're next, Owen Crewe!"

How did she know his name? As his feet pounded the sand and his lungs took in the hot, salty air, Owen told himself over and over not to be afraid. He had handled people like her before. It was his profession.

Yet something made him keep running, even when his shoes became heavy with water. He didn't stop until he reached the flat rocks of a jetty, where he threw himself down and panted loudly. He looked over his shoulder, expecting to see her behind him. But the beach was empty.

"You ass," he said to himself, turning on his back. "Some psychiatrist you are!"

He needed a place to rest and collect his thoughts. Then he would go back to the big white house, knock on the door, and confront Derek Miller face to face, as he should have done earlier. Then he might learn who that strange woman was. He climbed over the rocks to the public beach. Once he crossed them, he removed his sweat-soaked shirt and wet shoes and walked toward the crowds. God, how far away this all seemed from the loneliness of those woods.

He found an empty spot and sat down, bringing his knees up to his chin. Radios blasted all around him, children squealed, people talked loudly. Liza, who loved people, would love a place like this.

A sudden commotion in the water made him avert his eyes

from the jetty he'd just left. Two young boys in scuba gear were running to the shore, shouting something. The lifeguard stood up and blew his whistle at them. Curious, Owen got to his feet and shuffled to the small group that was gathering around the teen-agers.

"There's a car under the water!" one shouted, pointing. "We saw a body in it!"

"Sure, there is," the lifeguard drawled. "You think I'm crazy?"

"It's true," the boys insisted in unison. "It's true!"

"I think you'd better call the police," Owen said, staring at the innocent-looking blue water of Belle Bay.

He believed the boys. And, his stomach turning, he knew what the police would find when they came.

"Home at last," Melanie sighed to herself as she propped a grocery bag on one hip and unlocked the back door. Inside the kitchen she put two parcels down on the wooden table. Then she turned to go back outside, where two more bags were waiting in the trunk. But she decided she'd better go upstairs first to let them know she was home. She had been stuck in that traffic jam for twenty minutes.

Her voice, calling her children, rang through the house. But she heard no response. Melanie went upstairs to Kyle's room.

It was empty.

"What is this?" she demanded out loud.

She saw the Monopoly board on the floor, resting against the unmade bed, its pieces scattered everywhere. Kyle wasn't a messy child, but he was mischievous; he had probably used the golden opportunity of her absence to leave his bed. Melanie noticed his robe was missing from the closet and prayed he had taken it out himself.

She went out into the hall.

"Kyle?"

No answer. God, the house was quiet. Why didn't she hear the children talking or laughing? She went to Gina's room and when that proved empty, tried Nancy's. Then her studio and Gary's office. Why didn't her children answer her calls?

They couldn't have gone outside, she thought, her panic building.

Derek would know where they were. He'd tell her they were off playing somewhere. As angry as Melanie would be with Derek, she hoped to God that was the case. But Derek didn't answer when she knocked at the door. Thinking he might be taking a nap, Melanie carefully opened the door. She stepped into his room and cried out.

Like Gina, Melanie was at first too stunned to move when she saw the junkpile Derek's room had become. Sheets and blankets were torn from the bed, clothes strewn everywhere, swirls of crayon marked the headboard of the bed. Melanie almost screamed when she read the lipstick scrawling on the mirror.

MOMMY AND DADDY LOVE ALICEN

And below:

MOMMY AND DADDY KILL BAD CHILDREN

"Kill bad children," Melanie repeated, her voice choked.

Alicen's reflection appeared in the mirror. "They're all going to die," she sneered, in that horrible voice.

And suddenly Melanie recognized it.

"No!" she screamed. She went to Alicen and grabbed her roughly. "What have you done with my children? Where are they? Where are they?!"

"Mommy's going to kill them," Alicen said, in her own voice. "They're *bad* children."

"Oh, no," Melanie said, shaking her head. "No, they're good children. Why does she want to hurt them?"

Alicen shrugged. "I don't question my mother."

"Alicen, please," Melanie begged. "Tell me where she's taken my children."

Alicen shook her head and refused to answer. With a disgusted, frightened cry, Melanie pushed by her. She raced down the hall, crying loudly, *"Derek?"*

If he was there, he didn't answer. Neither did the children when she screamed their names. Derek must have kidnapped them.

It had to be. She couldn't possibly have heard that sneering voice a moment ago. It belonged to a dead woman.

(MOMMY AND DADDY KILL BAD CHILDREN)

"No," Melanie said. "No, this isn't happening."

She reached for the phone—it was dead. Trying to calm herself, she reached for her car keys and headed into the kitchen. She would drive to the police for help. She knew she couldn't handle this herself.

But the back door was closed tight, and locked.

"I *know* I left that open," Melanie cried. Quickly she opened the cupboard behind her to find the key. She was shaking so badly that she could hardly slide it into the lock. It clicked and turned, but the door wouldn't budge. It was as if someone had nailed it shut.

Without a moment's hesitation, Melanie ran to the front doors. She tried one, then the other. But they were sealed just as tightly, and she wasn't strong enough to break through them. She panicked for a moment, then realized the windows in the living room were big enough to crawl through. She hurried inside and saw to her shock that someone had snapped off their brass handles.

She grabbed the old slat-back rocker and lifted it high above her head. Using a strength unknown to her, she swung it forward, flying with it.

"Oh, God," she said, looking at the results. She had broken only a few panes, not enough to get out. Her shoulders felt as if she had torn them out, but she ignored the pain. She had to get to her children.

With a cry, she lifted the rocker again and tried to swing it forward. But she couldn't. Someone was holding it fast, behind her back. Melanie closed her eyes, afraid to turn around.

"Look at me, Melanie VanBuren," a voice said.

Melanie turned slowly, dropped the chair, and screamed.

"Are you so surprised to see me?" Janice asked. "You knew I was coming back, you murderess."

"No!" Melanie cried. "I'm not!"

"You are," Janice hissed. "You murdered me. You hit me across the head with a gun."

Suddenly Melanie remembered everything. She recalled the night of Gary's accident, when Janice had fallen under Jacob Armand's evil spell. She had tried to hurt Kyle, and Melanie had defended her son by hitting her with that pistol. But she had only stunned her. Jacob Armand was her murderer.

"No, it was *you*," Janice sneered, reading Melanie's thoughts. "*You*."

"Go away."

"Oh, no," Janice drawled. "Not until you pay for what you did to me."

Melanie found her legs and ran for dear life back to the—where? Where could she escape?

There was no chance. Derek was waiting in the dining room for her. As she lunged for the kitchen door, he tackled her and threw her to the floor.

"Let me go!"

She wrestled with him, feeling the sweat on his body,

220

hearing him growling at her. Her fingers found his eye sockets and dug in, yet somehow only scratched his eyelids. Giving a roar, Derek slapped at her hands.

"HELP! HELP, SOMEBODY!"

Down in the cellar, three terrified children cried softly as they heard their mother's screams. And in the dining room the smiling ghost of Janice Lors watched the two fighting. She wanted to see Melanie beaten, made to suffer for what she had done.

"Hurt her, Derek," she ordered, her voice filled with passion.

Melanie saw Derek's fist rise in the air. She screamed as it came down. There was a flash of pain, and then darkness.

Owen felt the muscles in the back of his legs tighten, and he started to breathe more deeply to calm himself. But no matter how hard he tried, he couldn't let himself believe the car being dragged out of the water wasn't his sister's. He was standing in the crowd, behind wooden police barricades. One look at the bumper sticker on the rusted, soaked automobile made him cry out and run forward, knocking down the barrier. It read:

FLORIDA: EVERY DAY IS SUN DAY

"Liza!" He screamed, running toward the car.

"Hey!" a cop shouted, lunging at him. He caught Owen by the arm.

"Let me go, damn you!" Owen shouted. "That's my sister!"

Still holding him fast, the cop turned and said, "Captain Davis? This guy says that girl's his sister."

Bryan Davis hurried to them and took Owen by both his shoulders. Owen's face was red with fury, his eyes flashing.

"Calm down, fellow," Bryan said gently. "Calm down and tell me what's going on."

"M-my sister has been missing for a week," Owen stammered. "I-I went up to the—"

His words were cut off when he heard the car door crash open, giving way to a crowbar. Jerking away from the policeman who held him, he walked in a daze to the car. Two other cops were pulling a corpse from the wreck, laying it carefully on the sand.

But, no, that couldn't be Owen's sister. That bloated, green, hideous thing wasn't beautiful Liza. Not when the face looked so round, the skin so tight it seemed ready to burst. And Liza had always smelled like roses. . . .

And she was nude. Someone had murdered her. And someone would pay.

Owen turned away from the horrid sight and started to cry. Bryan patted his arm gently, as pictures of the body were taken for evidence and notes were scribbled in reporters' pads.

When Owen calmed down a bit, Bryan at last said, "You were saying you went up somewhere?"

Owen nodded. "To that big house on the hill. My—my sister's lover lives there."

Bryan felt his heart jump. The VanBuren house?

"Come on," he said. "We're going up there."

"I want him to get the chair for this," Owen seethed.

"Yeah," Bryan said, not certain if Liza's boyfriend was the killer. But he didn't want to think of that right now. He gave orders to his men and had two cars follow him up the hill. Once at the house, he ordered them to stay put until called. If Derek Miller had murdered Liza Crewe, he might become violent upon seeing the police. So only Bryan and Owen walked up the stairs to the double doors. Bryan pounded loudly and rang the bell at the same time. No one answered.

"Open this door!" Owen shouted.

"Shh," Bryan said. "If he's here, he might be hiding. And there are other people in this house—innocent people. We don't want to scare them."

"What other people?" Owen demanded. "I don't care about other people."

He turned and continued to pound on the door. Inside the house, Melanie's ears perked to hear it. She turned, as if she could see the source of the noise through the walls of the kitchen. She tried in vain to cry out, but her mouth was gagged, and ropes held her fast to a chair—the same chair where Janice had sat seven months ago, when Melanie had killed her.

It had all come back to her, everything she had blocked from her mind since the night of Gary's accident. Jacob Armand hadn't killed Janice, *she* had. Janice had tried to hurt Kyle, and Melanie had stopped her. She had only meant to stun her friend but instead had killed her with that gun. Melanie understood now why she felt so guilty about Janice's death all these months. But it wasn't her fault. It was self-defense.

Now Janice and Derek were standing in front of her, their arms around each other. Derek's face was expressionless, but Janice's wore a smile, tasting the sweetness of revenge. She was making Melanie wait—death for a murderess couldn't be swift and painless. Melanie's tears made her all the more angry.

"Go ahead and cry," she sneered. "I haven't even begun with you."

The pounding on the front door stopped. *Oh, please,* Melanie thought. *Please come to the back door.*

Downstairs, the children had also heard the pounding. Had somebody come to rescue them? Was that why the knocking was so loud?

Little Kyle became so excited that he suddenly began to cough. Phlegm filled his throat, gagging him. He couldn't spit because of the gag.

He made strangling noises, falling forward. His coughing became so violent that Gina rolled toward him and tried to lift her hands from behind her and slap his back. But she couldn't. Someone had to find them before he choked.

Crying with fear and praying this would work, Gina lifted her bound feet and kicked the wall. They made a loud, satisfying thud. Again and again she kicked at the walls, and soon Nancy was joining her.

"What's that?" Derek asked, looking around.

"Those brats!" Janice cried.

She disappeared. Seconds later, Owen and Bryan were at the back door. Alerted by the pounding, Bryan had ordered his men to surround the house. Derek saw them through the window and ran from the room. There was a loud crash, and suddenly the door was hanging by one hinge.

"Oh, Lord," Owen said.

Quickly Bryan tore off Melanie's gag as another cop cut her ropes.

"She's got my children somewhere!" she cried, her voice hoarse.

"She?" Bryan echoed.

"You mean Derek Miller," Owen said.

"No," Melanie said firmly. "*She.*" She looked into Bryan's eyes. "Janice Lors."

Bryan backed away. Janice Lors? But she had been dead seven months.

And Jacob Armand had been dead nearly two hundred years on that November night when . . .

"Spread out over the house," he said over his walkie-talkie to his men. "We're looking for four kids, and a man."

No use telling them to look for someone they couldn't see.

"Where did the pounding come from, Mrs. VanBuren?" he asked.

Melanie shook her head. Where? It had come from everywhere, carried through every wooden beam of the house.

"Just find my babies, please," she cried, standing.

She hurried from the kitchen, Owen and Bryan at her heels. They broke off in separate directions, Melanie hurrying upstairs in spite of Bryan's protests. She knew where to find Derek. And she'd make him tell her where her children were.

He was in Alicen's room, holding the girl on his lap. Melanie stopped in her tracks. Why was her face so pale, her head hanging back like that?

Derek stared at her through tears.

"She's dead," he said softly. "Janice appeared to her, and when she saw it wasn't her mother, she collapsed."

"Oh, God," Melanie whispered, moving closer to them.

She reached out and touched Alicen's body. It was still warm. And then she drew back and screamed:

"Derek, where are my children?"

"I don't know," Derek whined.

"You have to know," Melanie cried. "She's got them somewhere, and she's going to kill them, too. Please, Derek!"

"I don't know where they are."

"Derek, this house is filled with police," Melanie said, her voice filled with rage. "They'll arrest you for murder if you don't tell me where Janice has my children!"

Just then, Owen and Bryan burst into the room. They took in Melanie, standing there with her fists clenched, Derek, crying softly, and the little girl flopped in his arms. When Bryan tried to pry the child loose, Derek spat at him and tightened his arms.

"I never wanted this to happen," he sobbed. "Jesus, she's just a kid. I never wanted her to die."

But Bryan had seen a soft rising in the girl's chest. He forced Derek's arm away and listened to the child's pulse. "This child is alive," he said, standing. "She needs an ambulance."

"Oh, Derek!" Melanie cried. "Can't you see what she's done? Janice almost killed your little girl. She's made both of

224

you her slaves. Don't give in to her, Derek. Please tell me where she has my children."

Derek rocked his daughter back and forth. Alive? She was alive?

"The—the cellar," he stammered. "She's got them in the storage room."

Without hesitation, Owen and Bryan ran from the room. Even as they hurried downstairs, Janice was standing over three cowering children, her eyes blazing.

"You wicked children," she said. "You tried to call for help, didn't you? And now Derek's sent help down here—but he'll pay for defying me."

She took a step forward. "But first—"

Gina screamed as best she could and kicked at the massless body. Janice laughed at her.

"Don't try to stop me," she said. "You deserve to die, all of you."

She grabbed Nancy's curls and lifted her off the floor. The child stuggled like a fish, with no arms or legs to flay. Janice shook her roughly and threw her to the ground. "You're all going to die."

But just then, the door crashed open. In the same instant Janice was gone, leaving Bryan Davis alone to gape in wonder at the children. Quickly, he untied them. Melanie appeared in the doorway now, and Kyle and Gina ran to her.

"Oh, my babies!" Melanie whispered. "It's all right."

"Nancy's hurt!" Gina cried.

Melanie looked up at Bryan, who had taken the child in his arms. He passed by her and carried her upstairs. Moments later, all three children were in the back of an ambulance. But Melanie wasn't with them.

"Where's my mother?" Kyle shouted.

"I don't know," Bryan said, hurrying back to the house. Owen was at his side, and Bryan turned and snapped, "Stay out here. This doesn't concern you."

"He killed my sister!" Owen yelled.

"Derek Miller didn't kill your sister," Bryan insisted.

He ran into the kitchen. Melanie was standing there, holding hands with Derek, speaking in firm tones.

And Janice was standing across from her.

"You can fight her, Derek," Melanie was saying. "You're a strong man. Don't let her control you."

"You fool," Janice hissed. "I *do* control him. Derek, I want her to die. *Now*."

Derek shook his head slowly. "No."

"What did you say?" Janice demanded.

Bryan took a step forward but stopped when Melanie spoke again.

"He isn't going to listen to you any more," she said. "Not since you tried to kill his daughter."

"Derek, you're my lover." Janice screamed. *"Kill her!"*

"Melanie, get out of this house," Derek said.

"Where am I going to go?" Melanie demanded. "I want to see this ended now, or I'll never escape her."

She began to cry again. Suddenly, infuriated by her tears, Janice pounced forward to grab her—but somehow Bryan managed to beat her to it. Without looking back, he dragged Melanie out to the ambulance.

"Get them to the hospital," he said to the drivers.

He turned back as the ambulance drove away, carrying a mother hugging her three children for dear life. Suddenly, Bryan realized Owen Crewe was now nowhere in sight. He raced to the house. Owen was in the kitchen, staring at something with wide eyes. Bryan turned to where his eyes were fixed.

Janice was on top of Derek.

"My God," he whispered. "She's tearing him apart."

He knew that he and Owen would be next if they didn't run *now*.

"Owen, get out of here!" he shouted, pulling at the other man.

He had seen so much in his years as a cop—so much gore and horror. But nothing would be imprinted in his mind more clearly than the picture of Janice Lors digging her hands into Derek's flesh, ripping at it. Clutching at his stomach, Bryan slid into his car and started the engine.

"I don't understand any of this," Owen said softly, watching the house. "I don't understand why Liza had to die. Why did Derek kill her? Who was that woman in there?"

"That house," Bryan answered vaguely. "It was that house. It ought to be burned to the ground."

Angrily he slammed his foot down on the gas pedal and sped into town—into the peaceful town of Belle Bay.

28

"Gary, I'm not going back to that house," Melanie said.

She sat with her husband on a couch in a hotel room, her head on his shoulder. They had been here two days, ever since the hospital checked them over and released them. Gary had been released at the same time and had found a place to hide from reporters just a few miles out of town. It was a small room, with only one king-sized bed, where Kyle and Nancy now slept away their fears. Gina was sitting in a chair, listlessly flipping through a magazine.

"Of course we won't," Gary answered, kissing his wife.

She looked at him in disbelief.

"You aren't going to argue with me?"

"No," Gary said. "We should have left that house seven months ago. We should have known this would happen again."

He squeezed her tightly. "I'm sorry I doubted you, Melanie," he said quietly.

"Lydia Browning tried to warn us," Melanie said. "Perhaps it was to make up for all the wrongs Jacob committed out of love for her."

She waved her hand. "But we're safe now—that's the important thing."

Gina stood up now and walked to them, putting her arms around Gary's shoulders.

"Daddy?" she asked. "Where are we going to go?"

"I was thinking of staying with your grandparents a few months," Gary said. "Would you like that?"

Gina nodded.

"That's a wonderful idea, Gary," Melanie said. "My parents have plenty of room."

"Are we going to leave the furniture?" Gina asked. "And all our nice things?"

"No, honey," Gary said.

"We can't go back to get them!" Melanie cried.

"I'll call a moving van once we're at your parents' place,"

227

Gary said. "We never have to set foot on that property again."

"Thank God," Melanie said. She looked at Gina. "Honey, it's late. Why don't you try to get some sleep?"

"I can't sleep," she said, shuffling her feet on the rug.

Melanie stood up and put her arms around the child. As she stroked her hair, she asked, "You aren't thinking of what happened at the house, are you? You shouldn't. None of it was our fault."

"Janice said you killed her," Gina said softly.

"Gina—" Gary cautioned.

"No, Gary," Melanie said. "She's old enough to hear the truth. Gina, I did kill Janice. But it was blocked from my mind until a few days ago. I believed Jacob Armand had done it."

"That's why she came back to haunt us?" Gina asked. "It was your fault?"

"Gina, please," Melanie said. "Janice had tried to hurt Kyle, and she had led you into Jacob's trap. I had to defend you—so I hit her across the back of her head with a gun. I didn't mean to kill her. I only wanted to save my children."

She had begun to cry. Now Gina was crying, pressing her head into Melanie's heaving breast. Her mother held her tightly. Gary, feeling helpless, reached for his crutches and got to his feet. Melanie and Gina moved closer to him.

"Go ahead and cry," he said. "It'll make you feel better. But don't worry. We're going to get as far away from that house as possible."

He looked at the two children sleeping in the bed.

"No one will ever hurt you again," he vowed.

"Wh-what about Alicen?" Gina blubbered.

"Alicen?"

"She must be so lonely in that old hospital," Gina said. "It wasn't her fault this happened. Janice made her do those awful things. And now she doesn't have a father or a mother."

"She's right, Gary," Melanie said. "We can't just leave that child."

Gary nodded. "I'm a lawyer. I know who to ask about taking care of her."

He kissed each of them.

"Alicen can come with us," he said. "And then, I swear to you, we'll never be afraid again."

* * *

228

Owen tugged at his mustache and stared at the carved double doors of the big white mansion. God, he thought, how could any place so beautiful hold so much evil? From talking to Bryan Davis, he knew now that his sister had been murdered by a ghost and that the ghost had also murdered Derek Miller.

But who would believe it? How could he tell his parents, who lived so peacefully in their Florida condominium, that their precious daughter had been murdered by a ghost?

"You don't have to tell them anything like that," Bryan had said as they sat together in the police station that morning. "We have a likely suspect. The man you first accused—Derek Miller."

"But he's innocent," Owen said.

"And dead," Bryan answered. "He can't defend himself. And who's going to defend him? A thirteen-year-old kid? Alicen's going to be in a hospital for a long time, and by the time she gets well, she won't remember any of this."

"Poor kid," Owen said. "But tell me about her father."

"Derek Miller had no family except for his daughter," Bryan said. "And only one close friend—a doctor named Mary Norton. I've already told her Derek was going slowly mad over the death of his wife Elaine, and she accepted that theory."

He lifted a pencil and bounced it a few times.

"Besides, I like the VanBurens," he said. "If we accuse Janice, they'll have all sorts of nuts bothering them the rest of their lives. But if we don't accuse someone, the blame will lie on them. And I don't want to see that happen."

God only knew the VanBurens had suffered enough. Bryan should have seen it coming when Gina was involved in that bus accident. The driver had been Janice Lors. She had taken little Alicen Miller into her power and had sent her to the police station with a story about the driver jumping from the bus. That mystery was now solved, too. Bryan would worry about what he'd say in his report later.

"Neither do I," Owen said, standing. "You go ahead and tell the papers it was Derek who killed my sister. But I won't rest until the real murderer gets what's coming to her."

"Stay away from that house," Bryan cautioned. "If I find you there, I'll have you arrested. That place is deadly."

Owen stared at him, considering the threat.

"All right," he said at last. "There's nothing I can do to a ghost anyway, is there?"

Yet now he was walking around the house to the back door, barricaded only by a rope since the door had yet to be fixed. A paper sign hanging on it said: POLICE AREA DO NOT CROSS. Owen climbed over it.

Pending an investigation into Liza and Derek's deaths, the house had been left exactly the way it was two days ago. Chairs were overturned, paintings knocked from the walls, the glass windows in the living room were shattered. Absently, Owen bent down and righted the rocking chair, setting it near the fireplace. He looked around in awe at the beauty of the room, with its plush sofa and antique furniture. And then he felt a touch on his arm.

"I knew you'd be back," a voice said. Owen turned and saw the woman named Janice smiling at him. "I noticed you alone among all those other people here the day I killed Derek. I knew I wanted you."

Stunned, Owen said nothing. Her eyes were powerful, holding him fast.

"I thought I wanted Derek," Janice said, moving closer to him. "But he betrayed me. He let those murderers escape."

She turned to stare through filmy eyes at the fireplace. "But I will have my revenge one day."

Owen found his tongue and was surprised to hear himself speaking to her as if she were simply one of his patients.

"Why do you want revenge so badly?" he asked. "So far as I know, Melanie was only defending her child. Jacob Armand had turned you into a madwoman. What was she supposed to do?"

"She had no right to kill me!" Janice snapped. "I was only twenty-eight. I was beautiful."

She leaned forward to kiss Owen, but he backed away.

"Don't do that," he said, feeling weak. What was it about her eyes?

"I want you, Owen Crewe," Janice whispered.

Calling himself a fool for coming here, Owen tried to turn and run away. But he couldn't feel his legs.

Janice pulled him down to the floor. "Make love to me, Owen," she whispered passionately.

"Let me go," Owen said, feeling powerless as a baby. This was happening too fast.

"I waited for Derek," Janice said, "because I needed him for something. That was a mistake—I lost him. But I won't lose you, my handsome Owen. I want you."

Her lips pressed his, her tongue pried them open. Suddenly Owen found his strength and tried to knock her away. She sat up and slapped him, hard, again and again. Her face changed then, bloated and turned green, and became Liza's face. Blood dripped onto Owen.

"No!"

"I want you with me, brother," Janice teased, in Liza's voice. "I'm so alone without you. Oh, so alone! Die, big brother!"

Owen closed his eyes and felt his heart jump. When he opened them again, there was nothing above him but stars and blackness.

EPILOGUE

When the moving company came Monday morning, they found Owen's body on the living room sofa. His arms were folded across his chest, his hair neatly in place. The effect was like a wake, but Bryan Davis insisted the death certificate should read heart attack. The coroner accepted a sum of money and obliged. Who was Owen Crewe to him?

Though she didn't know him, Melanie cried when she read the obituary. She was sitting on the porch of her parents' house, with Gary at her side and the children sitting nearby. They kept close to her these days. Nancy stood up from the game she was playing with Kyle and came to put her head on Melanie's lap.

"Mommy, why do we all cry so much?"

"Because many sad things have happened to us," Melanie said, gently rubbing the child's back. It was a hot day, and Nancy's sunsuit was soaked with perspiration.

"I don't want to be sad any more," Nancy said. "Daddy promised we wouldn't be sad—didn't you, daddy?"

"I did," Gary said. "Melanie, what are you reading there?" Melanie showed him the paper. "Don't think about it," Gary said. "You didn't even know the guy."

She leaned across the wicker sofa and kissed him. In spite of all that had happened, she still had her career, didn't she? And her beautiful family. Nothing bad could happen to them again. Not if they stayed away from that hateful, evil house.

Still, the next day, she couldn't help driving back to it for one last look. She didn't cry to see the high white towers and bay windows, nor the porch and bay windows. She felt a loss, of course, but also a joy that the terror was at last over. She would have sat there, near the car, looking at it for hours, remembering the good times they had had—and there had been many in spite of everything—if a sight in the upstairs window hadn't broken her spell. She saw two blond people. Melanie could barely make out the mustache on one. Was that Owen?

"My God," she said. "The papers were wrong. He didn't die of a heart attack—she killed him!"

She saw Janice pointing at her. Before those eyes could take her into their evil power, Melanie turned and ran to her car. It carried her at top speed to the highway, to safety. By the time she reached the main street of Belle Bay, she had forced herself to calm down. She had escaped. And it was over.

Her only worry now would be her career, and nothing else.

There didn't need to be any other worries, for Janice no longer wanted revenge. She had found something in Owen Crewe that satisfied her. He had become her total slave, easily forced into submission by the sight of his sister's face.

No one ever came back to the house after that, except for a crew to block the door and put up a condemned sign. Gary had wanted the place torn down but was told it would be too expensive. So now the house sat regally upon the hill, rotting and lonely. Winters passed and tore at the shuttered windows, summers made the white paint crack and peel. And as the house grew uglier, legends by the townspeople grew around it.

They called it the Ghost House. And sometimes, if the wind was blowing just right and imaginations were tense, people would swear they could hear the laughter of two people sounding from behind its ancient, dilapidated façade.

December 12, 1921

She was such a darling child. Bonnie Jackson was the little girl everyone wanted—bright, pretty, talented. At the tender age of five she'd already made a name for herself on Broadway, charming both audiences and critics with her incredible voice range and talent for acting. Even other actors, who saw kids and animals as proverbial menaces, enjoyed working with this cheerful, appealing child.

Sometimes, though, Bonnie wasn't very cheerful. On a particularly gloomy day in late autumn she sat in her dressing room and stared solemnly at the reflection in her vanity as her mother tied a frothy white bow in the child's shoulder-length black hair.

Bonnie was sad because her parents had just had an argument, one that left Mommy's mouth set hard and Daddy searching the room for a flask of bootleg whiskey. Bonnie's pink lips turned down in a pout, and her round cheeks flushed as she fought her tears. She hated it when her parents fought.

"Why the hell does that guy have to follow us to every theater?" Philip Jackson wanted to know.

"He's a friend, Phil," his wife answered. "Just a friend."

"I'm not an idiot, Margaret," Phil said. "I know what Aaron Milland means to you."

Bonnie looked up at her mother and in her desire to understand this argument dared to interrupt with a question.

"Do you like Aaron Milland, Mommy?"

Margaret glared at the reflection of her daughter's eyes, growing wider by the moment as Bonnie waited to be reprimanded. Sometimes Mommy became very angry with her. Sometimes, she even hurt her.

This time, however, she didn't say a word. Instead, she turned back to Phil.

"What does it matter, how Aaron and I feel about each other?" she demanded.

"Look," Phil said, "Bonnie shouldn't be hearing this. We can talk later in private."

Margaret sighed.

"All right, we'll talk later," she said. "Let's just concentrate on getting Bonnie ready for her debut."

As if by magic the stern look on her face fell away, replaced by a smile. Bonnie wished her mother would smile more often.

"Imagine," Margaret said, "our baby in the Winston Theater!"

"Only The Palace is bigger, Bonnie," Phil told his daughter.

Bonnie grinned at her father, her perfect white teeth glistening. He grinned back, caught a strand of his hair, and pushed it over his ear. It was plastered down with spice-smelling hair cream, parted in the middle and shining like the fender of a new Hudson Phaeton. Bonnie thought her daddy was very handsome. She loved him more than anyone, maybe even more than

Mommy. Daddy never hit her, or yelled at her, or put her in dark places.

But she wouldn't think about the dark places. She'd think only of the songs she'd be singing tonight on the bright stage of the Winston Theater.

"Stand up now, darling," Margaret ordered.

Bonnie did as she was told, and modeled the new dress her father had ordered from Paris. Its hem was just fingertip length, and when she twirled around, rows and rows of lace ruffles fluttered like wispy clouds. Her parents admired her from head to toe, taking in her white bow, dress, stockings, and finally a pair of white Mary Janes with pearl buttons. It was when Margaret's eyes reached the shoes that her smile disappeared again.

Bonnie stopped dancing and stared at her mother with eyes that silently asked what she had done now. She was glad Daddy was here. Daddy wouldn't let her be hurt. He never did.

"My God, Phil!" Margaret cried. "Her shoes are scuffed, and she's on in five minutes!"

Bonnie looked down at the offending shoes and noticed that a few black streaks ran over the very tips of her toes.

"For crying out loud, Margaret," Phil said. "They're coming to hear her sing, not look at her shoes!"

"She has to be perfect," Margaret said. "I have to make her perfect."

She lifted Bonnie up and sat her on top of a black costume-trunk, quickly unbuckling the Mary Janes.

"Do you have any lighter fluid?"

Phil took out his silver flask of whiskey and joked, "This stuff'll set 'em on fire."

Bonnie giggled, and Margaret snapped, "I'm not amused!"

And the little girl frowned again.

"Damn it," Phil said, reaching into the pocket of his pants. "Here, here's some lighter fluid. Jeez!"

Margaret went to work on the scuff marks. By the time she was done, Bonnie was being called on stage. Phil and Margaret took seats in the second row to watch her perform. The audience loved her here at the Winston Theater, as had audiences everywhere else— they applauded and smiled and cheered the tiny performer. Some of the women and men even felt tears in their eyes.

But they didn't know the melancholy sweetness in her voice was not part of an act. All the while she was singing, Bonnie couldn't help thinking of the fight her parents had had. When she was finished, she met them in the wings, and holding Margaret's hand, she hurried back to her dressing room.

"You were terrific," Phil said. "Which you would have been with or without the scuff marks."

Margaret shot a look at him and pushed open the door to Bonnie's dressing room.

"As a matter of fact," Phil said, "a performance like that deserves a reward."

"I don't think that's necessary," Margaret said.

"Sure it is," Phil answered. "I'm going to head over to F.A.O. Schwartz and buy a new doll for you, Bonnie."

"Oh, Daddy!" the child squealed with delight. She ran to him and hugged him around the knees.

"I love you so much, Daddy," she said.

"And Daddy sure loves you," Phil replied.

Margaret stared icily at them, but said nothing. Phil took his trenchcoat down from its brass hook.

"I shouldn't be too long," he said. He reconsidered that and glanced at his pocket watch. "Well, I guess the Christmas rush might delay me. Give me an hour."

"Phil, I think you're being foolish," Margaret commented.

But Phil only winked at Bonnie and left the room. Margaret began to see red, hating the fact that Bonnie was being rewarded simply for doing her job. What about Margaret? Why didn't Phil reward *her* for all the years she slaved to get the kid where she was? My God, she hadn't even wanted a baby! And look what sacrifices she'd made!

Her thoughts were cut off by a knock at the door. Bonnie watched her mother's face change once again from angry to cheerful as Aaron Milland walked into the room. The little girl shrank away from him, hating his gaunt cheeks and dark eyes. He reminded her of a skull. Ignoring Bonnie, Aaron pulled Margaret to him and kissed her neck.

"Mmm," she said. "Not here. Not here!"

She giggled and pushed him away.

Finally, Aaron noticed Bonnie. Bonnie didn't like Aaron Milland. He'd met her mommy last year during a preview run in Philadelphia, where he'd been stage manager. Now he followed them to every theater, always coming to see her mommy when her daddy wasn't around. Bonnie could sense there was something wrong with that.

"You kissed my mommy like my daddy used to," she said. "Why?"

Margaret gasped and put a hand to the low V-neck of her silky dress.

"How dare you ask such a question!" she cried. "Oh, Aaron, I'm so sorry. Sometimes she gets too big for her britches. It's this business, you know."

"That's okay," Aaron said. "No harm done. She's just a kid, Margaret."

"Nevertheless, I'd like you to excuse us," Margaret said.

Bonnie, though she didn't like Aaron, wished he wouldn't leave the room. What would her mother do to her? But he did, and now Margaret grabbed her by the arms, crushing the delicate organza of her puffed sleeves. Her long string of beads swayed forward, tapping the child's face lightly.

"You are rude, mean, and nasty," she hissed. "Aaron is my friend, and will be your daddy someday!"

"No!" Bonnie cried. "I only want my *real* daddy!"

Margaret slapped her little round cheek. Bonnie burst into tears and tried to pull away.

"You are a bad, bad girl," Margaret went on. "For being rude to Aaron, you'll stay in the closet until I come get you out!"

Bonnie kicked and protested with all her might as her mother pulled her toward the dark little closet. Why didn't anyone hear her? she wondered frantically. Why didn't one of the other performers come in and help, or even that Aaron? Bonnie decided then that she hated everyone in this theater. They didn't care what happened to her. They only cared if she made money for them.

Her mother shoved her into the closet. Bonnie's head struck the back wall, and she sat momentarily stunned as the door slammed shut and the lock clicked.

"Mommy, no!" Bonnie screamed. "No, please! I hate the dark! Please take the dark away!"

But the only reply was the sound of retreating footsteps and another door closing. Then laughter. Her mother was laughing, and so was Aaron! Bonnie recognized the deep voice of her mother's "friend."

"I hate you," she whispered, sniffling. "I hate you!"

She sat back and pulled her knees up to her chin, crying softly, rocking herself back and forth. Her daddy said he'd be right back. Maybe if she made herself small, if she closed her eyes, the monsters who hid in the closet wouldn't get her. Daddy would rescue her. Daddy always rescued her.

Cold and sick with fright, she collapsed into a deep sleep.

When her eyes opened again, it was darker in the closet than it had been earlier. Bonnie realized there was no light coming in from the room outside anymore. Had someone come and turned it off, not realizing she was in here? She crawled over to the door and tried to open it. Still locked.

"MOMMY!" she cried, pounding on the door. "MOMMY? PLEASE LET ME OUT!"

She would be good. She'd be a good girl if Mommy let her out. It was cold in here! And dark, so dark . . .

"I DON'T LIKE THE DARK, MOMMY!"

A door opened, there were footsteps, and suddenly Bonnie heard a key jangling in the closet lock. The door opened, but it was just as dark outside. She couldn't see who was there. Strong arms lifted her, and Bonnie started to struggle. Who was it? Who was going to hurt her now?

"Hey, it's me!" a man's voice cried. "It's your daddy!"

Bonnie relaxed, as her small hands found the familiar comedy/tragedy pin he always wore on his coat.

"Oh, Daddy!" She buried her face in his shoulder and sobbed.

"Did your mother do this?"

Bonnie nodded. "She said I was rude to Aaron," Bonnie answered.

"Aaron?" Phil echoed. "Aaron was here?"

Again, the child nodded. "Daddy, why is it so dark?"

"We've lost all the lights. Must be a fuse, honey," Phil said. "Here, I'll light a candle."

Bonnie felt herself being placed on a velveteen loveseat. Her father kissed the top of her head, then went groping across the room to a chest of drawers. After a lot of rummaging noise, he found a candle and lit it. A soft glow illuminated the room, and Bonnie immediately felt better. Her daddy had brought the light.

"You wait here," he said. "Daddy's got a few words to say to Mommy."

"Daddy, where is everyone?" Bonnie asked. "Why didn't anyone hear me?"

"Everyone's gone home, darling," Phil said. He stopped and thought. "Didn't you know?"

"No, Daddy," Bonnie said. "I fell asleep."

Phil rubbed his eyes.

"You've been in that closet for three hours," he growled. "God, I'm sorry about that! I called your mother—she said everything was okay."

And all that time she was screwing Aaron . . .

"You just wait here," Phil said. "I'll be right back."

He opened a drawer in a tall cabinet, reached way into the back and pulled out a gun, grasping it firmly in a white-knuckled fist.

And then he left. Bonnie sat staring at the candle flame, waiting for him. But soon the candle burned out, and still her daddy hadn't returned. Terrified to be alone in the dark, Bonnie slid off the loveseat and decided she'd try to find him. She shuffled her way toward the door and opened it, entering the long hallway outside her dressing room. She could see nothing in either direction, but she could hear voices. Yelling voices—two men and a woman.

"If I follow them," she said out loud to reassure herself, "I'll find Daddy."

But it was so hard to tell where they were coming from in the theater's maze of pitch black hallways. Bonnie walked slowly, listening, turning when the sounds seemed to grow louder. But none of the doors she opened led to Daddy.

All of a sudden she heard the sound of running footsteps. And then her mother's voice crying, "That child is more trouble than she's worth! You keep her! I hate her!"

Bonnie's eyes filled with tears. Her mother really did hate her, didn't she?

And her mother was going to hurt her now. That's why she was running. To catch Bonnie. To hurt her.

Terrified, the child pulled open the nearest door. At first, when she felt some hanging sandbags and lengths of coiled rope, she thought it might be the stage. But no, this couldn't be the stage. There was no light here. Daddy told her that all stages had a "ghost light," a single bulb that always burned at the apron so that no one would walk off it in the dark. This had to be a storage room.

"BONNIE JACKSON, HOW DARE YOU RAT ON ME?"

Margaret's shriek resounded throughout the building. And then Phil's angry voice boomed out of the darkness.

"DON'T YOU HURT HER! I'll kill you if you touch my baby."

Bonnie prayed her daddy would come get her. She poked a thumb in her mouth (Mommy would smack her if she saw her) and started backing away from the door, afraid her mother would enter.

Suddenly, from some faraway part of the theater, came a loud, cracking noise. The sound of a gunshot startled Bonnie so that she lost her footing and tumbled backwards into a dark void. She screamed, realizing too late that the blackout had also claimed the ghost light. She crashed to the floor of the orchestra pit, her head striking a metal chair. Blackness came, and all the life and sweetness of the little girl who had charmed Broadway drained away—as easily as blood flows.

ABOUT THE AUTHOR

CLARE MCNALLY attended the Fashion Institute of Technology in New York City where she studied advertising and communications. She has worked on a children's wear magazine, freelanced as an advertising copywriter and edited a technical magazine. She lives on Long Island. This is her second novel.

There's an epidemic with 27 million victims. And no visible symptoms.

It's an epidemic of people who can't read.

Believe it or not, 27 million Americans are functionally illiterate, about one adult in five.

The solution to this problem is you... when you join the fight against illiteracy. So call the Coalition for Literacy at toll-free 1-800-228-8813 and volunteer.

Volunteer Against Illiteracy. The only degree you need is a degree of caring.